The Day the Angel Came

Jean Ritchie is a successful ghostwriter. She has written, amongst others, the *Sunday Times* bestsellers *How Could She?* and *Little Girl Lost* with Barbie Probert-Wright. *The Day the Angel Came* is her first novel.

The Day the Angel Came

Jean Ritchie

arrow books

Published by Arrow Books in 2010

6 8 10 9 7

First published in Great Britain in 2010 by
Arrow Books
The Random House Group Limited
20 Vauxhall Bridge Road, London SW1V 2SA

www.randomhouse.co.uk

Addresses for companies within The Random House Group Limited can be found at:
www.randomhouse.co.uk/offices.htm

The Random House Group Limited Reg. No. 954009

A CIP catalogue record for this book
is available from the British Library

ISBN 978-0-0995-5647-3

The Random House Group Limited supports The Forest Stewardship Council (FSC®), the leading international forest certification organisation. Our books carrying the FSC label are printed on FSC® certified paper. FSC is the only forest certification scheme endorsed by the leading environmental organisations, including Greenpeace. Our paper procurement policy can be found at www.randomhouse.co.uk/environment

Typeset in 11.5/15pt Spectrum by Palimpsest Book Production Limited,
Falkirk, Stirlingshire
Printed and bound by
CPI Group (UK) Ltd, Croydon, CR0 4YY

For Ava

Acknowledgements

With many thanks to Kate Elton and Gillian Holmes, for the brilliant idea, and to Gillian for being a wonderful editor to work with. Also, many thanks as ever to Julian Alexander.

Prologue

Lisa unpacked her shopping on to the kitchen counter. There was nothing in her bag to show it was Christmas: no turkey, no crackers, no chocolates. The only sign of anything special was a large bottle of whisky, which she carried through to the small living room and put down on the coffee table, next to a letter that was poking out of the top of its envelope.

This room was not quite a Christmas-free zone. On the mantelpiece above the gas fire there were two cards. One, with a jolly Father Christmas on the front, came from the two girls who worked for Lisa at the shoe shop where she was manageress. Another, with a picture of a robin, came from the woman in the flat across the landing, whose cat Lisa fed whenever the neighbour went away. Lisa walked across and put a third card on the mantelpiece; it had a fat cherub and the words 'Peace on Earth' on the front, and had been given to her by Richard, the owner of the café next door to the shop. She hadn't given him one; she had been surprised when he'd handed her his. She had only bought three: one for her neighbour and one each for the girls in the shop. Christmas did not make a big dent in Lisa's budget, as it did for most people. She had bought the girls chocolates, and she had one present, already wrapped and on the chest of drawers in her bedroom, for Barry.

The thought of Barry made her start. He'd promised to come round tomorrow, Christmas Day, later on, when he could get away from his family. She smiled ruefully as she took a large bottle of pills from the bathroom cabinet and put them on the table, next to the whisky. Perhaps Barry would have the grim task of finding her body. She wondered, What would he do? She knew the answer: he'd run back home to his wife and children as fast as he could, after making sure there was no trace that he had ever been there. Barry's main emotion when he found her body would not be sorrow at her death, but fear that he might in some way become involved.

Well, she thought, he needn't worry. She would not be leaving any suicide notes, nothing putting any blame on him. It wasn't his fault; he'd be flattering himself if he thought she'd killed herself because of him. No, Lisa's despair went much deeper than Barry, with his occasional visits for wild but loveless sex. It's true he was about the only human contact she had outside her job, but there had been men before, and she'd learned from bitter experience that they were never the answer to anything. They used you; they let you down; they moved on. That's the way life went, and she had long ago given up expecting anything more. Occasionally, when she watched a TV soap or read a magazine, she saw glimpses of people who seemed to make life and relationships work, but she knew that was not for her. Closeness, true closeness with another human being, was something she had not experienced since she was a very young child, and she knew, with deep conviction, that it was not going to come to her again.

Lisa glanced at herself in the mirror above the mantelpiece. She was thirty-five years old, and she could spot the first signs of age beginning to crinkle the edges of her eyes, though you had to look closely to see them. She was not a great beauty, but she was pretty and she knew how to make the best of herself. Her fair hair was bobbed at shoulder length; her make-up was expertly applied; she knew how to choose clothes to flatter her slim figure.

She looked around the room. The flat was very neat, compact, with a small living room, a larger bedroom, a kitchen and a bathroom. She'd furnished it simply, in neutral colours relieved by sudden splashes of brightness: a deep turquoise throw across the settee, a matching vase. In the bedroom, a burnt-orange bedspread picked up the colour in the largest of the framed prints on the wall. She felt a pang about leaving it; she had worked hard to build up her home, and she was proud of it.

She was surprised at how calm she felt. She sat down on the sofa, poured herself a glass of whisky and took a sip. Her mouth twisted involuntarily as the sharp burn hit her tongue and the back of her throat. It would be easier, she thought, if she liked the stuff, but on the other hand, she had to be careful not to get so drunk that she failed to swallow all the tablets.

She picked up the letter and reread its contents. Tears slowly welled in her eyes. When tonight was over, when she was out of all this mess, nobody would care. She, without family and friends, would die and leave no trace. Not even a few memories. Her mind quickly conjured up her own funeral. Maybe Anne and Jodie from the shop would be there, but not both of them, or who would keep the shoe shop open? Maybe Mrs Smith, the owner of the cat. But that would be all. Barry definitely would not risk being seen among the mourners, and besides, by the time of the funeral he'd have moved on. Thirty-five years on this earth and nothing to show for it in terms of human relationships. Lots of people she had known, even loved, but none of them in her life now. Nobody, not one person, who loved her or cared about her.

These thoughts crystallised her resolve. She poured the tablets on to the table. They rattled down, scattering across the surface, two of them landing on top of the letter. It was these two she picked up first, putting them in her mouth and taking a big swig from the whisky glass to wash them down. Tears poured down her face. It was as if her first step on the road to peace, oblivion, a route out of this terrible life, was enough to unleash in her all her unhappiness. She sobbed and sobbed, clutching the letter to her.

As she surrendered herself to grief, myriad thoughts flickered through her brain. Her childhood, her parents, her sister, a couple of the men she had lived with . . . Jumbled, random images from her life, and none of them happy.

When the sobs began to subside, she reached forward to take two more tablets, but as she lifted them towards her mouth, she felt a hand on hers, a soft but very firm touch, strong enough to stop her action but, at the same time, so gentle that she could hardly feel it. Although she knew there was no one in the flat, she didn't feel frightened.

Eyes still blinded with tears, she turned to her right, towards the hand and arm that were restraining her. Through the mist of her tears she saw a bright, shimmering shape on the sofa next to her, a shape that, as she looked, resolved itself from a pool of light into the form of a young child with curly blonde hair. The form was clear, but somehow the radiance around it gave it an indistinctness, a quivering haziness that blurred the edges and made it seem as if the child was constantly renewing its human appearance.

Lisa felt calm and she was suddenly bathed in an overwhelming feeling of peace and love. She felt relaxed and inexplicably happy.

'Who are you?' she said.

'Don't you know? I'm your own special angel. I'm always with you, good times and bad. I love you.'

The voice was sweet and soft.

'But I've never seen you before.'

'You never needed to see me. You've never needed my help like you need it right now.' The angel nodded towards the scattering of pills on the table. Lisa started, shocked to be brought back to what she had been doing. Her hand opened and she dropped the tablets she had picked up.

'You see,' the angel went on, 'it's not your time. One day, you will come to the other side, to be with me for ever, to fulfil our destiny, but not yet. You have more to do.'

'Me? What can I possibly have to do?'

'You have to live. There are people who need you.'

Book One

1

Early Days

The midwife was panicking.

'Hold on . . . hold on. There's another one coming.'

Two minutes later, Margaret had another huge contraction and a second baby's head emerged into the world. Margaret's husband, Bill, who was holding her hand, began to shake with a mixture of emotions. They had tried so hard for a baby and now, without any warning, there were two. Two perfect little girls, small but strong and healthy.

'It's a bit like buses,' said a jovial doctor who had been summoned by the midwife's emergency alarm. 'You wait for ages and then two come at the same time.'

The babies were cleaned up; then Margaret had the chance to hold them briefly before they were whisked off to incubators.

'Why are you taking them? What's wrong?' Margaret asked anxiously.

'Nothing wrong at all, they're perfect, but because they weigh less than five pounds each, we'll keep them in special care for a couple of days. For twins, they're a really good size. And you've heard them cry – they know what breathing and living are all about,' said the midwife reassuringly.

A few minutes later, Bill was alone with Margaret, who was sipping a cup of tea that one of the nurses had thoughtfully brought.

'Well, my girl,' said Bill, who although not tall, was thickset, with muscled arms from years of working on building sites, 'what are you going to call the extra one?'

Margaret and he had already agreed on Lisa if their baby was a girl, but now, suddenly, they needed another girl's name. Margaret sipped her tea gratefully, elation sweeping through her. Twins! Two babies to take home. She luxuriated in the moment. She had feared she would never be a mother, had seen the sideways glances of her sisters-in-law and cousins, who all seemed to produce babies on demand.

'I think we should call her Dawn,' she said.

'Are you sure?' said Bill, who had endured long hours of Margaret agonising over names before 'Lisa' was settled on.

'I'm sure,' said Margaret, with a smile. 'It just came to me and it feels right for her.'

She closed her eyes and began to drift off to sleep. Tenderly, Bill took the cup from her hand and placed it on the cupboard. He stood up and began to tiptoe away when his wife woke and called to him, 'You'd better take that pram back to the shop. Change it for a double one.' Then she rested her head back on the pillow, smiling contentedly.

Twins were hard work, but Margaret revelled in it. She had happily given up her factory job when she was five months pregnant and had loved every minute of getting their small terraced house in Wolverhampton into shape for the arrival of a new baby. The second bedroom had been painted a pale lemon – ready for either a boy or a girl. Piles of baby clothes had been knitted, mostly in white for the same reason.

Now, at home with the twins, everything was very pink. Presents arrived – Babygros and matinée jackets, all pink. Flowers were delivered, all pink.

'You're well and truly outnumbered now,' Bill's brother said to him, clapping him on the back. 'A house full of women. You'd better get used to having a shower from the hose in the garden, because when they become teenagers, you'll never get a look-in in the bathroom.'

Bill beamed with pride. He, too, had been worried that this moment might never come, although he had kept his fears from Margaret. He adored his two little babies, his big hands holding them more gently than Margaret had believed possible. There were dark shadows under his eyes, from waking in the night to help with the long, difficult feeds. Like him, Margaret found herself permanently exhausted in the beginning, until magically, at five months old, Lisa slept through the night. A few days later, Dawn did the same. A pattern was set: Lisa, the older by two minutes, was the leader; Dawn was her very willing follower.

It was Lisa who first pulled herself up on to her feet, precariously hanging on to the coffee table. Dawn, a quiet, watchful baby, observed her daring elder sister and, a week later, followed suit. It was Lisa who first said a recognisable word. They both babbled the usual 'Mamamama' and 'Dadadada', to the delight of their besotted parents, but Lisa then clearly said 'Daw' for 'Dawn', quickly adding 'ball' and 'biccy' to her vocabulary. Dawn was slower: when she wanted milk or a biscuit, Lisa did the asking for both of them.

That's how it went. They were identical twins, impossible for anyone except Margaret and Bill to tell apart – and even Bill had to look carefully for the extra curl that Dawn's double crown gave to the top of her head. For the benefit of others, particularly the staff at the nursery where the girls went when they were four, Margaret developed a shoe code: red shoes for Dawn, blue shoes for Lisa. She never dressed them the same, however tempting it was, especially as well-meaning friends and family always bought them matching outfits. Margaret had read a book about bringing up twins and she knew it was important that they developed separate identities.

'One day, they'll have to lead separate lives,' she told Bill, who secretly hankered after seeing his little daughters looking like two peas in a pod.

'They need to develop separate personalities,' Margaret said.

'Oh, they're doing that, all right,' said Bill, smiling as he watched Lisa bossing Dawn about in a make-believe game with their dolls and teddy bears.

Lisa was fearless. Despite gradually introducing them to nursery, Dawn still clung to Margaret at the doorway and only went in if she was holding Lisa's hand. Lisa, anxious to join the other children in the sandpit or the Wendy house, often had to be called back to help her sister. When they encountered a dog behind the gate to their neighbour's garden, Lisa immediately put her hands through the struts to pat the animal, while Dawn held tight to Margaret's hand and pulled away. When Bill read them a bedside story, Lisa always wanted one with witches and goblins, but Dawn had nightmares if there was anything even slightly scary in the tale.

Despite the difference in their personalities, they played together all the time and rarely bickered like other siblings. When they were tired, they would lean on each other on the settee to fall asleep, thumbs in mouths, blonde curls tangled together. Although they had separate beds, they always ended up sleeping in one, their arms around each other.

At five, they started 'big school', the infants section of the primary school just across the park from their home. Every morning, Margaret walked them across the park, carrying their bags with their lunches and their painting smocks and PE clothes. And every morning when they reached the park, Lisa demanded to be allowed to go on the swings and slides in the playground area.

'Not now,' Margaret said firmly. 'After school, on the way home.'

So it was the swings and slides that filled Lisa's head as they walked home on that terrible day, the day that would change all of their lives for ever. Margaret was carrying the girls' schoolbags and struggling to hold both their hands. Dawn was chattering away about something that had happened in school, but Lisa was squirming and wriggling to be free because the park was in sight. When Margaret momentarily loosened her grip, the small girl made a dash across the road to get to the entrance. Round the bend in the road, a lorry was approaching fast. Margaret shrieked and ran after Lisa, dropping Dawn's hand, as all her energy was focused on saving Lisa. The lorry driver jumped on his brakes, which hissed loudly as the front of the vehicle skewed across the road. Margaret felt a rush of relief as the vehicle came to a halt four yards from Lisa, who was standing petrified in the middle of the road. Then Margaret heard the screams of other mothers. Halfway across the road, she turned to see Dawn running after her on her chubby little legs, just as a motorbike hurtled down at them from the opposite direction. This time, it was too late to apply the brakes and the monstrous machine, a blur of black and purple, ploughed into Dawn, catapulting her tiny body into the air.

Everything seemed to go into slow motion. One of Dawn's red shoes came off and traced an arc in the air, travelling higher and further than her little body. Despite the noise of the still-running engines, Margaret heard the sickening thud as Dawn hit the tarmac road, her limbs splaying in a strange and unnatural way, her blonde head, which had taken the brunt of the impact, lolling to one side. Time froze. People – other mothers taking their children home, shopkeepers, motorists who stopped – rushed to the scene. Someone took hold of Lisa and pulled her out of the road and held her tight as she screamed, a guttural animal shriek that would never be forgotten by anyone who heard it. Margaret dashed to Dawn, but a man held her back. It was clear, immediately, that there was no life in the little body.

Dawn was dead. And with her death, it felt as if Margaret, Bill and Lisa also died.

They didn't die, of course, but the light, warmth and happiness in their lives did. Margaret, ripped apart by grief and guilt, dragged herself from her sleepless bed every morning to feed and dress her one remaining daughter. Bill pulled back into himself, became a silent, brooding man, avoided by his workmates, who didn't know how to cope with his surly temper. Lisa, unable to fully understand what had happened, knew with a certainty deep within her bones that part of her was gone. Dawn, who had been the other half of her existence, was no longer there. Within days the bed was gone; the clothes were gone; the red shoes were gone. But Dawn would never be gone. They had always shared their toys, but the scruffy brown cuddly dog that had gone everywhere with Dawn now became Lisa's talisman.

Immediately after the accident, the house was full of friends and family. Lisa was taken to stay with her cousins for a few nights. She didn't cry, but she was sick every morning, physically sick as the memory flooded back.

The grown-ups who fussed around her urged her not to upset her mother and she took the message to heart, making sure her parents never saw her cry, which she did quietly in the depths of the night. Nobody ever asked her how she was feeling, not because they didn't care but for fear of stirring up more pain. Alone in bed, Lisa would dream of Dawn and feel convinced she could feel her sister's arms around her, her head against hers on the pillow.

Quite quickly the details of the terrible day faded, became muddled. Lisa did not think about it, but she thought about Dawn all the time. At school, the place where Dawn had hung her coat and left her wellies was given to a new girl. The other children soon forgot Dawn, but the teachers and mothers were always watching Lisa, looking for evidence of trauma, whispering to each other about her. Margaret felt excluded at the school gate, her terrible grief too much for her to share. She lived on tranquillisers given to her by the doctor and sat frozen in her armchair in the afternoons and evenings. Lisa by instinct knew to leave her alone and became a self-sufficient child who played on her own for hours. They walked to school by a different route and never, ever went to the park, with its swings and slides. At home, the photos of the two girls, proudly displayed in silver frames, disappeared, and nothing took their place.

As Lisa grew older, her solitude also grew. Occasionally she was invited to a birthday party, but she could never invite a friend back home and gradually the invitations dried up. Her own birthday brought the usual presents and cards from aunts and uncles, but it was not a day of celebration. Her parents were both too consumed with grief to celebrate Lisa's birth, as if by doing that they would also be celebrating Dawn's death.

There were flashbacks to the terrible day. Nothing clear in Lisa's mind, just a lot of noise, screams, the smell of burning tyres and the sight of her little sister's crumpled body, coupled with an overwhelming feeling of guilt. She could not remember what she had done, but she knew – without any shadow of doubt – that it had all been her fault. She taught herself to deal with the flashbacks: she took a deep breath, counted to a hundred and thought hard of something else. Sometimes she forced herself to do difficult sums in her head to distract herself. It seemed to work. She knew she could not speak of her grief or guilt to her mother or father: they were too immersed in their own feelings.

When she was eleven, Lisa transferred to the comprehensive school. It was a bus ride from home, and although her class-mates from primary school went as well, they were diluted by children from all over the area and Lisa no longer felt that people were watching her and talking about her. Now, she was just another girl. Life at home was still very strained, but her mother had started work – at the doctor's suggestion – at a local factory and was often not at home when Lisa returned from school. This suited her: she would grab a sandwich and take it up to her bedroom, her refuge, the room she had shared with Dawn. She'd play music, read magazines and spend hours in front of the mirror experimenting with make-up and hair-styles.

By thirteen, she had become a very pretty girl and modelled herself on her heroine, Kylie Minogue. The blonde curls of her childhood had gone – her hair was straight and fair – and one day, with the help of a home dyeing kit, she made her fringe bright blonde.

'What are you playing at?' her mother said angrily. 'You're making a show of yourself. Just wait till your dad sees it.'

Bill, roused from his usual silence, said, 'What do you think you look like? And don't go thinking we can afford money for things like that. You look a right mess.'

And so began a series of confrontations over the next three or four years. Margaret and Bill did not like her clothes, her music, her hair, the amount of make-up she wore or her boyfriends. Boyfriends had come on the scene in a big way by the time she was fourteen, and she was unerringly attracted to the bad lads, the ones who skipped school, dabbled in drugs and drank cider in the park in the evenings.

On more than one occasion Bill stormed down to the park to bring Lisa home after she had broken her 9 p.m. curfew. Since Dawn's death, he had become a man of few words, but when he was angry, his tongue was unleashed and he told Lisa in no uncertain terms what a disappointment she was to her parents.

'We didn't bring you up to behave like this. What do you imagine those lads think of you? You're making yourself into a little trollop and I won't have it.'

He never actually said it, but Lisa could hear the unspoken words: 'Your sister, Dawn, would never have behaved like this.'

This was her biggest problem: she always felt she was failing to measure up to an impossible standard, the perfect child/teenager/young woman that Dawn would have been.

I'm second best. If they could have chosen, it would have been Dawn, not me, who survived, she thought. *She was the good girl, I was the naughty one, and now it's me they're left with.*

Worse, she was sure she had caused the death of their beloved Dawn, and she knew they could never forgive her. Her own deep distress at having lost her twin, her soulmate, was paired with a deep resentment about the perfection that death had bestowed on Dawn. One morning, in a moment of bitterness, she took the cuddly dog that had shared her bed since the day of the accident and hurled it into the bin. When she tried to retrieve it after school that day, the bin had been emptied. Angry tears sprang to her eyes, but she blinked them away and shrugged resolutely. She didn't care, did she? She was on her own and she would get on with it.

She didn't attend school enough to do well in her GCSEs. In fact, she didn't even bother to turn up for most of them, spending the days in a café in the shopping centre with a group of other girls and boys who were also drop-outs. Although Bill and Margaret only gave her a small amount of pocket money, for the last year she had been working at weekends and evenings in a supermarket, so there was money for clothes and make-up and endless coffees. Besides, she had a boyfriend who was always happy to lend her a few quid. Johnno was three years older than her and a part-time roadie for a band. She never knew how he came to have money, but he had a motorbike and, it seemed, an endless supply of cash for anything he needed. He'd pick her up in the café and whizz her off on the back of his bike. She was smitten.

Margaret and Bill were very worried, but they had no control over her. Whenever they tried to talk to her, she stomped up to her room and slammed the door – or, worse, she stormed out of the house and sometimes did not return until the next day, spending the night on a friend's settee.

Bill tried anger; Margaret tried pleading. The school washed their hands: she was coming up to leaving age, so she was simply written off.

'What are you going to do with your life?' Bill asked her, provoked by Margaret's nagging. 'You've made it clear you've got no time for school, so what do you plan to do when you leave? Because if you think I'm going to keep putting my hand in my pocket for you, you've got another think coming.'

Lisa shrugged her shoulders and, five minutes later, went out.

Margaret brought home application forms for the factory, but Lisa refused even to look at them. The final straw came one day when Margaret was sent home early from work with a migraine. As she put her key in the lock, she realised that something was wrong. There was the sound of Oasis pulsing through the place, the house smelled of cigarette smoke, and as she pushed open the door to the living room, she saw Lisa and Johnno sprawled across the sofa, arms wrapped around each other.

She banged the door open noisily. Lisa sprang up.

'What are you doing here?' she shouted.

'I live here, in case you've forgotten,' Margaret retorted.

Lisa straightened her clothes, and Johnno stood up. He didn't speak.

'Come on,' said Lisa, grabbing his hand. 'Let's get out of here.'

'Where are you going? Your dad will want a word with you, madam . . .' Margaret's voice trailed off as Lisa snatched her bag from the table, picked up her jacket and followed Johnno out of the house.

'Come back,' Margaret shouted, but her voice was drowned out by the noise of the motorbike.

Lisa jumped up behind Johnno and they took off down the street at speed, neither of them wearing crash helmets.

That was the last time either Margaret or Bill saw Lisa. A couple of days later, when Margaret was at work, Lisa went back into the house, packed her clothes and records, and left, pausing on the doorstep to push her key back through the lock.

They'll be happier without me, she told herself. From the day Dawn died, they haven't wanted me around. Well, now they've got the place to themselves, and their precious memories.

2

The Baby

Johnno had a friend who lived in a squat in Crouch End, London. Lisa had never heard of Crouch End before – she'd only been to London once, on a school trip, and all she could remember was larking around at the Tower of London and having her picture taken with one of the beefeaters. Johnno, who, at nineteen, seemed very worldly-wise back home in Wolverhampton, had no more knowledge of London than she did, but he was anxious to get away.

'What's the matter?' Lisa asked him.

'Nothing much, but there's a couple of blokes who say I owe them money, so it'd be a good idea to clear out for a while.'

Lisa asked no more questions. She was mad about Johnno, with his tall good looks and dark, brooding eyes. The idea of going to London excited her: she'd finally be away, really away from her miserable childhood. Maybe, at last, she could be complete and whole, without the presence of Dawn always with her, without her parents' unspoken but constant comparison of her to her perfect sister.

Crouch End was an area of Irish pubs and Turkish and Greek kebab shops. It was just on the verge of becoming a trendy place, but there was still an air of seediness about it. The squat was on a road of tall, run-down Victorian houses, the kind that would be gentrified and sold for millions in the future, but were now mainly subdivided into flats and bedsits. The house the squatters had taken over had been empty for years; Johnno's friend had heard about it from an underground network of people who sold details of vacant properties.

There were about ten people living there, coming and going, some staying for weeks, some just for a couple of nights. The house was in a bad state. Lisa and Johnno managed to claim a bedroom for themselves, right at the top of the house, but there were floorboards missing on the stairs and the landings, so you had to walk carefully, and there was no electricity, making torches and candles essential. There was cold water, as one of the squatters had found the stopcock and turned it on, but there was no heating.

'It's a filthy hole,' Johnno said with disgust, but Lisa was determined to make the best of it.

'At least we're away and together,' she said, struggling to open a can of beans Johnno had 'liberated' from a local supermarket.

For all her bravado, though, there were moments when she pined for her neat, clean bedroom at home. Once, as she walked along the road, the mournful music of *Coronation Street* spilled out from an open window and tears welled in her eyes as she remembered how it had always been her mum's favourite programme.

'Much better than *EastEnders* – not so miserable,' Margaret used to say.

Lisa remembered how, when she was young, her mum wrapped her in a blanket after her bath, made her hot chocolate, then snuggled up with her on the settee to watch it.

For a moment, she wondered if her departure had made Margaret sad, or if her dad had gone to the police to report her missing, but she hardened her heart, remembering the bitter rows over her behaviour in the months before she left. She quickly pushed the thought away and carried on back to the squat.

The room in the squat had an old mattress, and Johnno fixed a lock on the door, so that they could leave their bags there when they were out. Some of the others objected to this – a posh bloke called Tim said it was 'against the ethos of the squat'. Lisa did not really know what he meant, but she was glad to have some privacy. In the first couple of days, she'd come back to find another girl wearing one of her tops, and when she'd said something about it, the girl had just laughed and told her not to be 'such a bourgeois capitalist'.

She soon realised she needed to get on with the others, because Johnno was not around much. He never told her where he was going, except to say that he was meeting 'contacts, about business'. Lisa guessed that his business was something shady, possibly drugs, but he never told her and she didn't ask. Lisa was achingly lonely, so she was delighted when a girl called Shelley befriended her. Shelley had dyed black hair and dressed top to toe in black, but underneath the goth look she was chatty and friendly.

Together they would walk into the centre of the borough for Shelley to sign on for benefits. Lisa was unwilling to claim anything: she knew that, even though she was over sixteen, her parents might be trying to trace her and she didn't want to leave any clues. She lived on money that Johnno gave her, when he put in an appearance. As usual, he always seemed to have money. He would hand her three or four twenty-pound notes every few days, enough for her and Shelley to eat in a café every day. If she wanted new jeans or shoes, he gave her more. The motorbike had gone and he now had a car, which he parked several streets away to prevent the others in the squat demanding to use it.

Life went on in this uncomfortable routine for several months. Lisa felt she knew the grey streets of Crouch End like the back of her hand. She supposed she should find work, but she felt so tired and sluggish all the time.

It was Shelley who noticed first.

'You not feeling good?' she asked one morning, as she scraped Marmite on to bread in the kitchen area, where a Calor gas hob was used to boil water for tea.

Lisa was pale and felt vaguely sick, not sick enough to throw up, but queasy at the sight of the food.

'No, must have been that kebab,' said Lisa.

'Are you sure?' Shelley asked. 'Only it's not the first time you've looked like death warmed up in the morning. What are you using?'

'Using?'

'Yeah, what contraception are you on?'

'Johnno uses condoms,' said Lisa. The question startled her. She knew that once or twice they had taken risks, when Johnno had come back late and didn't have what he called 'Johnno's johnnies'.

'How are your periods?' Shelley asked.

'A bit erratic, but what with the move and everything, I've lost track.'

Shelley looked at her. 'You may be up the duff, and if you are, you need to find out, because if you leave it too late, you won't be able to get an abortion.'

Abortion. Lisa had never thought about being pregnant and having an abortion. Abortion was something they had discussions about with the teacher at school who drew the short straw and took them for sex education, an excuse for the boys to make silly jokes and the girls to look bored, pretending they knew it all.

That morning, she and Shelley bought three pregnancy testing kits. 'Just to be sure,' Shelley said. Lisa tried the first one in the toilet at the back of a hamburger bar, while Shelley was wolfing down a cheeseburger. She offered up a silent prayer as she waited to uncover the result, but her appeal was ignored. The thin blue line confirmed what Shelley had suspected: she was pregnant.

Back at the squat, the other two tests, taken at different times, gave the same result. There could be no doubt. Besides, from the moment that Shelley had suggested it, Lisa had felt pregnant. Her breasts were tender; her tummy felt very slightly bloated.

'What do I do?' she asked Shelley.

'You need to get rid of it. You go to the pregnancy advisory centre. They ask you a lot of questions, but as long as you give the right answers, they arrange it all for you. That's what I did.'

'You had an abortion?'

'Yeah. Last year. It was from a one-night stand. I couldn't wait to get rid of it – didn't want anything to remind me of it.'

Lisa waited anxiously for Johnno to show up so she could talk to him, but he didn't appear for a couple of days, and when he did, he only came to the squat to collect some things.

'Moving out,' he said, before Lisa had time to tell him her news. 'Got a proper flat, electricity and all. Can't stick this dirty hole.'

'I'll pack my things,' said Lisa.

Johnno took her chin in his hands and looked down into her eyes. He kissed her on the tip of her nose. 'It's been fun, little one. We've had a blast, but it's time to move on.'

'What do you mean?'

'It's over, that's what I mean. We both knew it wasn't for ever, didn't we? And look, I got you to London, away from those miserable bloody parents of yours. You've got a place to stay. You've made friends. Now it's time to move on.' He spoke gently.

Lisa couldn't believe her ears. She tried to blink back the tears that flooded her eyes.

'Johnno, I'm pregnant,' she said, her shoulders shaking and her voice quivering.

Johnno's face hardened. 'What?' He loosened his grip on her and stepped back.

'I'm having a baby.'

'Fuck.' There was a moment's pause. 'Get rid of it,' he said. 'You can't be more than a few weeks. Get shot of it. I'll give you some money.'

'But—'

'Are you sure it's mine?'

'Of course. What do you think I am, some kind of slapper?'

'I've seen that bloke Tim ogling you, and I haven't been around much lately.'

'No, you bloody haven't.' Anger exploded from Lisa. 'You swan in and out, don't worry about what happens to me when you're not here.'

'Like I said, that's none of my business any more. Do what the fuck you like, but get rid of that.' He gestured towards her stomach. 'Now, I'm off. I've got a meet and I'm going to be late.'

He grabbed a rucksack, stuffed some clothes into it and left the room so quickly he was almost running. Lisa heard him clattering down the uncarpeted stairs. She knew she would never see him again. She slumped on to the dirty mattress and began to cry.

The clinic was bright and airy, and the staff were friendly. Shelley sat with her in the waiting room, but Lisa went in to see the doctor alone. She explained, with tears running down her cheeks, why she was unable to have the baby: she was living in a squat, not in a relationship, no money. The doctor was sympathetic.

It was agreed that Lisa would return the following Wednesday for what the receptionist called 'the procedure'. Afterwards, she and Shelley went to the pub on the corner of the road near the squat: Lisa had developed a strong aversion to the smell of coffee and could not bear to sit in their favourite café, with its steaming espresso machine. She sipped an orange juice while Shelley had a half of cider.

'What are you going to do for money, now Johnno's gone?' Shelley asked.

'Dunno. I'll have to get a job when this is all over.'

'You could sign on. Living in the squat, no rent or anything, it's enough to survive on.'

Lisa shook her head. 'Don't want them to find me,' she said.

'You could always work here.'

'Here?'

'Didn't you see the sign in the window when we came in? "Bar staff wanted."'

'I've got no experience.'

'How much experience do you need to pull pints and take money?'

'I'll ask them now,' said Lisa, determined not to let the impulse pass. She knew, from the past few weeks, how easy it was to lie around the squat all day doing nothing, and the aimlessness was beginning to get to her.

'I thought you said you'd wait until this was out of the way,' said Shelley, gesturing at Lisa's tummy.

'Yeah, well, I'll tell him I need Wednesday off next week. The woman said I'd be able to go home the same day.'

The young bar manager was called Eamonn and he, like

most of the customers, had a strong Irish accent. He didn't ask many questions.

'When can you start?'

'I can start now if you want. As long as I can have next Wednesday off.'

'Right, then. No time like the present. Come behind the bar now and work the lunchtime shift – it will be light today, so it's a good time to get the hang of everything. I take it you'd like to be paid cash?'

The Albion was a big, barn-like pub, with dark mahogany fittings and shiny brass pumps. Eamonn was right: at lunchtime, there were just a few pensioners, in for sausage and mash, and a handful of regulars, men who propped up the bar all the hours that the pub was open. The evenings – especially at the weekends – were non-stop, as the pub was packed and there was never any time for a break.

It was good; she worked through the weekend, which gave her no time to think about the abortion, or the baby growing inside her. Or even Johnno, who, as she guessed, had not been in touch. At the end of her evening shift, she was so dog-tired that she fell into a deep sleep, only to wake to the ringing of the alarm clock in time to get back to the Albion for opening time the next day.

On Wednesday morning, the alarm rang much earlier and she dragged herself into consciousness. Shelley was coming with her again and was ready downstairs, with a marmalade sandwich in her hand.

'Want a bite?' she said.

'No, I'm not allowed to eat until it's over,' said Lisa, rummaging in her bag for the letter giving instructions. 'It says here that I can have a few sips of water, that's all.'

They walked to the bus-stop and queued with the commuters, who were dressed in their neat office clothes. Shelley's goth garb attracted a few looks, but Lisa, pale-faced and with her hair fastened back, went unnoticed. She looked even younger than her age. Shelley could see that her friend was worried.

'It's for the best,' she said soothingly. 'Once it's over, you can put it behind you, forget all about Johnno. I've heard there's jobs in Clacton, working the funfair – we could move on, if you like.'

Lisa squeezed Shelley's hand. She appreciated her kindness, but she was not reassured. The bus was crowded and they stood up for the whole journey. Lisa felt shaky, clinging tight to the rail and feeling her stomach give way when they swung round corners.

That's my baby, she thought, making his or her presence felt. That's why I feel sick: there's a little one inside me, and he or she is letting me know that they're a part of me. It was the first time she had thought of the baby as either a boy or a girl. Until then, it had been an 'it' and she had never allowed her mind to linger on it. As the bus swayed to a halt at the stop where they had to get off, she felt a sudden conviction that her unborn child was a girl. There was no reason for the thought, but it swept over her, as if someone was telling her. 'It's a little girl, your little girl,' a voice whispered in her head.

She pushed the thought away. This was not a baby. It was a 'thing', an inconvenience, something she had to get rid of to start her life properly. It was no bigger than a thumbnail, and the operation ahead of her was simple and quick. She shuddered involuntarily. Shelley, holding her hand, turned to her.

'What is it? Cold feet?'

Lisa nodded. 'I'm not sure I can do this.'

'You have to. What else you going to do? You're living in a squat, no hot water, no bloke bringing in money. Believe me, when it gets to winter in that house, it's difficult enough for us to survive, no place for a baby. And what you gonna do? Even if you get benefits, it won't be enough for two of you. And no bloke wants to take on a girl with a baby.'

Lisa nodded sadly. It seemed there was no choice.

'You're right. I'm going through with it.' Lisa dropped Shelley's hand decisively as they stood outside the clinic. 'I'm being silly. I'll see you tonight.'

She turned and walked inside. The receptionist looked up. There were two others in the waiting room. One was a harassed-looking woman in her late thirties or early forties, and the other a smart young woman in her twenties who was reading a magazine and ignoring her surroundings.

After giving her name, Lisa sat down with them. The older woman looked sad, staring at her lap with an air of complete dejection. The younger woman's attitude showed that she just wanted to get on with it, get it over.

Lisa picked up a magazine and tried to read. The page swam

before her eyes and she couldn't take anything in. Then in some strange way the print on the glossy page rearranged itself, until it spelled out in big capitals the words 'Don't do it.' Lisa blinked, but when she looked again, the words were still there. 'Don't do it. You don't have to do it.'

With a start she looked up. Everything was the same as before: the receptionist shuffling paperwork on her desk, the other two women both absorbed in their own ways of coping. When Lisa looked down at the magazine again, it was back to normal, a spread of pictures of autumn fashion. But the words were in her head, and the gentle voice was whispering to her again, 'You have a baby. Give her a chance to live.'

Lisa stood up suddenly. The other women all glanced at her. She made her way to the receptionist and said, in a voice that cracked, 'I've changed my mind. Thank you.'

The receptionist came round the desk and put an arm around her. 'Would you like to be on your own to think?'

'No,' Lisa said decisively. 'No, I've thought. I've changed my mind.'

'All right. But you know where we are.' The receptionist picked up Lisa's file and checked the dates. Then she handed her a card with the clinic's phone numbers on it. 'You still have a little while to come back, you know. Quite a few girls find it hard, but when they think about it . . .'

'Thanks. I'll . . . I'll come back if I change my mind again.'

She walked to the door, aware that the others were watching her. Outside, in the sunshine, an exquisite relief flooded through her body. Her legs felt weak and she walked a little way along the street to a low wall, where she sat down. She was overwhelmed by a feeling of happiness. The voice, so soft it was more a feeling than a clear sound, whispered, 'Well done. You've made the right choice.'

3

The Birth

It was January, and Lisa was eight and a half months pregnant. It was bitingly cold and she pulled the bulky anorak that Eamonn had loaned her tight around her huge stomach as she walked towards the Albion. The pubs and clubs were beginning to fill up, but their doors were closed against the freezing weather and the sounds of weekend merriment were muted. Swirls of icy wind whipped eddies of leaves and chocolate wrappers into the air and banked them in corners with discarded drinks cans.

Lisa shivered. Her shopping bag was heavy, and her legs were aching. She hadn't had much sleep the night before, because the baby had been very active. She was on her way back to the flat she shared with Eamonn, above the pub. He had turned into an unlikely saviour. He was gay and had moved to England from Ireland to escape the outspoken disapproval of his family. Like Lisa, he had cut all ties with home, and the two of them had, in a way, made a little family for themselves. As soon as he had found out that she was living in a squat, he had suggested she move into his spare bedroom, and she was very glad of the heating and the hot water. The squat had been just about bearable in summer, when the nights were light, but living there in winter would have been terrible. Shelley had gone, hitching her way to Clacton, and the floating population of the squat had changed. The final straw had been when some of them had objected to Lisa having a room all to herself.

She still worked behind the bar at the pub, but only at lunchtimes. In the evenings and weekends, her sheer bulk was a problem, with the five or six other bar staff having to squeeze past her all the time. Besides, she felt tired now that the baby was big and heavy. She'd been to the hospital that afternoon and everything was going well with the pregnancy, but, for the second time, the hospital staff had arranged for a social worker to be there. The woman, who was pleasant but brisk, wanted to know what was going to happen to 'Little Pickle', which was the nickname she and Eamonn had bestowed on her bump. There were questions about the baby's father, and about her own parents and family.

'I don't keep in touch with my family,' she said truculently.

'But they may want to help you,' said the grey-haired, tired-looking social worker.

'I don't know where they live – they've moved,' Lisa lied.

'But the father, your boyfriend . . . what about him?'

'No! I never want to see him. I don't want him to know . . . and I don't know where he is, either.' This time she was telling the truth.

Eamonn told her she should keep the baby. He swore that he would look after them both, and that they would always have a home with him, but Lisa wasn't sure it would work. Eamonn had a succession of boyfriends; he seemed to like picking up unsuitable characters who treated him badly, and several times Lisa had found herself holding his hand through the night and talking him through another crisis. He was also, with his camp manner, a target for 'queer-bashers', lads who, fuelled with drink, randomly attacked him. On more than one occasion Lisa had washed away blood and iced bruises after he had been kicked around in the street.

Inside the pub, they both felt safe. The regulars were used to Eamonn and liked him for running the place well, apart from the odd occasion when he drank too much. Then he could be abusive.

'It's in the genes,' he would say ruefully to Lisa the next day. 'They're all alcoholics on me da's side of the family. And not much better on me ma's.'

On the whole, though, he kept himself in check. Occasionally a rowdy drinker would have a go at him, but he was quick with a funny retort, and if it ever got out of hand, there were a couple of heavies who were employed to keep order when the place was heaving with customers. Lisa, too, felt secure; she'd come to know many of the Irish building workers who frequented the place, and who treated pregnant women like princesses.

As the months ticked by, though, decisions were going to have to be made. The social worker was adamant: the baby would be taken into care if Lisa could not provide adequate details of where she was going to live and how she was going to care for it. Her home at the Albion was safe for the moment – the brewery who owned the pub thought she was Eamonn's partner and that the baby was his – but Eamonn was sulking because she refused to commit to bringing up Little Pickle with him. And she was scared. She had been to a couple of antenatal classes and she'd had two scans, but whenever she went to those appointments, she felt like an outsider, sitting with other pregnant women, who talked together about buggies and breastfeeding.

So far Lisa hadn't done any of the normal, exciting pregnancy things. The only clothes she had for the baby were a couple of lacy matinée jackets crocheted by one of the old ladies who came into the pub for cheap lunches.

'I've done 'em in lemon – then it doesn't matter what you 'ave,' Elsie said.

'Oh, I'm definitely having a girl,' Lisa told her.

That evening, as she arrived back at the Albion, she was bracing herself to tell Eamonn, definitely, that she had made a decision: she would keep the baby, with his help. She resolved to speak to him in the morning because Thursday nights were busy in the pub and he'd be behind the bar. To her surprise, he was upstairs in the flat when she dragged her aching legs and her shopping bag up the stairs. She stood in the doorway, in horror, as she saw him packing his bags. He turned to her when she came in.

'Sacked,' was the only word he said, before he plunged on to the sofa with his head in his hands. 'Got until the end of the week to get out, but I wouldn't give them the satisfaction. I'm off now.'

'What? What are you talking about?'

'They've sacked me. The brewery manager. Accused me of having my fingers in the till. It's rubbish, but I can't prove it. Said I'm not running the place to their standards.'

'But it's always packed!'

'I know, but when a brewery wants you out, they'll find something. They've no doubt got someone else lined up for the job, and my bet is, they're paying him less than me.' He jumped up and carried on packing.

'Where are you going?'

'To Roy's. He's offered me a bed until I sort myself out.' Roy was the latest boyfriend, and not someone to whom Lisa had warmed.

'What about me?' she said as she sank wearily on to the sofa. 'What about my baby? You were going to help me . . .'

Eamonn sat down next to her and put his arm around her shoulder. Then he took her chin in his other hand. He spoke gently. 'We both knew that wasn't going to work, didn't we? You never really thought we would do that. You should try to track down Johnno – it shouldn't be too difficult. And get yourself on the council list to get a flat. Or go back to Plan A and give the baby up for adoption.'

'But you said –' she blinked back tears '– you loved Little Pickle, you wanted her.'

'It won't work,' said Eamonn, and a sharp edge had come into his voice. 'Now, I need to get on. They'll let you stay here until the end of the week.'

'But it's Thursday now.'

'Yeah, so if I was you, I'd get looking.'

'What about my job here?'

'I should forget that. One of the things he said to me, Mr Big-Shot Area Manager, was that there had been complaints from the staff that I was paying my girlfriend a full wage when she was only working a few hours. Which I was. Except you were never my girlfriend.'

He got up and carried on stuffing his clothes into a brand-new suitcase with wheels and a handle. Then he stopped and pulled his things out. 'Here, you'd better have this for your things. You won't be able to carry a bag.' Then he took out an old, battered case and a rucksack. 'These will do for me. I'm leaving this place with nothing more than I arrived with. See, I've written down Roy's address for you. Let me know how you get on with the birth and everything.'

He hugged her and was gone.

Lisa sank further back on the sofa, her head reeling. Why did people say things they didn't mean? Were all men, even gay ones, unreliable and selfish? What was she going to do? Without her wages, she had no money for a flat – and with a baby due in a couple of weeks, who would give her a job? She could not bear the idea of going back to the squat; besides, they probably wouldn't let her in. Her anguish was too deep for tears; she felt emotionally frozen, as if making any decision was beyond her.

She went through to the small kitchen and made herself a cup of tea, then switched on the television. She heard the closing bars of the *EastEnders* theme tune, and that was how, for the rest of her life, she would know the exact time that it happened: 8 p.m. She sat down and immediately felt a pleasant sensation of something giving way deep inside her; an uncontrollable flow of water gushed out of her, more than she could have believed possible. She staggered to the bathroom and grabbed a towel to put between her legs. Then, hanging on to the rail, she hauled herself down the stairs to the kitchen area behind the bar. One of the staff was there, standing at the entrance to the back door, smoking.

'Can you call an ambulance?' Lisa said. 'The baby's coming. My waters have broken.'

It was a short, relatively easy labour: only four hours. Some of the pains were intense, but when she asked for gas and air, a cheerful midwife told her to try to keep going without it and two contractions later she gave birth.

'You have a beautiful baby,' the midwife announced.

Lisa, exhausted, just nodded.

'Don't you want to know what it is?' said the grinning midwife. 'That's what everybody asks.'

'She's a girl, isn't she?' Lisa said.

'She sure is. Did they tell you at the scan, or did you just have a feeling?'

'Just a feeling. A very strong feeling.'

'Well, you were right. And she's a healthy seven and a half pounds. Here she is, all fingers and toes counted. Everything present and correct.'

She helped Lisa prop herself up and then handed her the little bundle, wrapped in a clean blanket.

Lisa stared down at her in wonder. 'Hello, Little Pickle. Welcome to the world.' Her eyes filled with tears as she fervently prayed that life would be kinder and easier for the tiny girl in her arms than it had been for her.

'I can change my mind in the next six weeks?' Lisa asked the social worker.

'Technically, yes, but really you should be sure now. Your baby will go to foster carers for six weeks and then she will join her new family. That's when you will sign the final paperwork.'

'And I'll never see her again?'

'When she's grown-up, she may want to contact you. That's up to her. We give assistance tracing you if she wants to, but it will be up to you whether you see her. By then you'll probably be married with other children.'

Lisa shook her head. 'No, never again. I can't love another baby like I love this one.'

Little Pickle, whom Lisa now called Amy, lay in a hospital cot next to them in the bright office. She was six days old, and just glancing at her overwhelmed Lisa with love, making milk start to flow from her breasts.

The social worker glanced at the wet stains on her shirt. 'Ask one of the nurses for some breast pads. Don't worry, the milk will dry up in a day or two.'

Lisa looked at her, saying nothing. She could no longer cry: she had cried day and night since the birth, as the realisation hit her that she could not possibly keep her baby.

'Look,' the social worker said very gently, 'you're only seventeen. You can't give her the life she deserves. I'm going to find a place in a hostel for you, but you don't have anywhere to bring up a baby. She'll have a better life . . .' She nearly added 'without you' but checked herself.

Lisa nodded mutely. She knew it made sense. She had nothing and no one. The day after she came into the hospital, someone from the pub had brought all her possessions, packed into the new suitcase on wheels that Eamonn had left. Whoever it was had simply handed it in, not bothered to come and see her and her baby. While Amy was sleeping the next day, she rummaged through the bag to see if the slip of paper with Eamonn's address and number was there. It wasn't. There was nobody, not a single person, she could ring up to share the thrill of the birth.

The other women on the ward had swarms of visitors. The woman in the bed next to hers seemed to have at least half a dozen other children, who arrived in relays with their harassed-looking father. The girl in the bed opposite, obviously with her first baby, spent all of visiting time holding hands with her young husband, both of them staring in wonder and adoration at their tiny creation. Bouquets of flowers were delivered up and down the ward; the arrival of the post brought cards and presents for all the other mothers.

Lisa felt excluded. She didn't even have clothes for her baby, apart from Elsie's tiny cardigans, which she dressed Amy in, over the worn Babygros that the nurses had found for her. Some of the nurses were sympathetic, pulling the curtains round her bed during visiting hours and stopping when they could to coo over Amy and chat to Lisa. Others gave her short shrift: an unmarried mother who was giving her baby up for adoption.

The decision to hand Amy over was not as difficult as she had feared; it was born of the realisation that she could not care for this tiny scrap of life, and that Amy deserved better. She slept fitfully, in between Amy's feeding demands, but her dreams were full of pictures of her baby in a family home, surrounded by loving parents and grandparents. The dreams were peaceful and happy, and when she woke, she felt, more than heard, her secret voice telling her, 'This is right. This is where Amy belongs.'

The social worker had come to see Lisa the day after the birth and Lisa had agreed to start the adoption process. She pulled the curtains round her bed immediately afterwards and cried and cried. A kind nurse popped in, but seeing the state she was in, left her alone.

Later, bringing her a cup of tea, the nurse said, 'Ignore what anyone else says. I think you are the bravest woman on the ward.'

There were mutterings among the staff and the rest of the mothers on the ward picked it up. When they sat around chatting about nappies and breastfeeding and which kind of prams they had bought, Lisa was not invited to join in and sat alone in the bubble of her own bed with Amy's cot alongside her.

'We could take her straightaway. That would be best for both of you, before you bond,' the social worker had said on the day after the birth, but Lisa had insisted on a few days with her baby. She even secretly breastfed her. The staff had told her not to, as the baby needed to get used to being bottle-fed, but when no one was around, in the dark reaches of the night, Lisa snuggled Amy against her chest and let her suckle.

'It may not be for long, Little Pickle, but right now you know who your mummy is,' she whispered to her tiny girl. On day six, the day when she would finally say goodbye, Lisa borrowed a sheet of paper and a pen from one of the staff. She wrote a brief note:

To my Little Pickle, my Amy,

I want you to know that I love you more than anything in the world. I wish with all my heart I could keep you, but I know you will have a happier and better life with someone else.

Please never feel unloved and unwanted because somewhere, wherever I am, I will be thinking of you.

Have a wonderful life.

She folded the paper and put it under the blanket in the small cot. Amy was sleeping peacefully as the social worker trundled the cot to the office to complete the paperwork. Lisa followed behind, with her suitcase on wheels.

'Can I leave this note for her?' she asked, taking it from under the blanket.

'Yes, but she won't get it until she is eighteen, and then only if she wants it.'

'I hope she does. I hope she comes to find me, and I'll be able by then to give her everything she needs in the world.'

The social worker smiled tolerantly. She realised that Lisa was very young and immature. She was happy because she was today doing one of the best parts of her job: she was taking a healthy young baby and finding it a loving home. There was already a couple lined up to take the little girl, but first, for six weeks, Amy would live with experienced foster carers and gradually be introduced to her new family. Lisa would move on. She would never completely forget her baby, and she would probably always feel a pang on Amy's birthday, but she would now have time to grow up, find a proper relationship, start a family with support and love. This was the best outcome for everybody, the social worker thought.

'That's it,' she said, putting the forms that Lisa had signed back into her file. 'Here's the address of the hostel. They are expecting you. Will you be all right finding it?'

Lisa nodded, taking the slip of paper.

'Goodbye, then,' said the social worker. 'I'll be in touch in six weeks, but you can contact me before then if you need to.'

Lisa leaned over the cot and gave her daughter one last kiss. 'Goodbye, my Little Pickle,' she said. Then she straightened up, gripped the handle of her suitcase and walked out, along the corridor, down in the lift and through the bustling hospital foyer. She had an impulse to scream at all the normal people, going about their business as if nothing had happened, when for her it felt as if the world had ended. She stood on the steps outside, feeling the harsh bite of the freezing air on her cheeks after the central heating of the hospital. She was glad she still had Eamonn's anorak.

That's it, all over, she thought to herself, repeating the words of the social worker. That's it.

4

Chaotic Years

'What's eating you?' A skinny girl wearing a purple shell suit and with her hair pulled tight on top of her head by a lime-green scrunchie was monopolising the microwave in the kitchen of the hostel. Lisa, a cardigan pulled across her, and with her arms folded in front of her, was waiting to heat her Pot Noodle.

'Nothing,' she said, in reply to the question, which was asked aggressively. In only three days Lisa had learned the rules of living so closely with other girls, and rule number one, more important than all the stuff about not nicking shampoo, was never to draw attention to yourself.

'Nuffink?' the girl asked. 'Where d'you get that funny accent?'

'I come from up north. The Midlands,' Lisa said.

'What you doing in London?'

'Oh, you know . . .'

The girl walked out and Lisa took her meal back to the room

she shared with three others, sleeping in two bunk beds. Fortunately they were all out – down the pub, Lisa guessed. She'd been invited to join them the first day, but after she'd refused, they had decided she was standoffish and no longer talked to her.

Lisa was glad. She wanted to be alone with her misery. Amy was gone and yet her body was craving her. She was still bleeding; her breasts were still swollen and tender, even though her milk supply was fast drying up. She ached for the feel of her baby in her arms, a deep primeval longing she could not share with these girls, who talked of boyfriends, drugs, hair-dye and make-up.

At night, she stuffed a sock into her mouth so that the others would not hear her crying into her pillow. By day, she wandered the streets, but the sight of mothers with prams was unbearable. She deliberately did not go into a supermarket until the evening, because during the day the aisles were clogged with toddlers and mums with babies. Where was Amy? Was someone looking after her properly? Did they pick her up as soon as she cried? She tried to suppress the thoughts, but it was impossible.

'It will get easier all the time,' the social worker had told her. How long did she have to wait?

It would have been easy to find oblivion through drugs or drink – the others at the hostel would have been happy to help out – but Lisa knew she had to stay strong and healthy for Amy. It was a strange feeling; she'd had it before about Dawn. When she was growing up, she always felt she had to do everything for Dawn as well as for herself. Even at her most rebellious, resentful stage with her parents, she never blamed Dawn and always had secret talks in her head with her sister. Now she talked to Amy, murmuring her love as she imagined the tiny, downy head nestling against her breast.

She thought about going back home to her parents; at night, in her cramped bunk bed, listening to the sighs and snores of the other girls, she fantasised about her bed in the room she had once shared with Dawn, with her posters of Michael Jackson on the wall and her familiar Paddington Bear duvet cover, which she'd had since she was little. When daylight came, though, she put the thoughts away. One of her mother's sayings was, 'You've made your own bed. Now lie on it.' That, she thought, is exactly what I have done, and I have got to make the best of it.

The other piece of advice the social worker gave her was to find a job, 'something to keep you busy, keep your mind off things'. She knew the value of this: she'd learned in the past that the only way to suppress worries, fears and sadness was to be too tired to feel anything. So she found work in a factory, making boxes. Lisa couldn't help having a little smile to herself when she realised she was doing what her mother wanted her to do: working in a factory.

Once there, she soon discovered that there were rumours that the factory was closing down.

'Take no notice – they're always saying this place is closing and I've been here fifteen years,' Joyce, who was next to her on the line, said.

They talked loudly, to hear each other above the noise. Some of the older employees could lip-read, they were so used to the roar of the machinery, but Lisa wasn't interested in talking.

The good thing about the job was that it meant she could start saving for a deposit on a place of her own, and after six months, Lisa was able to move out of the hostel into a tiny bedsit. It was a room in an old house. There was a bed with a stained mattress, a wardrobe, a chest of drawers, an armchair and a small table, and Lisa was able to make it look cheerful with a vase of artificial flowers and a brightly coloured duvet cover.

She couldn't do much for the bathroom, however, which she shared with the other residents. On her first day, she cleaned, disinfected and bleached the bathroom and toilet, hoping that if she started with it clean, the other tenants would follow her example. It was a forlorn hope, and every bath Lisa had was preceded by ten minutes of scrubbing the tub.

Apart from a smiling Caribbean woman on the top floor, none of the other residents seemed to speak English, so Lisa kept herself to herself, spending her evenings with her small portable television and her ghetto blaster, playing Whitney Houston's 'I Will Always Love You' over and over, dedicating it in her mind to her daughter, Amy.

By the time Christmas came along, Lisa felt she had settled into a routine, but as she walked down Oxford Street one day, with Christmas lights glittering in every shop window, the loss of Amy hit her with full force, harder than ever since those first, grief-stricken days after the birth. On Christmas Day, she stayed in her room and buried her head under her pillow when she thought of a bonny baby girl gasping in delight at the fairy lights on the Christmas tree, and being helped by doting parents to open a pile of presents wrapped in glittery paper.

Amy's first birthday was even harder. Walking home a couple of days before, she stopped at the corner shop and lingered over the cards. Should she get one for her little girl? Would Amy ever see it? Would she even want to see it, when she was grown-up? Staring through tear-filled eyes at cards for one-year-old girls, cheerfully bright with pictures of Winnie the Pooh or pink princesses, Lisa reached out towards one with a pretty fairy on the front. In her mind, this was how she saw her little Amy, as a fairy, bestowing happiness around her. But she pulled back her hand and told herself off for being stupid.

Walking back to the bedsit, she repeated over and over again, 'She's happy, I know she is.' She said it out loud as she walked along a deserted stretch of pavement, telling herself, 'If I say it enough times, it will be true,' and suddenly her anxiety lifted and she was flooded with a deep certainty that everything was all right. It was as if someone had whispered in her ear, 'You're right – she's happy and loved. Don't worry.'

With this reassurance, which came to her whenever she began to worry about Amy, Lisa discovered that the social worker's advice was sound: her grief for her lost baby never went away, but she got better at coping with it. At times, when the thought of Amy intruded when she was busy, she would mentally say to the little girl, 'Not now, Little Pickle. I'll be with you later.' Then, in the privacy of her room, she would play their song and give in to her longing, talking to her daughter out loud.

These episodes grew further and further apart, and gradually Amy became a distant, unarticulated, dull ache. But she never forgot the certainty that came to her on Amy's first birthday; wherever she was, she was sure that Amy was safe and happy, and she couldn't ask for more than that.

'Hey, Lisa, d'you fancy coming out with us tonight?'

Lisa looked up in surprise at Carol, one of the younger girls from work, and realised that, after more than a year of grieving, she felt ready to go out and forget her sadness. So that Friday, she and a group of girls went to a local night club and she danced until her feet and head throbbed. After that, it became a habit and Lisa would go out and dance until all her troubles faded into oblivion, returning to her bedsit in the early hours of Sunday morning to sleep away the empty day. Even though she was a club regular, she never took the drugs she was offered to keep her awake, nor did she take any notice of the men who would dance close to her, eager for a casual encounter. She was too busy losing herself in the music, forgetting Dawn, forgetting Amy, trying to remember what it felt like to be glad to be alive.

One of her friends from work, Siobhan, said sex was nothing more than a physical need, like hunger and thirst, and there was nothing more to it than there was to a good meal or a drink. But Lisa wasn't able to make a complete disconnection between her body and her emotions, and just the thought of one-night stands made her feel sordid.

One day, as she took her place on the factory line next to Joyce, the older lady turned to her and said, 'You fancy coming to bingo tonight, love? It's a bit of a laugh. Gets me away from the old man for a few hours, and there's never anything good on telly any more.'

Lisa shrugged. 'All right, I'll come.' She was pleased to be asked. It was somewhere to go, something to do, to get her away from another lonely night in her bedsit thinking about Amy.

She wasn't surprised, when she arrived, to find she was one of the youngest there, but she didn't mind. She liked the kind and undemanding company of Joyce and her friends, and she settled at the table with a cup of coffee, quite happy to talk about their ungrateful husbands and their health problems.

After a few minutes, Joyce nudged her. 'Oooh, he's a bit tasty. And he's looking right at you. If only I was twenty years younger . . .' Joyce and the others cackled as they eyed up the man by the door. He was wearing a tux and a bow tie, and was flirting with the women as they streamed in, asking the oldest ones whether their mothers knew they were out, calling all the blonde ones 'Marilyn'. Lisa giggled and flushed.

Later, when she went out to the foyer to go to the ladies', he came across. 'Here with your mum?' he asked.

Lisa smiled. 'No, just a couple of the girls from work.'

'Girls!' he laughed. 'I think you're the only one in the whole building I'd call a girl. I'm Phil. And I can't help wondering why a beautiful girl like you is wasting her time with a load of old biddies playing bingo. You should be out being wined and dined at the best restaurants in town.'

Lisa laughed. 'I like them. Anyway, a girl can have too much of a good thing, don't you know?'

She surprised herself with her flirtatious banter. It had been years since anyone had shown such an interest in her, and she suddenly remembered how much she liked having someone making a fuss of her.

After that, they chatted for so long that Lisa didn't go back into the hall for the rest of the bingo session. She warmed to him as he told her how his marriage had broken up and his wife had taken their two children up north, to her family. He spoke movingly of missing his kids. She told him a few bits about herself, about how she'd left home because her family did not approve of her boyfriend, and about splitting from Johnno. She never mentioned Amy, and when he asked if she had any brothers or sisters, she shook her head. It wasn't as if she wanted to deny Dawn's existence, but it was always easier not to have to launch into a long explanation. In her head, she said sorry to her sister, but she was enjoying herself so much that she didn't dwell on it.

When the bingo session finished and a tidal wave of noisy women swept through the double doors, Phil pulled Lisa to one side.

'Wait here. Please don't go.' The seriousness of his appeal was very seductive, and Lisa pulled herself into an alcove, as Phil joshed and chivvied the women out into the street.

As Joyce swept past, she gave Lisa a broad wink and shouted, 'Clickety click. Full house? Don't be late for work tomorrow.'

Lisa's other workmates cackled at the innuendo, but Lisa just shouted back, 'I'll be there. On the dot.'

Phil drove her home. He was tall and rangy, his fair hair cropped very short, to disguise, as she later realised, that it was thinning. He had an attractive, crooked smile, and she liked the fact that he could be serious. They sat in his car outside her flat and talked. She found herself longing for him to take her in his arms, but Phil was playing the long game and only gave her a tender, brief kiss as they parted in the early hours of the morning, leaving Lisa to go to bed on fire with thoughts of him. He was, she realised, the first man she had felt attracted to since Johnno. She'd begun to wonder if she would ever feel like this again, whether having a baby had taken away her ability to love anyone else.

She took a lot of ribbing on the factory line the next day, but the joking stopped when the notice went up about the closure of the factory. The rumours had finally come true. It was being shut down at the end of the week, when the final order was filled. Some of the women walked out as soon as they heard. Others, like Lisa, stayed and worked their full shift. She felt sorry for the manager, Mr Shankar, who had always been a fair boss.

It was lucky she stayed, because as she walked out, she recognised Phil's car in the side street opposite the factory gates. He flashed his headlights at her.

Thank goodness I took my overalls off, she said to herself. She, Joyce and a couple of the others had ceremoniously removed their nylon overalls and draped them over the production line.

After hugging Joyce and one or two of the others, she hurried across the main road to Phil's car.

Two weeks later, Lisa moved into his flat. She was in love with him, but there was another reason: the factory closure had left her with only a couple of weeks' rent money, and it was harder than she thought to find another job. Moving in with Phil took all that pressure off her.

The flat was on the fourth floor of a ten-storey council block. There were three matching blocks, forming three sides of a square round a bleak space where, once upon a time, some city planner had envisaged grass and flowers. Now it was barren, hard-caked earth where boys played endless games of football, rode bikes or skimmed up homemade ramps on their skateboards. Inside, the flat was clean and tidy, and Lisa soon put her own stamp on it, buying colourful rugs and framed prints for the walls. It felt luxurious after the bedsit and the hostel.

Phil didn't want her to work, and there was never any shortage of money. 'Just be here for me. That's all we need, babes.'

In the first few months, it *was* all they needed: they were wrapped up in each other, spending hours in bed together. He was a considerate lover and Lisa was in love, which blinded her to everything else.

Phil went out every evening, to his various jobs on the doors of pubs and clubs, coming home very late on Fridays and Saturdays and sleeping until the afternoon. Tuesdays and Thursdays, he was at the bingo hall. It was an unlikely place to need a bouncer, but he told her later that the management liked a smart, burly presence in the foyer. Sometimes she went with him, hoping to see Joyce and her other friends. She never did, but it made a change from sitting on her own watching television and trying to suppress her creeping loneliness.

She chatted to some of the neighbours, but most of them were older than her, and even the young women of her age were mainly single mums with prams and buggies loaded with babies and toddlers. She looked at them and felt a rush of guilt. Could she, somehow, have managed to keep Amy? She pushed the thought aside, imagining Amy in a warm, comfortable house with all the toys and clothes a little girl could need – not on some bleak council estate like this, growing up among discarded syringes and crushed lager cans.

'How old are you?' she would ask the little girls who played along the landing outside the flat. When they told her, she would mentally calculate whether they were older or younger than Amy and try to gauge from their size what Amy would look like and would be doing. She had a very clear picture of her daughter: chubby limbs, a mass of curly blonde hair and always wearing red shoes. She knew that she was confusing Amy, in her imagination, with Dawn, but it was a confusion that comforted her.

Phil was generous with money. There was always a wad of cash in a kitchen drawer for her to use. He encouraged her to get blonde streaks put through her fair hair; he took her out to buy clothes, bags and shoes; he paid for driving lessons and took her out for practice in his car. He was affectionate and Lisa was grateful to him for rescuing her, but she was often alone, and after cleaning the flat and shopping, there was nothing to do.

Even when he wasn't working, Phil went out at night, and sometimes during the day, too. There were never any explanations.

'Babes, it's the way it is. I have my life. I have things to do,' was all he ever said when she asked, and after a while she accepted it as a matter of course. Sometimes he used the words 'doing business', which reminded her of Johnno. She was happy not to know the details of Phil's 'work', and he always took a lot of trouble to assure her he loved her and that there were no other women in his life.

Sometimes he would say, 'Get yourself tarted up, make a big effort.' They would go to a restaurant or a gambling club to meet up with his mum and dad and other members of his large family, including his two brothers and his sister and her husband. His dad, the leader of the clan, was a lean, fit man in his sixties, with a hard face. Even when he was smiling, there was a calculating look in his eyes, and Lisa was unnerved by the way he looked at her, as if weighing her up. Phil's mother was a brittle, dyed blonde, very slim and with as many gold bracelets, necklaces and rings on as you would see in a jeweller's window. She befriended Lisa, telling her where to get French manicures and chiding Phil for not buying her more jewellery.

'Always get gold,' she whispered to Lisa. 'Then you've got something of your own, whatever happens.'

The restaurants where Phil's father ate gave him private rooms or booths, or cleared space around his table, so that from time to time during the evening associates would drift in and talk to him. There was a lot of laughter, and a lot of expensive wine was drunk. Phil and his brothers hung on the old man's words. Lisa felt uncomfortable, out of place among the other wives and girlfriends, who seemed tougher than she was.

Once, when she had had a few drinks, Phil's sister, Marie, told Lisa about Phil's wife and children.

'She did a runner with them. Dad wanted to get her back

and sort her out. She'd have taken a bit of a beating. But Phil said no, said he was glad to be shot of her, but I think he just didn't want the kids to see it. He's soft about those kids. Shame he can't even see them now.'

'But he could have access, surely?' Lisa said, curious because, ever since the first night, Phil had always clammed up when his family was mentioned. She'd found some photos of a small boy and a baby, but had pushed them back into the drawer, knowing that Phil did not want her to pry in that part of his life.

'Probably wouldn't get it, not with his record,' Marie said, helping herself to another large glass of wine.

'Marie, you've had enough.' It was her father speaking, and Marie put down the glass.

Lisa was aware that he had been watching them closely while they talked. She realised she was frightened of him, and for the first time could understand why Phil's ex had wanted to get away.

There was a loud hammering at the door. Lisa groaned and pulled the duvet over her head.

'Open up. Police.'

Lisa sat up with a start and glanced at the clock by the bedside. Five o'clock.

'Open up. Now. Or we break the door.'

She staggered out of bed, heart pounding in fear, and pulled her dressing gown around her. The man sleeping next to her propped himself up on his elbows.

'Don't let them in,' he muttered.

'If I don't, they'll break the door, and what good would that be?'

'It will buy me a bit of time,' he said.

'Like I said, what good would that do?'

At that moment, they heard the strong impact of a heavy object being swung against the door. Lisa hurried through, shouting, 'I'm coming.'

She unbolted the door and six policemen pushed past her into the narrow hallway. One of them stayed with her while the others dashed into the flat.

'What's he done?' she asked the policeman desperately. She'd been living with Phil for two years now, and in that time he had been arrested a couple of times, but never with so much drama.

The policeman shrugged and said, 'Don't ask me. I'm not in charge round here.'

She stared in shock at the policemen rushing through the flat. 'Must be something bad to send so many of you,' she said.

Just then Phil was brought through from the bedroom, wearing tracksuit bottoms, a singlet and bare feet.

'Where are my trainers?' he said to Lisa, as one of the policemen clasped handcuffs on to him.

'Where you left them. On the floor in the lounge. What have you done?'

Before he could say anything, the most senior of the policemen said, 'Phil Stevens, we are arresting you in connection with a series of thefts from jewellers. You do not have to say anything, but—'

'Yeah, yeah, blah de blah. I know the form,' said Phil.

'I still have to say it,' said the cop, running through the rest of the standard arrest caution as quickly as he could.

Lisa pushed her way into the living room and came back with Phil's trainers and a sweatshirt. It was summer, but at five in the morning, there was a chill in the air.

As he was being led out, Phil shouted to her, 'Ring me dad. He'll sort out the brief.'

The police took him out on to the walkway outside the flat and led him towards the stairwell. Lisa glanced at the damage to the door – it had splintered – and then went across to the rail and watched until Phil and his escorts appeared from the stairwell at ground level. She waved as he was led to one of the police cars, but he did not turn and look up. Seeing the area deserted, without kids on bikes and skateboards, was a novelty for Lisa. She watched as the police cars pulled away.

Before she could go back inside, her neighbour Barbara, who lived two doors down, came out.

'You all right, honey?' she said, looking at Lisa's pale face, eyes wide with distress.

Lisa nodded.

'It's always worse when they come when you're asleep,' Barbara said. 'And that lot were noisy. Woke the whole bloody neighbourhood.'

'Sorry about that,' said Lisa.

'Not your fault, honey. Anyway, you get used to it round here. Got a fag?'

Lisa shook her head and then remembered that Phil had some in the flat. 'Maybe,' she said, turning to go in.

Barbara followed her, and Lisa handed her a packet of fags from the stash of fifty or so packets that Phil kept in a cupboard in the living room.

'I'll put the kettle on. You look like you need a cup of tea,' she said.

Lisa remembered Phil's instruction to ring his father. The number was on a pad next to the phone, with a couple of other numbers for emergency use. She rang and Phil's father answered with a string of swear words.

'Jesus, do you know what fucking time it is?' he said, before she could speak.

'It's Lisa. The police have taken him. He said to ring you to sort out the solicitor.'

The voice on the other end changed. 'You did the right thing. Do you know which nick they took him to?'

'No.'

'You should always ask. In future, remember to ask.' The phone went dead.

In future, Lisa thought ruefully. In future . . .

Barbara came through with the tea and they sat in silence for a minute or two, Barbara smoking a cigarette.

'Is this the first time you've been raided?' she asked.

'Yes,' said Lisa. 'He's been arrested before a few times, but never like this.'

'The first is the worst,' said Barbara. 'You'll get used to it.'

'I don't intend to,' said Lisa.

Barbara shot her a shrewd glance. 'Not thinking of leaving him, are you?'

'Maybe. I was thinking of it before this.'

'Be careful. His dad's got connections. They won't take it well if you leave him while he's in the nick. I know his dad. A right villain in his day.'

They drank another mug of tea each, and Barbara smoked two more of Phil's cigarettes. Then Barbara glanced at the clock. 'I'd better get ready for work,' she said.

Lisa told her to keep the packet of cigarettes. Then she went back to bed, pulled the duvet over her head and cried. Phil was all she had: what would she do now?

Seeing Phil in jail was a shock to Lisa's system. A visiting order arrived in the post and she rang to fix a time to go. Before his trial, he was held in a local London prison and it was easy to get there. The procedures were unnerving the first time: putting all her belongings apart from some loose change into a locker, then being escorted through locked doors by prison officers. She was patted down by a female officer, then was vetted by a sniffer dog before going through into the visits hall. Round each table, fastened to the floor, were four chairs, three brown and one yellow.

She waited at the table allocated her, sitting initially in the yellow chair until a woman at the next table leaned over and said, 'The yellow ones are for the prisoners. First time, is it?'

Lisa nodded.

When Phil came in, wearing jeans, a denim shirt and his own trainers, she felt a rush of pleasure at seeing him, but it was short-lived.

'Go and get us some food and a coffee, babes,' he said.

'What?'

Phil nodded to the small cafeteria being staffed by volunteers at the other side of the visits hall, next to a play area where children were being supervised by more volunteers. Other wives and girlfriends were queuing at the counter and she joined them. Phil wanted a bacon sandwich, a Mars bar and a banana.

When she got back to the table, he leaned across and kissed her. She felt self-conscious, which killed all pleasure and passion. She had already noticed that many of the other women were locked in public clinches with their men, but it felt unnatural to Lisa.

When Phil pulled away, he said, 'Got a date for the trial. Another four months, but they won't give me bail.'

'Why not?

He shrugged. 'I've got a bit of previous.'

'Are you all right in here?'

'Yeah. I know a few of the blokes. It's not bad here. It'll be worse later on.'

'Later on?'

'When I go down.'

'So they'll find you guilty? Even with your dad's lawyer?'

Phil gave a cynical laugh. 'Yeah. He'll help keep the tariff down, but I'll still get a few years.'

'A few years?' Lisa was shocked.

'Yeah, with luck only five, out in two and a half if I keep my nose clean.'

Lisa felt a cold hand clutch at her heart. She knew, from what Barbara had told her and from her own observations, that it would be nearly impossible to abandon Phil. And besides, where would she go? Yet for years ahead her life was going to revolve round visits like this.

'I passed my driving test,' she said, to change the subject.

'Good girl. You'll need the car if they ship me out to somewhere like Long Lartin.'

Phil's prediction proved to have been optimistic: at the end of his trial, he was sentenced to eight years. Lisa, who sat in the public gallery with his mum and one of his brothers, let out an involuntary cry. Even with full remission, her life for the next four years was on hold.

5

Drifting

'Hey, beautiful, why do you always look so sad?' Craig was in his forties, not particularly good-looking, but he had one great attraction for Lisa: he was kind to her, and obviously fancied her. He was a delivery driver at the supermarket where she worked, and he always went out of his way to find her and chat to her.

Lisa had now spent five years visiting Phil in different jails, going out shopping with his mother and sister, spending strained evenings having meals presided over by his bullying father, Victor. Her neighbour Barbara had warned her that she had to handle Phil's family with kid gloves.

'Don't mess with that lot. You won't know what's hit you if you upset Victor. Be a good girl, stay faithful to Phil, send him letters and visit him, and they'll take care of you, but you'll have to live like a bloody nun while he's inside or they'll know.'

They did take care of her. The rent on the flat was paid, and although Lisa took a job in the local supermarket to keep her boredom at bay, and she earned enough money to support herself, every so often one of Phil's brothers would turn up to give her an envelope stuffed with notes. She didn't want it, but she knew that to turn down the money would be another thing that went against the unspoken code of this family, so she took it and carefully hid it behind the microwave.

She was achingly lonely. Although she could talk to Barbara and one or two of the other women on the estate, she was aware of a slight reserve: they knew she was part of Victor's clan and they were wary.

Barbara arranged the job at the supermarket, and it helped. Lisa loved the work, chatting to people as their shopping crawled along the conveyor belt at her till. She got on well with the other staff, but never grew close to any of them.

There were always difficult questions. 'Have you got any kids?' was the worst. She said no, but even uttering the word caused a huge chasm of pain to open up inside her. Where was Amy? Was she betraying her by denying her existence?

Over coffee or lunch in the canteen, the others talked about their terrible childbirth experiences, for the benefit of one of the girls, who was newly pregnant. Lisa kept quiet, but watched the slowly swelling belly and dreamed of Amy.

Every year Christmas was hell, as she saw happy parents stuffing their trolleys full of toys at the supermarket. She kept to her annual ritual: the day before Amy's birthday, she looked through birthday cards, mentally selecting the one she would send. Once or twice she even walked towards the till with it, then realised what she was doing and put it back in the rack. On 12 January, the day of the birthday, she booked herself to do a double shift at work. When she got home, she crawled into bed with half a bottle of wine and drank herself to sleep.

What was her daughter like? Was she healthy? Did she know she was adopted? If she did, did she ever wonder about Lisa? The thoughts tormented her, but she still had the strange sensation of knowing – almost as if she was being told – that Amy was happy and cared for.

Lisa's life revolved round monthly visits to Phil, and these she found harrowing. She drove for up to three hours to different prisons across the south of England, then waited, sometimes for ages, before being searched. There was a camaraderie among the wives, girlfriends and mothers; she saw the same faces much of the time. They supported each other, knew when things were going badly, smiled with genuine joy when one had good news about parole or a move to a jail nearer home. Lisa looked sadly at the little children visiting their fathers and felt a surge of relief that Amy had been spared all this.

Eventually she would be admitted for two hours with Phil. This was the worst bit.

'Hiya, babes,' was all he would say, before grabbing her in a clinch and snogging and groping her as much as the prison staff allowed – some jails were freer than others. Lisa felt self-conscious, and her passion for Phil had died long ago. When they weren't holding each other, there was little to talk about. He had his own life in prison, and he told her nothing about it.

'Your mum sends her love . . . I've painted the bathroom. It's a nice pale-green colour . . . The car's been in for a service,' were the limits of the conversation, and she knew it was boring.

She never mentioned her job, partly because Phil didn't know any of her colleagues, but also because it was the only aspect of her life where she felt in control. Work had always been Lisa's salvation.

There had to be more to life, though. She was young, pretty, lonely and vulnerable. So when Craig asked her out, she thought, Sod it! Sod Phil and Victor and the rest of them. Sod living like a nun. I need to have some fun.

Craig made her laugh and she enjoyed herself. After not drinking much for such a long time, she was quickly drunk. He almost had to carry her into the lift at the flats, and she didn't think twice about letting him follow her into the flat. She passed out as soon as he helped her on to the bed.

When she stirred in the morning, it took her a few moments to remember what had happened. Craig was not there. She remembered him telling her that he started work at 5 a.m. She stretched, pulled a dressing gown around herself and went to run a bath. Had anything happened? She was sure it hadn't, that Craig had not taken advantage of her. He'd left a note for her against the kettle. 'Next time, I won't let you drink so much!' was all it said.

She smiled, remembering the fun of the night before, but grateful that she had not done anything she regretted. Glancing at herself in the bathroom mirror, she smiled again: her mascara had run down her cheeks; her hair was wild and unkempt.

As the bath was running, there was a knock on the door. Loud and urgent, it was as if a fist was being used, not just a knuckle. She pulled the dressing gown tighter and went through to the hallway, her head too muzzy from the night before for panic to set in. As she opened the door, a foot came inside and then the door itself was pushed back hard, wrenching it from her hands. Two men walked in. One was Phil's brother Dan; the other was someone she had seen hanging around the outskirts of the family.

'You're a slag,' Dan said, and with a swift move he slapped her hard across the face with the back of his hand. 'You treat my brother like shit and we won't stand for that. He's better off without a slapper like you. You've got till midnight to get out of this flat, you cow, right? It's his flat. We pay the rent. You're nothing.'

He'd been holding her shoulder, but now he dropped it, turned and walked out.

The other man followed, but turned as he got to the door to say, 'Tonight. Out. We'll check.'

'But where will I go?' Lisa stammered.

Dan, from outside on the walkway, said, 'Don't know, don't care. But don't hang around here. Phil don't want to see you now, or when he gets out. Got it? And be grateful it's not my dad who turned up to tell you – you might not have such a pretty face if he has to sort you out.'

The door slammed shut. Lisa shuddered. She had no doubt that Dan was speaking the truth about his father.

The sound of water slopping over the side of the bath on to the floor roused her. She rushed through and switched off the taps. She threw a pile of towels from the airing cupboard on the wet floor, starting to clear up. Then she plunged into the bathtub, causing more overflow, and sank her head beneath the water. All traces of her hangover had vanished. She washed her hair, soaped herself thoroughly, savouring the pleasure of the bath. She had no idea where she was going to go, but she knew from past experiences that clean, hot baths were not always on offer.

For the same reason, she cooked herself a full breakfast. Then she rang the supermarket to tell them that she wasn't going to be in for her shift that evening. Barbara knocked at the door and came in quickly, glancing along the walkway to check that nobody saw her.

'I saw them come,' she said.

Lisa nodded mutely.

'What are you going to do?'

'They've told me I've got to get out. The flat is in Phil's name, so I've got to go.'

'When? At the weekend?'

'No, by tonight.'

Barbara gasped. 'Bastards. Where are you going?'

Lisa shrugged.

'Back to your folks? No, you don't get on with them, do you?' Barbara asked. 'Got any friends who could take you in?'

Lisa shook her head. The seriousness of the situation was only just beginning to hit her.

'I'd help if I could . . .' Barbara's voice trailed off. Then she brightened and said, 'I've got this cousin who runs a bar in Spain. That's far enough away, isn't it? I've got his number. I'm sure he'd find you a job doing something.'

'Spain? Abroad?'

'Yeah. Have you got a passport? Any money?'

'Yeah, got a passport ages ago when we were gonna have a

holiday in Majorca, but Phil got arrested instead.' Suddenly she remembered the money. 'And I've got some money.' Lisa went through to the kitchen and pulled the microwave out of its slot in the fitted cupboard. She balanced it carefully while she slid one hand behind it and pulled out all the envelopes. There were a lot. She carried them through to the sitting room, where Barbara was lighting another cigarette. Lisa plonked her spoils down on the coffee table and Barbara's eyes widened.

'Bloody hell, girl. You kept that quiet.' She nodded at the pile of discoloured and splitting envelopes, all spilling twenty-pound notes.

'Yeah. Never wanted their money, but I'll damn well use it now,' Lisa said.

They counted the cash; it came to nearly £5,000.

Lisa pushed £200 across the table to Barbara. 'That's for being a good friend, and for phoning your cousin. I'll pack my things. I like the sound of going to Spain.'

The decision had been taken so rapidly Lisa hadn't really had time to think about it. The amount of money had surprised her, and until Barbara made the suggestion, she had never considered moving abroad. But it made a lot of sense: she needed to get well away from the tentacles of Phil's family. Something inside her, almost like a voice whispering in her head, told her that this was the right decision, that Spain was a good move.

Barbara went home to get the phone number, but was back five minutes later.

'May as well use their phone,' she said, picking up the landline. She punched in a long number and then sat back with a cigarette.

'*Holá*, Andy!' she said. 'It's Barbara.'

For a couple of minutes they talked about family matters. Then Barbara said, 'Got any work, Andy? I've got this friend and she wants to start a new life out there.'

There was a pause. Then Lisa listened to one half of the conversation.

'Yeah, I know it's the off-season, but you'll be needing to staff up soon . . . Yeah, very pretty, and hard-working.' She covered the phone and said to Lisa, 'Don't suppose you speak the lingo?' Lisa shook her head and Barbara said into the receiver, 'No, but she'll pick it up.'

The one-sided conversation resumed.

'Soon, in a day or two . . . No, not running away. She's just broken up with a bloke and she wants a fresh start.'

A few minutes later, Barbara put the phone down. She turned over one of the empty envelopes and wrote down a name, an address and a phone number. 'You need to fly to Malaga. Andy's place is in a small town about five miles from Torremolinos. Lots of hotels and bars, very busy in the season. We've been there for a couple of holidays off-season – Andy and Margie own some apartments, but they make money out of them in-season, so any family freebies are off-season. Nice enough place, though, and once you've got yourself sorted, you'll be able to move somewhere livelier if you want. Just a warning: don't mess with Andy. He's a real lady's man, but Margie's a tough bird and she'd leave you for dead if she caught him playing away.'

'You won't tell anyone where I've gone, will you?' said Lisa.

Barbara pocketed the money Lisa had given her and said, 'No, not a dicky bird. I won't even tell my old man. Listen, I've got to get going. Give me a knock before you go – on second thoughts, ring me when you're off. Victor's got spies everywhere.'

The two women hugged. Lisa was truly grateful to Barbara.

'I'll send you a postcard, but I won't put my name on – then people will think it's your cousin.'

When Barbara had gone, Lisa went into the spare bedroom, bent down and pulled from under the bed the suitcase on wheels that had been given to her by Eamonn what seemed like a lifetime ago. Just the sight of the case took her back to Amy's birth, but she pushed the thought away. Then she started sorting out her clothes. Summer dresses, shorts, tops, jeans and a couple of sweaters – that was all she reckoned she needed.

Before she packed, she hit the phone and arranged herself a flight. It was all very simple. She could fly out of Gatwick tomorrow, and tonight she would check in to a hotel at the airport.

Spain off-season was beautiful. Every year, as the hectic tourist season started to taper out, and the families with kids packed their bags and returned to Britain or Germany for the new school term, and the gaggles of young men and women who came in groups to get blasted and get laid staggered ruefully back to the airport, regretting their sunburn and their hangovers, Lisa relaxed and, gazing up at the mountains, silently thanked Barbara for fixing it for her.

The throbbing heat subsided a bit and the glare from the endless white concrete buildings softened. Off-season, in the spring and autumn, the customers were couples without children, older usually, with more money to spend but not wanting to stay up so late or drink so much. The town began to settle down and the locals, who at the peak of the season were lost among all the T-shirts and shorts and mottled red skin, began to appear in the streets and the market again. In the winter months, parties of retired people would take over the hotels that didn't close down, but they rarely visited the bar, preferring their full-board and bingo packages.

Lisa settled very quickly into life in Spain. She got on well with Margie, the wife of Barbara's cousin, Andy, and because she was always willing to work hard, the couple had taken to her. Off-season, she lived in the smallest of the apartments they had for rent: in-season, she moved into a box room above the bar, sharing their accommodation. It didn't bother her: at that time of year, she was so tired that she could sleep anywhere.

The pay was not great, but she got free board and lodgings, which was the most important thing. In-season, she picked up tips from the parties of drunks who stayed until the early hours in the bar, chatting her up, spilling beer and being sick all over the toilets.

Every morning, as the sun rose clear and hot and the tourists slept off the night before, her day started with a gallon of neat disinfectant, which she swilled round the washrooms and then diluted to wash down the floor in the bar. Finally, she poured it over the pavement outside, before unstacking the tables and chairs, and putting them out for the day. It was the worst part of her job, and when it was done, she showered and joined

Andy and Margie for breakfast, trying not to get caught in the constant bickering that was their relationship.

When the summer came round, she wore shorts and low-cut tops all the time, her limbs toasted a light honey brown. Andy and Margie encouraged her to look good: a pretty girl helped to bring in the punters. Lisa became good at back-chat with the leery blokes, who all believed they were the first to come out with the chat-up lines they used. They would stagger in at lunchtime or later, starting their boozy days with full English breakfasts, which Andy cooked. Then they would disappear to the beach or a hotel pool, to burn their skin and sleep some more, in readiness for long nights of rowdiness.

'They're mad, aren't they?' Margie said soon after Lisa arrived, as the two women watched a party of English blokes roasting in the full sun, swilling beer and eating pizzas and chips outside the bar. 'They'll go home burned and sore and convinced they've had a great time.'

When the evening came, Andy and Margie smiled if a bevy of young girls descended on the bar, smelling of suntan lotion and hair products, because the big-spending boys would flock around them, and while all the flirting and copping-off went on, money would make its way into the till. Girls always got their first jug of sangria on the house.

Lisa made sure she kept all the tourists at arm's length, giving as good as she got in the chat-up stakes but never following through. She was too tired, and besides, Margie had warned her against it.

'They're just out for a good time, and unless you want to be just a good-time girl, don't do it. This bar isn't a knocking shop. We've had girls out from England before, but the minute they start shagging the customers, they go.'

Margie was blonde, small and neat, with mahogany-coloured skin that was just beginning to wrinkle. She and Andy had been living in Spain for more than ten years when Lisa arrived, and both spoke Spanish well – their constant rowing could be in either Spanish or English. Lisa, too, soon picked up enough of the language to get by in the market and to chat superficially to neighbouring bar owners.

'*Cómo está?*'

The question – How are you? – came from Ramón, the son of one of the other café proprietors on the same street as Andy's Bar. Lisa's first long, hot, exhausting summer on the Costa del Sol was winding down into late September. Like Lisa, Ramón had worked flat out all summer, and she and he had only exchanged smiles and waves as he shot past on his motor scooter with panniers of bread and tomatoes. He was younger than Lisa, athletically built and with classically Spanish good looks: dark-brown eyes, near-black hair and a wide grin that showed one gold tooth among his beautifully white teeth.

'*Muy bien, gracias,*' she replied. Very well, thank you.

Ramón had sauntered up the road to sit on one of the metal chairs outside Andy's Bar. She brought him over a beer and sat with him to chat.

'I can teach you to speak Spanish really well,' he promised her, and Lisa laughed, perfectly aware that it was not just Spanish he wanted to teach her.

The flirtation blossomed into an affair, with the approval of Andy and Margie, who knew Ramón and liked his father. Lisa was a good worker, and if she was happy, she would stay, which suited them.

In the winter months, when the sunshine was watery and a cool breeze swept the leaves from the esplanade, they did not mind that Ramón spent many nights in the tiny apartment where Lisa lived.

Ramón was a gentle lover, with a great body and endless energy. They went out together: during the off-season, Margie was happy to give her days off in return for all the seven-day weeks through the summer. They went shopping in Torremolinos, took picnics up into the mountains, driving through olive groves and stopping at roadside bars for tapas and wine. Lisa travelled on the back of the scooter, clinging on to Ramón as they shot recklessly round bends.

Ramón, whose English improved as much as Lisa's Spanish, talked romantically of a future together, of their own little *niños* and *niñas* – he was determined to have at least six children, he said. 'You will make the best *mamá* in the world.'

Lisa laughed it off, but for the first time since Amy's birth, she began to think about having another child, of a steady future with one man. Would she be betraying Amy if she had another child? Would she be replacing Amy? Deep inside, she felt that she could never love another baby the way she had loved her Little Pickle, but she enjoyed the fantasy of having more.

In her mind, her children with Ramón were dark, not blonde like Amy and Dawn, which made it easier to think about them without opening up huge chasms of pain. And they were boys: a baby of the same sex as Amy was too painful to contemplate.

Soon the blissful off-season came to a close and Lisa had to move back into the tiny box room. Ramón went home to his parents' house, one of the white villas dotted around the hills above the town. Lisa half hoped she would be invited to stay there, but Ramón explained that his parents were good Catholics and could not let an unmarried girl stay under their roof, let alone share a room with their son.

'We'll still see each other,' he said. 'Besides, squeezing into your little bed together will be *muy romántico* – very romantic.'

But it wasn't. After long days working in the bar, serving, clearing, cleaning, all Lisa wanted to do was sleep, and by the end of the day, both she and Ramón smelled of greasy food and spilled beer. They made love, but Ramón would slope off back to his comfortable bed at the villa before dawn. Increasingly, they both looked for excuses not to meet after work, Lisa just too dog-tired to care.

Despite herself, though, she found herself watching Ramón as he served at the tables of his father's café a hundred yards down the street, flirting and chatting with the foreign girls who came out to Spain in droves and were desperate for a holiday romance to take home with their memories. They were easy picking for a good-looking young man, and Lisa was jealous, aware for the first time that she was five years older than him, and that all his grand talk of settling down with babies was probably only that.

He's just doing his job – like you are, she told herself as drunken Brits tried to slap her bum and endlessly propositioned her, but she also noted that with Ramón certain girls seemed to be singled out for special treatment, and there were some nights when he was more than happy to kiss her hurriedly goodnight and not follow her upstairs to her room.

For two years, she tolerated it. The off-season, when he was as attentive and romantic as ever, made it worthwhile. By the third year, however, the magic was wearing thin for both of them. Whenever Lisa told him they could not go on leading this irregular life and that they should make a commitment and rent a flat together, he made excuses. First, his mother was ill. Second, his sister was getting married and the family needed him at home.

The talk of marriage and babies came less frequently. 'Your babies will be so beautiful,' he said. 'But maybe not yet. We are still so young.'

She wondered if he said it to deliberately wound her, because while he was only twenty-four, she was now approaching thirty. In the end, it was clear to her that he was only staying with her for convenience. 'It suits him to have a girlfriend on tap through the winter, when there are no tourists available,' she told Margie miserably.

Facing the end of her romance brought on a melancholy mood and Lisa found she started to spend more and more time thinking about Amy. Whenever she saw a girl in her pre-teens, with endless legs and short shorts, she tried to imagine how Amy looked, now that she was twelve. The blonde curls would probably be gone – after all, her own hair had been blonde and curly when she was small and was now straight and darker. Perhaps she would be tall – Johnno, her father, had been tall. Lisa shuddered at the thought of Johnno and hoped that her daughter had not inherited too many of his characteristics. She smiled ruefully when she remembered how hard she had fought her parents over him, and how in the end they had been proved right.

Thoughts of her parents, which came infrequently, always caused her heart to jolt. Time had healed her resentments towards them and she regretted the way they had parted. Still, she told herself they were probably very relieved to see her go: without her they could grieve openly for Dawn.

When the summer came round again, Lisa was quite glad of the excuse to move back into the room above the bar.

'This time, we split up properly, for ever,' she said to Ramón.

He pulled a sad face and kissed her on the end of her nose, but he did not protest. 'Perhaps you are right,' he said.

In the coming months, he flaunted his affairs with the willing girls on their summer breaks, who loved having a handsome Spaniard on their arm and in all the pictures they would flash around back home. It hurt, but she could cope with it. It's his job, she told herself.

Towards the end of her fourth summer in Spain, Lisa noted another change: he had found himself a Spanish girlfriend, a local who wore dresses or jeans, not tiny shorts and bikinis. She was, no doubt, the girl his family wanted for him, and he seemed very happy with their choice. Lisa watched as they zoomed by on his motorbike, the dark-eyed girl clinging to his waist, her skirt fluttering behind.

'He'll be getting married soon and having his six *niños* and *niñas*,' Lisa said to Margie.

She could not bear it and knew she had to move on.

6

Back to England

Torremolinos was big, brash and anonymous, a sprawl of high-rise bleached-white concrete apartment blocks, awash with Irish and English bars and crammed with shopping arcades selling souvenirs of Spain. It wasn't hard for Lisa to find summer work when she left Margie and Andy and moved down the coast to the big town: the bar owners along the Calle San Miguel fell over themselves to employ a pretty waitress who spoke both Spanish and English. Lisa knew that in the winter months, however, they would not keep her on.

It was time, she told herself, to go back to England. The thought of 'home' – even though she did not have a home – crept up on her and she envied the tourists, packing their bags and taking the electric railway to the airport at the end of their holidays.

They have lives, families, people who care about them, she thought, and wondered why she, at thirty, was still alone. Was it a punishment for giving her baby away? Once, as she wandered towards the crowded beach, she heard the sound of Whitney Houston singing 'I Will Always Love You' drifting from one of the bars and the jolt of pain to her heart was so swift and so painful that Lisa had to stop and lean against a wall for a moment, as tears rushed to her eyes, blinding her.

'I have tried running away from you, my Little Pickle, but you follow me everywhere,' she whispered in despair.

'You all right, love?' The voice of a middle-aged woman intruded into her agony.

Lisa opened her eyes, nodded that she was OK and purposefully strode away. Get a grip, she told herself sternly.

The feeling of homesickness grew. She found herself picking up English newspapers discarded by Brits in the bar and nostalgically reading them. She chatted with customers about where they were from and tried to work out where, if she returned, she would like to live. Without ties, the choice was hers, but that made it harder, too big.

Steve came to her rescue. He was a builder, out in Spain to build a villa for a wealthy couple from his home town, Leeds.

'They don't trust the local builders,' he told Lisa as he enjoyed a beer in the bar where she worked. It was the end of September and the season was edging to a close.

'They're right, too – the standard of building round here is frightening. The worst bit is all the paperwork, especially if you don't speak the lingo.'

The bar was empty apart from the odd older couple drifting in for a beer or a glass of wine, so Lisa had time to chat. Steve was in his early forties, stocky and strong-looking. His colouring was the burnished gold-brown of a fair-skinned person who has been exposed to all weathers. He told Lisa he had three workmen from England with him.

'They are off on the rampage. I give them a late start on Saturdays and Sundays, so they're somewhere in the town getting hammered and complaining that there aren't any girls around. During the summer months they did all right, though,' he laughed.

'Why aren't you with them?' Lisa asked.

'Been there, done that, got the T-shirt. Now I'm getting to the age where I need a night's sleep before I'm safe tiling a roof.'

A couple of hours later, Lisa had agreed to help Steve with his Spanish paperwork. She said she would meet him at the town hall on Monday morning, to interpret for him in his battle with the bureaucrats.

It was a long morning. The planning clerk was determined that Steve had broken regulations; Steve was insistent he had obeyed the letter of the law. The clerk insisted that he would have to inspect the site and Lisa had to put a restraining hand on Steve's thigh as she saw him nearly explode with frustration.

Later, over lunch, he told Lisa, 'I'd have finished this villa a month ago if they didn't keep making problems, and we had full planning permission before we started. Normally the owners do all the hassling with them, but they're away on business in America right now.'

'Do you have a slush fund?'

'You mean money for extras? Like more building materials?'

'Yeah, but also for a little bit of bribery. An envelope stuffed with euros would do the trick.'

'You reckon? But what do I do – just hand it over?'

'I'll be there, if you like, when he comes to do the inspection tomorrow.'

'Can you get time off?'

'No problem. I only get paid for the hours I work, and not much then. I make my money from tips. It's so quiet now that my boss will be happy not to pay me.'

The site meeting went well. Lisa opened a sheaf of plans to show to the inspector and on top was the envelope. The man took the papers, discreetly pocketed the money and then told Steve that it looked to him to be perfectly OK.

When he had gone, winding his way down the hillside in his little Seat car, Steve hugged Lisa in delight. The other lads crowded round to thank her.

'Two more weeks, lads, and you'll be back with your wives and girlfriends in sunny Leeds.' The builders pretended to pull faces, but Lisa could tell that secretly they were all looking forward to the end of the job. Three months in the Spanish sun sounded good, but by now they were all feeling nostalgic for home and the people they loved. It underlined her sadness, realising they each had a place to go to.

For the next couple of weeks, Steve spent a lot of time at the bar and Lisa took more and more time off work to sit on the sunny hillside watching the work going on. The white villa was almost complete: the red roof was finished; the bathrooms were tiled; the luxury kitchen was being installed. Lisa helped Steve by speaking on the phone to suppliers who were holding them up.

Steve laughed. 'I wish we'd had your services all the way

through. Sometimes we've actually had to down tools while we waited for materials.'

'Yeah, we'd have finished four or five weeks ago if we hadn't had the hold-ups,' said one of the men.

Later, over lunch, Steve took hold of Lisa's hand and said, 'I'm glad we had all that messing about by suppliers. If we'd finished five weeks ago, I'd never have met you.'

That night, they slept at the villa. They took a picnic and some rugs, and watched the sunset over the hills. The next morning, they were both stiff from sleeping on the hard floor, but it had been a night of gentle passion, and they laughed together as they staggered about like two old crocks. They had to have cold showers, because the boiler was not connected, but the weather was still warm enough.

When the other workers flew back to England at the end of the job, Steve managed to persuade his bosses that he needed to do another couple of weeks' 'snagging' on the villa, and also to be there when the furniture arrived. It was a great time for them. Lisa now only worked at weekends in the bar, and after the arrival of the beds, they were able to move into the villa in style.

As the time for Steve's departure grew close, they began to talk of a future together.

'We could travel and live wherever we like. I can always get work as a builder.'

'And there are always bars and cafés where I can work,' Lisa added.

Steve had told her he was divorced and had no children.

'That means we're both free spirits,' Lisa said. 'We can go wherever we like.'

Parting at Malaga Airport was difficult. They clung together, kissing and whispering their love in each other's ears.

'Be sure to let me know you get there safely.'

'I will. And then you can join me in a couple of weeks.'

For the next few days, the texts and phone calls between them flowed.

'We'd get arrested if anyone listened in on these calls,' said Lisa, as Steve described in detail what he would like to do to her.

The season had now dried up completely, and the bar owner was letting Lisa stay in her room in return for some cleaning and bar work, but was no longer paying her. It was time to go. She had some money: one big advantage of working flat out, seven days a week during the season was that there was no chance to spend anything.

She rang Steve and told him she was on her way to Leeds. He sounded pleased and gave her his address. She booked her flight, gave him the details and he told her how he would crush her in his arms as soon as she came through the arrivals gate. Lisa couldn't believe her luck. This time it looked like she'd met a man who wouldn't let her down: another chapter of her life was beginning.

Steve was not at the airport. His mobile number no longer worked. The address he had given her did not exist, according to a taxi driver with an *A to Z*. Instead, she wearily asked the driver to take her to a cheap but respectable hotel, which he did.

She felt a fool. She should have guessed Steve would have a wife and family back home, that she meant no more to him than the casual pick-ups of the guys who worked with him. Why was she so stupid? Hadn't she learned by now never to trust a man? Didn't they all let you down sooner or later?

It was just her, she thought. She attracted the bad ones. It didn't happen to other women: she'd seen plenty of happy families on holiday in Spain. It was her. She deserved it. She couldn't complain about men letting her down. What did she do? She let people down. She had let Dawn down so badly. If it wasn't for her, Dawn would be alive now, married with lovely little children of her own. And Amy, she had let Amy down bringing her into this world when she wasn't able to look after her. Maybe giving her up for adoption was the right thing, but what if she was in an unhappy family? What if the people who adopted her didn't love her enough?

Lisa cried herself to sleep, crying as she had not cried since the early days after handing over her baby. In the intervening years, Lisa had built a hard shell round herself, rarely allowing deep emotions to penetrate it. She had found a way of living in the present, not thinking about the past, not even thinking about the future in any long-term way. Everything was about getting through the day. Now, alone between the crisp sheets of her bed in the small commercial hotel, she gave in to a huge wave of grief.

Eventually she slept, and when she woke the next morning and pulled back the curtains, there was an initial sense of shock. The bright Spanish sunshine was gone and she looked out on a busy street with grey, drizzly sky above it. Buses and cars splashed through puddles, and people scurried past under umbrellas, with coat collars pulled up.

After the shock came a feeling of relief and pleasure. She may not have a home – not an actual house or flat, or a man eagerly waiting to greet her – but she felt she was home again in England. Spain had been great, but she did not realise until this minute how much she loved her own country. The rain, the grey sky, the traffic, the crowded buildings, she liked it all.

She went down to breakfast and told the receptionist she'd like to keep the room until the end of the week. Then she sat over her bacon and eggs, in a dining room full of dark-suited men in the city for business, and pored over last night's *Evening Post*. She looked for flats to rent and then quickly scanned the jobs columns. Whenever any thought of Steve came into her mind, she sternly dismissed it.

What had made her think a man would take care of her? She knew from bitter experience that the only person who could take care of her was herself. She was alone in this life and she had better get on with it. If you don't trust or rely on anyone, you can never be let down, she told herself.

She made a promise to herself that she would, from then on, never allow anyone to worm their way into her affections. There was still a cold, hard stone in the pit of her stomach, a deep reminder of the betrayal and hurt that Steve, along with all the others, had inflicted on her. But it only reinforced what she knew: she was on her own, now and for ever.

Sharing a flat is fine when you are in your early twenties, Lisa thought, but it's not so much fun when you are ten years older. She had a job in one of the large department stores in Leeds and was enjoying the regular hours and time off – things she had not had working in Spanish bars – but the only decent accommodation she could afford was a flat-share. She'd looked at one or two really horrible bedsits in tough areas, in large houses full of floating populations of oddballs, but had opted instead for a large flat in a good location, with the downside that she shared with three other young adults.

She had no real complaints about the others, just a list of niggles. Mark could not be trusted with anyone else's food or milk, and in the end Lisa had bought a little fridge to keep in her own room. Alison left her underclothes dripping over the bath and spent such long hours in the bathroom that Lisa was forced to get up an hour earlier than she needed to, just to get a shower. Simon brought a succession of willing young women back to the flat, and as his bedroom was next to Lisa's, she could hear more than she wanted of his enthusiastic love life.

They all liked loud music, and none of them was very keen on the cleaning rota that Lisa tried to establish. She did not mind doing all the cleaning: she had two days off during the week when the flat was deserted, and cleaning it filled the hours. She loved her days off. She pretended to herself it was her own place, and she fantasised about redecorating it the way she would like it. When she heard the door slam as the last of the three went out to work, she could wander around in her dressing gown, luxuriate in the bath, watch daytime television to her heart's content.

She got on well at work and was soon promoted to a department supervisor. Her department was handbags and accessories, and she loved the smell of the new leather when she unpacked a fresh consignment of bags. She deliberately steered clear of making friends at work, remembering her new resolution to keep herself to herself and never rely on anyone else. She was sure the other girls thought she was a tough old cow, because she expected high standards: she'd tick them off if they wore too much jewellery or their heels were too high. The standard uniform was a smart navy skirt and blue and white shirt, but the young ones did everything they could to customise it and make it more individual.

She was also tough about timekeeping, and about extra time off. If one of them was late, she expected them to work through their lunch break to make up the time. If one of them pleaded to go early for a school sports day or a parents' evening, she would grudgingly allow it in return for extra time on another day.

The others moaned about her in the canteen.

'She's a dried-up old fossil,' said one eighteen-year-old.

'If she had a family herself, she'd understand the pressures,' said the older women.

Occasionally she surprised them by being considerate and lenient. When one woman, Mary, was having problems with a wayward teenage daughter, Lisa was generous with the time off she needed to go to the school to sort things out. She knew why she felt sympathy for Mary: the girl who was causing the trouble was the same age that Amy would be. Lisa hated the idea that Amy might be having a difficult time somewhere, just as she had herself been a difficult adolescent. Seeing Mary's genuine puzzlement and distress reminded her of her own mother and she felt a pang of remorse for what she had put her parents through.

'We've done everything for her, always loved her,' Mary said. 'She says we preferred her brother to her, but she's wrong.'

The words were almost the same as those her mother, Margaret, had used, pleading with her to go to school and not hang out with Johnno.

'It's probably just a phase. She'll grow through it,' Lisa said, agreeing to Mary taking the afternoon off.

Just a phase – in her case the phase seemed to have lasted a long time, she thought. Here she was, thirty-one years old, nothing to show for her life, no relationships except a series of unsuitable men. She envied the women she worked with, even the ones who looked worn out with the battle to hold a job and run a family, even the silly young girls who lived for their Friday nights out in the clubs where they would dance all night and probably be picked up by youths whom they would not remember the next day. At least they had everything ahead of them, these girls, whereas Lisa felt that her life was already over. She'd failed at the big fences: love, motherhood, a bond with her parents. Now she was just marking time, getting by.

It was a disastrous staff Christmas party, two years after she arrived back in England, that made her decide to move on again. She had too much to drink and ended up going home with one of the floor managers, a married man. She had not intended it to happen, of course – she had told herself she would have a couple of drinks, say merry Christmas and then slip out when everyone else was enjoying themselves so much that they wouldn't notice.

She had reckoned without the powerful effect of the punch,

which was served from a huge silver tureen. All the time she worked the bars in Spain, Lisa had been careful not to drink much, and even in her time off had limited herself to a couple of glasses of wine. Since she had returned to England, she had not even had one drink. The punch, sweet and innocuous-tasting, really did pack a punch and after two glasses Lisa felt slightly giddy. She knew she was struggling to find words and she had to be careful when she walked. If someone told her a joke, she laughed too much and too long.

'I bet you can't pull old iron drawers,' one of the other managers said to Alan.

'Not sure I'd want to,' he replied.

'Fifty quid on it.'

Alan looked at Lisa, who was flushed and tossing her head back when she laughed. She was very pretty, especially now that she was out of the store uniform. She was wearing a black dress, with just enough cleavage, and a gold chain round her neck. Steve had bought her the chain and at first, after his betrayal, she thought of selling it or giving it to a charity shop, but then she told herself not to be an idiot: it was at least something to salvage from the wreckage. Hadn't Phil's mother told her, 'Always get gold'?

'You're on,' Alan said.

He was known throughout the store as a bit of a player, one of the little band of men who always circled round any attractive new girl. He'd tried to chat up Lisa when she joined, but she'd rebuffed him, and the others, with her icy manner. But now, with the punch inside her, he could see that she had thawed and decided it was worth trying to make fifty quid to put towards the extortionate costs of Christmas with a wife and two toddlers.

He took a fresh glass of the punch across to Lisa and she recklessly drank it. They danced together for a short time, but she was by now so unsteady on her feet that Alan soon scooped his arm around her shoulder and took her to a quiet corner of the room. Fifteen minutes later, he was helping her into a taxi outside and then climbing in with her. She tried to protest, but she was too out of it to care, slumping back against the leather seat and falling asleep.

Back at her flat, Alan helped her inside and into her bedroom. She collapsed on the bed and he carefully removed her clothes and tucked her in. Then he left. He wasn't up for taking advantage of a drunken woman – and besides, he reckoned he'd done enough to win his bet. He'd been able to grin and put his thumb up to the other blokes as he had steered Lisa out of the party, and he now had a good description of where she lived, and the colour of her underwear. His bet was safe.

At work after the one-day Christmas break, Lisa was aware of the other women looking at her. When Alan came across to talk to her, she kept the conversation very short and businesslike. She felt a fool. She knew she had let herself down and the others were all enjoying it. She knew that nothing had happened, but she could not prove it, and besides, she did not want to discuss it with anyone. When she walked into the canteen, she felt the prickle of others looking at her and imagined they were all sniggering about her.

Back at the flat, the other three drifted back from their Christmas breaks away, at home with their families. They'd been shocked when they'd realised Lisa would not be going away and there had even been a couple of half-hearted invitations to join them, which Lisa had, to their relief, turned down.

The day after Simon returned was one of her days off, and she was annoyed to see that he had simply dumped his rucksack in the living room, open and spilling its contents everywhere. She picked most of it up and carried it through to his room. Among the debris left on the floor was a newspaper, which she was about to dump in the bin when something stopped her. She did not know why, but for the first time in a while she felt the whispering in her head, telling her not to throw the paper away. She made herself a coffee and settled on the settee with it.

The masthead at the top of the front page said, 'The *Allerby Gazette*.' She'd heard of Allerby; it was a picturesque town in the Yorkshire Dales. When she had saved enough money for a car, she intended driving around some of the famous beauty spots in the area. She opened the paper, as if she was on autopilot, at the page near the back where jobs were advertised. Her eye immediately fell on a classified ad, not prominently displayed: 'Manageress wanted for large shoe shop. Town centre. Experience essential. Good rates.'

Lisa picked up a pen from the table and put a circle round it. Then she turned to the property pages and looked in the list of homes to rent. She was amazed how much cheaper it was to lease a flat there than in the centre of Leeds. She scanned the list; there were at least two that would be suitable.

She picked up the phone and rang the shoe shop. She found herself talking to the head office of the chain. Yes, the job was still vacant. Yes, they would be happy to see her for an interview. Would Thursday be OK? Did she know the area? Never mind, the shop was easy to find – just off the High Street. Two p.m.? See you then.

She immediately started ringing the property numbers and within half an hour had programmed a whole day of flat-viewing around the job interview. She told herself she should not jump the gun – she may not get the shoe shop job – but the voice in her head reassured her, giving her a very strong, unspoken conviction that what she was doing was right. She felt strangely happy all day.

Later that evening, when Simon came home, she said, 'What's Allerby like?'

'Allerby? I dunno. Never been there.'

'But you brought a paper back. Here, look – the *Allerby Gazette*.'

'I didn't bring it back, unless I picked it up by mistake when I got off the train. I had so much stuff to carry . . . I've no idea where it came from.'

7

Shoe Shop

Allerby was picture-postcard pretty, a small market town on the edge of the Yorkshire Dales National Park, with impressive grey stone buildings in the centre, cobbled alleyways and shops selling fudge and tea towels to tourists. The remains of a medieval castle and a restored woollen mill, where visitors could watch the looms in action, brought coachloads of trippers to the town. Lisa, who had always thought of herself as a city girl, fell in love with the place from the moment she arrived. She moved into her small flat on a cold February day, two days before she was due to start work at the shop.

Walking into the town on the day she arrived, she felt a heart-stopping pang of guilt as she passed a card shop. The stress of the move had made her miss, for the first time in sixteen years, her annual ritual of choosing a card (that she would never buy and never send) for Amy's birthday, three weeks earlier. She hesitated, but then went inside. From the racks of cards she selected one that she thought would be right for a sixteen-year-old girl: no more My Little Ponies or fairy princesses, this one featured pop stars like J-Lo and James Blunt.

If I was sending it to you, Little Pickle, I'd have to write, 'Belated Greetings,' and that would be terrible, she thought, biting her lip. You'd think I'd forgotten you, but I haven't, I promise. I've just been busy.

'Can I help you?' The shop assistant's voice cut into her thoughts.

'No . . . it's all right. I've changed my mind.' Lisa slipped the card back on to the rack, as she had slipped cards back every year.

Why do I do it? she asked herself when she went outside. Every year, the same ritual. Why can't I move on?

The flat was in an old house that had been converted into six apartments. She shared the second floor with an elderly lady, Mrs Smith, who liked to chat whenever they bumped into each other. Lisa was polite and helpful, carrying bags upstairs for the old lady and offering to feed her cat when Mrs Smith went away to stay with her daughter or her son. She kept a respectful distance, though, never going beyond the threshold of the flat and never inviting Mrs Smith into hers. She was determined to stay self-contained. Sure, she needed people in a casual way, but nobody was going to work their way below the surface of her life ever again.

The shop was light and large, on a cobbled street leading down from the High Street towards the river, very well positioned for passing tourist trade. Unlike Spain, the tourist season in the Dales was not dictated by the school holidays; it lasted from early spring to late autumn, with pensioners on coach trips and serious walkers with hiking boots and rucksacks filling the cafés and shops.

Lisa had two staff working for her, supplemented by a couple of schoolgirls who worked on Saturdays and during their holidays. Anne was a middle-aged woman who had been there for many years, ever since her children had reached school age. Now she had grandchildren, and different members of her large family were always popping into the shop for a chat. Jodie was twenty, with a steady boyfriend and a habit of arriving late and leaving early, and always adding an extra few minutes to her lunch hour every day. Lisa soon realised Jodie avoided work, lurking in the stockroom until she or Anne dealt with a customer.

She said nothing about their work to either of them for the first couple of weeks, giving herself time to get their measure. She was polite and friendly, but when the shop closed for lunch between 1 p.m. and 2 p.m., she resisted their invitations to join them for lunch in Shenley's Tearooms next door, a café that did a very good line in teas with cakes and scones, but at lunchtime laid on simple meals at reasonable prices. Then, on a Monday morning two weeks after her arrival, she called a meeting, putting a notice on the door that the shop had closed for an hour 'for staff training'.

'I'm going to make a few changes,' she said. 'We need a new layout in the shop and head office are sending some men over to do the work.'

'Great,' said Anne, nodding her approval. 'About time.'

'Yes, we'll make the place more inviting, with better window displays that we will change regularly,' said Lisa. 'We also have some bigger changes. The first thing is lunchtime. Instead of closing the shop, I want us to take staggered lunch breaks, so that we don't miss out on the lunchtime trade. It's stuck in the dark ages to close for lunch. And for the same reason, during the busy season, from Easter until the end of October, we're going to open on Sundays.'

Anne shot a glance at Jodie, who was open-mouthed. 'But we've always had Sunday off. It's when I see my family,' said Anne.

'Seems to me you see quite a lot of your family during opening hours here,' said Lisa tartly. 'I'd appreciate it if they didn't regard this place as a social centre.'

'You can't change our conditions,' said Jodie, whose fiancé was a union man. 'We haven't signed on to do Sundays.'

'No, and I'm not expecting you to. I'll open the shop and I'm sure I can get some decent casual staff to help me. The Saturday girls may want to earn more money, and if not, I'm sure there are other bright schoolgirls who would be happy to come in. But what I am expecting from you, Jodie, is that you work the hours that are in these precious conditions you have signed up to. That means you are here on time, you leave on time, and at lunchtime you take an hour, no more.'

'But if I don't leave ten minutes early, I miss my bus,' Jodie whined. 'There isn't another one for half an hour.'

Lisa shrugged. 'You'll have to get used to it. It's not fair that Anne and I do all the clearing up at the end of the day every day. You have to pull your weight. I'm sure that's in your conditions. Now, let's get this shop open. We'll work as normal this week, while the men are here revamping the layout, but from next Monday there will be staggered lunch breaks. You can choose between you who goes early and who goes late.'

Lunchtime could not come fast enough for Anne and Jodie. They were careful not to leave before 1 p.m. on the dot and then hurried round to the café next door.

Richard Shenley, who ran the café for his father, knew them well – they'd been coming in for sandwiches and coffee for years – and he watched with interest as the two women sat down and started moaning.

'What a cow,' said Jodie, plopping herself down at the first table.

'Hypocritical old bag,' said Anne, 'playing us all nicey-nicey and then doing this.'

'Staggered lunch breaks! And me missing my bus home every night. It's not like I haven't been prepared to stay later when we've had stocktaking and things . . . She's a miserable old bitch. No wonder no man has married her.'

Pushing his unruly fair hair away from his forehead, Richard went over to the table. 'Well, my two beautiful girls, what's it to be today?' He was a tall man with a boyish face, and today he was wearing his glasses because once again he hadn't been able to find his contact lenses when he got up.

'Something to cheer us up, Richard,' said Anne. 'A glass of red wine each.'

'Drinking? At lunchtime? That's not like you two. What's happened?'

'It's her, Madam Stuck-Up, the new boss.'

'Yes, I've seen her,' said Richard. 'She doesn't look that bad, but she must be, to make you two so fed up.'

'Yeah, she's changing everything. Making us keep the shop open all lunchtime. And she's going to open on Sundays.'

Richard secretly thought that this all seemed to make good business sense, but he didn't say so. 'I'll tell you what – spaghetti Bolognese for you both on the house. How's that?'

Anne and Jodie looked surprised and pleased. Richard was happy to give them the free meal – they were good customers. Besides, the chef had just cooked far too much spaghetti for a family who had been in, and there was always plenty of sauce.

When he returned to their table with the food, they were still complaining about their boss.

'It's not as though she's even really friendly. She's polite. But what do we know about her? Nothing,' said Anne.

'She told me she used to work in Spain,' said Jodie, 'and just before coming here, she was at that big department store in Leeds, but that's all I know.'

'Mystery woman,' said Anne. 'Must be something wrong with her. Nobody gets to that age without having a family.'

'Maybe she's running away from something,' said Jodie.

Richard listened in on them as he moved about the café serving other customers. It was early in the year and he would not be run off his feet for another couple of months. He had moved back home to take over after his dad, a widower, had had a stroke. He'd intended it to be a temporary move, just to help out, but three years on he was still here. He didn't mind: after his marriage broke up five years before, he had been rootless, and the café, and looking after his dad, had put a framework on his life. When he was younger, he'd been adamant that he didn't want to be involved in the family business, but now he was enjoying it.

He was interested in Lisa. She had struck him as attractive the first day he had seen her, but she had never been into the café to eat, and although she always answered his 'Good mornings' pleasantly, she never lingered to engage in conversation. She had not noticed him at all, he felt sure.

The next few months were tricky for Lisa. Anne and Jodie accepted the new arrangements, but they were as mutinous and uncooperative as they could possibly be without giving her grounds to reprimand them. As usual, she survived by keeping very busy, working a seven-day week. When she closed the shop at 4 p.m. on Sunday, she would usually stay behind for a couple of hours, doing paperwork or a new window display.

She loved opening shoeboxes. Again, the smell of new leather was always a pleasure. She enjoyed planning how to display the shoes both in the window and inside the shop. She persuaded head office that she should stock a range of walking boots and a rack of umbrellas, and these proved popular. By staying open seven days a week in the tourist season, she increased sales of sandals and even wellies. Anne and Jodie complained about trippers 'who only come in to get out of the rain', and it was true that when the weather was bad, the shop would fill with women in damp-smelling raincoats, but Lisa would invariably sell them something, even if it was only shoe polish.

She knew when the children were due to go back to school and always gave over the prime displays to the kind of shoes they could wear with their uniforms. She watched as teenagers tried to persuade their mothers that two-inch heels were allowed, reminding her of herself at that age, but she made sure one of the other staff served them: she could not bear to be so close to a girl of Amy's age.

One Sunday afternoon, as she began a display of small shoes for babies, toddlers and pre-school children, she opened a box and drew out a pair of bright-red shoes. She felt her breath catch in the back of her throat. Normally, she tried not to think about Dawn, suppressing thoughts as soon as they entered her head, but the red shoes brought the memories flooding back. She could picture the two pairs of shoes, one blue, one red, tucked under their beds. And, horrifically, she visualised the awful moment when Dawn's red shoe had flown off when the motorbike had tossed her little body into the air. She had never been able, in her memory, to see Dawn's crumpled body; all she ever conjured up of the scene was the lone red shoe.

She concentrated hard on not crying, packed the red shoes back in their box and decided it was time to go home. She would come in half an hour early tomorrow to finish the display. As she was locking up, Richard came out of the café next door. He still had two customers, a pair of lovebirds who were lingering over cups of frothy coffee, more interested in each other than their surroundings.

'How's it going?' he said chattily to Lisa.

She nodded her head and muttered, 'OK,' turning and

walking away. The emotion of the red shoes was too great for her to trust herself to speak more.

Richard could see that she was on the verge of tears. He looked after her.

Hmm. Perhaps you are the snotty cow the girls think you are, he said to himself.

Barry came into Lisa's life when she was at a low ebb.

Lisa was used to being lonely, but this was the worst it had ever been, because she did not even have the casual chatty friendship of the women she worked with. Anne was beginning to thaw, but Jodie, she knew, loathed her and called her 'the Battleaxe' and worse names behind her back. During Jodie's lunch breaks, when she was alone with Anne, the atmosphere became almost pleasant, as they'd talk together about the customers and the new stock, but the minute Jodie was back, Anne's shutters came down. Lisa disliked the situation not just for her own sake but because she believed customers picked up on whether a place was happy and well run, and that this affected how long they stayed in the shop, browsing and buying.

It was Mrs Smith who introduced her to Barry, but she would have met him anyway eventually. He worked for the owner of the block of flats, a man who lived abroad. Lisa had dealt with a pleasant girl at the estate agent's when she took on the flat, but Barry, apparently, was in charge of managing the block. Any complaints about maintenance had to go to him.

'I've heard he can be very nasty with people who don't pay their rent,' Mrs Smith told her. 'There were some hippies downstairs once, strange smells and loud music and girls wearing black lipstick. He got them out in no time. I've only had good dealings with him, though. When my boiler broke, he was round with workmen the next day, and he'll change the light bulbs on the stairs as soon as they go.'

One day when Lisa arrived home at 7 p.m., she was about to put her key in the lock when Mrs Smith called to her. She came out of the doorway of her flat and a tall, dark-haired man with a swarthy complexion followed her. He was so dark he did not look English, but when he spoke, he had a broad Yorkshire accent.

'This is Barry,' Mrs Smith said, 'Barry who looks after everything here. He's just been sorting out my electric. Very good – fixed it straightaway and came two hours after I called him.'

Barry flashed Lisa a complicit grin and winked behind the old lady's back. 'It wasn't difficult,' he said. 'All you'd done was trip the fuse box. Remember what I said – you need to go down to the hardware shop in the High Street and get Bernie there to put a new plug on that kettle of yours. That's all it needs. And don't use it until then.'

'No, I'll boil water in a pan,' said Mrs Smith.

Throughout this exchange, Barry was looking at Lisa, who found herself smiling back at him.

'Now that I'm here, perhaps I should check out your flat, Miss Heywood.'

Lisa smiled. 'Just call me Lisa,' she said, opening the door for him.

He followed her inside, calling his goodbyes to Mrs Smith.

'Lovely old dear,' he said, after Lisa's front door closed behind him, 'but she's always doing that. I must have been out four times because she plugs in old equipment she's had since the dawn of time, and I think the cat chews the plugs.'

'It could be dangerous,' Lisa said.

'No, the trip switch throws. She's never figured out how to get the electricity back on, and I prefer to keep it like that. I'd rather come out every time one of her gadgets blows a fuse than have her messing about in the fuse box.'

'Very conscientious,' Lisa said with a smile.

'Well, I reckon you're the conscientious one. I've been wanting to meet you, but every time I come round, even on a Sunday, you're out. Always at work, according to Mrs Smith.'

'Just for a bit. I'm putting in a seven-day week. I'll ease up soon, when I've got my staff trained. Is this a full-time job for you?'

Barry laughed. 'Full-time and a half. Chet Ainsworth owns a lot of properties and I look after them for him. They're not all easy like this block. They're all over Yorkshire, and they're in rough areas of Leeds and Bradford. I've got a few blokes who I can call on when I need to – and I need to sometimes.'

'So how come you turn up here in the evening two hours after an old lady's kettle blows a fuse?' Lisa asked.

Barry laughed. 'That's because I live in Allerby, and I always know what will be wrong, so it's not worth calling out an electrician. Plus, it's a good excuse to get out of the house.' He winked broadly again.

'You have a family?' Lisa asked.

'Yeah, a couple of lovely sprogs and a wife who treats me like dirt. I'm always glad to get out for the evening. She can't complain, because I'm bringing in the money, aren't I? She's got no idea it's only a blown fuse. So how about you and me go and have a drink, to celebrate my escape?'

Normally Lisa would have said no. She didn't want anyone in her life, and she certainly didn't want a married man with problems, but Barry was very attractive, and as they had been talking, he had edged closer to her and she found herself melting into his dark eyes. It was a pure animal attraction. His swarthy colouring reminded her of Ramón, but it was more than that; she was engulfed by a visceral desire to touch him. It was a long time since she had felt herself swept off her feet by a man, but Barry was having that effect on her.

Over a few drinks, he told her the story of his life. Chet Ainsworth was a villain who had made a lot of money through protection rackets back in the 1960s. He was more or less straight now, with all his ill-gotten gains invested in property. Barry had become involved, doing 'a few little jobs' for him, and when Chet had left to live in Spain, he had asked Barry to become his property manager.

'You don't say no to Chet. That would have been writing my own suicide note,' he said. 'Chet's got the sort of connections you don't argue with. Anyway, it's a good job. Hours are irregular, but the pay is OK. Chet's tough, and pretty mean, but he knows the size of the investment I'm protecting, so he pays me a decent wage. Besides –' he winked again '– I've got my own deals going down and Chet knows nothing about them.'

'Isn't that dangerous?' Lisa asked. She was surprised that he was telling her so much, but sensed that he, too, had nobody to talk to.

'I'm careful,' he said. Lisa had been aware that in the pub, where one or two men seemed to know him, he kept a respectful distance from her and did not publicly chat her up, which only increased the sexual tension between the two of them. When they got back into his car, a Jaguar, he drove clear of the town and pulled into a layby. As soon as the engine was off, they were in each other's arms, hungrily kissing and holding their bodies against each other.

'Back to your place, I think,' he said, when he finally pulled himself away from her.

They parked the car round the corner so Barry could sneak in without any of the other residents seeing him, and they made love until daylight began to seep through the gap in the curtains. After he left, Lisa soaked for ages in the bath, then slept for a couple of hours before going into work. Every sensible bit of her screamed that Barry meant danger, but she was forced to recognise that she enjoyed sex and had missed it badly. She had even enjoyed the companionship of going for a drink with someone, having someone to talk and listen to.

8

Barry

For a few months, the affair with Barry was all-consuming. She lived for the times when he would turn up at her flat. If he rang her in advance, she'd shop for food in her lunch break and make an effort to get home from work early, to peel and chop and prepare meals for him. She'd buy wine, and flowers to make the flat look lovely. She shopped for new bed linen, bought paintings for the walls, made the place into a cheerful home, and for the first time in ages she haunted the boutiques and clothes shops in the town, trying on their latest stock and buying dresses and tops that flattered her shape and colouring. At work, she made full use of her staff discount to buy strappy, high-heeled, sexy shoes.

'She's got a bloke,' Jodie confidently told Anne. 'Why else would she be buying shoes like that?'

Sometimes Barry would turn up without telling her in advance, so she was always there for him, hastily brushing her hair and applying a slick of lipstick in the couple of minutes from the entry phone buzzer going to him reaching her door. She had no other social life and he soon realised this. Her flat became a second home to him, except that he was always careful to leave in the early hours of the morning. She stopped slobbing around in jeans and sweaters after work every day and instead changed into one of her new outfits in case he turned up. She stayed up later than normal, because at times he showed up really late, usually too drunk to do anything other than fall asleep on her settee. On those nights, she would set her alarm for 4 a.m., so that she could shake him awake and push him out of the door.

I'm sending you back to your wife, she would think bitterly. I'm supposed to be your lover, but I don't even get sex out of the arrangement.

Every time she resolved to end the affair, he would turn up with expensive presents for her, a disarming smile on his face. He brought her gold necklaces and bracelets, and although she resented the feeling of being a kept woman, she had learned from bitter experience that she should take whatever she could from a man, because it would invariably all end with him deserting her one day. The advice from Phil's mother – 'Always get gold' – rang in her head again.

Barry became more confident about being seen out with her, taking her to a couple of pubs in the town, and sometimes to a restaurant on a hill overlooking Allerby, with a view down through lush trees to the river.

'I don't give a damn if the wife finds out – I'd happily divorce her tomorrow if it wasn't for the kids,' he said.

Lisa smiled wryly to herself but said nothing. Wasn't this the classic married man's get-out clause, 'I'm only staying because I love my children'?

Barry always seemed to have business to do when they went out. Lisa would see him in urgent conversation with men who would turn up expressly to see him. Although she sat outside hearing range, she could tell from his expression and gestures that he was being tough with these men, putting pressure on them. Sometimes envelopes would change hands and Barry would bend his head while he flicked through the notes inside. Lisa shuddered, involuntarily, the first time she saw one of the men hand him an envelope, as it reminded her of her unhappy time with Phil's family. The men, too: they were the same sort of thugs who hung around Phil's father.

When they went to the restaurant, Barry would make sure Lisa was settled at a table, and the obsequious proprietor, Enrico, would bring wine and breadsticks to her. Then, if the restaurant was fairly empty, he and Barry would sit at a far table out of earshot and whisper to each other. Later, just as she was beginning to feel the effects of the second glass of red wine, Barry would rejoin her and they would be served a meal. They always left without Barry paying anything, but he would be at pains to leave a generous tip for the staff.

'Always keep the little people on side,' he said. 'You can never be certain how much they know. You need them to be grateful; that buys their silence.'

'What are you involved in?' Lisa asked him one night, when they lay back on the pillows after energetic lovemaking. Experience had taught her that these were good moments to get information from men, when they were drowsy and contented. She was worried that Barry was heading for trouble.

'Business. Got some of my own deals going. Nothing to do Chet.'

'You'd better be careful. Those men you are dealing with, I don't think you can trust them. And I wouldn't trust Enrico, either.'

A hard edge crept into Barry's voice. 'What's it got to do with you? You don't know anything. Do you?' The question was asked menacingly.

'Of course not,' said Lisa truthfully. All she had was a premonition, but her instinct to protect Barry had misfired. The aggression in his voice made her feel slightly sick.

The mood had been broken and Barry got up, dressed and left without kissing her goodbye.

The relationship had slipped a gear. From then on, Barry was more offhand, less tender in his dealings with her. He turned up just as often, and there were still occasional presents from him, but Lisa knew that her flat was just a convenient place for him when he did not want to go home until his wife was in bed and asleep. She didn't ask questions about his family, partly because her way of dealing with the guilt of being a mistress was simply not to acknowledge their existence, and partly because she had learned not to pry into Barry's life. He had made it clear what the terms of their relationship were. He was in charge, and everything was done to service his needs. He told her once that he had only married his wife because she was pregnant, and that he had felt coerced into it. Whenever he mentioned her, it was in derisory terms: 'She's a lazy cow.

Sits around all day watching TV and eating chocolates. She's let herself go.'

Lisa gave herself lectures, telling herself she was being a complete fool and that she shouldn't be taken in by this 'my wife doesn't understand me' routine, but she found his company addictive.

She tried to convince herself she'd always been happiest when she was on her own, but the sad fact was, she was more alone than ever, and she knew it.

She understood that all his talk of leaving his wife meant nothing, and that even if he did one day split from her, he would never want to live full-time with Lisa. She didn't want him full-time: she was determined never to let any man have that much hold over her ever again. Even so, on the occasions when she didn't see him for a couple of weeks, she missed the casual companionship he gave her, and there was an anxious feeling in the pit of her stomach as her eyes raked the traffic for his car. She still got a buzz from seeing him. Sometimes, if there was a knock on her door in the evening, she would rush to open it, her heart thudding and a huge smile on her face, but these days it was more likely to be Mrs Smith, asking if she would look after the cat. Realising it wasn't Barry left her feeling flat and miserable.

Things had not improved much at work. Anne was a good worker, but Jodie was insolent and deliberately worked slowly. Telling her to clear up the stockroom meant she would disappear for an hour and not much would happen. She talked endlessly on her mobile phone and Lisa had to ban her from using it out in the shop, in front of customers. This caused her to flounce around for the rest of the day. Her attitude to customers was poor, as if they were a nuisance who had interrupted her day.

Lisa spoke to head office about her, but was told that there were insufficient grounds for sacking her and the company did not want to have to pay her compensation for unfair dismissal. It infuriated Lisa that she and Anne were carrying a passenger. At first Anne was Jodie's ally, but gradually she, too, became irritated by her.

One day when Anne went next door for her lunch, Richard came and sat at her table, the only one occupied in the café.

'I don't see so much of you girls since you've staggered your lunch breaks,' he said.

'No, I usually just buy a sandwich now. It's different when there's someone to sit and chat with.'

'You can always chat with me,' said Richard, giving her a grin.

'You're always so busy. I'm waiting for my daughter today, but she's not going to be here for another ten minutes.'

'How's it going round there?' Richard nodded his head in the direction of the shoe shop.

'It's OK. Well, it's better really. We're doing a lot of business, and head office are very pleased, apparently.'

'I've noticed it's a lot busier. How's the boss?'

'She's all right. Jodie can't stand her, but that's because she doesn't let her get away with things. She's strange, though, Lisa. Keeps herself to herself. I've heard she's going out with a bloke with a bit of a reputation.'

Richard raised an eyebrow. 'What sort of a reputation?'

'Bit of a thug, according to my son. A gofer for Chet Ainsworth, that bloke who lives on the Costa del Crime. He was in the paper. This bloke, Barry Shields, does a lot of fixing for him. He's done time himself, I've heard.'

'I'm surprised she'd go for someone like that,' Richard said. 'I know Barry Shields – we were at school at the same time. He was a lowlife then, a thug and a bully. She struck me as a bit too stuck-up to get involved with that sort.'

'She's not really stuck-up.' Anne repeated what she had said earlier: 'Just keeps herself to herself. Apparently he's got her wrapped round his little finger. But I don't really know, because she never talks about her private life. Doesn't talk much at all, beyond the weather and stuff to do with the shop. But our Bill knows someone who lives in the same block of flats as her and he sees it all. This Barry is coming and going at all hours, he reckons.'

'Well, it's a shame. Seems to me she deserves more than a bloke like Barry Shields. But there you are – women always go for the bad 'uns. Think I'll have to get myself involved in a couple of fights, toughen up my image,' he laughed.

'Ooh, don't tell me you fancy her?' Anne said.

Richard laughed again. 'Not a chance!'

To his relief, he saw Anne's daughter struggling in through the doorway with a pushchair. He leaped up to help her, ending the conversation.

It was true, he admitted to himself, he did fancy Lisa. From the first day he saw her, she had intrigued him. She was pretty, but it was more than that. There was something about her aloofness that made her seem vulnerable. He felt she was mysterious, and he wanted to know what the mystery was. Like the women who worked for her, he knew she must have a history, but she had emerged from nowhere and seemed to have no connections. He had never known her go away on holiday, or even for the weekend. Did she really have nothing and nobody?

He'd talked to her a few times, when they both emerged from their premises at the same time, but it had been routine, banal conversation about the weather, about the state of business in the town, about the tourist trade, about a burglary in one of the other shops. Nothing personal, although she did once ask him how his father was getting on, just after his dad had come home from another spell in hospital. Anne must have told her, he thought.

He was disappointed to hear she was going out with someone, anyone – he recognised the feeling as pure envy – but the news that she was involved with Barry Shields both disgusted him and, at the same time, made him feel even more protective towards her. For all her appearance of being self-contained and in control, she really needed someone to take care of her, not make her problems, whatever they might be, worse.

Two years after she came to Allerby, Lisa made her annual pilgrimage to the card shop in the market square. It was the day before Amy's eighteenth birthday; she was coming of age.

This will be the last time I do this. Lisa told herself the same thing every year, but this time with more force than before. She's grown-up now. I have to let her go.

Still, she lingered over the cards, all decorated with popping champagne bottles, balloons and streamers.

Is she having a big party? Has she got a boyfriend? Please, God, let her be happier than I was at her age. Let everything work out better for her. She said the silent prayer, then walked out of the shop without buying anything.

She walked briskly down to the river, choking back tears. Her Little Pickle was officially grown-up. Lisa wondered if, now that she was able to, Amy would make enquiries about her birth mother, but she hastily pushed the thought away. She didn't want to live in hope of something that would never happen. Besides, wouldn't she be a terrible disappointment to her daughter?

'I did the right thing by you, all those years ago,' she whispered. 'I gave you the best chance – a life much better than I could give you.'

She stood by the river, dabbing her eyes with a tissue, unaware that Richard Shenley was watching her. He'd strolled down for a break from the café and had caught sight of Lisa as she emerged on to the river bank.

He was about to move towards her, but checked himself when he saw she was crying. His impulse was to comfort her, but from what he knew of Lisa he sensed that she would prefer to be left alone. He watched as she pulled her shoulders back, lifted her head and walked purposefully back towards the town.

Although Lisa knew in the logical part of her brain that Barry was not good for her, and that she should ditch him, she was afraid of the loneliness that would seep back into her life if she did not have him, the emptiness of long evenings alone in the flat, the terror of having nothing at all to look forward to. Besides, she was worried about how to break with him: she was very convenient for Barry, and she knew it. She also knew he was not a man to cross.

One evening, she tried to warn him about something she had seen.

'I saw Enrico today, in the town. He was with that bloke you meet in the Spread Eagle. They were going into the Crown together, and they looked round before they went in, sort of secretive.'

Barry erupted. 'Bastards!' He launched into a tirade of swear words and grabbed his car keys. Before he rushed out, he turned to Lisa. 'What's it got to do with you, anyway, bitch?' His right hand shot out and hit her full force, with an open palm, on her left cheek. The impact sent her sprawling back against the wall. By the time she recovered, the door had slammed and Barry was gone. Trembling, Lisa looked in the mirror. The powerful slap had caused a bright-red mark to spread across her cheek, and she gingerly fingered her jaw to check that no real damage had been done. The shock hurt more than the physical pain. She had only been hit once before by a man, and that was when Phil's brother used the back of his hand against her face.

Her practical side kicked in. Thank God, she thought, that he had not given her a black eye or cut her lip, injuries she would not be able to conceal the next morning for work. With luck, the red mark would have subsided by then, and if not, she could cover it with make-up. A few minutes later, as she made herself a cup of tea and ladled sugar into it to calm herself down, she dissolved into tears.

I'm thirty-five years old. I have nothing at all to show for my life. I have hurt the two people I loved most, Dawn and Amy, and been a terrible daughter to my parents. No wonder men treat me badly – I'm not worth anything. What's the point of this life? What's it all about? I just lurch from one terrible man to the next. Maybe it's the punishment I deserve: I killed Dawn and I rejected Amy. I deserve to be slapped.

What am I going to do? I've tried cutting myself off completely and it never lasts – I always make a fool of myself with some bloke or other. Why do I bother going on?

She cried herself to sleep. The phone rang in the middle of the night, but she ignored it, certain that it was Barry, grovelling and promising it would never happen again.

Her resolve not to see him lasted three days. She did not pick up the phone or open the door to him on the first day, and then he stopped trying. Everything went quiet, until he turned up on her doorstep on the third day, with a bunch of roses and his usual sheepish grin. Despite herself, Lisa opened the door and allowed herself to be seduced by him all over again.

'You know I didn't mean it, don't you? It was just that I was angry about something. It'll never happen again, promise.'

The sex was good that night, better than it had been for months, and Lisa, ignoring her own sensible warnings, accepted him back into her life.

The summer passed with no further incident, but Barry

showed up less frequently, and when he was there, any warmth and affection they had once shared was gone. Lisa considered breaking up with him, but was scared that he would react badly to her calling the shots. She was even more afraid of the loneliness that would be the inevitable result.

The relationship drifted on, and before long another Christmas was approaching. Lisa knew that she would spend it alone, as she had for many years. Christmas was the worst time of the year for her and she longed to be able to hibernate through it, through all the build-up with shops full of jingly Christmas songs, and their windows packed with boxes wrapped in bright Christmas paper, and stars and angels and tinsel and Christmas trees. At work, she loved doing the window displays, but her heart was not in the Christmas ones and she always asked Anne to do them.

Cynically, she thought of all the money she saved, having no great list of presents to buy. She knew Anne put money away all year to buy shiny new toys for her grandchildren, and to provide the extra food that her family would consume over the break. She listened to Jodie and Anne moaning about how difficult it was to buy presents for their fathers and brothers – 'I just never know what to get men,' they said – and she heard them comparing notes about what to buy their mums, their sisters and Anne's grown-up daughters. Christmas for them started at least two months before the big day, and for Lisa there was no escaping it. The whole town was infected by it.

Worse than the build-up for Lisa was the actual break itself. In the big cities, shops now opened on Boxing Day, but in little towns like Allerby, Christmas was still a two-day complete break, when everyone would stay home and eat too much, watch too much television and have a couple of drinks too many. It was a family time, and if you had no family, all that was left was a lonely couple of days in front of the television, which would be showing back-to-back programmes of Christmas jollity.

There was no escaping it, but Lisa dreaded it every year, with every fibre of her being. She had a large supply of sleeping tablets in her bathroom cupboard, amassed over the years from doctors who prescribed them easily, but she made sure to get yet another prescription. Maybe she would take just enough to sleep deeply for two whole days, she thought, waking up when it was all over. Maybe she should simply sleep for ever . . . That would be the easiest option of all. The thought was surprisingly comforting, not frightening.

Barry promised her he would visit on Christmas Day, as he had done the last couple of years.

'How can you get away? Isn't that the one day of the year you are supposed to stay with your family?' She asked the same question every year.

'Yeah, but who's to say when a pipe bursts or a fuse blows at one of the flats? My job doesn't stop for Christmas. I'll be there for the kids opening their presents and the boring lunch with her mum and stepdad moaning on at me, but I'm buggered if I'm sitting around all evening listening to her dad snore and burp and her mum whine about what a lousy husband I am. I'll see you early evening.'

At least, she thought, he's given up lying that he's coming because he can't bear to be apart from me, which is what he had always said before. At least he's being honest: he can't stand his in-laws.

One lunch break in the week leading up to the holiday, she bought the cards, wrapping paper and chocolates for the girls in the shop. Then she went into the traditional men's outfitters in the marketplace to look for a present for Barry. She told herself she was mad buying him something, but it made her feel human and normal to have a present to buy. She glanced at the displays of cufflinks and tiepins, the sort of gifts men received and then stuck in a drawer, and moved on to the shirts and ties. She settled on a blue shirt with a coordinated tie, packed together in a sturdy box. Barry usually dressed smartly, in slightly flashy suits, and she knew he liked clothes and prided himself on looking good. It was an expensive shirt, very much his taste.

All the residents at the block of flats had their own individual postboxes in the entrance hall, which they unlocked to collect their mail. At Christmas, with so many cards to deliver, the postman would leave the overflow on a table in the hall. Lisa never had to look there: her box was more than adequate for the small amount of post she received, just bills and junk mail. On Christmas Eve, she paused in the hallway to check her box before setting off for work. There was only one letter, a gas bill, which she stuffed into her handbag.

Just as she was letting herself out of the heavy front door, Lisa heard a voice calling her name down the stairwell. She went back and looked up, to see Mrs Smith leaning over the banister, waving a slim white envelope.

'Oh, Lisa, I'm glad I've caught you. This was put in my box by mistake. It's for you.'

Lisa felt a twinge of exasperation, wondering why the old lady hadn't just put it under her door, but she went back up the stairs, knowing that she had plenty of time to get to work.

'Here,' said Mrs Smith, handing her the envelope. 'I was worried I wouldn't catch you. I'm going away this afternoon, and I thought I'd missed you.'

Lisa thanked her. She didn't recognise the neat handwriting on the front.

'At least it doesn't look like another bill,' she said cheerfully to Mrs Smith. 'I've just had one of those from the gas people – a nice Christmas present! Have a lovely break.'

'I'll be back next week – only going for five days this year,' the old lady said. 'Don't want to outstay my welcome. You know what it's like at Christmas, such a lot of work . . .'

As she spoke, Lisa slipped her thumb under the flap of the envelope and opened it. She smiled at Mrs Smith and then glanced down at the letter that she pulled out. A small photograph, passport size, slipped out as well and fluttered to the floor. Lisa blanched as she read the first two lines of the letter, then covered her confusion by bending down and picking up the photograph. Her fingers trembled as she grasped it.

'Are you all right, Lisa, love?' Mrs Smith said, as Lisa straightened up. 'You look as if you've seen a ghost.'

Lisa recovered her composure quickly. 'No,' she said. 'Just a letter from an old friend. I'll pop it back into the flat before I go.'

'Well, take care, then. And have a lovely break – you work too hard, you know,' said Mrs Smith.

'You enjoy yourself – and be good! I don't want to hear of

you misbehaving,' Lisa chided the old lady affectionately, at the same time opening the door to her flat and stepping inside.

She flopped down on the settee and read the letter. Then she read it again. She felt physically weak. She put her head in her hands and sat there for a few moments. She pulled the photograph out of the envelope and stared at it, not moving. At last, she stirred and glanced at her watch and, realising she was late for work, left the letter on the coffee table and dashed out.

She got through the day on autopilot. Luckily, the shop was busy, which did not give her much time to think. She gave Anne and Jodie their chocolates and they gave her cards. At 4 p.m., she let them both go home: she could manage the last two hours of business on her own, and, besides, it was a strain having to keep cheerful with them. At least now she only had to smile at the customers, and they were thinning out.

What am I going to do? she thought. She tried to stop herself thinking about the letter, telling herself that she had to hold herself together until she was back in the flat. Then she could break down, but right now she had to keep a tight rein on her thoughts and feelings. No matter how hard she tried, though, the words kept coming back to her. She felt terrified, exhausted and alone, and she could think of only one way out of the mess of her life.

Methodically, she tidied away all the shoes in the stockroom, put the cash in an envelope to leave in the bank safe deposit and finally, at dead on 6 p.m., locked up the shop.

As she stepped away from the door, Richard came out of the café next door.

'Hey! I was hoping to see you. Here's your card,' he said, walking across the wet pavement towards her.

Lisa was surprised and embarrassed. 'Oh, thank you,' she said, taking the large, stiff envelope. 'I'm sorry – I didn't get one for you.'

'I wasn't expecting one,' said Richard. 'I hope you are going to have a good couple of days.'

Despite not wanting to reveal her feelings, Lisa pulled a wry face. 'I'll be glad when it's over,' she said.

'If I'm honest, so will I,' said Richard, 'but I'm making an effort, for my dad. He's very sentimental about Christmas. Will you be on your own?'

Lisa nodded, and Richard could see she was biting her lip. He felt a strong impulse to put his arm around her and cuddle her. Instead, he said, 'Well, you're always welcome to join us. Plenty of food, that's for sure. I got the chef to prepare all the vegetables for me, so I don't have to do it all. My sister and her family will be there for Christmas lunch, but there's room for another one.'

Lisa looked at him. She had never really taken much notice of Richard – he was just there – but she could see he was a good-looking man and she wondered why he had no woman in his life. She knew he was divorced; perhaps he had been very badly hurt.

'No, I'm fine, but it's kind of you to offer. I shall be having two days of complete rest, which doesn't happen very often.'

They both stood together awkwardly.

'Well, I'd better be going . . .' Lisa said, at last.

'Me too. Haven't wrapped any presents yet . . .'

'I'll see you in two days' time, then.'

'Yeah, merry Christmas.'

'Merry Christmas.'

Lisa walked away through the glistening streets. She went home via the marketplace, to put the envelope in the bank safe-deposit box. There was a huge Christmas tree in the square, gaudily lit with twinkling lights, and round it a group of singers were getting themselves organised for a carol concert. People were coming into the square to listen to them. Lisa weaved her way through the gathering crowd and went into one of the few shops still open, the off-licence. She bought a large bottle of whisky. She had made up her mind.

She walked on towards her home, the strains of 'O Little Town of Bethlehem' following her. Christmas, she thought sadly: a time of miracles and angels and goodwill to all men. A happy, cheerful time. But the saddest time of the year if you are on your own. And, even worse, if you have problems like mine, all this happiness is just there to mock you.

She bit her lip, determined not to cry until she was behind her own front door. It will soon all be over, she told herself.

Book Two

9

The Angel

The hand that reached out to stop Lisa swallowing the tablets felt as soft and gentle as a feather, but there was an underlying strength that made it impossible for her to resist. Dropping the tablets in her hand, Lisa sank back on to the sofa next to the angel, overcome with a feeling of tiredness and release, as if a huge burden had been lifted from her. At first she had not noticed the wings, but now the angel unfolded them and wrapped them around Lisa. They enclosed her completely in a bright light that radiated love towards her and into her, penetrating the core of her being. She felt warm and deeply content, all her fears and worries washing away. Although she was engulfed by the light, and could feel the down-soft touch of the angel's wings, she could still see the room, as if through a hazy white mist.

'You are very tired,' the angel said, in her low, gentle voice. 'You need a sleep, but not like this.' She gestured towards the pills that were spread across the coffee table, shaking her head at Lisa. 'This is not your way. Now, come with me.'

The angel bore Lisa up, her whole body supported by the ball of shimmering light. She could no longer see a human shape in the light, but she was aware of the presence of the angel, and she could feel the delicate touch of the arms that carried her through to the bedroom, supporting her whole weight as if she were no heavier than a breeze, and very gently laid her down on the bed.

Lisa tried to sit up, but the angel said, 'Lie down, rest, slumber.'

The angel then sang to her, in the sweetest of voices, music that Lisa had never heard before but that seeped into her like a drug and made her sleepy. She could feel the angel massaging her limbs gently, until they felt weightless and her whole body was relaxed, as though it were floating on a cushion of warm, enveloping air. The familiar shapes and contours of the bedroom melted and slowly Lisa drifted off into a profound sleep.

She did not stir all night, breathing easily and peacefully, dreaming that she was being cuddled and held in the arms of someone who loved her very deeply. It was the sweetest, most refreshing, untroubled sleep she had ever known, and when she woke the next day, she felt an overwhelming sensation of tranquillity and peace.

At first, as her eyes flickered into wakefulness, she could not remember what had happened the evening before. She was still drowsy, but not in that heavy-lidded way when sleep has been disturbed and too short. This drowsiness was a pleasant state between sleep and waking, a lovely interlude when her body was still completely relaxed and her mind was full of delightful memories and thoughts. She saw pictures of happy childhood moments – playing in the sand with Dawn on their first trip to the seaside, holding tight to her dad's hand on a visit to the zoo, cuddling up on the sofa with her mum when she felt unwell. She saw a picture of herself with Amy, feeding her tenderly in the middle of the night, when the rest of the hospital ward slept. And she saw glimpses of people who had been kind and caring to her in her adult life, people whom she had worked with and even men she had loved, in the heady days before disillusion and disappointment set in.

She was suffused with an intense happiness. The despair of yesterday was all gone; she did not remember it. Slowly, she surfaced into full wakefulness. Faintly, through the window, she heard the sound of church bells ringing out Christmas morning and she remembered what a special day it was. Instead of feeling overwhelmed by her own loneliness, she thought about the spiritual meaning of the day, a day in which goodness and forgiveness came down to earth, and the message in the bells seemed to be just for her. Looking at her watch, she realised she had slept for twelve hours, longer than ever since she was a tiny child, when she slept in her sister's bed, their arms encircling each other.

As she sat on the edge of the bed, she remembered the angel. There was no sign of the celestial being, although the room was lighter than usual for a dull December morning. There was a soft radiance that made everything look bright, clean, lovely. Lisa looked around, as if seeing her own bedroom for the first time, and felt a rush of pleasure at her surroundings, and a deep sense of gratitude that she was still here to enjoy them.

She walked through the flat to the kitchen, enjoying the sight of everything as if it were all new to her. She made a cup of tea and went into the sitting room. When she saw the letter, the whisky bottle and the scattering of sleeping pills, the memory of last night came back to her and she stood for a moment, remembering the details. But the desperation did not return. She picked up the whisky and put it away in a kitchen cupboard, and then she gathered up the tablets, returned them to the plastic bottle, carried it through and put it in the rubbish bin.

Only then did she sit down again with her tea and pick up the letter. She opened it to read one more time, but before she could unfold it, she felt the same light touch on her arm that she had felt yesterday. Turning, she saw again the vibrant golden glow next to her, shimmering and quivering and finally forming itself into the shape of the angel, the beautiful cherub with a mass of curls that flowed and moved as if caught by a breeze.

'Let's read it together,' the same soft tones from yesterday evening spoke, the gentle sound washing over Lisa like no human voice. It was almost as if she felt the words, rather than heard them. The hand released her arm and Lisa opened the letter, which yesterday had tipped her into her suicide attempt. As she pulled it from the envelope, a small photograph fell to the table.

Lisa read the words out loud, holding the letter in her left hand. Her right hand rested in the angel's hand, and as she started to read, she felt a small, comforting squeeze.

It was handwritten on white paper, neat writing that looked as if it had been done with extra care. At the top was an address in Benting, a small village very close to Allerby. Lisa had never been there, but she had seen buses leaving the market square with Benting as their destination. At the top of the letter there were two phone numbers, a landline and a mobile, but the mobile was underlined.

Dear Miss Heywood,

You may not want to have this letter, and I expect you will just throw it away, but I want to make contact with you because I believe you are my birth mother. I was born in London eighteen years ago, on 12 January, and given up for adoption straightaway.

When I reached the age of eighteen, I was allowed to start looking for my birth mother. I have had help, but it has taken a few months. I have been given a letter that was written by my birth mother, which says I was loved when I was born and that my mother would always think of me.

My birth mother gave me the name Amy, and although that is not the name my parents gave me when they adopted me, it may prove to you that I really am your daughter.

I would like, if you agree, to meet you. My mum and dad are happy about this and they have helped me trace you. I am really surprised to find you live so close to me.

I will try to understand if you do not want to see me.

Yours sincerely,

Nicola Bradley

PS I enclose a photo.

The teenager looking out of the picture reminded Lisa of herself at that age. Like her, this girl Nicola (she could not quite think of her as Amy yet) had dyed her hair blonde and was smiling from the passport-sized photo with a look that reminded Lisa of her own mother. It was something to do with the way her eyes crinkled. She had dark, arched eyebrows, like Lisa's.

Yesterday, Lisa had hardly dared look at the photo and had stuffed it straight back into the envelope. It had frightened her. She had always known that Amy was alive and well somewhere, but she had accepted she would never meet her.

'Why were you so afraid when you opened this letter?' the angel asked gently.

'Because . . . I can't explain it. I used to want to meet her, but that was when I felt I would be settled by now, with a house and a family and something to offer her. Instead I've got nothing, and my life has been a failure. What kind of mother would I be?'

'You would be *her* mother,' the angel said.

'But it sounds as though she already has one who loves her,' Lisa said.

'It is a very hard lesson for many human beings to learn, but there is no limit to the amount of love a person can give or can have poured into them. Love is infinite. The more love, the better. Love, real love, is not competitive. Love is the greatest gift one human being can give to another.'

'She might not want my love.'

'Why do you think she has written to you?'

'I dunno. Maybe just curiosity. It's weird to think that she lives so close. She might have been in the shop without my realising . . . Of all the places in the whole country, she's here. That's a really bizarre coincidence, isn't it?'

Lisa heard the angel laugh, a tinkly, high-pitched chuckle, the sound of a fast stream running over rocks.

'I don't think it is a coincidence. Coming back from Spain to Yorkshire, then leaving Leeds for Allerby – I didn't find it too hard to arrange.'

'You did this?' Lisa turned to look at the angel, who was tenderly stroking her hand. The smooth, fair face gazed back at her, the grey eyes, so like Lisa's own, shining a beam of light, bright but not dazzling, on to Lisa's face.

'I can only make happen what you want to happen,' said the angel, smiling. 'Angels tell people the best course of action, but human beings often don't listen, don't open themselves to hear us whispering our advice. You listened because you wanted this to happen. You didn't have to come to Allerby – you could have thrown that old newspaper away, and you nearly did. I was whispering to you as hard as I could, and thankfully you listened.'

A puzzled frown crossed Lisa's face. 'But I *don't* want this to happen. I'm not ready. I can't see her. She will probably hate me. She probably hates me already for giving her up. What kind of mother gives up a baby?'

'A very loving mother. One who puts the baby's happiness and well-being ahead of her own emotions. Don't you remember the Judgement of Solomon? You had a book of Bible stories, remember?'

Lisa was surprised that the angel seemed to know everything about her life, for she remembered the story: two mothers each claimed a baby was theirs, and the wise King Solomon said the only way to settle the dispute was to cut the baby in half and give them half each. The true mother immediately gave the baby to the other woman: she loved her child so much that she could not bear him to be hurt. Solomon knew from this that she was the baby's real mother.

'I remember . . .' Lisa said.

'The mother who loved the child more was the one who wanted the best things to happen for him and was prepared to give him away. That was you: you wanted to give your Little Pickle everything you could not provide.'

Lisa started at the words 'Little Pickle'. They came back to her down the years and tears started to flow as she was transported back to the hospital, nearly nineteen years ago. She saw a young girl, her long fair hair, streaked with blonde highlights, falling round the face of her tiny baby, as she held the child close to her and watched over her through the night, cut off from the rest of the silent, sleeping ward by brightly patterned curtains.

'That girl is you,' said the angel, sharing the vision. 'She isn't an uncaring, hard-hearted girl who wanted to give her baby away so that she could get on with her own life. That girl thought long and hard, and did what was best for her child. You must never, ever blame yourself for that decision. It was the right one, and it took a lot of courage to make it.'

The angel stretched out a hand and wiped the tears from Lisa's cheeks. The touch seemed hardly to brush the skin, but immediately Lisa's sadness lifted. The light that shimmered around the angel moved to include her, bathing her in its gentleness. The feeling of tranquillity, warmth and hope that had filled her when she woke up came back to her.

'Have you always been with me?' she asked. 'Were you there when I gave Amy away?'

'Yes. I was there. I was telling you that it was the right thing to do, and you listened.'

'Who are you?'

'I am your guardian angel. You have always had a guardian angel, but it was not always me. Don't you know who I am, Lisa? Look at me. Don't you recognise me?'

Lisa turned to face the angel and the realisation flooded over her. The form of the little girl with the blonde curls was now clearer and she said, 'Yes, yes, of course. You are Dawn . . . You are my sister.' Her voice broke into a sob, which she fought to hold back.

'Yes, I am your twin sister. When we were little, we knew that we would always be together, just as we were together in the womb. Death could not separate us, and as soon as I became an angel, I took over looking after you. Haven't you felt my presence? Why do you think you didn't go through with the abortion? Who do you think helped you to escape to Spain so easily? And who was it that brought you here, to Allerby, to your daughter? Our daughter. Because, Lisa, even though I died in human form, I live on, and I'm always with you, sharing your life.'

Lisa felt as if her heart were breaking. 'But I've made a bad job of it. You would have done better, I know you would.'

Dawn, the angel, slowly shook her head and smiled. 'You've always thought that. You've always tried to judge yourself against some impossible standard you think I would have achieved. But, Lisa, human beings all fail in different ways. Nobody is perfect. I wasn't perfect, and if I had lived, I would have led an imperfect life. You have done the best you could. You haven't been bad, just misguided at times. You have chosen to live your life alone, and that is the toughest choice of all.'

'I didn't choose to be alone – it is how it has worked out,' said Lisa.

'Yes, but you've always had the strength to walk away from bad places. That's a great strength, but it's also built a wall around you, and you've missed much that is good in other human beings because of this. Now, you must not turn your back on your daughter.'

'It sounds as though she has done all right without me.'

'Yes,' said Dawn. 'She's been loved, and that's the main strength and help she could possibly have had, but there's a hole inside her, a deep longing that can only be filled by one person: you. You made the right choice for her all those years ago. Now you must make the right choice again.'

Lisa sighed and read the letter again.

'Don't make any decisions now,' Dawn said. 'Relax and let's enjoy our time together. I've been with you all this time, but this is our first chance to talk and share our thoughts and feelings.'

For the next few hours they chatted away together like old friends meeting after years apart. At times Lisa had to remind herself that she was talking to an angel, to her dead sister, the conversation was so normal. They reminisced about their childhood, but also about the whole of Lisa's life. The terrible times seemed much easier now that Lisa relived them with Dawn, and she even managed to laugh at some of the situations she had found herself in.

'Remember the motto our grandmother had on a sampler on the wall: "A trouble shared is a trouble halved,"' Dawn said, and instantly Lisa was back with her twin, in the dark hallway of their grandmother's little terraced house, where the old lady sneaked sweets into their pockets when their mother was not looking.

'Yes, I remember,' said Lisa, 'but sharing with you does more than halve my troubles: it makes them go away completely.'

'That's your doing, not mine,' said Dawn. 'I'm here to help you, to love you and guide you, but I can't live your life for you.'

At some stage, Lisa went into the kitchen to get some food. She cooked herself a very simple omelette and ate it with salad and bread. She laughed. 'Do you realise, the whole of the country is tucking into roast turkey and stuffing, sprouts and roast potatoes right now?'

'We never liked sprouts, did we?' Dawn said, giggling, and they clutched each other, laughing at the memory of their mum struggling to get them to eat their green vegetables.

Every mouthful of food tasted delicious to Lisa, as though her taste buds had been activated for the first time. Just as the room looked bright and more beautiful than she had ever realised, food and drink seemed to acquire mellower flavours.

The day passed peacefully and happily, and Lisa had no concept of time. When she lay in a hot bath, Dawn sat beside and held a hot flannel to her forehead. When she towelled herself dry, Dawn's gentle touch could be felt teasing out the knots in her wet hair. Sometimes Dawn was just a shimmering, indistinct presence; at other times, particularly when they were sitting together on the sofa, the light resolved itself into the shape of the little blonde-headed girl whom Lisa remembered. At one time, Lisa dozed and awoke to find she had leaned herself into Dawn, and although she could not feel the firm substance of a body next to her, she was supported and held, and her hair mingled with the blonde curls, just as it had done when they were little.

It was a ring on the doorbell that roused Lisa. She jumped up and spoke into the intercom. 'Who is it?'

'Merry Christmas, beautiful!' said Barry's voice.

Lisa started. She had forgotten that he was coming round.

'Don't let him in. You don't have to. He's trouble. He's not good for you,' Dawn whispered.

'But I can't leave him outside. I've got to see him,' Lisa said.

'You don't have to,' the whisper was urgent, but Dawn's shape and luminous glow were fading.

Lisa hesitated; then there was a loud knock at the flat door. Lisa, with a quick glance at the soft flush that was all that remained of Dawn's presence, went across and opened it.

'You forgot to buzz me in,' said Barry. 'I had to use my master key. I thought for a minute you had someone here with you.' He glanced around suspiciously.

'No, I'm all alone. I've had a very quiet day,' said Lisa, taking his coat off him.

'God, I wish I had. It's been bedlam with that lot all day.'

He put his arms around her and kissed her. Lisa pulled away.

'I could do with a stiff drink,' Barry said.

Lisa fetched the bottle of whisky and a glass from the kitchen, and Barry poured himself a large one. 'Aren't you having one?'

'No, I don't feel like it,' Lisa said. 'I don't like whisky. And hadn't you better be careful if you are driving?'

Barry looked at her, irritated. 'What's eating you? It's Christmas Day. Have a drink, for God's sake. If I want to be nagged, I can get plenty of that at home.' He pulled her down on to his lap and began fondling her breasts.

'No, Barry, not today. I really don't feel like it.'

A flash of anger crossed his face, but he subdued it quickly and turned his most charming smile on her. 'What's the matter with my little girl?' he said. 'Come on, let Barry kiss everything better.' He picked her up in his arms and carried her through to the bedroom.

She knew, remembering how hard he had slapped her face, that it was better not to resist him and she mechanically went through the motions of having sex with him. There was no pleasure in it for her, and it was quick and passionless for him.

He sensed her lack of willingness and participation, and when it was over, said, 'What's up?'

'Nothing,' she said. 'Just a bit tired.'

'Tired? You? You didn't have to get up at five with a couple of kids bursting to open their presents, or sit around trying to be nice to the in-laws all day. You've got it made. Don't tell me about being tired. I didn't get in until three a.m., either.'

Lisa lay back on the pillow and sighed. She had not wanted to see him today, especially after her lovely time with Dawn; even so, she could not help but feel a pang of jealousy when he said he had been out late last night. Wherever he had been, she had not been invited.

She got up and went across to the chest of drawers, where his neatly wrapped present was lying. She handed it to him.

'Merry Christmas,' she said, sitting on the bed next to him and leaning over to kiss him. She knew how stupid it was, but she still wanted him to love her.

'Thanks, beautiful,' he said, as he tore open the packaging.

He liked the shirt and tie, just as Lisa had known he would.

'I'll have to leave it here for the time being. The wife would be a bit suspicious if she found this in my car. I'll take it with me next week, say I bought it.'

'Yeah, she'll think you got it cheap in the sales,' said Lisa bitterly. 'Don't suppose you got anything for me?'

Barry gave her his most winning smile and shrugged apologetically. 'You know how it is . . .'

Lisa felt like saying no, she didn't know, but she held back. There was no point in provoking a row. It was clear Barry had only called in for a break from his family and some quick sex. She, like an idiot, had given into him, despite what Dawn had said.

She was relieved when, after he'd dressed and downed another whisky, Barry said he would have to go.

'I'd love to stay here, you know I would, but it's the one day of the year when I can't stay out late, not with the bloody in-laws clocking me out and clocking me back in. I told them I'd been called out to a flat in Leeds where there was a flood, which gave me as much time as I could get, but . . . well, you know what it's like. Bloody Christmas. You're the luckiest person I know, not having to bother with all the bloody fuss. I'll make it up to you about the present.' He turned his smile on for her again.

Lisa looked away. She knew, had Dawn not intervened, Barry would have had a bigger problem than a flood in a flat in Leeds on his hands. He would have arrived to find her dead body. Then, perhaps, he would have had a glimmer of understanding about what Christmas on your own without 'all the bloody fuss' was really like. Except that he would not have wasted time thinking about her – his mind would have been totally pre-occupied with how to get himself out of a sticky situation.

She no longer cared. He gave her a goodbye peck on the cheek, and when the door closed behind him, Lisa sat down again on the sofa. She looked around the room expectantly, hoping that Dawn would reappear, but there was nothing to show the angel had been there. The bright colours of the room had faded back to their original tones; the only light came from the electricity supplied to the two table lamps.

'I'm so sorry, Dawn,' Lisa whispered. 'I didn't take your advice. You were right. He's bad for me. I just wish I had the strength to get him out of my life, but you have no idea what it is like to be lonely.'

She picked up the box containing the shirt and tie and stuffed it into a drawer. Then she crumpled up the shiny paper she had so carefully wrapped it in and took it to the bin.

It was only as she walked back that she paused to look at the three Christmas cards on her shelf. The one from Richard, with the cherub on the front, did it look just a little bit like Dawn?

10

Meeting Nicola

Sleep was not the happy, restful balm of the night before. Lisa tossed and turned, angry with herself for letting Barry in, disappointed in herself for letting Dawn down.

I've behaved just like I always do. I've thrown away something good for a bloke who isn't worth it. Will I never learn anything?

She hated herself, the same feeling that on Christmas Eve had propelled her into sleeping pills, whisky and a promise of oblivion. Why, why, when everything had been going so well, did she have to ruin it?

When morning came, she got up not because she was rested but because lying in bed, replaying in her head everything that had happened the day before, was miserable. She knew she had been privileged to meet Dawn, her guardian angel, yet she had done exactly what she had always done: turned her back and gone her own, stupid way. The bliss of the early hours of the day had been contaminated and defiled by Barry – and by her, because she hadn't listened to Dawn, hadn't refused to see him.

She was so angry with herself. She moved around the flat quickly, pummelling the cushions and scrubbing the kitchen worktops. As she worked out her anger, it was replaced with a feeling of deep desolation and tears welled up in her eyes.

'I don't deserve you, Dawn. I'm sorry – for everything. I don't suppose you will come back now. I have killed you again, just like I killed you when you were little . . . If you can hear me, I'm so, so sorry. I want to be stronger, I really do, but I've let you down.'

Lisa was standing at the kitchen sink as she said this aloud to Dawn, looking out over the quiet rooftops of the town. It was Boxing Day and everyone else was still asleep, enjoying a lie-in after hectic Christmas mornings with children, or too many drinks with their Christmas celebrations. Daylight had broken and the sky was grey, but there were still tiny pinpricks of stars, glinting in the heavens.

The tiled roofs glistened with light frost, and as Lisa watched, one of the stars seemed to get bigger, taking on a luminous glow that set off a thousand little sparkles in the frost. The light grew even larger and came towards her, turning into a stream of dancing pinpricks of brightness, moving closer at speed until it passed through her window and once again she was engulfed in warmth and radiance.

'Dawn, is it you?' Lisa asked, turning to follow the light as it moved through into the sitting room.

'Yes, it's me. You didn't really believe I would desert you, did you?'

'I deserve to be left alone,' Lisa said. 'I didn't do what you told me to do yesterday.'

'I can never tell you what to do. We angels, we can suggest and guide, but in the end you humans make your own choices. Just because you don't do what we think you should doesn't mean we would ever desert you, or that we don't love you. Even in your darkest times, Lisa, I've been by your side. There have been times when I have been entreating you, begging you to take more care of yourself, but even though you have ignored me, I've always stayed with you.'

'I didn't feel you with me during the night.'

'No, I can't soothe all your fears and problems. Letting Barry in wasn't a good thing, because he is bad for you, but you have to realise this for yourself. I have to let you suffer for your own actions, or you'll never learn. Just like when we were little, we had to learn not to run too fast or we would fall – the scrapes and cuts on our knees taught us the lesson.'

'I ran too fast one day. That's why you died,' said Lisa, with a catch in her throat as she fought back tears. 'I killed you.'

'You need to stop thinking like that. You didn't kill me. When our mother ran after you, another lady took hold of my hand, but I wriggled and squirmed and then, in desperation, I bit her hand until she let go – just so that I could follow you. What happened wasn't your fault. I behaved very badly myself. Besides, if Mum hadn't run after you, screaming at you to stand still, *you* would have died. In the end, on that terrible day, one of us was going to die. And you were the one who did what you were told: you stopped running. I didn't.

'Now, I want you to put all feelings of guilt out of your

mind. You didn't kill me. It was my time. These things are ordained; we don't decide them. And I've been very happy ever since, even though I have always known how much grief and unhappiness my death brought to those of you left behind. The main sorrow I have is watching you make mistakes, but I know that you'll try to learn from them.'

As she spoke these words, Lisa felt the shadow of blame passing away, out of the room. She felt as if something bad had left her. Could it really be true? All her life she had shouldered the guilt for Dawn's death. Was it possible that she wasn't to blame?

Dawn was able to tell what she was thinking: 'You've lived your life with a permanent sense of guilt. Now you must learn to live without it,' said Dawn. 'You didn't kill me. It wasn't your fault.'

'Really? It's hard . . . to accept. I always thought . . . I can't imagine you doing something like that. You were such a good little girl.'

'I wasn't as perfect as you seem to believe,' Dawn said. 'I was just a little girl like you. A bit quieter, but just as capable of getting into trouble.'

Lisa paused, still unable to take in Dawn's version of events on the day of the accident, but aware that she felt lighter, less troubled. Then she remembered: 'But it's not just you – what about all the pain I gave to Mum and Dad?'

'Yes, you did give them pain, but they, too, had a very large battle to fight, coming to terms with my death. If you think you felt guilty all these years, just imagine how Mum felt. She may have seemed to reject you in some ways, but that was because she could hardly bear to look at you and be reminded of her own failure to keep me alive. We were as alike as two peas in a pod – how could she look at you and not think of me? She acted instinctively that day: she ran after you. She has never freed herself from the anguish of leaving me to run to my death.

'And Dad, he couldn't cope with her guilt. There was a bit of him, which he tried hard to suppress, that really did blame her, a bit of him that said he would never have let it happen. So there they were, two tortured souls, trying to comfort each other and still be good parents to you. Can you imagine how hard it was for them?

'They thought that the best thing for you was to remove all trace of me, to not mention me, then you would forget because you were so young. They were very wrong, but it was what they genuinely believed was right.'

Lisa nodded mutely. It was only since she gave birth to Amy that she had been able, in any way, to understand her mother. Nevertheless she tried her best never to think of her parents; it was too painful. Whenever she saw an elderly couple who were about their age, she felt a pang, but she pushed it away. She didn't even know if they were still alive. Today was the first time she had ever really thought through the accident from their point of view, and she knew, as Dawn spelled it out, that her mother had had to fight a terrible battle to carry on living with guilt and loss bravely. She suddenly felt ashamed for wanting to kill herself: her mother's pain and guilt put hers in the shade, yet her mother had carried on.

Dawn spent the whole of Boxing Day with her. At one point,

they even went out together. They walked through the park and across into another area of the town, where a small mini-mart opened up even on bank holidays, so that Lisa could buy milk and bread. Dawn had insisted: 'I may not need food and drink, but you do. We have to keep you strong, don't we?'

Walking with her was a strange experience. It was as if a ball of light was bouncing alongside Lisa, and they were able to carry on talking. Lisa soon realised that other people could not see her angel; they walked past her, oblivious. Occasionally someone shot her a puzzled look and Lisa realised she was speaking out loud to Dawn.

She laughed. 'Well, I always said I would turn into an old dear who muttered to herself in public,' she said.

Walking back across the park, Dawn persuaded her to sit on a bench for a few minutes. They watched a father running behind his son on his brand-new Christmas present, a two-wheeler bike, while his daughter proudly pushed her new toy pram.

'You have avoided parks and playgrounds for many years, haven't you?' Dawn said.

'Yes,' Lisa whispered. 'After you died, we never went to the park. And when I grew up . . . well, it has always seemed easier to walk round rather than stir up memories.'

'We're dealing with those memories, aren't we?' Dawn said.

Lisa nodded. 'Yes . . . yes, everything seems a lot easier to bear.'

Back at the flat, Dawn said, 'Now, we have the most important thing to do.' She gestured at the table, where the letter still lay.

'You have to speak to your daughter, Nicola.'

'Amy,' Lisa said.

'No, you must get used to her now being Nicola. Amy suited her for a time – it was the right name for her while she was in your arms – but when she found her other loving mother, she became Nicola. That, too, is the right name for her. A name is given to you by those who love you; it is their gift, and their right to choose. You must respect that.'

'What do I have to do?'

'You must ring her.'

Lisa nodded, opened the letter to see the phone number and picked up the receiver. Before she dialled, though, she put it down again.

'What can I say to her? I don't think I am ready for this.'

'Just tell her who you are and that you would like to meet her.'

'I'm not sure I can meet her . . . It's too terrifying. I'm not good enough. I'll be a huge disappointment to her.'

'You won't. But think of this: if you don't ring her, she will feel you have rejected her. Again. She has had a happy life, but however happy they are, many adopted children feel that they were rejected by their birth parents, that in some way it was their fault, that they failed at the first hurdle in life. If you don't tell her otherwise, she will always feel that she was unloved at birth – and however well loved she has been since, there will always be a feeling of loss.'

'I hadn't thought of that.'

'No, you've been thinking about how you feel, and about how you may be a disappointment to her, but the much bigger disappointment will be if you don't ring her.'

It took two or three goes, with Dawn reassuring her all the time, before Lisa could actually dial the number. By this time it was 8.30 p.m. She pressed the numbers into the keypad and willed there to be no answer, still unsure how she could cope with speaking to her own daughter.

But after four rings a girl's voice said, 'Hello.'

Panicking, Lisa pressed the red button and hung up. She looked at Dawn. 'I just couldn't.'

At that moment, her phone rang. She glanced at the screen. It was Nicola calling her back.

This time, it was Lisa's turn to answer with 'Hello.'

'You called me just now,' said the girl's voice.

'Yes, sorry . . . It was a wrong num—' Lisa started to say. Then she felt Dawn's gentle gaze on her and she said, 'No, sorry, it wasn't a wrong number. No . . . I . . . er . . . You sent me a letter.' She stumbled over the words. The pit of her stomach seemed to fall away, to be replaced by a big ball of anxiety that gnawed at her. So much rested on the next few seconds, and on Nicola's response.

There was a silence at the other end of the line.

'You *are* Nicola, aren't you?' Lisa asked.

'Yes . . . yes, I'm Nicola.' The voice sounded fainter than before and Lisa realised that the girl was just as nervous as she was. In the background she could hear music playing, and after a slight hesitation, Nicola said, 'Hold on a minute. I'm just going to go outside.'

There was a pause, the sound of a door opening, and the music faded to a very faint murmur.

Nicola spoke again. 'That's better. I'm . . . I'm in the pub with some friends . . . I wasn't expecting you to ring today . . . or ever, maybe.'

'I didn't know whether to or not,' Lisa admitted. 'I didn't know if you really wanted to see me.'

'Yes . . . yes, I do.'

The girl still sounded hesitant and Lisa put her own nerves aside and took the initiative in the conversation. 'OK. When would you like to meet?'

There was another pause. 'I can see you after work on Thursday if you like. I finish at four thirty on Thursdays. I work in Allerby.'

Lisa felt her heart lurch. The girl – Nicola, her daughter – worked so near. 'All right. How about a quarter to five at Shenley's Tearooms. Do you know it?'

'Yes, it's next to the shoe shop, isn't it?'

Nicola even knew the shoe shop.

'Yes, I'll see you there,' Lisa replied.

'How will I know you?'

'I don't think there will be that many people in there. I'm sure we'll know each other.' Lisa said goodbye and the phone went dead.

She sank back into the sofa, shaking. Her heart raced, and there were beads of sweat on her forehead. Dawn held her hand but said nothing, giving Lisa space to calm down.

'I must have seen her. We must have passed each other in the street. Perhaps I've sold shoes to her.'

There were two whole days to fill before the meeting on Thursday. Lisa felt a mixture of excitement and fear, and she coped by filling her days with work. The shop had reopened and she was busy doing the window and re-ticketing all the shoes that were going to be in the post-Christmas sale. She half heard the chatter of Anne and Jodie, the recounting of what they were given for Christmas and what disasters there had been with overcooked turkey, with elderly relatives snoring in front of the TV, with temper tantrums from Anne's toddler grandchildren. They both politely asked if she had had a good time and she was able to answer sincerely that she had.

'It was a really great Christmas,' she said, smiling.

Behind her back, Anne and Jodie glanced at each other: as far as they had been able to establish, their boss had spent the holiday at home, on her own. Yet she seemed very relaxed and happy, and definitely full of energy, as she made them tidy the stockroom and fill the racks with sale shoes.

By Wednesday evening, Lisa's nerves were kicking in. She put a honey-gold rinse through her hair to lift the colour and applied a face pack. She wanted to look her best for her daughter. It was hard to sleep that night. The excitement in the pit of her stomach felt like hunger, but she could not face eating.

On Thursday morning, she told Anne and Jodie that she would be taking her lunch break at the end of the day, leaving work early. Anne, who was in charge whenever Lisa wasn't there, was entrusted with the keys to lock up if Lisa was not back before six. By half past four, Lisa was feeling very jittery.

She had still not been able to eat, which made her light-headed. She had dressed carefully that morning: her navy-blue work suit was, for the first time the other staff could remember, teamed with a pink shirt instead of the regulation white one. The touch of colour added warmth to her own colouring, making her face prettier and softer.

Her mind raced. Would Nicola be angry with her? Would she blame her? Would she feel a rush of love for her, like she had for the tiny baby she had held in her arms all those years ago? Would there be a connection, or would they be polite strangers? This meeting seemed like the most important thing she had done in her life and she desperately wanted to get it right.

She agonised about whether she should go early and be in the café when Nicola arrived, or whether it was better to wait until the girl was already there. Dawn whispered to her, 'Don't think of yourself. Think of her. She is going to find this every bit as hard as you do, and she is much younger. It is down to you to be the grown-up one, to do everything you can to make her comfortable. Get there before her.'

So she went into Richard's café at twenty to five. There were two tables occupied, each with a couple of women shoppers sitting at them. Richard greeted her when she came in, and she ordered a cappuccino. Then, before he had time to froth up the milk, she called across to say she had changed her mind: she was suddenly worried about having a frothy moustache when Nicola arrived.

'I'll have it black,' she said.

Richard brought it over. 'Meeting someone?'

Lisa nodded. She did not want to talk to him. She wanted him to go away, so that when Nicola walked in, she was on her own. It was seven minutes before Nicola arrived and it seemed like seven of the longest minutes Lisa had ever endured. When the large clock behind the till creaked past a quarter to five, she became convinced that Nicola was not going to turn up. One minute, two minutes . . . each one seemed like an eternity.

Then the door swung open and a young woman came in. She turned to close the door behind her, shutting out the icy blast of winter wind that had followed her in. It gave Lisa a few seconds to look at her. Nicola was slim, average height, with shoulder-length feather-cut blonde hair. She was wearing jeans, slouchy fur-lined boots (Lisa knew they were a copy of fashionable Ugg boots, exactly like ones she sold in the shop next door) and a black pea coat with a blue scarf. When she turned towards the room, Lisa gave a small start: this was the girl from the photograph, the girl with her eyebrows and her mother's eyes.

Within a couple of seconds, those eyes rested on Lisa, who forced herself to smile. She half rose from her chair and Nicola came over. They looked at each other, stiffly, for a moment, and then Nicola sat down. Before either of them had time to speak, Richard was at the table, asking Nicola what she wanted.

'A Coke, please,' the girl said.

When Richard walked away, Nicola said shyly, 'Hello. Thank you for meeting me.' It sounded like something she had rehearsed, and Lisa was glad of it – breaking the ice was the hardest bit. Somehow words did not seem adequate for an occasion like this; it was too enormous to take on board.

'I'm very happy to see you,' she said, and she smiled. For a moment the two pairs of grey eyes rested on one another, each trying to drink in everything they saw. Up close, Lisa saw that Nicola had a pretty face, longer and thinner than her own. With a jolt, she realised she could see something of Johnno in her. Johnno – in all the hours she had spent thinking of this meeting, she had virtually forgotten that the girl she would meet would have a large helping of his DNA as well as her own. What would she say if she asked questions about him?

'What do you do for a job?' she said.

Nicola seemed very happy for Lisa to take the initiative, and after a series of questions Lisa found out that Nicola worked as a receptionist at a large veterinary practice in the town, that she loved Lily Allen and Kate Nash, that she hated the fact that Benting was so cut off and that she had to go everywhere on the bus. In return, she told Nicola that she worked next door, in the shoe shop.

'I knew I'd seen you somewhere!' Nicola exclaimed. 'I don't go in there much now – I'd rather go shopping in Leeds, much more choice – but when I was little, my shoes came from there—'

Richard interrupted them. 'Would either of you ladies like something to eat?' he asked.

Lisa turned to Nicola. 'Would you . . . ?'

'No, thanks. Mum will have my tea ready for me when I get home.'

Mum. The word jolted Lisa. This girl, her daughter, had another mum who was busily cooking a meal for her as they were sitting here. A mum who had been absorbed in all of her life, who had bought her school shoes, walked with her to school when she was little, held her hand when she went to the dentist, clapped like mad at her appearance in the Nativity play, tried to help her with her homework, comforted her when she had silly quarrels with her friends . . .

'No, we're fine, thanks,' she said to Richard, who moved away. 'Does your mum know that you are meeting me?' she asked. She said the word 'mum' without hesitation, trying to forget its meaning.

Nicola shook her head. 'I didn't want to worry her. She thinks I'm meeting a friend.'

'Why would she worry? I thought you said she knew you had traced me?'

'Well, obviously she's worried that I might get too close to you and she would be cut out.'

Lisa was irritated. She'd given up Nicola (or Amy) as a baby, and by doing so, this other woman had had the privilege of bringing up *her* child, had enjoyed all those moments that Lisa had missed. What right had she to feel worried? How could she possibly object to Lisa now wanting just a little time with Nicola?

'She's had you to herself for a long time,' she started to say.

Nicola looked up quickly. Their eyes met and each looked directly at the other.

Nicola bristled at the implied criticism of her adoptive mother. 'She's been great. It cost money finding you, I'll have you know. We had to register with an agency and it cost a couple of hundred pounds. Mum and Dad paid for it.' She said it with a slight defiance in her voice.

Again, Lisa felt a prickle of irritation. It had never occurred to her that tracing someone could be expensive, but even so, Nicola complaining about the cost was a bit rich, on their first meeting.

'Would you like me to pay some of it?' she asked, with a visible hint of annoyance.

Nicola, every bit as sensitive as Lisa, responded sharply, 'Of course not. If you think I've just traced you for money, you don't know me.'

'No, that's the trouble, I don't,' Lisa said, more softly. She regretted the way the conversation was going. 'We don't know each other at all, but I think I would like to get to know you.'

A sullen look had come over Nicola's face and she answered Lisa's questions but never elaborated or asked any in return. It was hard work, like pulling teeth. Lisa learned about her GCSE results, about her dog, about an older brother, also adopted, but Nicola ventured no details, other than the bare minimum, and if she could get away with just saying 'yes' or 'no', she did.

I've lost it, blown my chance. I'm never going to have a relationship with this girl, Lisa thought. She could tell that Nicola was regretting ever making contact. For a second, she thought, Maybe this isn't such a bad thing. Maybe I can just walk away and lay to rest the ghost that has haunted me for more than eighteen years. Maybe that's why Dawn wanted me to see her, just to get her out of my system. As soon as she thought it, though, a cold hand clutched at her heart and the pit of her stomach. No, this wasn't what Dawn had planned . . . She'd messed up again.

She made one more attempt to be friendly. 'Would you like another Coke? Tell me about your dog.'

Nicola looked at her watch. 'It's time for me to go,' she said. 'It's time for my bus.'

She picked up her bag. Lisa could see a look of relief on the girl's face, relief that the ordeal was over.

'Do you want to meet again?' she said, without much hope.

'No . . . no, I don't think so,' said Nicola, and turned and walked out.

Lisa watched her go, then drained her coffee. She sat still for a few seconds, trying to memorise Nicola's face in detail, sure that she would never see it again. Then, with a sigh, she took out a ten-pound note to pay Richard.

'I guess she didn't get the job?' he said, bringing her the change.

'What?' Lisa was preoccupied and had no idea what he was talking about.

'Well, I guessed you were interviewing her for a job at the shop, and from the way she left in a hurry I guess she didn't come up to your high standards. Am I right?'

Lisa looked startled. 'No,' she said, but then realised that she did not want to say any more, to Richard or to anyone. 'Yeah, you're right. I won't be taking her on,' she said, pulling her thick winter coat round her shoulders and walking out.

Richard watched her go. As the bell on the door pinged, he shook his head. Would he ever have any idea what made her tick? Somehow, it hadn't been a normal work interview, he knew that. There was something about the girl . . . Still, it was none of his business, he thought, as he picked up the empty coffee cup and Coke glass.

Lisa intrigued him. There had to be more to her than just a snooty cow who spent her time off with some rough bloke . . . She seemed vulnerable, sad. She was also unreachable, he told himself. Not for me. Stop thinking about her, the sensible part of his brain told him. She's trouble.

Back at the shop, Lisa let Jodie and Anne go early. It was quiet; there were no customers in the days before the sale, as everyone was waiting for the reductions. She locked the door half an hour early. As she tidied the stockroom, she went over the conversation again and again, as if it was on a loop that kept playing itself round and round in her head. She had blown it. She had upset Nicola. She had not come up to her daughter's expectations, which was what she had feared all along. Dawn would be very disappointed in her – again.

A wave of exhaustion came over her and she sat on a large delivery box. 'What have I done?' she said out loud, and suddenly her entire body was wracked with sobs. She cried for Nicola, for herself, for her failure, for Dawn. 'I've messed up big time, like I always do,' she said when she had enough breath to speak.

Pulling herself together, she went into the little kitchen at the back to get some tissues and make herself a cup of tea. To her astonishment, Dawn was waiting for her. The angel said nothing, but folded Lisa in her gentle arms, her wings wrapping around them both to create a little tent of warmth and solace.

'I failed,' said Lisa bleakly. 'She never wants to see me again.'

'Yes, she does,' said Dawn.

'No . . . she said she didn't.'

'Everyone says things they don't mean. It was all too much, for both of you. You need time, to take things slowly.'

'We won't get time. She won't see me again. She didn't like me, I could tell. And she seemed spoiled. She wouldn't talk to me properly. She was barely polite, and she couldn't wait to get away.'

'Remember what Richard said?' Dawn asked.

Lisa looked puzzled. 'Richard? No. What did Richard say?'

'He said she had not lived up to your high standards. Maybe you set the bar too high. Maybe you are forgetting that you are dealing with a teenager, confused and in need of help, not judgement. She's not spoiled. She just didn't know how to talk to you.'

'But Richard had no idea what was going on.'

'No, but it is out of the mouths of innocents that we hear the truth. You do expect a lot from other people, even though you know, from your own life, how hard it is to live up to such high standards.'

Lisa paused, thinking about Dawn's comments. From anyone else she would have resented the criticism, but from Dawn it felt more like encouragement.

'But she loves her other mother too much to ever let me in,' said Lisa bitterly. She thought again of all the pleasures and privileges she had handed over to a complete stranger when she gave Nicola up for adoption. 'She said her mother was worried about me coming back into her life – you'd think after all I've given her she wouldn't begrudge me a little bit of my daughter's time.'

'Yes, you gave her a very precious gift, but you are only thinking of yourself again. Think of Nicola's mother, a woman who found, through no fault of her own, that she could not have children. A woman who loved children so much she thought her heart would burst with the sorrow of not having them. A woman who took the precious gift you gave and nurtured her and loved her. Not just through the happy moments, but also difficult times. Times like when her husband lost his job and she had to scrimp and save and put money away to pay for Nicola's dancing lessons. Like when Nicola was rushed to hospital with meningitis and she sat by her bed, praying and praying that the precious gift would not be cruelly snatched away from her. Times like the teenage strops when her daughter threw it back in her face that she was not her real mother. Her road has not been an easy one, either. You have both struggled.'

'How do you know so much about Nicola's family?' Lisa asked.

Dawn gave a brief, tinkly laugh. 'Oh, I may be your guardian angel, but I can still visit other people. You are my priority, but to look after you, I've also kept an eye on the people who are important to you . . . Now, I want you to answer this question: what was the thing you wished for most when you thought about your Little Pickle all these years?'

'That she was happy,' Lisa mumbled, aware now how unfair she was being.

'Yes, and she couldn't have been happy if she didn't love – or wasn't loved by – the woman who mothered her. So the price you pay for her happiness, the thing you wished for more than anything, is that she can't instantly replace her new mother with her old one.'

'I didn't ask her to—' Lisa began, but Dawn interrupted.

'No, not outright, but you felt resentful about the other mother. We've talked about love before. It's infinite, and love doesn't look for trouble. Nicola has love enough for both of you, and you have to accept that. That's part of the deal of loving her.'

Again Lisa realised that she had been selfish, seeing everything from her own perspective. 'How can I make it right?'

'Send her a text right now. Ask her to give it another chance.'

Lisa fumbled with the keypad on her phone. She hardly ever sent texts; she had nobody to send them to. Her fingers felt clumsy and it took her a few minutes. She wrote, 'I'm sorry about this afternoon. I would love to see you again. Please.'

She pressed the 'send' button and sighed. She was sure she would never hear from Nicola again, and she dreaded the inevitable moment when they bumped into each other in the street. Perhaps it was time to pack her bags and leave Allerby.

Just as she was thinking this, her phone beeped. It startled her and she nearly dropped it. 'One new message,' it said on the screen.

Lisa pressed 'open' and the words popped up: 'Wd lk 2 C U 2.'

11

A Drink with Richard

Lisa walked out of the shop feeling wildly happy, yet also tired and drained. It had been an emotionally exhausting day, and she suddenly remembered that she had not eaten anything. As she was locking up, Richard was coming out of Shenley's, also with a bunch of keys in his hand.

'I didn't think you closed so early,' Lisa said, surprised to see him locking up. The café normally stayed open until 7 p.m., to serve coffees and snacks to workers heading off to the cinema or a night out.

'It's deadly quiet. The week between Christmas and New Year is always like this – people stay home to try to make up for everything they've spent over the holiday.' He walked across to her. 'Fancy a drink? I might as well enjoy shutting up early and having a bit of time to myself.'

Lisa's instinctive reaction was to say no, to keep herself closed off from other people, but the exuberance that was bubbling inside her because of the text, and the light-headedness caused by her hunger, combined with Dawn whispering in her ear, 'Go on. Relax,' made her impulsive.

'Why not?' she said. 'That would be very nice.'

They walked together uphill towards the market square, past a couple of closed souvenir shops, a dress shop where the elderly owner catered to a clientele of equally old ladies from the town, and a men's outfitters where the genial manager gave them a wave as he, too, locked up for the night. It was a wide cobbled road, and glancing back, Lisa could see the dark, glistening stretch of the river, so pretty in the summer.

It was below freezing and the cars parked on the far side of the street were covered in frost. The pavements were treacherous, coated with black ice, and twice Lisa's high-heeled boots skidded from under her and Richard had to grasp her arm to keep her upright. They laughed together.

'You'd think, running a shoe shop, I'd have the right footwear for the weather,' Lisa said.

They reached the Feathers, an old-fashioned hotel in the middle of the town's wide market square. Years ago, it had been a coaching inn, a stop-off point for stagecoaches, with stabling for horses through a large cobbled archway. Inside, it was dark and gloomy, and they were the only customers.

'I don't think it's been decorated since the days of the stagecoaches and highwaymen,' Richard whispered to Lisa. She giggled.

An elderly lady came out from behind a curtain to serve them at the bar. When they had walked out of earshot to a table, Richard said, 'And I think some of the staff go back that far, too. On the other hand, it's the quietest place in town. I must be getting old, but I can hardly hear myself think in some of the pubs around here, the music is so loud.'

Lisa nodded. She was grateful to sit down, suddenly feeling quite faint.

Richard glanced at her. 'You look very tired – when did you last eat?'

Lisa confessed that she hadn't had time for anything all day.

'You should have had something while you were interviewing that girl,' he said.

Lisa winced. 'No, no, that wasn't the right time.'

Richard sensed that he was in danger of breaking the happy mood that had borne them through the wintry streets and into the hotel. He did not want to shatter the spell, so quickly changed tack. 'Right, I'll go and see what we can get. If they don't do food here, we can go up the road.'

A minute later, he came back from the bar. 'Well, the dining room doesn't open for another half an hour, which is too long for someone who hasn't eaten all day, so I've ordered soup, bread and a big bowl of chips, which they can do now. How does that sound?'

'Marvellous,' said Lisa, meaning it.

They chatted about business, and Richard told her how his father was getting on. He told her a funny story about his ten-year-old nephew, who smuggled a rabbit into the house without his parents knowing and tried to keep it in his room without anyone finding out.

'A boy at school gave it to him. He put it under the bed and barricaded it in with toys so it couldn't escape. Shirley, my sister, couldn't work out why he was suddenly keen to have salad for his tea. He only managed to keep the rabbit secret for about three hours – long enough for it to chew through an electricity lead and fuse the whole house!'

Lisa laughed. Richard looked at her and thought, I'm right about her. There's a lot more to her than she lets people see. She's not cold and hard, like the girls at the shop think.

He said, 'You should laugh more. It suits you. You are far too serious most of the time. I always think you look as though you've got the worries of the world on your shoulders.'

Lisa felt a strong urge to tell him all about Nicola, but she managed to suppress it. She did not want to jinx her chances with Nicola by talking about her. Instead she said, 'What happened to the rabbit?'

'Oh, they let him keep it. Only in a proper hutch, not loose under his bed.'

'You never had children?' Lisa asked him.

Richard shook his head, and his expression changed. 'No, sadly. When I was married, we tried, but my wife wasn't very keen. I discovered she was secretly still taking the Pill. That's what finished it, really.'

'Oh,' Lisa said, unsure how to react to someone else's sadness. 'I'm sorry. I think you would have made a good father.'

'So do I,' said Richard, brightening. 'But I've got my sister's kids and I'm very close to them. Guess who bought the rabbit hutch?'

Lisa laughed. 'Would that be Uncle Richard?'

'You got it. But what about you? I've seen you around the town with a little girl. Is she your daughter or your niece?'

Lisa went rigid. Her pale face became even paler, and she clutched her hands together tightly.

'I think you must be mistaken,' she managed to say, after a pause. It must be a mistake. He can't possibly have seen Dawn.

'No, I'm sure it was you. I saw you in the park on Boxing Day. I waved, but you didn't see me.'

Lisa stood up abruptly. My God, she thought. Her head was spinning.

'It wasn't me,' she said, as forcibly as she could. She grabbed her coat and bag and headed for the door.

Richard, completely nonplussed, called after her, 'Wait, Lisa, wait . . . The chips are just coming . . . Wait, I didn't mean to upset you . . .'

He started to run after her, then remembered he hadn't paid. He rushed back, put some money on the bar, grabbed his coat and ran out. By the time he reached the street, there was no sign of Lisa. For a brief moment, he thought about following her to her flat – he knew where she lived; they'd talked about it – but then he grew worried that she would feel he was stalking her. He felt deflated and miserable; he had been enjoying her company. He was also puzzled. He could have sworn it was her he saw with the child. And if it was a simple mistake, why was she so upset?

Perhaps the girls in the shop were right about her all along, he thought. She's unapproachable. Don't waste your time, he told himself. And yet . . . she was under his skin, and he felt disappointed in her for running away and annoyed with himself for letting it happen, just when everything had been going so well.

'Dawn, Dawn, where are you?' Lisa called frantically when she arrived home.

'I'm here,' the familiar ripple of a voice whispered.

'But I can't see you.'

'No, I need to teach you to hear my voice even when you can't see me. That's what goes wrong, when I whisper in your ear and you ignore me. I was there, in the Feathers, and I was telling you to stay with Richard. You were safe there. He is a good man.'

'But he knows about you. He's seen you.'

Dawn chuckled. 'That happens from time to time. Sometimes a person sees another person's guardian angel. It is rare, but it does happen. It is nothing to worry about. It confirms what I was telling you: he is a good man.'

Lisa was going to ask more, but at that moment her phone beeped. It was another text message from Nicola: 'I'm not working next Wed. C u for lunch, same place, 12.30 p.m.'

Lisa's heart leaped. Nicola really did mean it when she said she would see her again. Perhaps it would have been better not to be at Shenley's, now that Richard was involving himself in her life, but she didn't care; all that mattered was that she was seeing Nicola again.

She danced an exultant little jig around the room, and when she turned round, she could see Dawn, sitting on the sofa, laughing at her exuberance. She plopped down next to her.

'I think you are truly exhausted. You have had a very powerful day,' said Dawn. 'It's time for sleep.'

And she folded Lisa into her arms and carried her to bed, where, once again, Lisa snuggled down and fell into a deep, tranquil sleep, filled with happy dreams.

Late the next afternoon, Richard put his head round the door of the shoe shop. Lisa's heart leaped; then she remembered how she had run out on him. A flush crept up her cheeks and she was about to apologise, but Richard spoke: 'You couldn't do me a big favour, could you?' he said, acting as if nothing had happened between them the day before. He had decided this was the way forward with Lisa. She was easy to offend and he did not know why, so the best thing was to ignore it and start again.

'What is it?' Lisa asked.

Richard pushed the door open properly and came in. He was carrying a cat basket, from which an elderly tabby peered out. 'It's my dad's cat. My sister has just dropped him in to me, so that I can take him to the vet after I shut the café. She normally does this kind of thing, but my nephew's got football practice and she has to pick him up. The problem is, I'm not allowed to have an animal on the premises, health and safety and all that, so I wondered if I could leave Lurch in your stock cupboard for twenty minutes, until I finish clearing up.'

'Of course,' said Lisa. 'But why do you call him Lurch? That's a terrible name.'

'It's not his real name. He's really called Sam, but we all call him Lurch because, in his youth, he was a bit of a monster, terrorising the neighbourhood birds. And he's not exactly a pretty, dainty cat. But he's past that bad behaviour now. All he does is sleep – and smell. But there's still a nasty streak in him: he'll give me and the vet hell tonight. If you see me covered in scratches tomorrow, don't go imagining it's because of some passionate encounter.'

Lisa laughed. Being around Richard somehow made her relax. She found a place for the cat basket on a pile of boxes in the stockroom. When Richard came back to collect Lurch, he brought with him a small bunch of violets and handed them to Lisa.

'I didn't bring them earlier, when your gossipy staff were around. They'll start rumours about us, so I waited until I saw them go. I just wanted to say sorry for upsetting you yesterday.'

'No, it's me who should apologise,' said Lisa, gazing down at the pretty little purple faces of the flowers, too embarrassed to look at Richard. 'I overreacted . . . I'm sorry.'

Richard paused for a moment, half hoping she would offer an explanation, but Lisa said, 'These are beautiful. I didn't know you could get them at this time of year.'

'Well, I expect they've flown a long way and have a huge carbon footprint for such little flowers. Do you fancy a trip to the vet with me?' Richard asked. 'I could leave Lurch in the back of the car while we went for a drink afterwards.'

Lisa was about to say yes when she remembered with a jolt that Nicola worked at the vet's. She didn't want to bump into her before Wednesday – it would seem pushy.

'No . . . I need to carry on here for a bit. I've got all my paperwork to do.'

'Well, maybe I could pick you up after I've deposited Lurch back at home and we could get a meal?'

Lisa was very tempted. She felt she could hear Dawn whispering to her to say yes.

'No . . . it's very kind. I'd like to . . . another time. I need to get home tonight.' She was worried that if she chatted to Richard for too long, she would tell him things that were better kept secret. He had the knack of making her want to open up. Her relationship with Nicola was so new, and so precarious, that she wanted to keep it secret for a little while longer.

Richard smiled. He was not offended. 'As long as you mean it when you say you'd like to, we'll do it another time.'

He picked up the cat basket and walked to the door. Lisa watched him, and just as he opened it, he turned back and caught her gaze. For a second, they both looked startled, like children caught doing something naughty, then Lisa looked away hurriedly and Richard was gone.

It was raining as she walked home, icy sleet that made the skin on her cheeks feel raw. Tomorrow was New Year's Eve, she realised. The start of a whole new year. A time when people made resolutions about changing their lives, then broke them within the week. A time for hope, new beginnings.

Please, God, please let this be a new beginning for me, she prayed silently as she hurried as fast as she could through the bitter weather.

As she turned the corner to the road where she lived, her footsteps checked and slowed. She could see the familiar sight of Barry's Jaguar, pulled into a parking bay at the front of the block of flats. Once, not so long ago, her heart would have leaped with excitement at the realisation he was there, but now it sank. She hadn't seen him since Christmas Day, and there had been so much going on she hadn't thought about him.

I'm really over him, she thought. I don't want to see him ever again. She knew, though, that getting rid of him was going to be tricky. She'd had one small experience of his anger and violence, but she was sure it could be a whole lot worse.

Letting herself in through the front door, she found him in the entrance hall, talking to one of the other tenants, a pretty girl who had recently moved in with her boyfriend. Barry was smiling at the girl and had one hand on the wall, above her head.

Full chat-up mode, Lisa told herself cynically.

She nodded a greeting to them both and then made her way upstairs. Ten minutes later, after she had unwrapped herself and begun chopping onions for a meal, there was a knock at the door.

'You don't have to let him in,' Dawn whispered to her, and for a moment Lisa paused.

'He'll make trouble if I don't,' she said out loud.

'He *is* trouble,' Dawn's melodic murmur continued.

Lisa sighed as the knock on the door came again, louder. She wiped her hands and went across to open it. She could not face a confrontation.

Barry walked in, took her in his arms and kissed her. Then he released her, wrinkling his nose. 'God, you stink of onions.'

'I didn't know you were coming,' Lisa said, going back into the kitchen to wash her hands.

'Well, I wouldn't mind some grub. I've only had a sandwich all day.'

'I haven't got enough for two,' Lisa said levelly. She was pleased with herself: in the past, she would have cooked the meal for him and watched him eat it, pretending she wasn't hungry, and many a time she had thrown food away, bought in the hope that he would turn up.

'Oh, well, in that case I can't stay long,' he said. 'I'm starving. Still, there's always time for a little bit of fun.' She noted that he didn't invite her out for a meal.

He grabbed her round the waist and began to propel her towards the bedroom, sweet-talking to her all the way. 'I know I've neglected my little girl, but it's been a difficult time. I'll make it up to you, don't you worry, my sweetest. I'm here now. Barry's all yours.'

As he spoke, he was nibbling her ear, and when he got her through to the bedroom, he pulled her towards him and then launched them both down on to the bed. He could sense her reluctance, so propped himself up on one elbow, looking down at her.

'I'm really sorry I haven't been round,' he said, speaking seriously. 'There's been a bit of trouble. Chet's not very pleased with me, and I'm not sure what I'm going to do.'

He looked genuinely anguished and Lisa, despite herself, felt sorry for him. He lay back on the bed, and it was her turn to prop herself up, stroking his cheek. She was at her most vulnerable when he did his little-boy-lost act, and Barry knew it and exploited it.

'It'll be all right,' she said. 'It always sorts itself out, you know that.'

Barry nodded. It had worked: he had won her over. She'd always been a sucker for a hard-luck story, especially a true one.

Half an hour later, after making love, Barry showered. Despite her rush of sympathy for him, Lisa had found the physical encounter repulsive, but had gone through with it because she was not strong enough to say no. She was frightened of him, and he knew it.

'Got my new shirt?' he said.

Lisa brought his Christmas-present shirt and tie to him and he opened the box, grumbling about the number of pins used to hold it in shape. He put it on, then looked at himself in the mirror.

'Good choice. You've got a fine eye. Well, course you have, running a shop all on your own.'

'Not on my own. We're part of a big chain.'

'Yeah, but they more or less leave you to your own devices, don't they? I mean, they don't make spot checks on you or anything.'

'No, of course not,' said Lisa. He had never shown any interest in her work before. 'As long as my paperwork all adds up and we're making a good profit. Of course, the area manager does come in from time to time, but he always lets me know first. We usually just go for a coffee and have a chat about the new lines.'

Barry nodded, still admiring himself in the mirror. He finished dressing, gave Lisa a peck on the cheek and said, 'I definitely won't leave it so long. I'd love to stay, but I've got to meet a couple of people.'

He used to take me with him on his business deals, Lisa thought. But she was glad not to go.

As he went out through the door, she asked, 'What are you doing for New Year's Eve?'

Barry pretended not to have heard her and dashed down the stairs.

Back in the flat, she pulled her dressing gown tight around her and went into the kitchen to resume making her meal. Tears streamed down her face. It's only the onions, she said to herself.

'But it's not, is it?' It was Dawn's voice.

'I've let you down – again,' Lisa said, leaning hard on the kitchen counter, her eyes blinded with tears.

'No, you haven't. You have to stop feeling guilty. If you have let anyone down, it is yourself. But you shouldn't be too tough on yourself, either. He's very persuasive. Just think, though, you could have been having a meal with Richard right now.'

Lisa felt a pang as she remembered Richard's offer. 'Yes, that would have been much better.' She found herself thinking about Richard and realised that she cared about what he thought of her. She was glad he didn't know about Barry; she would go down in his estimation if he did. She smiled to herself as she wondered if Lurch the cat had survived his trip to the vet. Then she thought, I wonder if Nicola was on duty this evening, whether she saw Richard. Saw Lurch. Just the thought made her feel close to her daughter.

New Year's Eve was the first day of the sale and Lisa and all her staff were run off their feet. It was good: there was no time to think. She saw Richard briefly as she popped out to the back of the shop with two black bin bags filled with packaging. Richard was talking to his chef, who was taking a cigarette break after a hectic lunchtime. Lisa waved across.

'Hi. How's it going?' Richard called.

'Bedlam. Did the cat survive?'

'Oh, sure. Lurch is indestructible, but I've got a few battle scars up my arms.'

Lisa laughed, then went back into the fray.

When she finally left work, she turned to glance at Shenley's and was disappointed to see that the café had already closed and there was no sign of Richard. She had been intending to wish him a happy New Year.

She walked home through streets that were already busy with people who had spilled out of their work into the pubs. There was the sound of music and laughter from every corner. She felt relieved that she did not have to join in. She had spent lonely New Year's Eves before, often crawling into bed to sleep the magic hour away, but tonight she was looking forward to it: she had a good bottle of wine and a box of chocolates, and she had treated herself to an expensive bubble bath.

As she reached the market square, she saw a gaggle of young girls tottering along on the other side in precariously high heels. Despite the weather, they were wearing skimpy sequinned tops and short skirts and they had no coats. They were giggling and clutching each other to stay upright on the frosty pavement. Lisa paused and pulled back into a doorway, recognising

Nicola among them. The girls turned into the wine bar, and Lisa watched until they had gone.

Fancy letting her go out without a coat, she said to herself, blaming Nicola's mother. Then she checked herself, remembering what she had been like at that age.

When I was your age, she silently said to Nicola, I'd already given birth to you, abandoned my mum and dad, and messed up my life. You are doing OK – even if you will catch your death of cold.

12

Lunch with Nicola

'You don't look much like me,' Nicola said, her bottom lip pouting slightly. 'I expected we'd be more similar.'

'We've got the same colouring,' Lisa said. 'Fair skin, fair hair, same colour eyes, and the eyebrows . . .'

The lunch was not going well. Lisa had prepared carefully. The day before, her day off work, she had gone to Leeds and had shopped for hours to find a present for Nicola. Should she buy a top, or was that too intimate? Should she buy music CDs? All she knew was that Nicola liked Lily Allen and Kate Nash, and she probably had all their music. She didn't want to buy anything too expensive or Nicola might think she was trying to buy her friendship. In the end, she settled for three bangles that were meant to be worn together. She even asked for advice from the shop assistant, who was about the same age as Nicola. She wrapped them prettily and put them in a gift bag.

Now the shiny blue bag sat on the table between them,

unopened. Again Lisa wished that their meeting could have been somewhere more private; she was aware of Richard glancing her way every now and again. Luckily, the café was very busy.

'At least you are young. Well, youngish,' said Nicola. 'My adopted mother is very old, much older than you.'

'Well, I was very young when I had you.'

'Yeah, but she's really old. She was over forty when she got me.'

'That doesn't matter, does it?'

'I'd have liked a young mum,' said Nicola, still looking down and pouting. 'She's older than everyone else's mums.' Then she shot Lisa a baleful look. 'At least their mums are their real mums. They kept their babies.'

'I would have kept you if I could have done.'

'Oh, yeah? Doesn't seem that hard – they'd have given you a council flat and benefits. I reckon you got rid of me because it was easier.'

Lisa could hear the challenge and was determined not to rise to it. 'I wanted to do what was best for you, and it was best for you. You told me last time that you love your mum and dad. You do, don't you?'

Nicola glanced up, a bit shame-faced, and nodded. 'They're all right. They've been good. But I've always felt different because I was adopted. It's just not the same as my friends. My mate Julie is pregnant and she can talk to her mum about what it's like to go through pregnancy and childbirth. I can't do that 'cos my mum's never had a baby of her own. And my friends are always saying things like they take after their mums for some things and their dads for others. I can't join in.'

'That doesn't seem like a big problem – I don't suppose they talk about it that much. And what you have to remember is that your mum would have loved to have had her own children – she really wanted to have a baby. Think how painful that must have been for her.'

'Yeah, so we're second best. She got us because she couldn't have her own. That makes me feel really good.' Nicola pushed her hair away from her face and looked defiantly at Lisa, as if she was goading her.

'I wasn't saying that. Your mum and dad chose you . . . That makes you very special to them.' She nearly added 'and to me' but bit the words back – this girl did not want to feel connected to her.

Lisa was floundering. This was the sort of conversation Nicola should be having with a welfare worker, not with the woman who had given her up for adoption.

'What about your brother? He's adopted, too, isn't he? How does he cope with it?'

'He doesn't care. He's happy. Says he never thinks about the mother who had him, because Mum and Dad are all he needs.'

'Well, they say boys are less likely to look for their birth parents.'

'Do they? Who is "they"? Have you been reading up about all this?' Nicola's voice was accusatory.

'A bit,' Lisa said. She did not want to admit that since their last meeting she had rung an adoption helpline for advice. It was the woman she spoke to who had suggested a small gift, and also said Lisa should take some photographs of herself as a young woman, and of her parents. It was only later that Lisa realised she had no pictures of her own mum and dad, and precious few of her own life. She had always avoided being photographed, always volunteering to be the one who pressed the shutter. It was as if she wanted no record of her life because she felt it was wasted and unworthy.

'That's typical,' said Nicola, after Lisa's admission that she had read up about how to handle this tricky meeting. Nicola threw down her knife and fork and turned her head to study something out of the window.

In profile, she looks more like me, Lisa thought, but she said nothing.

Nicola had turned up today ready to find fault. She wanted to punish Lisa, and Lisa could understand why. Even so, it was miserable sitting through it.

Eventually Nicola turned back to face her. 'Why didn't you try to look for me? Why didn't you register with the agencies to say you wanted to find me? It was a big disappointment that you didn't, but I suppose I was just expecting too much as usual.'

'I . . . I didn't think I had the right to come back into your life, after what I did. I didn't want to intrude, and I was afraid you wouldn't want to see me.'

'Me, me, me. That's what it is with you. Always put yourself first, like you did when I was born.'

There was an awkward silence, Nicola staring out of the window again and Lisa looking down at her plate.

'I need some information,' Nicola said coldly, after a pause that seemed to Lisa to last for an eternity. She was very shaken by Nicola's allegation that she was selfish. 'Then we can say goodbye. For good. I've done what I needed to do: I've seen you. I'm glad I don't look like you. You haven't been anything to me all my life, and you are nothing to me now.'

Lisa felt her stomach lurch. This was not how she wanted it to be, not how she meant it to be. In recent years, she'd given up on the thought of ever seeing her daughter again, but in the days when she used to fantasise about it, this was not how it was. She didn't want to take Nicola from her adoptive parents, but she wanted them to be able to have a different, happy relationship.

Since their last meeting, she had started to think it would be possible. OK, they'd got off to a rocky start, but the adoption welfare woman had warned her to expect the first meeting to be difficult, as they both came to it with so many expectations. But I can build bridges, she thought, make a friendship. She had brief glimpses in her imagination of them shopping together, laughing together, going out for meals together. When the new stock arrived for when the sale was over, she'd spotted some particularly pretty shoe boots, with little button details, that she immediately wanted to buy for Nicola.

Now these modest dreams were in ruins. Nicola did not like her, did not really want to get to know her. She was a disappointment to her daughter. When the letter had arrived, it was this fear of being a terrible let-down, and of having nothing to offer her daughter, that had tipped Lisa to think of suicide, but Dawn had reassured her, built up her hopes again. Was that deliberately cruel? Was Dawn also punishing her? She bit her lip, hard, to prevent tears welling in her eyes. A physical pain could distract her from an emotional one.

'What do you want to know?' she said quietly. Her food was cold and congealing on the plate; she had not eaten a single mouthful.

'About illnesses and things. My friend Becky is diabetic – have you got anything like that? Any stuff I could pass on to my children, or things I might get myself?'

Lisa shook her head. 'No, I'm very fit and well.'

'What about your mum and dad, your grandparents?'

Lisa gave a small start, which Nicola noticed. This was not easy.

'I . . . I don't know. I lost contact with them before I had you, but they'd always been well.' She realised she did not know if her parents were still alive, and was pretty sure her grandparents would not be.

'They threw you out 'cos you were pregnant?'

Lisa felt a spark of sympathy from the girl, and for a second she was tempted to lie, but she could not. 'No . . . no. They never knew about you. I just left.'

''Cos you knew they would be upset with you for getting knocked up?'

Lisa winced at the expression. It seemed Nicola was determined to shock and upset her, but she remembered Dawn's words: 'However hard this is for you, it is even harder for her. And she is very young.'

'No, I'd left home before I got pregnant with you.'

There was a pause.

'Were they horrible? Did they beat you up, get drunk, that kind of thing?'

Lisa shook her head. She was feeling very tired. It was as if she was on trial, in the dock, trying to account for her life.

'No, nothing like that . . . They were good people.'

'So it was down to you? Not very good at relationships, are you?' said Nicola. 'First your mum and dad, then me. And you are not even married with kids now, are you?'

'No, I'm on my own.'

'What is it with you? Can't you get on with anyone?'

Lisa sighed, paused for a moment and then looked up, meeting Nicola's eye. She breathed in deeply and said, as calmly as she could, 'I think you are right, I'm not very good at relationships, but that's not why I gave you away. I really, genuinely believed I was doing the right thing for you. And I still think that. There's nothing great about being brought up in a council flat by a single mother.'

'Well, my mate Julie has worked out OK and that's what her mum did. Then she got married and had more kids, but Julie's always been with her.'

Lisa bowed her head. She felt ashamed. This girl, her own flesh and blood, was mouthing the words she threw at herself whenever she thought about her life. She'd failed to keep one strong relationship going. She'd run away – literally and metaphorically – from every situation that needed to be worked at. She'd abandoned her family, and God knows they were doing their best, bringing her up as well as they could under the cloud of Dawn's death. She'd thrown their love back in their faces. She'd abandoned her daughter, because at the time it seemed the best course, but maybe she should have fought harder to keep her baby. Maybe she had just taken the easy way out.

As for romantic relationships, she'd always thought she was a really bad picker of men, but perhaps the truth was that it was her fault, not theirs. Perhaps she brought out the worst in them. She'd never told any of them about her baby, never trusted them enough. I'm damaged goods, she thought, the woman who gave her baby away.

She was staring at her plate, at the cold lasagne. She sensed that Nicola was waiting for her to say something.

'Maybe I could have kept you, but I think you've had a better life with your mum and dad. They are obviously good, steady people, and they seem to have done an excellent job of bringing you up. So ask me any questions you want and then I'll go. You are right. Perhaps we should never see each other again.'

'Bit difficult when you work in the only shoe shop in town,' Nicola sniffed. 'But don't stress – I'm moving to Leeds soon. Going to share a flat with one of my mates, just as soon as we've sorted out jobs.'

Lisa looked up, startled. This really was going to be the end of their brief relationship. She said nothing for a moment, and then, 'Yes, you probably want to live somewhere bigger than Allerby at your age. Just remember to keep in touch with your mum and dad.'

'Oh, don't worry,' said Nicola, with heavy sarcasm in her voice. 'Some of us can keep relationships going. I'd never dream of turning my back on Mum and Dad. After all, I've got to be grateful to them – they took me in when my real mother didn't want me.'

This was turning into a torture session.

'Is there anything else you want to know?' Lisa asked quietly, looking down.

'Yeah, I want to know about my dad. I want to trace him, too.'

Lisa flinched and Nicola saw it.

'I guess he's another one you managed to ditch along the way,' she said.

'It wasn't like that . . . He ditched me.'

'Because he didn't want to have a baby?'

'Yes . . . well, maybe he would have ditched me anyway. I thought we had a lasting relationship. He thought differently. I was very young.'

'Not that young. Not much younger than I am.'

'No, but maybe I was more immature. Maybe I just got it all wrong.'

'Tell me about him.'

Lisa had been expecting this and over the past couple of days had rehearsed in her head what she would tell Nicola about Johnno. She knew the girl would ask: it was natural to want to know about the other half of your genetic package.

'He was older than me, by about three years, which seemed a lot at that age. He was tall, good-looking. I can see him in your face. It's the same shape as his.'

Nicola involuntarily touched her own cheek, as if to feel the imprint her missing father had made on her. 'What did he do?'

Lisa shrugged. 'This and that. He knew about cars and motorbikes, so he could have worked as a mechanic.'

'Could have? You mean he didn't work?'

'No, he didn't. Not really . . . Well, he did work, but not in a regular job.'

'Are you telling me he was a criminal?'

'Not exactly.'

'What does *that* mean?'

'He wasn't a big-time criminal. He probably sold drugs in a minor kind of way.'

'Probably? Don't you know anything about him?'

'I never really knew how he got money,' Lisa said, looking down at her plate again. There was a pause; then she forced herself to go on. 'But I can tell you some things about him. He only had a mum – his father had left home when he was a kid. He had a sister. He was clever, but not in a school kind of way. And, like I said, he was good-looking. You take after him in that respect.'

'What was his name? It wasn't on the birth certificate.'

Lisa paused again. 'No. Like I told you, he didn't want to know me when I got pregnant. I don't know where he went and I've never heard of him or seen him since. If I give you his name and you trace him, he'll just deny he was anything to do with it.'

'There are ways around that. I could get a paternity test.'

Lisa was shocked. 'Why would you do that? He's never been involved.'

'And you think you have? You're the one who gave me up for adoption. If you'd given him time, he might have come round. It was probably just the shock of finding out. He might have insisted you keep me and supported you.'

Lisa shook her head. 'Try not to have a rosy-coloured view of him. He offered me money for an abortion. Then he drove away, leaving me no way of tracing him.'

'So you're telling me my dad was a right bastard?'

'We were both very young.'

'So my dad was a bastard who wanted to get rid of me, and my mother was a woman who thought more about herself than anyone else and couldn't wait to get me off her hands. That's it, isn't it? That's my happy family background.'

Irritation mounted in Lisa as she realised the girl was deliberately provoking her. 'No,' she said forcibly, looking Nicola in the eye. 'Your happy family background is with the mum and dad who have brought you up since you were tiny. They are your family. I may have got an awful lot of my life wrong, Nicola, but giving you a stable, loving family is not one of those things. And . . . and . . . although I dreamed about one day meeting you and being part of your life, I can see that it won't work out. I am bringing you pain. I am very sorry that I cannot give you a full medical history for both of your parents, but that's the way it is.'

'Yeah, well . . . thanks for nothing. I'd better be getting back to work.'

'Yes, me too. I'm really, really sorry that we are parting like this.' Tears filled Lisa's eyes and threatened to trickle down her cheeks. She used her napkin to wipe them away.

'Seems you've got a lot to be sorry for.' After delivering this last barb, Nicola grabbed her coat from the back of her chair, picked up her handbag and marched towards the door.

'You've forgotten this . . .' Lisa called after her, half rising and holding up the gift bag containing the bangles.

'Keep your poxy present. I don't want anything from you.' Nicola said this loudly, from the doorway, and marched out, not bothering to close the door behind her.

A gust of icy cold wind swept into the café and an elderly man at the nearest table levered himself up and shut the door. He looked towards Lisa with a sympathetic smile and said, 'Kids, huh? Don't know they are born,' before turning his attention back to his companion.

Lisa nodded. Inside, she was thinking, You're wrong. That girl knows she was born. She knows she was born to me, and that's what's troubling her. Once again, Lisa, you have brought disaster and suffering into other people's lives. Why, oh why, did I ever make that phone call? Why did I think it could be all right? Have I learned nothing over all these years? She felt momentarily angry with Dawn and thought, You say you are always with me, but where were you when I needed your help? You got me into this. I'd never have laid myself open to this if it hadn't been for you. It's your fault.

She sat forward in her chair, her shoulders hunched and her arms tightly folded across her front. Looking at her, Richard felt he could almost touch her misery. He had observed them, her and Nicola, throughout their meeting and had suddenly realised, as he caught a sideways glimpse of Nicola, that she was related to Lisa. Daughter, I guess, he thought. Their conversation had been too intense, too unhappy, for the girl to be a niece. Lisa had never mentioned an ex-husband, a child or children, though. Strange – the first thing most people tell you about is their kids, especially women, he thought. And the girls in the shop, Jodie and Anne, they'd never told him about her having a daughter, and they were pretty hot at getting any gossip or scandal.

Whatever the story, he felt very sorry for her. Her pain was palpable, and he did not want to intrude on it by clearing away the plates of uneaten food. He left her alone for a few minutes, busying himself with other customers, who were paying their bills and saying goodbye.

When the café had emptied, he made a strong cup of espresso coffee and carried it across to her table. He put it down without a word. Lisa glanced up at him, but her eyes were full of tears and she knew that if she spoke, she would break down. Richard simply nodded and walked out the back to the kitchen.

When he returned, she had gone, leaving money on the table to cover the meals, far too much money. Richard put her change to one side of the till.

13

Pressure from Barry

Back at the shoe shop, Lisa went immediately to the small rear washroom, avoiding making eye contact with Anne, who was the only other member of staff working that day. She splashed her face with water, then reapplied her make-up. She stared at herself in the mirror.

Get a grip, girl, she said to herself. The show must go on.

Anne was curious: she could see that her boss was upset, but she knew from experience that it was impossible to pry into Lisa's life. If you asked a direct question, Lisa would simply rebuff you. If you tried fishing, she would never take the bait. It was not that she was rude, but she made it completely clear that her private life was off limits. Jodie said it was because she was a frigid old cow, but Anne felt sorry for her, sure that there was an unhappy past.

When it was time for coffee, Anne popped next door to Shenley's, ostensibly to buy a couple of takeaway cappuccinos, but also to pump Richard. She knew Lisa had been to lunch at the café, and she wanted to know who with, who could make her return so visibly upset.

Richard would not be drawn. 'Yeah, she was in here with someone, a young woman, but I didn't take any notice of them. The place was really busy and I was run off my feet. She seemed OK. Left me a decent tip.' He smiled, winking at Anne. Whatever Lisa's troubles were, they would not be made easier by having Anne and Jodie poring over them, he thought.

'Well, she came back in a bit of a state. I reckon she'd been crying. But you know her – no point asking. She doesn't ever tell you anything.'

'No, she keeps herself pretty close,' Richard said thoughtfully. 'Maybe she was just interviewing for more weekend staff.'

'Yeah, that's what I thought when she went out, but to come back so upset . . . She rushed straight out to the toilet when she came in without a word to me. She normally wants to know how business has been.'

Richard laughed, still trying to defuse Anne's interest. 'That's maybe something to do with my lasagne,' he said. 'I made it myself this morning because the chef is off and I've only got a temporary one from an agency in the kitchen. It's probably my cooking sent her dashing to the loo.'

Anne smiled and Richard quickly asked her a question about her daughter, to change the subject. He felt very protective towards Lisa, even though she never let him, or anyone else as far as he could make out, inside her shell. Except the girl – the girl definitely got inside, he thought.

'Have them on me,' he said to Anne, who was fumbling

for the cash to pay for the coffees. He was tempted to give her Lisa's change, but decided against it. It would give him an excuse to talk to her again. Lisa was really getting under his skin; he found himself thinking about her whenever the café was quiet.

Fortunately for Lisa, the shop was very busy that afternoon. There were mothers wanting new school shoes for their children; there were middle-aged women bringing back the slippers they had been given for Christmas in the wrong size or colour; there were passers-by drawn in by the sale racks. With only two of them working, it was hectic and there was little time to think. Whenever she did get a moment to draw breath, Lisa had to force herself not to replay the lunchtime confrontation with Nicola.

I'll deal with it later, she thought. She began to think about moving away from Allerby, a long way away. Perhaps she would go abroad again. Wasn't it a waste, her speaking such good Spanish and not using it? Wouldn't it be great to get away from these miserable British winters? Or maybe she should go somewhere else in Britain? After all, she had no ties. None at all, she reminded herself bitterly.

At closing time, 6 p.m., the shop was still busy, so there was no time to clear up before the last customer left. Anne volunteered to stay late and help put everything away, but Lisa said no.

'It's OK – there's not a great deal to do. You get along. I'll be finished here pretty quickly. I'll do the paperwork tomorrow morning, before it gets manic again.'

After Anne had left, Lisa busied herself pairing up stray shoes, putting them back in the right boxes and stacking them in order in the stockroom. While she was out in the back, she heard a loud knock on the front door. She hoped it would be Richard, but when she walked through into the brightly lit shop, she saw Barry outside, hands in his pockets, nonchalantly looking at the men's shoes in the window. His Jaguar was parked immediately outside, on the double yellow lines that ran down this side of the street.

Lisa's heart sank, but she went across and unlocked the door to let him in. He had never visited her at work before.

'You can't stay long – your car will be ticketed,' she said.

'That's a great greeting,' said Barry, putting his arms around her. She shrugged him off.

'Not here. The lights are on – people can see in.'

'So what?'

'What do you want?' Lisa said coldly. Right now, Barry was the last person she wanted to see or talk to.

'Come back here,' he said, taking her hand and pulling her into the back of the shop. First he pushed open the door to the washroom, then the stockroom. 'Ah, this is big enough. Come on in here, my lovely girl.'

Lisa allowed herself to be pulled in, glad to be out of the glare of the fluorescent strip lights in the shop, on show to any passer-by in the gloomy street.

'You shouldn't be here,' she said. 'It's after closing time. I've locked up. What if someone came?'

'You said yourself nobody comes to check up on you. Have you cashed up?'

Lisa's heart plummeted and she said angrily, 'What do you want? You are not taking money from here.'

Barry put both his arms around her and pinioned her against the wall of shoeboxes. 'Shush, shush, my little spitfire. Of course I'm not taking money from your till. But *you* are mad if you don't, you know. It would be easy to fiddle yourself a bit of extra income here, as they leave you to your own devices.'

'It's because I'm honest that they leave me alone,' Lisa said icily. 'Stock control is centralised – they know what I sell and how much money I take.'

Barry chuckled and put one hand under her chin to tilt her face towards him. 'Don't worry, I'm not seriously going to steal sweetie money from your till. That's not my league. I'm here to see you . . . Mind you, a pair of those black brogues in the window could easily go missing without anyone noticing, couldn't they? Have you got a size nine?'

Lisa looked startled and angry, but before she could say anything, Barry kissed her, keeping his mouth against hers for a long time. Lisa was determined not to respond, but her anger subsided. The best way to get rid of Barry, she thought, was to give in to him. He wanted sex, and when that was over, he'd be out of her hair.

'No, he won't. If you give in to him again, he will always come back for more. You will never be rid of him.' It was Dawn's voice, whispering in her ear. 'One day, you have got to stand up to him. He's a liar, a thief and he uses you. Why do you let him? You have to say no.'

Lisa pulled herself away from the kiss and tried to move

Barry's hand from her shirt, where he was fumbling with the buttons.

'No, not here. Not any more. I don't want this,' she said.

Barry pulled his face back but kept his body pressed hard against hers. 'What? You don't want it? Of course you want it. You're always mad for it. That's what I like about you. Always ready to go.'

His voice was harsh, not his usual sweet-talking, persuasive tone. Lisa struggled to free herself.

'Oh, no, you don't,' he said, holding on to her tight. He had unbuttoned her shirt and was trying to unhook the back of her bra.

'Barry, I don't want to do this. I don't want to see you any—' Lisa spoke urgently, but before she could finish what she was saying, Barry's hand came over her mouth. She tried to bite him, but the pressure of his hand was so great she could not open her mouth.

'What's eating you?' he said, pulling her skirt up to her waist. 'You love this. You've always loved it. It's the only thing you're any good at, isn't it? And you can't get enough of it. You've probably got half a dozen other blokes on the go as well as me. I don't care, but just don't come the old "Oh, Barry, no" with me.'

Lisa realised that whatever she did, he was going to have sex with her, even if he had to rape her. She gave in. Let's get it over with, she thought. She found Barry repugnant; she'd never noticed before, but he smelled of stale sweat and cigarette smoke. His suit was too shiny and made him look like an old-fashioned spiv; his hair was carefully combed over to hide where it was receding at the front. How could she ever have found him attractive? How had she let him seduce her? I was lonely, she told herself. He's disgusting and I am, too, allowing him into my life.

The sex was quick and unsatisfactory for both of them. When he had finished, Barry scowled at her. 'Marks out of ten? No more than two,' he said, watching her straightening her clothes. 'Have you lost your taste for it, or is it me you've lost your taste for? Got some other bloke to keep you warm in bed, have you?'

His whole way of speaking to her was crude and insulting, and Lisa was humiliated. It's what I deserve, she thought. It's what I'm worth. She knew that the easiest way to get rid of him was to say nothing, not to rise to the bait. And she knew about his violence; she did not want to experience it again. She looked down submissively, as he roughly cradled her chin in his hand.

'I have to lock the shop up now,' she said. 'You'll have to go.'

Barry began prowling around the stockroom. 'Those brogues – where would they be?'

'You can't do that.' Lisa was angry now, but also scared.

'Who says I can't?' Barry laughed at her obvious discomfort.

'Before you lock up again, I've got a present for you,' he said. He walked out of the stockroom, through the shop and to the car. Opening the boot, be carried back with him a large carrier bag, which she could tell, from the way he held it, was heavy.

For a brief moment, Lisa thought he had actually brought something for her, but after he closed the door behind him, he pushed past her back into the stockroom.

'Come in here,' he commanded.

Lisa obeyed, now worried about herself and the shop.

'I need to leave this here,' he said.

'You can't.'

'Oh, yes, I can. And anybody who tries to stop me will find out that I'm not always Mr Nice Guy,' he said, with serious menace in his voice.

The threat terrified Lisa. 'What is it?'

'Never you mind. It's nothing to do with you.'

'If it's drugs, I'm telling the police.'

Barry grabbed her arm and pulled her face up against his. 'You do that and you won't have a pretty little face any more. And at your age, you need to be able to attract a man or two, or you're heading for a lonely old age.' He dropped her arm and turned on a more conciliatory voice. 'Anyway, who said it's drugs? It definitely isn't drugs. I give you my word on that. And it's not something the police would bother about, so tell them if you must . . . Chet Ainsworth, on the other hand, would not be at all pleased about my little freelance efforts. If he found out, he'd be after me. And if he comes after me, I come after you.'

The threat had crept back into his voice. Seeing Lisa's alarmed expression, he softened: 'Look, I'm not asking you to do any more than store this package for a few days, somewhere out of the way, where your staff won't notice it. A couple of weeks at the most. If you want to have a nosey in there, I can't stop you – you'll do it when I'm gone. So I'll tell you what's in there, save you the trouble. It's money. A lot of money. And I know exactly how much, so don't get any fancy ideas about it . . . Now, where are we going to hide it?'

Lisa felt a great, cold hand enclose her heart. This man treated her so badly, and now he was involving her in his dodgy activities. If only she had the strength to tell him to take his package and get out of her life. But that would require a great deal of strength, physical, mental and emotional, and she was not equipped for it. Once again, the easiest thing was to give in and do what he told her.

'Back here,' she said, taking him through into the small kitchen area. There was an oven, a sink, a kettle and a microwave. 'Put it in the oven.'

Barry looked dubious. 'Won't the others find it?'

'No, we never use the oven. We never have time to actually cook anything – the most we ever do is stick something in the microwave, and that's not very often. The only time I tried to use the oven, it didn't work.'

Barry turned the knob on the oven and waited to see if it started to warm up. It didn't. 'OK, that's good. Don't want my small fortune to be incinerated, do I? You're responsible – don't forget. I know exactly what's in there, and I'll be back for it.'

He stashed the money in the oven and then walked through the shop. He called back to her from the doorway, 'I haven't got time now – got to be somewhere – but don't forget those shoes I want. Size nine. Take care of yourself, and be good.'

Lisa followed him to the door, intent on locking up as soon as he had gone, but Barry turned round unexpectedly, caught her wrist and dragged her outside. He kissed her hard and long, pushing her back against the window frame. It was a lascivious, slobbering kiss, and he tried to prise her mouth open to slip his tongue inside. Lisa struggled, but he was strong. Then, just as abruptly as he had started, he pulled away. He turned and grinned at the window of the café next door and nodded his head. Lisa looked, still supporting herself on the glass, and saw Richard moving away from the window next door.

Bright red with humiliation and anger, she threw herself back inside. Richard had seen it! How could she ever face him again? Barry had deliberately dragged her out there because he knew someone was watching. What a bastard! Her flesh crawled at the idea of Richard witnessing her shame.

Richard had only looked out of the window because he had caught a glimpse of a car parked out there. Then the door of the shoe shop had opened and, with a start, he had recognised the man who emerged. They had been at Allerby High School at the same time, although they had never mixed.

So she's still seeing him, he thought. Barry Shields. A no-good toe rag all his life. A flash dresser with a flash car. God, women are a mystery. What does she see in him? He was a thug at school and he's a thug now. She's never going to be interested in me if that's her taste. But he doesn't make her happy, that's for sure.

Just as he was thinking this, Barry had dragged Lisa outside and pulled her into the rough clinch. As he thrust her aside to leave and turned to grin at Richard, Richard realised that the whole pantomime had been for his benefit. Not content with treating her badly in private, Barry had set out to deliberately humiliate her in front of someone else.

He was crushingly disappointed in Lisa. He knew, because the girls had told him, that she'd been seeing Barry, but he had pushed the thought from his head in the past few weeks, as he'd got to know her better. She was pretty, funny and obviously able to look after herself. What made her turn to a bloke like Barry Shields? He was embarrassed and angry that he had been dragged in as a witness, but overriding all these feelings, and despite himself, he felt a deep sorrow for Lisa.

She's got herself into something she can't get out of, he thought. But perhaps I'm being a fool. Perhaps she enjoys it. Otherwise, why does she keep seeing him?

He tried to convince himself that it was none of his business, but he could not get the scene out of his head.

It seems I'm not very good at choosing the women I go for, just like she's not very good at choosing men . . .

Lisa locked the front door quickly. For a moment she stood still, leaning back against it, then remembered that the shop was lit up and anyone passing could see in. She hurried through to the bathroom and sat down on the lid of the loo. Richard had seen! She could never face him again. She was rigid with shame. If a hole had opened up, she'd have willingly crawled into it.

What does it matter who had seen? she told herself fiercely. What mattered was that Barry had left a parcel in the kitchen; getting rid of Barry and his unwanted goods was what was really important. But Richard kept seeping back into her thoughts. Perhaps she should run next door and try to explain? But how could she? There was no excuse or explanation for what he had seen. He would despise and ignore her now, and he would be right to do so, she told herself.

She made herself get up. She walked back through to the stockroom. She had almost finished clearing it before Barry arrived, but having rough sex in there had caused a few boxes to fall to the floor. She carefully put everything back in place, all the time thinking about the package in the oven. What if the police came looking for it? She'd lose her job. The thought made her sad; she took pride in the way she had built up this business; she enjoyed the fact that the men in suits at head office respected her and praised her. She realised, with a pang, that she did not want to leave Allerby. She did, after all, have some roots. Here, this small town, now felt like home to her, and she would like to stay. At the very least, she did not want to be driven out in shame.

Now she not only had the worry about Nicola, and the risk of chance meetings in the street; she also had to worry about Barry and the fact that he had made her an accomplice to his crime by storing his ill-gotten gains on her premises. And how could she avoid bumping into Richard?

When she had finished sorting out the stockroom, she walked through to the kitchen, opened the oven door and pulled out the heavy package. Inside the carrier bag was a parcel, wrapped in newspaper, which was bound together with lashings of Sellotape. Lisa looked at it and decided that she could repackage it easily enough and Barry would never know. She took a pair of scissors and cut through the packaging. The bundle split open and there, on the tiny sink in the shop kitchen, was a huge number of wads of used banknotes, with elastic bands holding them together. Lisa had never seen so much money.

She quickly counted the number of twenty-pound notes in

each wad. There were twenty-five in each. She then counted the number of bundles: eighty. She did a rapid calculation. There, in front of her, was £40,000 in untraceable money. For a second, she thought, I could take this, go away, and nobody would ever find me. This could be the answer to all my problems. It would be enough to set myself up with a new life . . .

'But that would be doing what you have always done – running away.' She could hear the sweet, gentle cadence of Dawn's voice, whispering softly in her ear. She turned, but could not see her guardian angel.

'I'm here, even if you can't see me. Listen to me, Lisa – you have much unfinished business in this town. Do not run away again. Believe me, that is not the way forward. If you run away, trouble will catch up with you. You will never feel free or happy. Stay here. Face up to yourself.'

Lisa paused, then walked through to the shop and picked up the free newspaper that had been pushed through the letterbox. She took a roll of Sellotape from behind the till and carefully replaced the large bundle of notes inside the pages of the paper, putting it back inside the carrier bag and then into the oven.

When she locked up the shop, she glanced at Shenley's. She was relieved to see that the café was all in darkness. She could not bear the memory of Richard, with his back to her, walking away from the window while Barry grinned at him. For a time – just a short interlude – she had dared to hope that Richard liked her.

What a joke, she told herself wryly. It was best to forget about Richard; she'd let him down the way she let everyone else down. He'd seen Barry forcing himself on her – he wouldn't want anything more to do with her. No normal, respectable man would. She walked home feeling as low as she had ever been. Was this the worst day of her entire life? No, but it came close behind those two terrible days: one when Dawn had died and the other when she had handed her baby over for adoption.

14

Nicola in Trouble

Nicola's birthday, 12 January, was always a difficult day for Lisa. Every year, she made sure she was extra busy on that day, and never alone. It was a day when, if she gave herself time to think, she became again that frightened seventeen-year-old who gave birth without anyone to help and support her, but who fell instantly in love with her baby girl, her Little Pickle. A girl who had made the biggest decision of her entire life with no one to guide her, no loving hand to hold hers.

This year, she knew, was going to be the worst ever. Nicola was living just a few miles away and working every day at the other end of the town centre, barely a twenty-minute walk. The fuzzy picture Lisa had, over the years, built up of her daughter was now in sharp focus, crystal clear. She knew what Nicola looked like, how her voice sounded, the way she scrunched up her forehead when she frowned, how her eyebrows arched when she was annoyed.

She had not heard from Nicola since their disastrous lunch, and she had been careful to avoid bumping into her. She no longer went to the hairdresser's salon that was close to the vet's, but had found another one in the opposite direction. She avoided the market square at the time that the bus to Benting was leaving – she'd even gone to the trouble of picking up a timetable, to make sure. But still, despite herself, she found herself looking at every young woman in the street and in the supermarket. Once, at the beauty counter of the large chemist in the square, she was sure she recognised the back of Nicola's fair head, giggling with a friend over the racks of lipsticks and nail polish. She turned quickly and rushed out of the shop.

Barry had not been in touch, either. She was relieved; she dreaded her next confrontation with him. The way he had treated her, forcing her into having sex, without even the slightest hint of romance, had left her degraded and humiliated. Worse still, he had shamed her in front of Richard. In relationships, Lisa had very little self-esteem, but Barry had driven her to an even lower depth. She believed that no decent man would ever want her, and she felt that, at thirty-five, her chances of finding lasting happiness were now remote.

Good men, men like Richard, would not look twice at someone like her. He had been kind to her, because that was his nature, but now he was avoiding her. She had forced herself to go back into Shenley's for coffee and sandwiches at lunchtime, and she noticed how he always seemed to be busy out in the kitchen, leaving his young waitress to serve her. When she'd taken the rubbish out to the bin behind the shop one day, he'd been at the back of his premises. He hadn't ignored her – he gave her a wave – but he hadn't stopped to chat. It's what I deserve, she told herself, feeling desperately sad that their friendship was over.

It was the day before Nicola's birthday and she wanted to buy a present for her: a real present, a gold chain or bracelet. She reminded herself that Lisa hadn't even opened the last present she'd tried to give her, the cheap bangles. But perhaps, without disturbing Nicola or her adoptive parents, she could give her something she would keep for the rest of her life. Something to remember Lisa by, even though they were not part of each other's lives. She agonised about whether this would be wrong, whether she was intruding too much on a girl who had clearly said she wanted nothing more to do with her.

However much she argued with herself, she found herself lingering outside the window of the best jeweller's shop in the town. She had savings: she found her wages more than enough to live on and she was able to put some money into a savings account every month. What was she saving it for? There could be no better way to spend it, she told herself, than to buy something lovely for Nicola. She would send it, to the vet's address, with a note saying that there were no strings attached, that she did not want to impose on Nicola, but that she would like her to have one small thing to always remember her birth mother by.

She spotted a pretty gold locket, but changed her mind about it. A locket was too personal – Nicola would probably think she had put a picture of herself inside it. Instead, she saw a lovely opal pendant on a fine gold chain. It was expensive, but she knew it was perfect.

Pushing the heavy door of the shop open, she was surprised to see Richard inside, looking at the display cabinets.

'Looking for something special?' she said, forcing a polite smile.

Richard turned round, startled to see her, and blushed slightly. 'No, just lurking while they put a new battery in my watch,' he said. 'What about you? Buying yourself something nice?'

Lisa shook her head. At least he wasn't blanking her. 'No, I'm buying a present for someone else,' she said.

At that moment, a shop assistant appeared from the door leading to the back of the shop and asked Lisa if she could help.

'Yes, the opal pendant in the window – I'd like it, please.'

The girl opened the back of the window and brought the pendant to the counter. 'Is this the one?' she said.

'Yes, that's it,' said Lisa, fingering the delicate chain before fishing in her handbag for her wallet.

Richard came across. 'Wow,' he said. 'That's really nice. Must be a present for someone very special.'

'Yes,' Lisa said. She didn't say any more, suddenly regretting letting him see what she was buying. When she saw him in the shop, she could have easily asked about something else, a small charm for her bracelet, anything. Or simply walked out. She could have come back another time. Once again, she'd left herself open and vulnerable.

Richard sensed that she was not going to tell him who the present was for and intuitively realised it must be for the girl he had seen with her in the café, the one who looked like her.

'Well, I expect they'll be very pleased with it,' he said, as another assistant emerged from the back with his watch. He paid the small amount due and turned to leave. Lisa was choosing a box for the pendant and it was clear she was not going to involve him.

'Bye,' he called.

Lisa turned and replied, 'See you around.'

Yes, Richard thought, I'm bound to see you around. We work next door to each other. But I don't think you want to see me in any other way, and I'm a fool for ever thinking you would.

On the eve of Nicola's birthday, Lisa was at home on her own. She hadn't sent the little package containing the pendant to the vet's address. She'd been close to doing it, but felt something stopping her. It wasn't the clear whisper of Dawn's voice in her ear that she had heard lately, but it was the same sort of feeling she had had many times in her life, like when she ran away to Spain, or when she decided to move to Allerby. It was a strong conviction that this was what she should do – or, in the case of the birthday present, not do. The little parcel stood on the side, next to her handbag. She still felt sure, somehow, that she would give it Nicola, but the feeling told her not to put it in the post.

'If it's you, Dawn, you're not coming through loud and clear. The station's off tune, but I think I'm getting your message.'

There was no reply, but Lisa accepted that she should not send the present, while at the same time being sure she would, at some point, hand it over.

It puzzled her. She had no intention of seeking Nicola out. She had held the door open after their first, unhappy meeting, and she could not do it again. Nicola had the right to make the choice, just as Lisa had made the choice nineteen years ago. Nicola's choice was not to see her again, and she had no right to feel critical or resentful about that. Why, then, was she being told so obliquely but firmly not to send the parcel?

She cooked her evening meal but could not face eating it. It was this night, all those years ago, that she had come home to the pub to find it wasn't really her home, that, just when she was at her most vulnerable, she was homeless. Perhaps it was the shock that had made her go into labour, and in the early hours of the next morning her perfect little daughter had entered the world.

To prevent herself dwelling on the anniversary, she switched on the television. The room was gloomy, with just a table lamp in one corner and the flickering brightness of the television in another. She lay back on the sofa and began, eventually, to doze.

Suddenly the room was filled with a very bright light, as if a switch had been thrown. Lisa jerked back into wakefulness, rubbing her eyes. Dawn was there, but this time there was an urgent pulsating feel to the sheen that surrounded her, and it was a sharper blaze of light than the gentle glow that Lisa had become used to.

'Dawn?' she said, sensing that something was wrong. The voice that answered was as soft as ever, but there was an animation to it that underlined to Lisa that something was different. The light around Dawn danced and flickered more vibrantly than ever before.

'Get up and get your coat,' Dawn said. 'We have to go out.'

'Out?' Lisa glanced at the clock on the wall. It was nearly midnight. 'Out? At this time of night? Where are we going?'

'Get ready. Hurry,' Dawn insisted, without offering an explanation.

Lisa pulled her boots, which she had dropped on the floor, back on to her feet. She put her coat on.

'Here – you need your scarf and your gloves,' said Dawn, pointing to them. 'It's a cold night.'

'Where are we going?' Lisa asked again, as she let herself out of the front door. Dawn's brightness subsided into a glow as soon as they were away from the privacy of the flat, and when they got out into the street, she was nothing more than an intermittent twinkle. Nevertheless at all times Lisa could feel the warmth of her, walking alongside, her tiny hand firmly clutching Lisa's, her voice giving directions. She did not answer Lisa's question, but simply insisted that Lisa go where she led her.

They walked hurriedly towards the town centre. It was a Thursday, so the streets were not as busy as they would be at this time on a Friday or Saturday, but there were people around. Lisa heard car doors slamming and happy voices as groups arrived home and young couples scuttled past, their arms around each other to fend off the cold. The nearer they got to the market square, the more people they saw, coming out of restaurants. When anyone passed, Dawn's light would disappear completely, but Lisa could still feel her presence, and the voice, inaudible to anyone else, continued to give rapid instructions.

'Come on, walk faster. Go right here, then across the road. We need to hurry. It will be too late if we don't get there soon.'

Lisa quickened her pace until she was almost running. She brushed past one man, who had emerged from a pub long after closing time and was lurching unsteadily down the street, and nearly knocked him over.

'Oi, you,' he shouted after her, before shrugging his shoulders and staggering away.

Without knowing why, Lisa had picked up Dawn's urgency, and anxiety knotted her stomach. Within minutes they were through the town centre and heading towards an area of town Lisa did not know well. It was an estate where there was often trouble, even in a quiet town like Allerby. She'd heard Jodie and Anne talking about it; Anne had been very upset when one of her sons moved into the estate.

They hurried past blocks of flats. There were no high-rise buildings, but the solid blocks went up four storeys. The icy wind whistled round the bulky buildings, making the night even colder. Lisa shivered and pulled her scarf around her without pausing. Dawn was hurrying her along at a pace that was almost running and Lisa was fighting to catch her breath.

'Come on, not far now,' Dawn urged.

They came through the other side of the estate to a passageway, illuminated by one inadequate street lamp. Lisa shuddered as she hurried along it. It led to a small industrial area, which was dark and deserted. In the distance, Lisa could see a yard lit with floodlights, and the faint figure of a man with a dog, patrolling it. Nearer to her, though, the buildings were just black outlines. Dawn pulled her down a small service road, towards the jagged shape of a burnt-out warehouse, the steel frame outlined black against the faint glow from the distant lights. Lisa remembered reading about the fire, a few months ago. In front of the warehouse was a car.

'Quick, quick, oh, hurry.' There was a tremor in Dawn's voice; she was on the edge of tears.

Lisa broke into a run, pelting as fast as she could towards the building. At one end, an office block was largely untouched by the fire, although the bricks were blackened. As she got near, Lisa, so agitated that she was unaware that Dawn had slipped her grip and was gone, could hear muffled sounds. She went towards them, pushing open a metal door into the building. The smell of burned wood caught her throat.

It was pitch-black inside, but Lisa could hear the sounds clearly now, very close.

'Stay still, bitch, or it will be worse for you,' a man's coarse voice said savagely. 'Keep fucking still or I'll lay you out.'

There were other sounds, muffled, and Lisa guessed the man had his hand across someone's mouth. There was a crash, as if the two were fighting and had fallen. The girl's mouth had been uncovered in the struggle and she let out a piercing scream. In that instant Lisa knew it was Nicola.

'Right, that's it, you little cow. You'll get it now.' The man's voice was frantic and vicious.

Lisa stumbled her way through the darkness towards the noise, tripping over debris to get to an opening into another room. Just as she got there, she heard a sickening thud, a groan, and at that moment the room lit up.

'Thank you, Dawn,' Lisa inwardly murmured as she flew

across the space in a frenzy, towards the body of her daughter, who was slumped on the floor, face down. Her ankles were bound together with rope, and another length of rope was attached to one wrist. Her skirt was pulled up around her waist, and her underwear was ripped. The man was standing over her, his trousers unbuckled, holding a heavy lump of wood, which he had used to knock her out. The light shocked him into silence and he turned to see Lisa coming towards him like a fury. His mouth fell open and he dropped the wood.

'You leave her alone,' Lisa screamed, with a power to her voice she did not know she had. She grabbed the man's arm and pulled him away. His trousers, unfastened, slipped to his ankles, and as he tried to lash out at Lisa, he tripped and sprawled on to the floor, letting out a stream of guttural swear words.

Lisa took hold of the block of wood with both hands. She raised it above her head and was about to bring it crashing down on him when Dawn's voice stopped her: 'No, no, look after Nicola. Leave him – he's nothing. He'll pay for his sins.'

Lisa's rage abated and she rushed across to Nicola, who was not moving. As she put her head down to the girl's face to listen for breathing, she became aware of the man staggering back to his feet. She spun round, groping with her hand for the lump of wood, but the man stared at her for an instant, hitched his trousers up, turned and blundered his way out. She heard him staggering and swearing as he tripped on the debris; after a few seconds' pause, there was the roar of a car engine accelerating away.

Lisa dropped back to her knees beside Nicola. Nicola's clothes were torn; a red weal was coming up on her bare leg. Lisa noticed that one of her shoes – red shoes – was still on her foot, but the other was across the room. Her handbag was on the floor next to her, spilling its contents. She gently twisted Nicola's head so that she could breathe more easily, but did not move her, remembering from first-aid classes that more injuries are caused by well-intentioned help than by the original accident.

Dawn spoke: 'Cover her with your coat, then get help.'

Lisa pulled her mobile out of her pocket. 'No signal.'

'Go outside.'

'I can't leave her.'

'I'm with her. You go. You get help. Get an ambulance. Now.'

Dawn was giving orders, just as she had when they had rushed together through the town. Lisa obeyed, pushing her scarf under Nicola's head without moving her neck, then covering her with the coat. She ran out, Dawn's light showing her the way.

She quickly dialled 999.

'Which service do you want: fire, police or ambulance?' said a woman's voice.

'Ambulance, please.'

'Hold on.'

Another voice came on the line, and Lisa, by now beside herself, gabbled, 'You have to come. Come quick. It's a girl. She's been hit on the head. She's unconscious.'

'Address, please,' the polite young woman on the other end of the line said.

'I . . . I don't know.' Lisa began to describe the location, and then remembered the security guard. She ran towards the lights of the factory, calling out, 'Help,' as she ran. The 999 operator stayed on the line, and as the security man and his dog ran towards her, Lisa thrust the phone at him, panting heavily.

'Please . . . It's the 999 operator. Just tell her where we are. We need an ambulance,' she gasped.

The man gave the right directions and then hurried back with Lisa to the warehouse. There was no sign of Dawn, but his flashlight illuminated the scene. Lisa dropped to the floor next to Nicola and stroked her hair. The girl was breathing steadily, but was unconscious, and still lying in the awkward, splayed way that Lisa had left her. More bruises were appearing, and there was a trickle of blood from the back of her head, which was congealing in her hair.

'Please, please . . . make sure he doesn't come back,' Lisa pleaded to the security man.

'He wouldn't dare. The dog would 'ave 'im,' the man said.

Within minutes, they heard the sound of the ambulance and the security man went outside to wave his flashlight and guide them to the right spot. The next few minutes seemed to pass like a speeded-up film to Lisa. The ambulance men cut the rope that bound Nicola's ankles, then levered the girl with great care on to a stretcher, reassuring Lisa that she had not damaged her spine in the fall and that it looked as if she would be all right.

'But we're not making promises – it's a head injury,' said one of them.

Lisa gathered up Nicola's belongings. She picked up the red, high-heeled shoe, and the ambulance man handed her the one from Nicola's foot.

'You may as well take them both,' he said.

Lisa scrabbled on the ground to find everything that had spilled out of the handbag. There was a lipstick, a phone, a wallet and a piece of paper. There was no time to check for anything else, because the ambulance men had carefully picked their way through the debris with the stretcher and were calling for Lisa to follow them. She hastily thanked the security guard and climbed into the ambulance. She wanted to hold Nicola's limp hand, but the men insisted that she was belted in.

The blue flashing lights went on and the ambulance sped through the streets. Nicola stirred, sighed and muttered something and the paramedic bent over her.

'Is she OK? Will she be all right?' Lisa asked.

'They'll tell you at the hospital, but she's showing signs of coming round, which is good.'

When they reached the brightly lit Allerby General Hospital, on the outskirts of the town, the stretcher was gently unloaded and pushed on a trolley through to A and E.

'We'll leave you now,' said one of the ambulance men. 'You can give the nurses her details. And the police will be coming – they'll want a statement.'

Lisa nodded. She sat on a hard chair next to the bed in Nicola's cubicle, watching as she began to move and murmur to herself as consciousness gradually returned. Lisa clutched the red shoes. How could she explain it to the police? How could she give them Nicola's address – she didn't know it? She pulled the piece of paper out of Nicola's bag, in the hope that it had her address on it. It was thin, fragile with age. She opened it up and read:

To my Little Pickle, my Amy,
I want you to know that I love you more than anything in the world. I wish with all my heart I could keep you . . .

Tears swam in Lisa's eyes and she began to sob. Nicola was carrying with her the note that she, Lisa, had so carefully worded nineteen years ago. Perhaps, after all, Nicola did feel something for her. Perhaps there was hope.

15

The Hospital

A doctor and a nurse bustled into Nicola's cubicle within minutes of her arriving in the hospital. The nurse took her pulse while the doctor listened to her breathing. Nicola moved and sighed.

'She's stirring. No need to intubate. She's protecting her own airways,' the doctor said to the nurse.

'What?' said Lisa, who was still clutching a damp tissue and fighting back sobs.

The nurse turned to her and patted her hand. 'Don't worry. I think your daughter is coming round. If she wasn't, we might have had to put a tube into her throat to help her breathe, but the fact that she's muttering means that she is breathing on her own perfectly well.'

Lisa gasped slightly when the nurse said 'your daughter'. Nobody had ever used those words before. For a moment she was prepared to leave it, say nothing, but with a pang she said, 'I'm not her mother.'

The nurse and doctor ignored her, because Nicola's eyes were flickering open.

'Hello, young lady,' said the doctor. 'What's your name?'

'Nicola,' she whispered, and began to pull herself up against the pillows.

'That's great,' the doctor said, 'and do you know where you are and why you are here?'

Nicola frowned. 'I don't remember . . . I remember being dragged into a car . . . I remember . . .' She closed her eyes.

'That's fine,' said the doctor. 'You are doing well. Your mum is here with you. She'll talk to you.' He turned to Lisa. 'It's a good idea if you keep talking to her for a little while, try to keep her awake.'

'Will she . . . will she have any permanent damage?'

'No, I don't think so,' said the doctor. 'She has come round quickly enough. Of course, we'll have to keep her overnight at least for observation, but it's looking good.' Addressing the nurse, he said, 'She needs a couple of stitches in the back of her head. Can you cut her hair round the wound and get it ready for me?'

Lisa took hold of Nicola's hand and the girl looked at her with gratitude.

'Thank you.'

Lisa's eyes filled with tears again. 'Don't thank me. I'm just so glad it worked out as well as it did.'

The doctor returned, and while he and the nurse busied themselves with the gash on the back of Nicola's head, Lisa slipped a lock of the fair hair, which the nurse had cut away, into her coat pocket. After waiting a couple of minutes for the local anaesthetic to kick in, the doctor carefully stitched the wound.

'Thank you, Dawn. Thank you a million times,' Lisa whispered, suddenly overwhelmed by the enormity of what had happened, and aware fully for the first time how vital Dawn's role had been.

The nurse turned. 'Sorry – I didn't catch what you said.'

Lisa, who hadn't realised she had spoken out loud, said, 'Nothing. Nothing important. Just talking to myself.'

'It must be such a relief for you. Thank God you were there. If it wasn't for you, anything could have happened,' she said, packing up the tray of implements. 'We'll leave you alone for a while, but we're relying on you to keep her awake and talking. I expect the police will be along soon. Shout if you need me.'

Nicola tentatively leaned back against the pillows, gently lowering her head so that the dressing was not disturbed. She closed her eyes, but Lisa took hold of her hand and squeezed it. 'They don't want you to sleep. Not yet.' She laughed out loud. 'Whether you like it or not, we're going to have to talk to each other.'

Nicola smiled.

'Tell me what happened, everything you can remember,' said Lisa.

'I went out with my friends to celebrate my birthday,' she said.

Lisa glanced at her watch; it was two o'clock in the morning. She grinned. 'Happy birthday,' she said. 'It's exactly nineteen years ago, almost to the minute, that you were born.'

Nicola smiled back at her. 'Only you would know that. When people asked me what time I was born, I never knew the answer.'

'Well, now you do. Five minutes past two in the morning precisely. But tell me what happened. Where did your friends go?'

'We were going home. It had not been very lively at the club – we should have waited till the weekend. I decided I was going to get the last bus home – the others all live in a different direction, and one of the girls has a boyfriend with a car who came to pick them up.'

'Why didn't he take you, too?' Lisa was angry, outraged that some young man would leave a girl to make her own way home at that time of night.

'Well, they don't live near me, like I said. And he'd already had to cram five of them into the car. I've used the last bus before. It's normally OK.'

'What about your mum and dad? Won't they be worried that you are not home yet?' Lisa had been tempted not to mention them, enjoying her time alone with Nicola, but the idea that they were distraught that their daughter had not come back, and may be walking the streets looking for her right now, was too much to bear.

'No,' Lisa shook her head. 'They think I'm staying at Tracey's.'

'So why didn't you go to Tracey's? How did that man get you?'

'I realised I'd forgotten to bring my uniform for work, so I had to go home. I was waiting for the bus when he pulled up. He asked me which was the road to Leeds. I started to tell him . . .' She broke off, and her voice caught with a sob.

Lisa squeezed her hand and leaned forward to smooth the hair on her forehead. 'Don't worry. You don't have to tell me. It's over, and it's worked out all right.'

'No, I want to say what happened. I want to try to remember . . .' Nicola's voice trailed away again. Then she looked at Lisa with startled eyes. 'He could do it again to someone else, couldn't he? And they might not have anyone to help them. So I've got to remember as much as I can, to try to stop him.'

Lisa nodded. 'But maybe not right now.'

Tears ran down Nicola's face, but she said, 'Yes, now, while I can still see it. He grabbed my arm and dragged me into the car. He was very strong. I kicked and screamed, but he drove a bit and then stopped and tied me up, my arms and my legs. He said that if I screamed, he would make it so I never screamed again. Then he drove some more.'

She broke down in sobs and Lisa leaned across and cradled her, awkwardly, making sure she did not disturb the dressing on Nicola's head. She kissed Nicola's hair and inhaled the fresh shampoo smell. For a second, she was transported back to the hospital ward, where she cradled her newborn baby and marvelled at the lovely smell of her downy hair.

When Nicola was calmer, she encouraged her to carry on: 'Then he dragged you into that burnt-out warehouse.'

'Yeah. I tried to kick, but he was too big and strong. I knew there was no point screaming because I could see there was nothing around, nobody to hear. I . . . I managed to get one of my hands out of the rope and hit him in the face, but that just made him more angry. I don't remember any more, not properly.' She paused, a long pause. 'That nurse said you found me. How did that happen?'

She turned to look directly at Lisa, who was no longer leaning across but was still holding her hand. The movement caused her to flinch, as the wound on her head dragged slightly on the pillow.

'Stay still,' said Lisa soothingly. 'Don't hurt your head.'

'But why were you there? How did you know?'

Lisa shook her head. 'I can't really tell you. All I know is, I just felt this strong urge to go there. I knew exactly where it was somehow.'

'And you pulled him off.' Nicola's eyes filled with tears again. 'He was going to rape me, wasn't he?'

Lisa nodded mutely. The thought was too terrible to bear.

'Don't think about it now,' she said, rubbing Nicola's hand. 'The main thing is that you are safe. And you are going to be OK. He didn't do any permanent damage.'

'No, but they've cut my hair. I'm going to look gross with stitches on the back of my head.'

Lisa laughed out loud, a huge feeling of release flooding through her body. 'If you are vain enough to be worried about what the back of your head looks like, you are definitely OK,' she said.

Nicola smiled. 'At least it's winter, so I won't look odd wearing a hat. How much did they cut off? Have a look, can you?'

She pulled forward and Lisa stood up and looked at the back of her head. 'It'll be fine. The long hair on your crown will fall down over it. And besides, it will all grow back. That's the great thing about hair – even if you let the hairdresser do something disastrous to it, it grows back.'

'Have you ever had a terrible haircut?'

'Course. I had a dreadful perm once, one of those very tight, bubbly ones. I thought it would make it easy to take care of – instead it looked awful, like a circus clown, and even worse when it was growing out. I ended up having a really short cut, just to get rid of it, and that definitely didn't look good.'

Nicola was watching her as she spoke and then suddenly stretched her other hand out to Lisa, who grasped them both. Nicola smiled broadly. 'I like talking to you,' she said, almost shyly. 'My mum is great – I love her and all that – but she's not interested in hair and make-up and clothes.'

Lisa felt a warm glow. She and Nicola were building bridges and maybe, just maybe, her fantasy about shopping together and having lunch together and sharing news about the latest boyfriend would one day become a reality.

'What do you think told you where I was with that man?' Nicola said, turning back to the present.

Lisa paused, unsure whether she should reveal Dawn's role, but decided against. Her daughter might think she was a bit weird if she started talking about angels. Maybe later, one day, when they knew each other better.

'I can only describe it like I said before, an urge. I just knew you needed me. Maybe it's my way of making up for all the times I haven't been there for you.'

There was a brief silence; then Nicola said, 'Why did you give me away? I need to know what made you do it.' She pulled her hands away from Lisa's and looked intently at her.

Lisa felt worried. Was this the end of their lovely, warm chat? Was Nicola going to get angry with her again?

Looking down at her hands, she noticed a splinter sticking out of the ball of her thumb. She tried to pull it out, but it was too deeply embedded. Nicola looked down to see what she was doing.

'Don't pick it!' she exclaimed. 'You may infect it. I expect that nurse has some tweezers to get it out . . . Where has it come from?'

'When I picked up that block of wood to hit him,' Lisa said.

'I wish I'd seen you do that. I must have been out for the count by then.'

Lisa smiled. 'You were. Dead to the world.'

'Did you clunk him?'

'No, he got away.'

'But the police will catch him?' Nicola sounded anxious, so Lisa reassured her, even though she was not completely convinced herself.

'Of course they will. They've probably got him already. He won't cause you any more bother.'

'No, but if they don't catch him, he could do it to another girl – and she might not have a guardian angel to come looking for her.'

Lisa was startled by the words 'guardian angel', but realised straightaway that Nicola had said them innocently, thinking of Lisa as the guardian angel.

'Don't worry. They'll keep him locked up for a long time.' She squeezed the girl's hand again and Nicola lay back, looking more relaxed. She closed her eyes.

'Don't get too comfortable. You remember what the doctor said about not falling asleep.'

'Yeah. Tell me about my birth.'

'It wasn't difficult, not physically. You came out quickly and easily, a beautiful baby weighing seven and a half pounds.'

'I know what I weighed. They told Mum that bit. She needed to know to check that I kept putting on weight, I suppose.'

'Yes, I suppose so.' Every mention of the other 'mum' was a knife in Lisa's heart. She felt the yawning gulf of Nicola's childhood opening up between them, years when this other woman was the closest human being to her little daughter. She pushed the thought away, determined not to let anything spoil this precious time together.

'How long was I with you?' Nicola asked.

'Six days. Six days, that's all,' Lisa said, and a sob caught in the back of her throat. It was Nicola's turn to squeeze her hand.

'Tell me about it. I want to know why you couldn't keep me.' Nicola's voice was not combative, but gentle and curious.

'Well, I was only seventeen, living in a squat—'

'In a squat?' Nicola interrupted, astonished.

'Well, yes, at the time I got pregnant,' said Lisa wearily. 'I'd left home, very stupidly, to be with a boyfriend I thought loved me, but he didn't. When I found I was pregnant . . . There wasn't even any hot water. The place was dirty.'

'What did you do? Why didn't you have an abortion? You said that was what your boyfriend wanted.'

Lisa looked at her. 'I thought about it, nearly did it, but something told me not to go through with it . . . and thank

God I didn't.' She smiled at Nicola, her eyes glistening with tears. 'We wouldn't be here now, would we?'

Nicola was also crying, and shook her head mutely. For a few seconds the two of them held hands tightly. Then Lisa pulled one hand free to grab a box of tissues from the locker. They both wiped their eyes.

Nicola suddenly laughed, looking at Lisa. 'You've got mascara all down your cheeks. And I bet I have, too.'

Lisa smiled. 'Yep, we both look a bit the worse for wear.'

'Tell me more. I want to hear about it all.'

'I didn't have any friends or family. I thought I might keep you – I shared a flat with a gay guy while I was pregnant and he said he would help me, but it didn't work out. I literally had nowhere to go. Somebody brought my suitcase into the hospital for me and that was all I had. I didn't even have clothes for you – just a couple of little cardigans an old lady had knitted.'

Nicola nodded. 'Lemon-coloured?'

'Yes, that's right,' said Lisa, surprised.

'They gave them to Mum with me and she kept them, because she knew they came from my birth mother. I've got them at home.'

Tears swam before Lisa's eyes. For a moment she was transported back to the pub, where old Elsie had handed over the little matinée jackets, wrapped in tissue paper.

'Strange to think that's all you've ever had from me,' she said.

Nicola shook her head. 'No, I've got the letter.' She gave a start. 'What happened to my bag, my things?'

Lisa patted her hand reassuringly. 'They're here. I picked everything up. At least, I hope I got everything. I picked up the letter.'

'That's all that counts. I've carried it with me ever since I got it, a year ago, from the adoption agency. Tell me more about what happened when I was born.'

'There's not much more to tell. They wanted me to give you up for adoption, so I agreed.'

'Who's they?'

'The social workers and nurses and everybody.' She looked at Nicola pleadingly. 'I was too young. I didn't know what to do. All I wanted was what was best for you . . . It wasn't because I didn't love you. I loved you and loved you. While the other mothers were trying to get as much sleep as they could between feeds, I was staying awake so that I could have every minute with you before they took you away. And when you went . . . well, I cried so much I thought I was going to die of crying.'

Nicola stretched out to hug Lisa, but flinched with pain as she moved.

'Don't hurt yourself,' Lisa said solicitously, jumping up to rearrange pillows.

'I wanted to hold you. I wanted to say thank you for having me.'

'I loved having you, and I am so pleased and proud of how you have turned out. I just wish I could have been with you all these years, but it wasn't possible. I hope you can forgive me. I really wanted to do the best for you.'

'There is nothing to forgive. I've wondered about you, lots of times. But Mum and Dad have been very good. I would not like to have missed having them in my life.' After a pause, she said, 'I think if it was me, I'd have done what you did.'

The words were music to Lisa's ears; she felt this was her complete absolution. Not only did Nicola not blame her, but she felt she would have done the same thing in Lisa's position.

'My biggest fear, all down the years, was that you were unhappy, but something deep inside me told me you were OK, that the people who took you were good and kind. That was all I could ask for.'

'For me, I just wanted to know what you looked like, and whether you ever thought about me. Also, I wanted to know if I had any brothers or sisters.'

Lisa shook her head. 'No, I always felt I couldn't love another baby the way I loved you. I know this sounds strange, but I did not want you to ever feel that I had replaced you with another baby.'

'I don't think I would have thought that,' said Nicola, smiling. 'I used to think it would be great to have a sister – I've already got a brother. I'm glad now, though, that I've got you to myself.'

They sat in silence for a couple of minutes, holding hands, comfortable in each other's company.

'I suppose I'm even glad that man attacked me,' Nicola said eventually.

'What?' Lisa looked at her with an expression of shock. 'Glad that he attacked you?'

Nicola smiled broadly. 'Yes, I know it sounds strange, but I'd decided I didn't want to see you again. I told myself I just wanted to know what you looked like, and whether there were any health things I should know about, and that was it. I didn't want to have you in my life. But thanks to that man . . .'

'Well, I don't think he deserves any thanks,' said Lisa, feeling a sudden rush of anger towards Nicola's attacker.

Before she could say any more, the curtain round the bed parted and the nurse popped her head in.

'Oh good, still bright and alert. Well, if you're up to it, I've got the police here to talk to you. If you really can't face it, I can ask them to come back in the morning.'

'No, we can do it now, can't we?' She turned to Lisa for reassurance.

'Yes. I expect they want to talk to me, too.'

The detectives, a man and a woman, in plain clothes, squeezed into the cubicle, sitting in two chairs on the opposite side of the bed to Lisa.

The older one, a bulky man in a beige raincoat, introduced himself as Detective Constable Wilf Atkins.

'And this is DC Susan Morris,' he said, gesturing to the woman next to him.

'Just call me Sue,' she said, smiling sympathetically at them both. She had an open, friendly face.

'First,' DC Atkins said, 'we've got some good news. We think we know the man who attacked you.'

Lisa was amazed. 'That's fantastic! How did you know?'

'The security guard who helped out – he jotted down the number of the car when the bloke drove in. He stupidly drove past the yard where the guard was. Nothing happens around there at night, so the guard makes a note of anything out of the ordinary.'

Lisa sighed audibly with relief.

The young woman detective picked up the story. 'We checked out the number and the car belongs to someone we have had dealings with in the past. He's got a record. It's now just a matter of picking him up.'

Lisa's temporary relief was over. 'You mean you know who he is, but you haven't caught him?' she said sharply.

'Not yet. He didn't go back to his home – not really a surprise – but we've got an alert out for him, and we'll have him in custody in no time, trust me.'

Lisa tried not to let her alarm show, because she didn't want to worry Nicola, but her face betrayed her agitation.

DC Atkins reassured her. 'He's not a great criminal mastermind. He won't be on the run for long. In fact –' he glanced at his watch '– I daresay our colleagues have rounded him up already. Nothing for you to worry about.

'We're going to check the CCTV from the other premises on that estate, but we can't do that until the morning. It's only belt and braces – we're very sure we know our man. But we'll need a statement from you both, and we may have to ask you to attend an identity parade, in the fullness of time. Will you be happy to do that?'

They both nodded. DC Atkins's pocket radio crackled into life and he went outside to talk.

When he returned, he said, 'That's even better news. We've got him, safe and sound. All locked up and out of harm's way.' He gave them a grin.

DC Morris said, 'We'll take the formal statements tomorrow, when you're feeling better. But right now, if you are up to it, can you tell us a bit about what happened?'

The detectives took Nicola through the same story she had told to Lisa.

'Well, you've learned a big lesson, I hope,' said DC Morris. 'You must always arrange for someone to take you home. No wandering around on your own at that time of night. Even a quiet town like Allerby – it's just not safe.'

Nicola nodded.

Then it was Lisa's turn to be questioned.

'Just how did you come to be there?'

'It's . . . it's very hard to explain. I just had this very strong feeling . . . It was as if I was being guided there . . . like I had some sort of homing device . . . I didn't even know what I was going for. I didn't know it was Nicola in danger until I got there . . . I know it sounds spooky, but it's what happened.'

The older detective nodded. 'I've heard of stranger things,' he said. 'The power of love . . . well, you just don't know. I've known a skinny little seven-stone woman lift a car all by herself because her child was trapped under it. It should be impossible, but . . .'

'Anyway, it's a bloody good job you did get there,' said DC Morris. 'You had a very narrow escape,' she said, turning to Nicola. 'Thank God your mother is so close to you she can pick up your distress, even at a distance. But take more care – don't rely on it.'

The other detective smiled. 'No, you aren't always going to have Super-Mum coming to the rescue.'

Lisa realised that they had not fully explained the situation. 'I'm not her mum,' she said hesitantly.

Both the detectives looked surprised.

'Yes, you are,' said Nicola.

'You certainly look like her mum,' said DC Morris, glancing from one to the other.

'Well, I am, in a way.' She hesitated, drew in a deep breath and then continued. 'You see, Nicola was adopted when she was a baby, but I'm actually her birth mother. I haven't brought her up, and we've only got in contact recently.' It felt weird saying all this out loud, revealing a lifetime's secret to two strangers. 'So, you see, I don't feel as if I can call myself her mum.'

'Yes, you can. You are my mum.' Nicola beamed at the detectives. 'I guess I'm just lucky I've got two super-mums.'

As they drove away from Allerby General Hospital, the older detective turned to DC Morris and said, 'What do you make of that? You don't think she set up the attack just to rescue her daughter?'

DC Morris laughed. 'Don't be daft. You've been in this job too long. You're too cynical for your own good. No, it's like you said back there. It's the power of love. A mother's love is an amazing thing. Amazing. That kid had a lucky escape.'

Back inside the hospital, Nicola's bed was moved from the busy, bright A and E to a quiet ward, where all the other patients were asleep. The doctor had told her it was now all right for her to rest, and the exhausted girl lay back against the pillows and was soon deeply asleep.

Lisa was tired, too, but she fetched a cup of coffee to keep herself awake. She was determined not to miss a single minute of this time with her daughter.

Just as she had stayed awake with her Little Pickle in the hours after her birth, now she stroked the fair hair from the forehead of her sleeping daughter and rejoiced in her gentle, regular breathing, grateful to be there.

Book Three

16

Barry Returns

Early in the morning, while Nicola slept peacefully, Lisa went to freshen up and get herself another coffee. As she made her way back to the ward, she saw, ahead of her, DC Sue Morris walking in with two people. Lisa pulled back and stopped. She knew, without being told, that this small, plump woman and her rangy husband were Nicola's adoptive mum and dad. A sharp pang went through Lisa's chest. She knew, of course, that they had to be told and would come as soon as they could, but it felt as if a precious interlude was now over, and that she was going to have to share Nicola again.

She did not feel up to meeting them; the whole episode had been emotionally draining, and she could not face the awkwardness of being introduced by a policewoman. Besides, they would only want to be with Nicola right now, and it would be cruel to suddenly appear in their lives. They had enough to cope with.

Luckily, she had her coat and bag with her – the only thing left by Nicola's bed was her scarf. She turned and walked slowly out of the hospital, and her luck held because she found a cab outside.

Back home, she lay in a hot bath. She knew that if she went to bed, she would not wake up in time for work. A storm of emotions raged through her: terror, at the thought of what might have happened to Nicola; joy that she had spent so long talking happily to her daughter and had been reconciled with her; sadness that the long night was over; and envy of the two people who were now sitting by the bedside, Nicola's true mum and dad.

She sighed, dunked her head under the water and vigorously lathered her hair with shampoo, symbolically washing away all the negative emotions.

I must stop thinking of myself and simply rejoice that Nicola is safe and well, and that she wants me in her life, she lectured herself.

As she tentatively opened her eyes after rinsing away the shampoo, she saw that her small bathroom was bathed in Dawn's soft light.

'Oh, Dawn, you're here,' she said excitedly. 'Thank you, thank you a million times. You saved Nicola. I can't thank you enough.'

She climbed out of the bath and vigorously towelled her hair. Dawn watched her from the doorway, smiling.

'You did it,' she said, 'not me. I told you to go there, but you didn't have to listen to me. And you did the rest.'

'But without you . . .'

Dawn chuckled. 'Let's not argue about who gets more stars,' she laughed. 'We sound like two little girls! All that matters was that it was the right result for Nicola. And for you. Now, you must make yourself a good breakfast because you have to get through today without having had any sleep.'

Despite her tiredness, Lisa was on a high all day. She was so cheerful that Jodie and Anne exchanged glances.

When Lisa was out of earshot, Jodie said, 'What's making her so happy?'

Anne shrugged. 'No idea, but enjoy it while it lasts.'

At coffee time, Lisa popped next door to get three takeaway cappuccinos. As usual, when he saw her coming in, Richard picked up some dishes and carried them out to the kitchen. He was trying, for his own sake, to avoid Lisa. He could not figure her out, but after seeing her with Barry, he had convinced himself she was bad news and that he should move on. It was already too late, though: he was completely fascinated by her and would have loved to sit down and talk to her, to find out why she had let a man like Barry into her life. He was also baffled by the small child he had seen with her, and her refusal to explain. Then there was the grown-up girl she rowed with: who exactly was she?

Lisa stood at the counter while Richard's waitress, Michelle, frothed the milk for the coffees. 'And I'll take three of those cupcakes, please,' she said. 'They look fantastic.'

The girl smiled. 'I made those,' she said proudly, holding out the tray of brightly coloured cakes.

Lisa chose three.

'Where's Richard these days?' she said artlessly. She would have loved to see him this morning, now that everything was so good in her life. Then she remembered that he had seen her with Barry and a prickle of shame crept up her neck and flushed her face.

'He's out the back. Shall I call him?' the girl said.

'Oh, no. No. I . . . I just wondered because I hadn't seen him lately.'

Richard, lingering behind the doorway to the kitchen, caught his breath. She missed him. Maybe there was hope. He was about to walk out and speak to her, but he hesitated too long and he heard the ping of the door, which told him she had left.

The awareness that Richard was avoiding her was the only cloud in Lisa's sky that day. Her happiness about Nicola kept her buoyed up, despite her lack of sleep. She said she would take a late lunch and allowed Jodie and Anne to go out together for theirs: a rare treat, as they now had to stagger their breaks.

'Your boss seems happy today,' said Richard, serving the two of them with bowls of minestrone soup and toasted panini.

'Yes, we can't figure it out,' said Jodie.

'Not that we can ever figure her out,' said Anne, 'but we are enjoying it while the sun shines. She even bought us cakes this morning.'

'Yes, I heard,' said Richard. 'Perhaps she's kicked that dodgy boyfriend of hers into touch.'

'Yeah, I don't think he's been seen round her flat as much,' said Anne. 'Never understood why she took up with him. My son's mate says he's a bad lot. Treats his wife and kids really badly. Probably treats her badly, too.'

'Some women like that,' said Jodie almost wistfully. She was still struggling to get her fiancé to commit to a wedding date. She moaned frequently to Anne that he was too cautious, insisting they save more before taking the plunge.

'Well, women like that are stupid,' said Anne firmly. In her life, she had known a couple of friends who had been the victims of domestic abuse and she could not find anything to recommend it.

'I don't think *she's* stupid,' said Jodie, nodding her head towards the shop next door.

'No, but even the most sensible women do stupid things for men they love,' said Richard, thinking about the mystery parcel he had seen being taken into the shop by Barry. 'Let's hope she has got rid of him. She deserves better.'

Anne shot him a sharp look. 'Someone like you, you mean, Richard?'

Richard laughed and turned away so that they would not catch him blushing. 'Oh, no, I'm far too boring for Lisa.'

He sensed Anne looking at him shrewdly, so he changed the subject. 'What did you think of the cupcakes? Can I tempt you with another one now? Or pudding? We've got a great apple crumble.'

'Get thee behind me, Satan,' said Anne, laughing. 'We'll have to buy new work clothes if you keep tempting us. I can hardly do up my skirt now.'

After they had left, Richard smiled to himself. Perhaps Lisa is sorting herself out, he thought.

Twenty minutes later, when it was her turn to come in for her lunch, he did not scuttle away to the kitchen, but instead went across to serve her.

'I think I'll have the soup and a toasted sandwich,' she said. 'The girls have just come back raving about their lunches, so I'll go for the same.'

'Coming up,' Richard said, with a smile.

Lisa felt a sudden rush of happiness as he walked away from her. Everything was going right today. Now even Richard was no longer avoiding her. 'Thank you, Dawn,' she whispered, and felt a tiny squeeze of her hand in reply.

When he brought the food to her, Richard said, as casually as he could, 'How are things? You are looking well.'

Lisa flushed, then laughed. 'I'm fine, thank you. Things are great. How about you? How's your dad? How's the rabbit?'

The café was nearly empty – the lunchtime rush was over – so Richard sat down at a chair at the next table to Lisa's. He did not want to crowd her, but she was obviously inviting him to chat.

His young waitress came over and facetiously said to him, 'What can I get you, sir?'

'I'll have a latte, please, miss,' he said, with a straight face.

Lisa laughed, and the girl went to fetch the coffee.

'Sitting down in the middle of the day is a rare privilege,' he said. 'I expect it is for you, too.'

'Yes, although we take it in turns to have a sit-down in the stockroom. I don't let the girls sit down in the shop.'

'They used to, before you came.'

'I know, but it didn't look good.'

'No, well, that's all a long time ago.' Richard nodded approvingly. 'And they seem happy enough now.'

'Yeah, they've settled down. Even Jodie.'

They chatted for half an hour, while Lisa ate her meal. They talked about Richard's nephew, his dad and the cat, Lurch. He told her about the Sunday-league football team he played in.

'I used to be in the first team, but a knee injury, old age and too many good lunches mean I'm now in the third team. It's actually a lot more fun – we don't care whether we win or lose. We just meet up for a damned good kick-around and then fall into the pub afterwards to undo all the good work we've done running around the pitch for ninety minutes.'

Lisa laughed.

As usual, he noted, he was telling her a lot more about his life than she was about hers.

'You used to live in Spain?' he said, trying to find out more about her. Anne and Jodie had filled him in, when Lisa first arrived, on the sparse details of her life that they knew. 'Do you speak the lingo?'

'*Si, señor*. I spoke it really well when I was out there, but it's a bit rusty now.' She paused. 'I've been thinking about moving back there . . .'

Richard felt himself grow pale.

'. . . but I've decided not to. I like Allerby. It does seem a shame not to use the language, though.'

Richard's relief was palpable. 'I'm glad you're not going,' he said, looking at her. For a second their eyes locked; then they both looked away, embarrassed.

Lisa stood up. 'I must be getting back,' she said. 'I'm tough with the girls about their breaks – I mustn't overdo mine.' She took out her purse.

'Have this one on me,' Richard said.

'No, no . . . I insist.'

He shrugged and let her pay, but as she was leaving, he gave her a bag. 'Three choc-chip cookies. They'll keep till tomorrow if the girls don't want them this afternoon.'

Lisa smiled widely at him. 'You are a good bloke, Richard,' she said, and left the café.

Yeah, I just hope I'm good enough, Richard thought. Or maybe, in your case, bad enough.

He felt happier than he had felt in days as he polished the coffee machine.

Lisa, too, felt another surge of happiness. Was it just to do with Nicola? She realised, as she pulled the café door closed behind her, that mixed with her joy about Nicola was a sense of tender excitement about Richard. Would a man like that really look twice at her? She bit her lip and pushed the thought away. No, she should not expect the moon. She should be content with what she had: a burgeoning new relationship with Nicola.

By the end of the day, Lisa's lack of sleep was catching up with her and she began to feel drained. When Anne and Jodie went home, she sat down to do the day's paperwork and to get the cash from the till bagged up for the night-safe at the bank. As she worked, she nibbled one of Richard's cookies. I need the sugar boost, she told herself, to justify the extra calories, and thought longingly of an early night.

I wonder if Nicola has gone home from hospital. Should I ring her to see how she is? She decided to leave it until the next day because she felt too tired to take any more emotional stress that day and she wanted to give Nicola space with her family.

Just as she was wearily collecting her things together and putting her coat on, she heard a loud banging on the shop door. Her heart sank. Throughout all the excitement, she had put thoughts of Barry out of her mind. She had spun through the day in a haze of happiness and relief, which had made her lack of sleep bearable, but now, realising that Barry was outside, she felt bone-tired and sick to her stomach. Why, when anything good happened to her, was it always followed by something bad?

'Don't let him in. Stay in the stockroom – he doesn't know you are here,' Dawn whispered in her ear.

'I know you are there, Lisa,' Barry shouted loudly. 'Open this door or I'll break it down.'

Lisa scuttled out and opened it, hurrying him inside. She glanced up and down the street, hoping that there was nobody – especially Richard – about to witness her humiliation.

'I'm sorry, Dawn. I didn't have a choice,' she whispered.

'What?' Barry sprung round to look at her, his face contorted with rage. 'Did you say something, you cow?'

He held her arm and roughly drew her towards him. Lisa shook herself free.

'I wasn't speaking to you. I don't think I've got anything to say to you, except take your parcel and get out of here – and get out of my life, if you don't mind.'

'Ah, but I do mind,' said Barry. 'And I'm not taking that parcel anywhere – and you, bitch, can do nothing about it.'

Lisa's heart sank. Barry's attitude towards her was even more vicious than last time: he'd given up any pretence of sweet-talking her. She knew that she no longer mattered to him – if she ever had. The only good thing that could have come from his visit was the removal of the package – then she could, perhaps, finally be free of him.

The presence of the package of money had been a constant worry from the day he left it there. Lisa had found herself following her staff out to the kitchen if they were heating up lunch, just to make sure that nobody tried to use the oven. She was particularly worried about the extra weekend staff, who might not know it was broken. In the end, she had stuck a note to the front of the oven: 'Broken. Do not use.'

Now Barry went through to the kitchen and pulled open the door. He removed the package, pulled away the newspaper and roughly checked that the full amount was there.

'Good girl,' he said to Lisa, with a sneer. 'Not been tempted by Uncle Barry's loot, then?'

'I wouldn't touch it,' said Lisa disdainfully.

'Well, I see you touched it enough to find out what it was,' he said, rolling into a ball the local newspaper she had wrapped it in. 'I distinctly remember wrapping it in something more classy than this rag – the *Daily Telegraph*, if I recall correctly. Now, get me another paper.'

Lisa fetched a discarded newspaper from the wastepaper bin and without being asked brought the Sellotape from the drawer behind the till. She watched as Barry rewrapped his parcel and stowed it back in the oven.

'When will you take it?' she asked.

'As soon as I can, my petal. As soon as the nasty man Chet is no longer angry with little Barry.' He pulled an over-the-top sad face, which in the past would have made Lisa smile, but she was not smiling for him tonight.

'I just hope that is very soon. I want it out of here. And I want you out of my life. I mean it, Barry.'

He crossed the tiny kitchen in one step and took hold of her under her chin. 'Right little bossy boots tonight, aren't we? Come in here.' He dragged her into the stockroom. 'This is our little love nest, remember?'

Lisa struggled and almost pulled herself free, but with a deft movement of his left arm Barry struck her across the face. Panic set in; if she resisted, he would beat her up and she would have to explain away the cuts and bruises. Right now, with everything going so well with Nicola, she did not need this complication. She sighed and stopped resisting him.

Once again, Barry crushed her up against the wall of shoeboxes and began pawing at her.

'I'm so glad you wear a skirt for work,' he said. 'Trousers are more of a problem. I can always rip tights.' As he said this, he pulled her skirt up to her waist, tearing at her underwear, and began to have sex with her.

Lisa did not participate, but she did not resist, moving her body when he ordered her to. It was a cold, horribly orchestrated performance and she found herself wondering how Barry could do it.

He's just an animal. He could easily be a rapist. He doesn't need any tenderness or romance. He doesn't even need a woman who agrees to it.

She was overwhelmed with disgust at herself, that she had ever felt attracted to this man and excited by his presence.

I must have been desperate, she thought.

When the act was over, Barry pulled himself away from her and quickly went through to the washroom. She heard water splashing; then he came back into the stockroom fully dressed and with his hair combed. Lisa was standing where he left her, numb with disgust and self-loathing.

'You going to stay there all night?' Barry said roughly. 'You look a mess. You should get a grip on yourself.' He laughed, a hollow, mocking sound.

Lisa roused herself. 'Are you going now?' she said quietly.

'Yeah, things to do, places to go, people to see.' Walking jauntily, Barry left the shop, and within seconds she heard the roar of the Jaguar engine.

Slowly, her cheek throbbing, Lisa removed her ripped tights, cleaned herself up and went back into the shop. The fluorescent lights were still on and the brightness made her flinch. It was so different to the gentle light that Dawn brought to a room.

Lisa took a pair of tights from the display, then went back to the washroom to put them on. She conscientiously put the money for them into the cash bag and altered the day's takings. She took her old, ripped pair and went out to the bin at the back of the shop, even though it was dark out there. She did not want to leave them in the shop for the early-morning cleaners to find.

Outside, there was a pool of light spilling from the back entrance of the café next door and outlined in the door frame she saw Richard, standing still and looking across at her.

'Working late?' she called, as brightly as she could, trying to suppress the sob that threatened to choke up from deep inside her.

'Yes. You too, I gather,' said Richard curtly. He turned and went back inside, closing the door behind him.

'Oh God,' Lisa whispered to herself. 'What am I going to do?'

Her perfect day, the day when she finally felt accepted by her daughter, had descended into misery and anguish. Even as Barry was forcing himself on her, she had found herself fervently hoping that Richard had gone home, had not seen the flashy car parked on the yellow lines outside. Now those hopes were dashed.

But why should I care? Richard is never going to feel anything for me, so why shouldn't he know just what a lowlife slag I am?

Richard, too, was bitterly disappointed. He'd allowed himself to believe that Lisa was free of her entanglement with this small-town villain. He'd enjoyed talking to her again at lunchtime. But then, the flash car had zoomed up and Richard had watched from the front window of Shenley's. As Barry banged on the door, he had felt a welter of mixed emotions. He could see from Barry's posture and the way he shouted at Lisa to open up that she was being threatened, and part of him wanted to run outside and tell Barry to leave her alone, get out of her life. He wasn't physically intimidated by Barry: Richard had known him since they were kids and knew he was a bully and a coward. He would back off if someone stood up to him, just like he did when he was at school, throwing his weight around in the playground.

He plays the big tough guy, but he's just a plastic gangster, a creep who can big it up in a small place like this, Richard said to himself.

As well as the anger he felt towards Barry, though, he was bewildered by Lisa's behaviour. Why did she let him in? If she was frightened he would break the door down, why didn't she call the police?

Even as he thought this, Richard could see that the situation was too complicated. Perhaps this man was the father of her daughter, the girl he had seen her with. Perhaps she was tied to this lowlife in ways that could not easily be undone.

She's not for you, he told himself resignedly, but she needs help, that's for sure.

He had gone to the back of the café after Barry left because he did not want to bump into Lisa in the street as they locked up. It was at times like this that he would dearly love a cigarette – he'd given up four years earlier and on the whole was not bothered by cravings any more. Right now, though, he would have loved to light up.

Then Lisa had walked out to the bin. Instinct had made him want to jump the fence and put his arms around her, to protect her, but he could not remove the picture of Barry from his mind, and he had turned and gone inside.

By the time Lisa arrived home, she was close to collapse. The combination of the tiredness, the high of being reconciled with Nicola, the secret thrill of her flirtation with Richard, followed by the huge crash of her emotions when Barry appeared, and all the humiliation and shame that went with that encounter, had left her barely able to walk.

Once in the flat, she flopped on to the sofa. Immediately she was enveloped in Dawn's soft glow, and the gentle touch of the large feather wings comforted her.

'Dawn . . . I'm so sorry.'

'Shush, shush, don't talk.' Dawn bore her up and carried her through to the bedroom, keeping Lisa in her arms until she was deeply and soundly asleep, all the conflicting emotions subdued.

17

Barry's Wife

Sleeping beside Dawn was a blissful, healing experience, and when Lisa woke – late – the next day, she felt refreshed and content. The sharp pain of Barry's visit had been anaesthetised and she was able to think clearly about how to get him out of her life. Dawn was still there when she woke and sat with her while Lisa enjoyed a leisurely breakfast. It was her day off work and she felt relieved that she would not have to bump into Richard.

'I blew it again, didn't I?' she said to Dawn.

'It's very hard. You were caught. Whatever you did there would have been trouble. Don't blame yourself. And at least you saved your bosses from having to pay for a new door,' Dawn chuckled, and Lisa, relieved to find her so understanding, smiled too.

'But I can't go on like this. I have to get rid of him,' she said.

'The time will come – and very soon – when you will be

able to put him completely out of your life. But, you know, even bad things happen for a reason. Human beings learn more from the sad and bad things that happen to them than from all the easy happiness that falls their way. The most compassionate people are those who have experienced pain themselves, and that allows them to help others.'

'Well, I've certainly learned my lesson. I'm going to be a lot more choosy about men in the future. I'd much rather be alone than in a bad relationship, and I'm just hoping I'll have the strength to remember all this when I'm feeling lonely.'

'You need never be lonely again.'

'I know. I've got you now.'

'Not just me.'

Lisa looked puzzled, but Dawn didn't elaborate. After a brief silence, Lisa said, 'It makes me sorry for other women, trapped in abusive relationships, but I can't help them.'

'There's one woman you can help.'

Lisa looked puzzled. 'Who?'

'Get dressed. We're going out,' said Dawn. 'Warm clothes.'

Obediently, Lisa dressed in jeans, a sweater and a pale-blue quilted jacket. She went to get her scarf and then remembered she had left it by Nicola's bedside. The thought of Nicola brought a smile to her face, and Dawn smiled too, knowing what she was thinking.

'Yes, your Little Pickle is doing well,' she said. 'Later on today, you can ring her, but right now, we have important things to do.'

Taking Lisa by the hand, she led her out of the flat. Immediately they were outside, Dawn's light faded and she disappeared to sight, but Lisa could feel her presence and the warm touch of her hand. They strolled leisurely; there was none of the urgency of the last time that Dawn had guided her. It was chilly, and there was a light drizzle falling, so Lisa put up her umbrella. Dawn snuggled up to her under the umbrella.

'Don't you remember when we were little, sharing an umbrella? The sound of the rain pattering on it always made me feel very safe and secure,' Dawn said.

'Yes. Do you remember our umbrellas? Mine was green, with ears and eyes like a frog, and you had a red one, like a lady-bird.'

'Red, to match my shoes,' Dawn said.

Lisa felt her breath catch. Red shoes always brought back memories of the terrible day Dawn died.

'Shush. Don't worry,' said Dawn, squeezing her arm. 'That's all a long time ago, and as you know, it happened for a reason. Don't let it upset you any more.'

As she said the words, Lisa felt lighter and happier.

'Where are we going?' she asked, as they headed across the car park at the back of the market square.

'Not too far, I promise. I'll have to leave you when we get there – at least, I'll still be with you, but you won't feel me touching you, and you definitely won't see me. Most of all, you mustn't talk to me, or they'll be thinking you're a mad woman.'

Lisa laughed. 'I think anyone who has walked past us this morning already thinks that. All they see is this crazy woman who laughs out loud and talks to herself.'

On the other side of the car park was a large supermarket. Lisa knew it well: she bought her shopping there every week.

'You're going to have a cup of coffee and a cake in the café,' Dawn told her. 'I'll take you to the right table. Then you must keep your eyes and ears open and you will learn something, something very important.'

Lisa was baffled, but went into the busy little café, full of women shoppers having a break before or after pushing their trolleys around the aisles. There were clusters of young wives with children too young for school playing in the nearby nursery corner that the supermarket provided, and lone pensioners making full use of the cheap meals for senior citizens.

Lisa went to the self-service counter and chose a pot of tea and a flapjack. At the checkout, she added a newspaper to her bill. Taking her tray, she felt a firm pressure on her elbow as Dawn guided her to an empty table in the far corner. Settling down, Lisa looked with interest at her neighbours at the adjoining tables. On one side was a middle-aged man with a newspaper open at the racing pages. He was engrossed in marking up his possible bets with a red pen. Not him, surely? Lisa thought.

She turned the other way. This was more promising: two young women, each with a toddler in a buggy, talking earnestly together. Lisa surreptitiously moved her chair slightly closer to them and began to eavesdrop. She opened her newspaper and pretended to be reading. The women took no notice of her.

'. . . You just don't have to put up with it, Angie. He's going to kill you one day. It'll be on my conscience – I can see it coming.'

'But there's nothing I can do.'

'There's a battered-wives place in Leeds. I've found the details for you.'

The woman speaking had bright-blonde hair and was wearing a tracksuit. Her face was carefully made up, and she wore gold hoop earrings. Lisa could see her clearly, just by glancing diagonally across the café. Her companion was sitting further along on the same banquette as Lisa, making her more difficult to look at without Lisa turning her head, which might attract attention. Out of the corner of her eye, she could see that this woman had her head down, staring at the table. Her voice was low and Lisa could hear that she was close to tears.

'How can I take the kids to a place like that?' she said, and Lisa could hear the anguish in her voice. 'They're used to having their own rooms, toys . . .'

'It's better than staying there and getting beaten up,' said the blonde woman. 'Honest, Angie, peace of mind is worth more than a big house. He's going to kill you one day, I just know it. I can hardly bear to look at you today. God, if he was here now, I'd give him a piece of my mind.'

'No,' said the other woman, Angie, sounding slightly panic-stricken. 'Whatever you do, Shaz, don't say anything to him if you see him. He'd really kill me if he knew I was talking to you. You've no idea what Barry can be like.'

Barry! The name cut into Lisa like a knife. Now she understood why Dawn had brought her here. This was Barry's wife.

Shaz was talking. 'Of course I know what he can be like. I've seen what he does to you. Look at your face today. You're wearing sunglasses in January! Don't you think everyone who sees you knows why?'

'Yeah . . . I used to stay in for a few days when I looked like this, but I'm sick of that, too. I don't care what people say or think any more. I just want it to stop. Sometimes I think it would be better if I just wasn't here at all. It's me that seems to wind him up.'

Shaz spoke sharply. 'Rubbish! It's nothing to do with you, so stop blaming yourself. He's a drunken bully, and if he wasn't doing it to you, he'd be doing it to whoever else he was with. Wouldn't surprise me is he isn't a bit heavy with his hands with some of those other women he knocks about with.'

At these words Lisa unconsciously put her hand up to her cheek, to the spot where Barry had slapped her hard.

'Yeah, and that's another thing,' said Angie. 'He's definitely got someone new on the go. He hasn't been home at all two nights this week. Not that I care – it's so peaceful for us all when he's not there.'

Lisa did not feel the slightest stab of jealousy when she heard that Barry had another woman. She'd suspected it: the frequency of his visits had tailed off. She, like his wife, was grateful for his absence, and just fervently wished she did not have his parcel of money stashed away at the shop.

'And don't kid yourself he won't take his temper out on the kids,' Shaz was saying.

'Yeah, he's already given our Adam a couple of hard clouts,' said Angie. 'That's what I'm most afraid of. When he's in one of his rages, he just lashes out, doesn't care who he hits. I've kept them safe by getting them out of the way when I see he's in one of his moods, but I'm scared I won't always be able to protect them.'

'So which is worse, the battered-wives place or living in constant fear for your kids? He'll come smarming round you later today, sweet-talking you and buying you presents. Don't be taken in by it again. Switch your phone off.'

'I can't do that – suppose Adam's nursery wants me?'

'Well, just ignore his calls.'

'He'd kill me later.'

'So what are you going to do? Can't you go to your mum and your stepdad's?'

'No, he'd find me there straightaway. I tried it. He scared the life out of them – I think that's why my mum had that stroke. It was four weeks after he turned up there, shouting the odds and threatening them. He broke the windscreen of their car with an iron bar. They were terrified. My stepdad has told me not to get them involved again. He's not been that well, either.'

'They came at Christmas?'

'Yeah, but only for one night. They love the kids, but they couldn't wait to get away. I told you, didn't I, that the bastard went out to see one of his women on Christmas Day? With the kids so excited over their presents and everything, he buggered off and came back smelling of whisky and someone else's perfume.'

Lisa's head sunk lower behind the newspaper.

'Your sister can't help?'

'No, Barry knows where she lives, and her old man would side with him.'

'But you've got to get away, Ange.' Shaz was speaking more softly, pleading with her friend. Lisa saw her lean forward and grasp her friend's hands in hers. 'Is there nowhere and nobody?'

'If I had some money, I'd go to the other end of the country, get myself a job, maybe use a different name, but I'd have to have train fares and enough money to put down the deposit on a flat. I'd need hundreds, probably thousands, because I might not get a job straightaway and there would be childcare costs.'

'Can't you take some of his money?'

'No, he never leaves money in the house. I know he's got loads – he was counting great piles of it out only a couple of weeks ago. God knows what he's done with it. I don't think he would put it in the bank, because I'm sure it's hot money. In my dreams I see that Chet Ainsworth catching up with him and doing serious damage to him . . . That would be great.'

She said the last bit with relish. Lisa, staring at her cold tea, found herself agreeing. What Barry needed was a dose of his own medicine.

One of the toddlers, whose buggies were parked side by side behind the table where their mothers were sitting, began to grizzle and squirm.

'Uh-oh. She's awake,' said Angie, getting up and going to release her daughter.

It was the first chance Lisa had to look at Angie properly. She was an attractive woman of about thirty, with auburn hair hanging loose around her face. Probably deliberate, Lisa thought, to help hide her injuries. As Angie turned to bring the little girl back to sit on her knee, Lisa, without staring, took in the dark glasses and the ruddy bloom of a bruise on Angie's left cheek. Lisa looked down quickly and turned the page of the newspaper in front of her, keeping her eyes glued to the page.

Shaz gave a short laugh. 'You've made a pig's ear of that fringe. You'll have to get Maria to cut it properly.'

'No, I'm not going to Maria. She'd ask questions. I'll go to one of the hairdresser's where they don't know me. I had to do it. Look,' Angie said.

Shaz let out a sigh. Lisa did not lift her head, but could tell that Angie had pulled her fringe aside to show more injuries to her forehead.

'You could get him arrested,' Shaz said. 'You need to take some photographs. Here, I can take some on my phone. You can use them for evidence.'

Angie shook her head. 'He'd kill me, properly kill me, before we got near a court,' she said. 'I've thought it all through. I'm saving from the housekeeping, but he's such a mean bastard I can only put away twenty pounds a week. I have to hide it from him – he's always going through my purse when he's a bit short.'

'Where are you hiding it?' asked Shaz.

'At the moment, it's in the oven. He never goes in there. Course, I have to remember to take it out before I cook anything.'

The two women laughed briefly and Lisa felt like joining in. She knew an oven where Barry did go looking for money.

Angie was still talking: ' . . . years before I have enough to run away with, but it's a start. It makes me feel I'm doing something.'

'I'd help if I could, you know I would,' said Shaz.

'I know, but you've got less than I have.'

'Yeah, that mean so-and-so doesn't even give me enough to cover the rent some weeks. God knows what he thinks we live on.'

The two women launched into a discussion of the problems Shaz was having with her husband. Lisa listened just long enough to know that Shaz's husband was a feckless drinker, but was never violent towards his wife or children.

Picking up her tray with the cold tea and the uneaten flapjack, Lisa began to make her way out of the café.

'Are you not eating that, love?' said the man who was sitting on the other side of her, nodding towards the flapjack.

'No . . . no. Have it.' She held the tray out and the man took the flapjack and began to eat it greedily.

'Ta. You're a good lass,' he said.

Lisa forced a smile. If only I was, she thought. She felt wretchedly guilty about Angie, knowing that she had added to this family's unhappiness. Telling herself that if it wasn't her, it would have been someone else didn't make it any better.

Lisa walked around the aisles of the supermarket, picking up a few bits of shopping. She kept an eye on the café and saw the two young women leaving with their buggies and bags of shopping. Angie walked slowly, limping slightly. She loaded her little girl into the car seat of a hatchback, wincing at the effort of picking up the toddler, then hugged her friend and got into the driving seat. Before she left the car park, Lisa saw her having a tearful phone conversation.

I bet it's Barry, she thought, telling her how sorry he is, how it will never happen again, all that stuff.

As she headed back towards home, she felt Dawn at her side again, gently touching the hand that held the carrier bag of shopping.

'Oh, Dawn, it's terrible,' Lisa began, tears pricking the back of her eyes.

'Hush, let's wait till we get home. Then we'll talk about it.'

They walked in silence, but Lisa could feel Dawn's presence and was comforted by it. She was devastated by what she had heard and felt vaguely sick. Unbidden, a flashback to the real, naked fear she had felt when she was under threat from Phil's family, all those years ago, came into her brain. She understood something of the terror that ruled Angie's life. She knew how unpredictable Barry was, how even in her short encounters with him she felt as if she was walking on eggshells to avoid triggering his displeasure. How much harder it must be for Angie, spending her whole life with him.

Back at the flat, Dawn became visible and the two of them sat down together.

'She's trapped . . . She needs to get away from him. If I was her, I wouldn't worry about money. I'd just pack up and go.'

'That's easy for you to say,' said Dawn. 'You haven't got two small children to think about. You've always been able to run away; she can't.'

'Maybe she should just stand up to him more.'

'Ha! Did you see the state of her face? That's what answering him back gets her. And those are only the bruises you can see. Did you notice how carefully she was walking? She's black and blue, maybe even got a couple of broken ribs. You can't stand up to a man who is bigger and stronger than you and has a vicious temper. How well did you get on with standing up to him? You haven't got any of her ties, yet you can't get him out of your life – how much harder is it for her?'

'But she could go to the police.'

'You heard what she said, and she's right. Short of the police putting a couple of full-time bodyguards on her, he'll do much more serious damage to her. Violent men like Barry don't think rationally when they are angry. They just want revenge.'

'She deserves a lot better life than that.'

'Yes, she does,' said Dawn. 'But remember, you deserve a better life, too.'

18

Richard

Richard Shenley was troubled and he did not like the feeling. He had lost his dreams when his ex-wife had walked out and had spent hours, days, weeks trying to work out what went wrong. In the end, he had had to accept that she simply didn't love him. He wasn't the sort of person who worked out a plan for life, but somehow he had always taken it for granted that he would find romantic love and live happily ever after with one woman.

Well, he told himself after his marriage broke down, the biggest lesson he had learned was never to take anything for granted in future. Moving home to run his dad's café had, at first, felt like a failure, but he had soon realised that it was what he loved doing. There was a simple satisfaction in making sure it was well run, that the food was good and the service friendly. He got a real buzz from people telling him how much they had enjoyed their meal.

He felt he had brought an equilibrium back into his life. Allerby was his home town; he knew people here; he felt he belonged. He loved being so close to his sister and her children, and he got on well with his brother-in-law. His dad was recovering well and was visibly delighted to have Richard around. The old man didn't make demands, but was grateful for everything Richard did – in particular, taking over Shenley's. If Richard had not returned home, the café would have closed, ending two generations of Shenley family involvement in the business, because it was Richard's grandfather who first opened it, as an ice-cream parlour, way back in the late 1940s. He looked at the old photographs that hung on the walls and felt a glow of pride that he was part of its history, that he was now the third generation. He wondered idly on occasion if his nephew or niece would one day take it on; sadly, it wouldn't be handed down to one of his own children.

Now there was a problem in Richard's new life. His contentment was at risk of being destroyed, sacrificed on his growing fascination with the woman who ran the shoe shop next door. Lisa had wormed her way into his life, and whether he liked it or not, he could not get her out of his mind.

Since he'd come back home, his sister had busied herself trying to find a new partner for him. Every eligible single woman, divorcee or even young widow that she knew had been casually paraded in front of him at barbecues, pub quizzes, karaoke nights, even the football-club Christmas party.

Richard's brother-in-law, Bill, had complained to Richard over a pint after football on Sunday, 'I wish you'd get yourself a new bird, mate. As long as you are single, Shirley's on a mission. It's costing me a fortune, all these "events" we have to hold, just to put you next to some woman or other.

Why can't you choose one and let me get back to normal life?'

Richard laughed. 'I wish she'd stop, too. I'm just not interested in settling down again. Been there, done that, got the T-shirt. Life's pretty good – and one reason for that is I haven't got anybody telling me what to do.'

Bill sighed. 'Yeah, I envy you that bit.'

And now here was Richard, feeling more and more involved with a totally unsuitable woman. True, unlike some of those his sister had attempted to line him up with, Lisa didn't have a posse of children in tow, and she didn't want to talk for hours about her rat of an ex-husband, which seemed to be a common theme among Shirley's choices.

That was just the trouble, in a way: she didn't want to talk about her past life at all. Getting any information out of her was hard work. She was funny and pretty and laughed at his jokes (an important attribute), but he felt it was always him giving and her taking.

Even worse, there was the problem of Barry Shields. Why the hell was she involved with him? Richard had asked one or two questions to establish what Barry had been up to since school; it wasn't hard in a small town like Allerby to find out about someone. He knew Barry was a married man; he heard about his unsavoury connections; he even heard a rumour that the man's wife walked into a lot of doors – in other words, she frequently had black eyes and bruises.

He could see the guy was good-looking in a flash sort of way, and he knew he had a reputation as a womaniser, which meant that Lisa wasn't the only one to fall victim to him, but why didn't she get rid of him? From his own observations, he knew that whatever relationship she had with Barry was not happy. Why had he got a hold over her?

Common sense told Richard to run a mile, but he'd tried avoiding her, tried to put the relationship on a friendly-but-distant footing. It hadn't worked. When she'd come into the café the other day, he'd retired to the kitchen, but found himself hovering by the doorway to catch a glimpse of her, straining to hear any conversation she had with Michelle, the chatty waitress who served her.

He was intrigued by her life. There was the teenage girl who looked so much like her. Was she her daughter? It was certainly an emotionally fraught relationship: on the two occasions he had seen them in the café, the girl had left in a hurry and it was clear that Lisa was very distressed. And what about the little girl, the one with blonde curly hair? He'd seen her twice now with Lisa. The first time was when they were in the park together at Christmas, and the second time was yesterday, when he drove into the supermarket car park with Shirley to pick up some shopping for their dad.

Lisa hadn't seen him. She looked preoccupied. She was walking away with a bag of shopping, and holding her hand was the small blonde child. Lisa wasn't talking to her or paying any attention to her, as she had been in the park. There was something odd about it. Nobody else in the car park seemed to notice the child: he saw Lisa walk right past an elderly couple and it was as if the child just floated round them. Very strange. Lisa had reacted so oddly when he mentioned the kid that Richard had begun to think he was imagining things.

'Look at that,' he said to Shirley in the car park, nodding in Lisa's direction.

'Oh, yeah, that's the woman from the shoe shop, isn't it?'

'Mmm. But who's she with?'

Shirley looked in Lisa's direction. 'I don't think she's with anyone. That couple, they're just walking alongside her; they're not with her. See, they've gone to their car.'

'Yeah,' said Richard, turning away. It was clear that Shirley could not see the child. He must be imagining it. Time for the funny farm, he told himself.

Lisa picked up her phone and pressed Nicola's number into the keypad, then saved it in her list of contacts. She had not dared do this before; it seemed presumptuous. Before the night of the attack, Nicola had clearly said she did not want to see her again. But now, well, Lisa was hoping that everything was going to be different.

The anger and self-loathing that the encounter with Barry's wife had caused evaporated when Dawn reminded her that it was time to ring her daughter, to see how Nicola was getting on. She'd been dying to know but had resisted ringing before, wanting to give Nicola space with her family. She pressed 'call' on the menu and within seconds Nicola's phone rang. It was answered on the first ring.

'Hello, Lisa?' said the now familiar voice. 'It's really weird – I was just getting my phone out to call you when it rang. It's our psychic bond again, the same thing that brought you to rescue me.'

'Yes, I guess,' said Lisa, grinning at Dawn, who pulled a face and shrugged her shoulders to show she hadn't been involved in this telepathy.

'So how are you? Are you still in hospital?'

'No. They only kept me overnight. As soon as they could see I didn't have concussion, they let me come home. I'm taking the rest of the week off work, though. They said I should rest. And anyway, my hair's such a mess, I don't want anyone to see me.'

Lisa laughed. 'I already told you, vanity is a sign that you are feeling OK. Does your head hurt?'

'I have to be careful not to lie on the stitches, but not otherwise.'

There was a pause. Lisa was not sure what to say next.

Nicola spoke: 'Mum and Dad are really grateful to you. I've told them everything about our meetings. They want to meet you.'

'Oh.' Lisa didn't know how to reply. She was deeply worried about meeting Nicola's adoptive parents, almost as nervous as she had been about meeting Nicola for the first time.

'Here, Mum wants to speak to you,' said Nicola, thrusting her phone into the hands of her mother.

'Hello, Lisa,' said a shy voice.

'Hello, Mrs Bradley,' Lisa said, feeling very awkward.

'Oh, please, call me June. And my husband's Tony. We just want to say thank you, a million times, for what you did. Saving Nicola. And . . .' She stopped. Lisa was about to speak when she hurriedly continued: 'And . . . and . . . for giving her to us in the first place. I can't tell you how happy she has made our lives.'

She began to cry. Lisa also felt a sob surge up into her throat, and her eyes misted.

'That's just Mum being soppy,' said Nicola's voice. She had taken the phone back from her mother. 'Anyway, what Mum would have said if she hadn't started crying is that we'd like you to come for tea. Are you able to come on Sunday? Mum'll make a cake – she makes wicked cakes.'

'Then I'll definitely come. Can't resist a wicked cake,' Lisa said, smiling though tears were running down her cheeks.

'Great. About four o'clock. Is that OK? Have you got the address? There's a bus from Allerby at three thirty. I can meet you at the bus-stop if you ring. We're only five minutes' walk away.' There was the sound of a doorbell ringing at the other end and Nicola said, 'Ooh, that's my mate Tracey. I'd better go. She wants to see my bruises before they fade.'

Lisa laughed. 'Off you go. Milk it as long as you can . . . See you on Sunday.'

The conversation had cheered her up. She knew that shock could set in at any time, but so far it sounded as though Nicola was dealing with the trauma well.

As for tea with the family on Sunday . . . She felt nervous already, and she knew that as the time approached she would feel even worse. Could she go through with it? How could she face the people who had brought her daughter up? What would they think of her? It was all very well thanking her for giving them their daughter, but wouldn't they secretly, deep down, despise her for not keeping her own child?

The questions raced through Lisa's brain, pushing thoughts

of Barry's wife, Angie, to one side. It was only later, over supper, that Lisa began to replay in her mind the scene from the supermarket café.

Something has got to be done about all that, she said to herself, but what? Today was a day for questions, but no answers.

Early at work the next day – the café opened at seven to sell coffees, sandwiches and croissants to people on their way to work – Richard watched from behind the steamed-up window as Lisa arrived next door. He saw her crossing the cobbled street carefully in her high-heeled boots, the same ones she had been wearing the night she had clung to him to stop her slipping on the ice. His heart missed a beat when he thought about that evening. He had never been closer to her; it had all been going so well. Then the child – the mystery, non-existent child whom only he could see – had come between them. The very mention of the child had sent Lisa scuttling away. He wondered if he had missed his chance for ever.

Later in the morning, Lisa came in to buy a sandwich.

'Not sitting down for a proper lunch today?' Richard asked.

'No, Jodie's had to go to the dentist, and for some reason we're really busy today, so it will be lunch on the run, I'm afraid,' she said.

'Not good for you,' said Richard. 'Here, have a cupcake to help you get through the long afternoon.'

Lisa opened her mouth to protest but he cut her off.

'On the house. A very, very small present from me to you.'

Lisa smiled. 'You won't want to give me presents when I'm the size of a bus from eating all your delicious cakes and cookies,' she said.

'Ah, then you really don't know me . . . I'm not that shallow. Although I must admit, when you can no longer fit through the door and I have to bring the cakes out to you, I might have second thoughts.'

Lisa laughed. 'Well, that could be any day now if you don't stop feeding me.'

Richard handed her the change and she was turning to leave when a thought struck her. She was about to say something when she hesitated; just because Richard chatted and flirted with her, she couldn't presume to ask him a favour. It was not fair on him, and she didn't want to give him the wrong idea.

Richard, seeing her pause and frown, said, 'What's up? Anything I can help with?'

'I . . . I don't really know. I need to ask someone a favour.'

'Won't I do?'

'Yes . . . but I don't want to put on you.'

'Fire away.'

'Do you know anything about cars?'

'Well, I'm a bloke, aren't I? I watch *Top Gear*, and the smooth lines of a Porsche or a Ferrari are almost as exciting as the smooth lines of a woman who hasn't eaten too many cupcakes . . . but I don't spend my days off flat on my back under the car with an oily rag in my hand. Why do you ask?'

'I'm thinking of buying one. The garage down the road have a great repayments deal, and there's a nice blue Honda on the forecourt.'

Richard laughed. 'Blue! It's the colour that attracts you, isn't it? You aren't concerned about what's going on under the bonnet.'

'That's why I asked you, 'cos they say that garages are much more likely to try to con a woman than a man.'

'Shall I come with you to look at it? Would that help?'

'Would you mind? It's really kind of you. I'd be very grateful.'

'I'm warning you, I can talk the talk, but I'm no expert mechanic,' Richard said.

'That'll do nicely.' Lisa beamed at him. 'When are you free?'

'Can you slip out this afternoon? We get a bit of a lull here at about three o'clock, when lunch is over and afternoon tea is only just beginning. Michelle can cope without me.'

'Yes, that would be great. As long as Jodie comes back – you know what she's like, the slightest excuse and she's off sick.'

'I'll pop in at about three, and if you can get away, we'll walk down there.'

Jodie did come back, moaning about her numb mouth, so Lisa was able to go with Richard when he came round. Anne and Jodie watched them leave together.

'That's a much better bloke for her than that Barry,' Anne said.

'Nah, she's just using him. She doesn't go for nice types like Richard,' said Jodie, whose instinct was to think and say the worst about anyone.

When they reached the garage, the sales assistant, predictably, ignored Lisa and addressed Richard, who dutifully asked lots of questions about previous ownership, mileage, fuel consumption, the after-sales warranty. He bargained for a six-month tax disc, interior mats and other bits and pieces that Lisa would not have thought about. She was happy with the little car and signed on the dotted line.

As they walked back up the hill, she said, 'It's years since I've driven, and the last time was in Spain, on the wrong side of the road. I think I'd better book a couple of lessons just to ease myself back in.'

'You'll soon get used to it. If you like, I'll come with you to collect it and you can drive around with me in the passenger seat for a while.'

Lisa laughed. 'Are you sure? It might be a bit of a white-knuckle ride.'

'Oh, I've got a strong stomach. And nerves of steel. And a good insurance policy.'

Lisa laughed and playfully punched him. 'It won't be that bad, I hope.'

It was growing dark the next afternoon when she and Richard again walked down towards the river to the garage. She'd arranged her insurance, and the garage had organised everything else to do with the finance package. Lisa felt strangely excited; she'd never owned a car before.

'She'll have to have a name,' she said to Richard, as they sat together in the car on the garage forecourt, while Lisa familiarised herself with the controls.

'She? She? It's a female car, is it? Why can't it be big and butch with a name like Arnie or Tyson?'

'That sounds like a pit-bull terrier. No, she's definitely a she.'

'Maisie,' said Richard.

'Yes . . . Actually, that sounds right for her. Maisie. OK,

Maisie it is. Come on, now, Maisie,' said Lisa, sliding the gear-stick into first and slowly driving out on to the road.

She drove cautiously, gradually getting used to the controls and the road signs.

'See – just like riding a bike. You never forget,' said Richard. 'Now, take the next turn on the right – we'll get out of the town and give little Maisie a blast on a bigger road.'

'I'm not sure about the blast bit – even when I was used to driving, I never enjoyed doing it in the dark,' said Lisa.

Within a couple of minutes they were out of the built-up area and on a main road heading towards Leeds. A car zoomed towards them with headlights on full beam.

'Tosser!' Richard shouted at him as he raced past.

Lisa laughed. 'Yep, I reckon you really are a bloke. Swearing at other drivers . . . Jeremy Clarkson would be proud of you. I'm surprised you didn't give him a two-fingered salute.'

'I would have done, if it had been daylight and he could have seen me . . . Anyway, what's all this about me really being a bloke? You didn't have any doubts, did you?'

Lisa laughed. 'No, of course not.'

'Pull over in this layby. You need to practise stopping and starting a bit.'

Lisa slid the car down through the gears and brought it to a standstill in a long layby. A few hundred yards in front was a small roadside café. The owner was putting up shutters for the night. Caught in the headlights of the little car, he glanced at them, then carried on locking his small shack.

Richard leaned across Lisa and snapped the lights off. She

turned to look at him, puzzled, but before she could ask a question, he put his arms around her and pulled her towards him. They kissed, a lingering, gentle kiss.

What am I doing? Lisa's mind raced. She was enjoying the kiss, enjoying the warmth of Richard's body near hers, the slight smell of the café food on his jacket, but before she could relax into the embrace, Richard pulled away. He held her for a moment, looking at her face, then straightened himself.

'Come on,' he said. 'Let's get on with the driving lesson.'

Lisa glanced sideways at him. He was looking directly ahead and she wondered if he regretted what he had just done.

'Lights on, start the engine, then pull out when you are sure there are no cars coming up.' He spoke in a businesslike way, and Lisa, bewildered by what had happened, followed his orders.

They followed the main road to a roundabout, turned round and headed back into Allerby. At first there was an uncomfortable silence, but they quickly resumed their normal chat.

'Where would sir like me to take him next?' Lisa asked.

'Oh, I think my chauffeur should take me back to the café now. And next time I expect you to wear your peaked cap.'

Lisa drove to a public car park off the market square, just a hundred yards from the café and the shoe shop.

'I won't normally bring Maisie to work,' she said.

'No, there's room in the car park now because it's winter, but when the tourists are in town, it's a nightmare. I get a space because I'm here so early. From where you live, it's easy to walk.'

They walked together back up the street. There was a slight distance between them, a sense they both had that the kiss had changed something. At the door of the shoe shop, Richard said goodbye without turning to Lisa.

She shouted after him, 'Thanks, Richard. Thanks for everything . . .'

He turned and smiled before going back into Shenley's.

Lisa was just in time to close up the shop for the day. As she cashed up she replayed the kiss, over and over, in her brain.

Did it mean anything? Surely Richard had seen her with Barry – he wouldn't want anything to do with her. Perhaps he thought she was loose, promiscuous, and he was just testing her. Should she have resisted? What was he thinking about her right now?

She'd enjoyed it, and she could still feel the pleasure of being held tight by a man she really wanted, but was it right to want Richard? Did she really want him, or was she, once again, jumping at any man on offer?

Questions, more questions.

You've made a pact not to get involved again, she told herself sternly. Besides, until you have sorted out the Barry situation, you are not free.

The thought of Barry was like a cold hand clutching at her heart. She went through to the kitchen and checked the oven. Yes, the package was still there. She was, whether she liked it or not, still involved with Barry.

19

Nicola's Home

By Sunday Lisa was in an agony of indecision. She didn't know what to wear to meet Nicola's parents. Should she go for something casual, the sort of thing she normally wore when she wasn't working, a sweater and jeans? Or should she go for something more formal, like one of the navy-blue suits she wore for work? She settled for something in between: a smart pink shirt and blue skirt, but with a cardigan on top. She made her face up carefully. Did she look too young? Too old? What would they be expecting?

She'd bought flowers, lilies, but now she was worried that they looked funereal. It's a shame it's not spring, she thought. I could have got something more cheerful. She wasn't sure whether she would take them at all. She'd bought a box of chocolates, too, and she wondered if that was more appropriate as a present. Or should she take both?

She was also unsure about the opal pendant she had bought

for Nicola's birthday, which was still sitting in its wrapping on the sideboard. Would this be the right time to give it to Nicola? Would her mum and dad think that she was trying to buy her way into their daughter's life?

She was unable to eat anything all day, she felt so sick. She rang Nicola to tell her that she would be driving to Benting and asked for directions to the house. She left home so early that she found herself in the village half an hour before she was due to arrive, so she pulled over into a small car park on the common. It really was a tiny village, very pretty, but she could understand why Nicola, at her age, wanted to move to Leeds. There was a church, a shop and post office and an unattractive village hall, around which a clutch of teenagers were hanging out, some with bikes and a couple with skateboards. Four or five boys were kicking a football around in the yard of the hall, and a row of girls, heavily made up and with their hair pulled back in scrunchies, were sitting on the wall, jeering at the boys.

Lisa felt a protective surge. She hoped Nicola didn't join this crowd when she wasn't working. Looking at them more closely, she realised they were several years younger than her daughter. Perhaps, when she was still at school, Nicola was one of these bored kids. Lisa suddenly remembered herself at the same age as these youngsters; she had cafés and a shopping mall to hang out in, but she was just as aimless and restless as these teenagers. And, she reminded herself, she hadn't managed that stage of her life very well at all. So what right did she have to be critical of these kids?

At five to four, she started the car and drove the couple of hundred yards up a lane to the house where Nicola's family lived. It was one of a row of pebble-dashed semis, all neatly kept. The front garden had been converted into hard standing, and there were a car and a van parked there. Not wanting to block them in, Lisa parked further down the road and walked back. She made a last-minute decision, leaving the lilies in the car but taking the chocolates and Nicola's pendant, which she slipped into her handbag. She could make up her mind about it later.

By the time she walked back, Nicola was outside the house, waiting for her.

'Saw you drive up,' she called. 'Smart set of wheels.'

'Yes, I've just bought her – I mean it. The car,' Lisa said. Then she grinned and added, 'She's called Maisie.'

Nicola smiled and held the door open for her. Hovering in the hallway were her parents, June and Tony, and Lisa could tell at a glance that they were every bit as nervous as she was. They all shook hands and Lisa was ushered through into a comfortable, clean and cheerful sitting room. A tall youth disengaged himself from his computer game and stood up to say hello.

'This is my brother, Giles,' said Nicola. 'All you need to know about him is that he's a nerd who plays on his computer or messes with his car.'

Giles grinned, lunged at her and tried to give her a playful punch. Nicola moved back, so his hand did not connect with her.

'Oh, and he's a bully, too, as you can see,' she added, pulling a face at him.

'Stop it, you two,' said June. She was short, plump and looked to be around sixty. Her brown hair was peppered with grey, and she had a pleasant, round face with a ready smile.

Turning to Lisa, she added, 'Honest, they're at it all the time, these two. Ever since they were little . . . I don't know,' she sighed, but she was looking at both her children proudly. It was clear to Lisa that the only bickering that went on in this household was in jest.

'Now, sit down,' said June. 'Tony, put the kettle on.'

'Yes, boss,' said Tony, with a big wink at Lisa. He was the physical opposite of his little wife: tall and skinny, over six feet, but slightly stooped. He was not quite bald, but his hair was rapidly thinning. He went out to the kitchen. Lisa perched on the other end of the sofa from Giles, who was looking at his flashing screen again.

'Put that away, Giles,' said his mother. 'It's a wonder you can see properly, the time you spend on that thing. I'm sure it can't be good for your eyes.'

'Or your brain,' Nicola added.

'Well, at least I've got one,' Giles retorted. He unwound his gangly limbs and stood up, turning to Lisa and saying, 'Nice to meet you, but I'm afraid I've got to go out now.'

'Don't be late tonight,' his mother said. 'You've got to get to Leeds for college in the morning.'

After Giles left the room, she said to Lisa, 'He's an apprentice electrician, which means he has to do one day a week at college. It's the bit he doesn't like, but he's got to do it to get proper qualifications. Excuse me a minute.'

She bustled out to the kitchen. Nicola came over and sat

next to Lisa, taking hold of one of her hands. Lisa realised she was still clutching the chocolates.

'These are for your mum and dad,' she said. She felt shy and awkward.

Nicola took them and looked at the box. 'These are Mum's favourites. How did you know?'

'I didn't. I just thought the box was pretty.'

Nicola gave her a sly grin. 'It's that psychic things of yours working again.'

June and Tony came back in, June carrying a tray of china cups and saucers, Tony with a teapot.

'Fetch the cake and the plates, Nicola,' June said. She glanced across and realised for the first time that her daughter was sitting with Lisa, holding hands. She blushed and looked awkward.

'No, stay there. Tony, put the teapot on its stand and go and get the cake.'

'No rest for the wicked,' said Tony, with another grin at Lisa, who had quietly slipped her hand out of Nicola's. She did not want June to think she was taking over.

'Look what Lisa's brought you, Mum,' said Nicola, brandishing the chocolates.

'Oh lovely. Thank you. Perhaps we should open them now. Maybe you'd prefer a chocolate to a piece of cake?' she asked Lisa.

Lisa smiled. 'No, they're for you. I'm looking forward to a piece of cake. I've been told it's wicked.'

June flushed with pleasure. 'Well, it's only a lemon drizzle cake.'

'My favourite,' said Lisa, keen to put this kind woman at ease. She felt a rush of happiness. Yes, all those years when she had no contact with her daughter, she had a strong feeling that Nicola was in a happy household. Now she knew it for a fact.

They all sipped tea and nibbled cake awkwardly for a few minutes; then June went across to a dresser and brought over three albums from the top of it.

'I thought you might like to see some photos of Nicola,' she said timidly.

'Oooh, I'd love to,' said Lisa. Funnily, she hadn't thought about this, but she realised when June said it that it was what she wanted most of all.

Nicola pretended to squirm. 'Oh, Mum, not all those pictures of me when I was little . . .'

'And why not? Lisa hasn't seen you sitting on your potty,' Tony said, grinning at his daughter. 'Mind you, I'm saving those for your first serious boyfriend.'

Nicola picked up a cushion and threw it at him. Then she moved along the settee and said, 'Here, Mum, you sit next to Lisa.'

The first book June opened was a large scrapbook, and on the first page was a picture of Nicola in a cot at the hospital, taken a day or two after her birth. Lisa's body tensed with shock. She had no idea the picture had been taken.

June turned to look at her and involuntarily patted her on the hand. 'The social worker from the adoption agency gave us this. They said it was a good idea to do a baby book, so that we could talk it through with Lisa while she was too small to know any different. She's always known she was adopted.'

On the next page was a picture of the hospital frontage, then a picture of a tiny baby in the arms of a tall, smiling older woman.

'That's the foster mum who had Nicola for the first six weeks,' June explained. 'We visited her, then one day we took her out in her pram, and then two days later we took her home with us.' Her eyes were glistening with tears as she told Lisa the history of those early days, immediately after Lisa had parted with her precious daughter.

'I always wondered what the procedure was,' Lisa said. For her, the emotion went too deep for tears. She felt as though she was functioning on autopilot. Her throat was dry and she had to swallow hard before speaking.

'We were so pleased to be given her. I can't begin to thank you,' June said, turning to Lisa and grasping her hand. Lisa nodded mutely.

'We were living in London then, though we're Yorkshire born and bred. Tony was working for a firm that had a factory down there, and they sent him down for three years. He's good with the machinery . . .' Her voice trailed off. She turned the page to a picture of herself and Tony, holding Nicola, and a plump toddler hanging on to June's hand.

'We already had Giles. I . . . I couldn't have babies myself. It took us a long time to find out . . . It was hard . . .'

She was visibly upset and Nicola, sitting on the other side of her, put her arms around her. 'But it worked out for the best, didn't it, Mum? You got me. And Giles. What more could any mother ask?' She said the last bit with a wide grin, hugging her mother.

June laughed. 'You're right. It definitely worked out for the best.'

Tony, who had said very little, turned to face Lisa. 'We know it must have been hard for you,' he said softly, 'but we want you to know that having our children was the making of us. I don't know what Junie would have done if we hadn't been able to adopt. She was put on this earth to be a mother, but life isn't always fair with things like that.'

'Hush, Tony,' June said. 'It's a long time ago, but we've never forgotten what you did for us, and we've never stopped thanking you, even though we didn't know you. All they told us about you was that you were very young and unmarried.'

Lisa nodded. 'That's true. I wanted to keep Amy – Nicola – but I could see it was impossible. All these years, I've just prayed that she was all right, but I've always felt, inside me, that she was safe and happy. Now I know it's true.'

The emotion in the room was too much for Nicola, who broke the mood by saying, cheerfully, 'After all this, I'll be glad when you get to the potty pictures!'

'Yes,' said June, brightening. 'Let's show Lisa you at your best.'

She began to turn the pages of the baby book. Each picture was carefully captioned in neat handwriting: 'Nicola in the bath'; 'Nicola and Giles'; 'Tony cuddling Nicola.' They came to the one of Nicola sitting on a potty and Lisa and June both laughed, happy to relieve the tension.

The albums were comprehensive, taking Lisa through every year of Nicola's life. There was her first day at school, Nicola in her Brownie uniform, Nicola making sandcastles on the beach, Nicola as a sheep in the nativity play, Nicola in her first school uniform, Nicola on a school skiing trip. There was even a photograph of Nicola, with a wan smile on her face, sitting in a chair next to her hospital bed, with a drip on a stand next to her.

'That's when Nicola had meningitis. She's recovering in that picture.'

'Check out the horrible green dressing gown,' said Nicola, peering over Lisa's shoulder.

'Your auntie Emm gave you that dressing gown the Christmas before you were ill,' said June reprovingly.

'Yes, well, if you saw the way Auntie Emm dresses, you wouldn't be surprised,' said Nicola.

'That's enough,' said June, with a smile. She turned to Lisa. 'Tony's sister, Emily, is a bit of a hippie.'

'A failed hippie,' Nicola added.

June turned another page of the album. 'Tony's always liked photography,' she said, almost apologetically. 'He takes pictures of everything.'

'It's lovely to have such a good record,' Lisa said politely, struggling to hold back her feelings. Everything she had missed out on was being paraded in front of her and she was experiencing a mixture of delight that Nicola's life had been so happy and deep regret that she had not been part of it.

Tony, perhaps sensing that his wife was overdoing it and that Lisa was finding it hard, stood up and said, 'I think that's enough pictures for today. How about another pot of tea, Junie? Or would you like something stronger?' he asked Lisa.

'Oh, no, I'm driving,' Lisa said.

'She's just bought a car,' Nicola chipped in.

'Oh, what make?' Tony asked, and when Lisa told him, he asked her questions about it, obviously feeling more comfortable on the solid ground of cars and their performance. He asked where Lisa bought it, how old it was, what the mileage was.

'You have to be careful buying second-hand cars, but that garage has a good reputation – I know the chap who owns it and he wouldn't do you down.'

'No, and a friend came with me to help me with the right questions to ask,' Lisa said, blushing slightly at the thought of Richard.

June came in with another pot of tea, and after politely drinking a cup, Lisa said, 'I think I'd better be going.' She didn't want to overstay her welcome, and she felt that, emotionally, they had all covered a lot of ground. She wanted time to herself, to take in everything she had heard, seen and felt. It was as if a whole lifetime, Nicola's, had flickered in front of her eyes like a movie in a couple of hours and she needed to step back and let it all sink in.

'Oh, are you sure?' June asked. 'We'll be having a sandwich tea soon. You're very welcome to stay.'

'No, I've got to get back. I've got something on,' Lisa lied.

'Can I get a lift with you?' Nicola asked.

'Where are you going, young lady?' June asked. 'You've still got stitches in the back of your head, remember?'

Nicola pulled a face. 'As if I could forget. I'm not going where anyone can see me. Just to Tracey's. I've promised to put a rinse through her hair.'

'How long are you going to be out? How are you going to get back?' June fussed.

'I'll pick you up,' Tony said quietly but firmly.

Nicola looked for a moment as if she was going to protest, but she agreed. 'OK, Dad, but don't embarrass me by tooting your horn. Just call me on my mobile when you are there.' She smiled at Lisa. 'Dad's an old dinosaur – never uses his phone much. Have you ever sent a text, Dad?'

'No.' Tony grinned sheepishly. 'And I'm not about to start. I'll be there at nine o'clock. That's late enough. You be ready.'

As they drove off, Lisa glanced at Nicola. 'Thanks. Thanks for introducing me to your family. They're very nice.'

'They're OK,' said Nicola, pretending to be grudging but clearly pleased that the afternoon had gone so well.

Following Nicola's direction, Lisa took her to the estate on the far side of Allerby where her friend Tracey lived. As they pulled into the kerb, Lisa reached behind her to the back seat and pulled her handbag on to her lap.

'I got you a birthday present,' she said to Nicola. 'It's only a few days late . . .'

Nicola took the small package and began to open it. Suddenly, she froze and a look of guilt and misery came across her face. 'You gave me a present once before and I wouldn't take it.'

Lisa laughed. 'Don't worry about that. This is a much nicer present. Promise.'

'I don't care. It was very rude of me.'

'Shush. We were both a bit . . . well, you know . . . It wasn't easy for you.'

'Or you.'

'No, but it's better now, isn't it? Open your present.'

Nicola removed the wrapping and snapped open the small leather box. Nestling on the padding was the pale-blue opal, its colour enhanced by the royal-blue velvet backing.

'Oh, it's beautiful. Beautiful. I've never had anything so beautiful.' Nicola's face showed that she meant what she was saying.

'Here, try it on,' Lisa said.

When the girl had removed the delicate gold chain from the box, she scooped her hair up while Lisa leaned across and fastened the chain round her neck. Then Lisa pulled down the sun visor on the passenger side of the car to reveal a mirror. 'Take a look.'

Nicola moved the mirror until she could see the opal, resting against her throat. 'It's perfect,' she said. She flung her arms around Lisa's neck. 'Thank you. Thank you. I'll always keep it. It's the most special present I've ever had.' Then her face looked troubled. 'Not that Mum and Dad don't give me nice presents. They gave me this watch for my eighteenth.' She thrust her wrist forward and Lisa admired the watch. She felt very moved by the girl's determination to play fair to her adoptive parents.

'That's a fabulous watch,' she said. 'You are very lucky to have them as your mum and dad. They are good people, and they love you very much.'

Lisa and Nicola looked at each other, and there were tears beginning to well in both sets of pale-grey eyes, but at that moment Tracey's front door opened and Nicola's friend came towards the car.

'Hi, Nicola,' Tracey called and waved.

'I'm off,' said Nicola, giving Lisa another hug and a kiss. 'I'm sure you've met enough people today without having a dose of Tracey. She's a heavy trip. Can we have lunch again when I'm back at work next week?'

'Of course. Whenever you like.'

'Wednesday is good for me. We don't have an afternoon clinic.'

'Wednesday it is. I'll see you then.'

Nicola was out of the car by now but leaned back in. 'Wednesday, one o'clock, at our usual place.' She grinned as she said it, then added, 'And thanks again for my lovely prezzie.'

Back at her flat, Lisa poured herself a glass of wine. She could hear the bells of the large church in the centre of Allerby ringing for evensong. She felt happy and relaxed; any doubts she had had about Nicola's family had been completely dispelled. She felt a deep envy of them, for all the years of Nicola they had enjoyed, but also compassion for June, who had so clearly wanted to have a baby of her own. It was as if they were part of the same shared fate: that her anguish at losing her tiny daughter had assuaged June's anguish at not having her own child, and that between them they had done well by Nicola.

As she sat there, running through the day's events in her mind, she became aware of Dawn's soft glow appearing on the sofa next to her, a mellow, golden light that not only illuminated the room but warmed it, too. Lisa, overwhelmed by the day, had not switched the gas fire on, and the evening was chilly.

'Oh, Dawn,' Lisa said, turning to the sweet face of her sister,

'I've had such an amazing day. I need to tell you all about it.' She stopped, and laughed. 'But I don't have to tell you anything. You were there, weren't you?'

'Of course,' Dawn's sweet fluting voice replied. 'I've told you, I go with you everywhere. The great thing about being a guardian angel is that I'm there for the good bits as well as the times of trouble. I'm so glad you enjoyed it, but it was emotionally stressful for you, too. Put down the wine, switch the fire on and then cook yourself a meal. You haven't eaten all day, apart from some cake.'

Lisa laughed again. 'Are you my sister or my mother? You nag like a mother. Just like June nags Nicola.'

Dawn's laughter tinkled through the room. Lisa, with a smile, obeyed her and began to prepare some food.

'They are a very happy family,' she commented to Dawn.

'I know,' Dawn said simply.

Lisa looked at her. 'The feeling I had, all those years, that she was OK and was with good people – were you behind that?'

'Yes, or, at least, I did my best. When you started to worry about her, I whispered in your ear that she was safe, loved and happy.'

'That's all I asked for,' said Lisa. Then, without warning, she began to sob. She flung herself down on to the sofa next to Dawn, who gently wrapped her wings around her, and she cried until there were no more tears left and she was heaving long, dry sobs from the very pit of her being.

'Shh. It's OK,' Dawn said.

'But why am I crying?' Lisa gasped between sobs. 'I should be happy, shouldn't I?'

'You have just released a huge amount of tension. Years of quiet worry about your Little Pickle have finally been washed away in those tears. You have let go of the biggest fear, worry, shame and unhappiness in your entire life. You are crying in relief. They are the tears of a mother who has finally seen the child she loves settled on a happy course in life.'

'Yes . . . yes . . . you are right.'

Dawn squeezed Lisa into a hug and then released her. For a few moments the sisters sat quietly, side by side, neither of them speaking. Lisa was still giving an occasional sob, as if her body was slowly switching off the emotional tap that had been in danger of flooding just a few moments earlier.

It was the ping of the oven timer that broke the sweet silence and Dawn laughed. 'There you are. That's what you need – shepherd's pie. Something hot and substantial. A good meal will make you feel completely better.'

As Lisa ate, she said to Dawn, 'I haven't had any experience of normal family life. Not since you died and it all went pear-shaped at home with Mum and Dad. Not in my adult life, not at all. But now I've seen a really happy family and I wish all children could be brought up like that. I hate to think of children in a house where the parents are rowing and hating each other.'

'Are you thinking of Barry's children?'

Lisa nodded. 'It just goes to prove that natural parents aren't necessarily the best thing for children. Not when you compare Barry's family with Nicola's. And having one good parent is better than being stuck in an abusive family, even if there are two parents. I wish there was some way I could help Angie.

After all, I've been part of the reason why her life is so miserable.'

'Don't worry about it now. You need some sleep.' Dawn folded her wings around Lisa and gently bore her through to the bedroom.

'Go to sleep thinking happy thoughts. Think about Nicola and how she is starting to love you.'

As she murmured gently in Lisa's ear, Lisa fell into another blissful sleep where soft dreams chased themselves across her unconscious mind, leaving her feeling refreshed and serene when she awoke.

20

Angie

'How's my friend Maisie getting on?' Richard gave his familiar grin and, without waiting for an invitation, sat down opposite Lisa as she ate her lunch at Shenley's the next day. She'd had a busy morning in the shop and rewarded herself with a proper sit-down hot meal, instead of her usual sandwich.

'Oh, she's great. We went out for the day yesterday. She had a good time. She told me.'

'Glad to hear it. Seriously, you do need to give her a good run when you take her out, as she's not going anywhere most days. Where did you get to?'

Lisa paused. 'Well, not that far, actually. Only to Benting and back. But I'm determined, now I've got her, to explore the Yorkshire Dales. I'm still a bit nervous about driving into Leeds, with all that traffic.'

'Don't be. It's well enough signed, and you're a competent driver, even though you were a bit rusty at first.'

'Just a bit,' Lisa laughed, remembering the crunched gears and the jerky braking that Richard had endured on the day she first drove Maisie.

'What's in Benting?' Richard asked.

Lisa blushed and he immediately kicked himself. If he wasn't careful, she'd clam up, just as she always did when he tried to get close to her private life.

'Oh, just some friends . . . I went there for tea,' she said lightly.

Richard felt relieved. It looked as if she didn't mind and wasn't going to make a hasty excuse to get back to the shoe shop. He called the waitress over and asked for two more coffees.

'If you want me to come with you when you go on a long drive around the Dales, or on your first trip into Leeds, I'm happy to come. I can navigate for you,' he said, stirring his coffee purposefully so that he didn't have to look at her. He was unsure where he stood with her and was waiting for a rebuff.

Instead, to his surprise and pleasure, she said, 'Would you? I'd be very grateful. It's the city I'm more worried about than the winding lanes and steep hills – I think I can cope with them – but one-way systems, multi-storey car parks and endless traffic lights . . .' She grinned and shrugged.

'Yeah, I know. All a bit frightening when you haven't tackled them for years. Mind you, if you drove in Spain, that took some guts.'

'Yes, but there you drive with one hand on the horn and the other hand ready to give the finger to anyone who cuts you up, which they do.'

'That's two hands. What do you steer with?'

'Your elbows. You get used to it.'

They both laughed.

'So when do you want to go?'

'I'm taking another Sunday off next weekend. I was thinking of trying Leeds then, because I figured it would be quieter.'

'Yes, although there will still be quite a lot of shoppers on the road. But you're right, it won't be as busy as a weekday. I'm happy to come with you, if you really want.'

'That would be great.' Lisa was struck by a sudden thought. 'Don't you play football on Sunday mornings?'

'Oh, they can manage without me, I reckon. Probably be glad I'm not there, outplaying them all. Give some of the others a chance to shine.'

Lisa laughed. 'Are you sure?'

Richard looked straight into her grey eyes and paused for a moment. Then he nodded and said, 'I'm sure.'

Lisa glanced down at her empty plate, feeling flustered and aware that her cheeks were reddening.

'So that's agreed, then,' Richard added, pleased to see the effect he had on her. She must feel something for him, too, he thought. Maybe, if they spent a whole day together in Leeds, had a meal together away from the prying eyes of his staff and the girls from the shop next door, just maybe . . . Don't get ahead of yourself, he told himself firmly. It's only a driving lesson.

Lisa fumbled in her bag for her purse. 'Yes, that's great, as long as you really are free. What about your dad?'

'Oh, my sister, Shirley, is always around on Sundays with her gang. It will be good to get away from all that mayhem.'

'Is the rabbit still going strong?' Lisa, too, was happy to get back on to safe, impersonal ground.

'Yep. We collect all the carrot peelings and cabbage leaves in the kitchen here, so it's the best-fed rabbit in Yorkshire.'

Lisa stood up and walked across to the counter. She insisted on paying for her meal, even though Richard tried to wave her aside.

'What time will I see you on Sunday, and where?' she said.

'Well, as you are the driver, you'd better pick me up. I'll pop the address and directions on a piece of paper and drop them into the shop. Is eleven o'clock a good time?'

'Perfect.'

Lisa walked back next door feeling, if it was possible, even happier than she had before. Nicola, Nicola's mum and dad, Richard, there were good people in the world, and some of them seemed to like her.

There was only one cloud in her blue sky – well, two, when she thought about it. The first was Barry; she had to get rid of Barry. That was now her top priority. The second was Angie and her children. Getting rid of Barry would be great, but she knew she would always feel guilty about Angie. Even though, she told herself, that if it had not been her, Barry would have had some other girlfriend on the side, she still felt responsible for the times when Barry should have been with his family but instead was with her.

Not only that, she felt that Angie deserved a break. Nobody should have to stay in an abusive relationship, but she could see how difficult – impossible, really – it was to make the break when two little children were involved. But what could she, or anyone, do?

The shop was quiet all afternoon, which gave Lisa time to think. She let Anne and Jodie go home early. Even Jodie was pulling her weight nowadays and Lisa appreciated it. Jodie was happy to take charge of the shop on Sundays because it earned her extra money to put towards her long-delayed wedding.

After turning the key in the lock at 6 p.m., Lisa did her paperwork and then went to the stockroom to check that it was tidy. As she passed the kitchen door, she glanced at the oven and on impulse went in and opened it. The package was still there. She pulled it out.

How much would Angie and the kids need to start a new life? Wasn't it unfair that Barry had all this money stashed away, while Angie didn't have enough to get away from him? Would he notice if she took some out?

She gave a short, humourless laugh as she asked herself this last question. Of course he would notice. She'd probably get a good slapping – and more – if she messed with his money. A cold shiver ran through her body. She was afraid of Barry.

But still . . . the thought formulated in her brain. She would not steal all his money. She did not want it; it was dirty money. But some of it would help Angie, and that would only be fair. If she had to pay a price, so be it. What could Barry do? He could not go to the police and complain that his money had been stolen. Wherever this money came from, she was sure it was not something he wanted to share with the law. If it had to be hidden, and not kept in a bank like normal people do, it was hot money, and even if the police were not after him for it, his dodgy boss, Chet Ainsworth, probably was.

She opened up the parcel of money and looked thoughtfully at the wads of notes stacked on the kitchen draining board. Five thousand pounds should be enough, she thought. That would pay for Angie to move well away from Yorkshire, and give her enough to put down a deposit on somewhere to live, with enough left over to tide the family through a couple of months until she sorted out work and benefits. Lisa did the sums in her head, then counted out £5,000. She started to pack the rest back into a fresh couple of pages from the local paper – she didn't care that Barry would realise it had been opened. He'd know soon enough anyway. At the last minute, she pulled out another £1,000. Just to be sure, she said to herself.

The re-fastened parcel did not look noticeably smaller when Lisa put the carrier bag back into the oven. She found a large envelope behind the counter for the £6,000, sealed it with Sellotape and thrust it into one of the shop carrier bags. It was too bulky for her handbag.

Then she locked up the shop and walked briskly home, only pausing to post the shop takings in the bank safe deposit. She had no real plan of what to do next, but she wanted to get rid of the money quickly. She figured that the evening was a good time to call on Angie: Barry was always out in the evenings. She knew from experience that his 'business' life involved meetings in pubs and clubs, and with a new girlfriend on the scene, he was very unlikely to be at home playing happy families with Angie and the kids.

Lisa slipped out of her work clothes and put on jeans and a sweater. She was about to pull her high-heeled ankle boots on, but at the last minute decided on trainers. She didn't like to formulate the thought, but at the back of her mind she knew she might be glad to move quickly. With her thick quilted jacket on top, she went to get her gloves and scarf – remembering, again, that her favourite scarf had been left at the hospital with Nicola. The thought of Nicola brought a sudden rush of happiness and a smile sprang to her face. Thinking about Nicola's happy family life increased her resolve to help Angie. Just before she left, she wrote, in block capitals, on the front of the envelope containing the money:

ANGIE,
THIS MONEY IS FOR YOU. BARRY KNOWS NOTHING ABOUT IT. USE IT TO GET AWAY FROM HIM.
FROM A WELL-WISHER

She knew Barry's address: she remembered it from the days when he used to take her out in his car. Sometimes, when he'd left her outside houses or pubs where he called in to 'do business', she'd idly gone through the glove compartment and she had seen letters – bills mostly – addressed to his home.

He lived on a new executive-style housing estate on the outskirts of Allerby, which Lisa found easily enough. The houses, all five or six bedrooms, she guessed, had open front gardens and drives where cars like Barry's were not out of place among the four-wheel drives and the top-of-the-range convertibles. It was a haven for successful men who commuted to offices in Leeds or other Yorkshire cities, but who preferred quieter surroundings for their wives and families. As she drove into the estate, Lisa wondered what the neighbours made of Barry, with his irregular hours and his flash clothes. She felt another surge of pity for Angie, realising that the girl she had seen in the supermarket probably felt out of her depth and unhappy in these surroundings, where the children of her neighbours would go to posh prep schools and the other wives would look down their elegantly made-up noses at Angie.

The road where Barry's family lived was not difficult to find: there were only four or five roads in the whole estate. All the houses were set at an angle to their neighbours, so that nobody overlooked anyone else. In the dark, using only her car headlights, it was difficult for Lisa to pick out any numbers – and besides, most of these houses had names and there were no numbers to be seen. She drove slowly along the short road twice and then decided to park the car and walk.

She approached one house. If she could see a couple of numbers, she could work out the rest. As she walked up the drive, a security light came on and a dog started barking; the shock made Lisa retreat hurriedly. But she had glanced at the number and guessed that Barry's house was further down on this side of the road. Counting, she came to the one she thought was his. There was a small car on the drive with two child seats in the back; this looked promising. There was also a doll's pushchair on the porch, and some toys littering the lawn. Again Lisa felt a pang; Angie was not part of this set, with their manicured lawns and au pairs.

She went up to the house and, after checking it was the right number, quickly thrust the package through the letterbox. It was a squeeze getting it through, and as she struggled with it, she could hear a child crying. Her heart was pounding. Hastily, afraid of being seen, she retraced her steps back to the car, wanting to run but telling herself to stay calm, and drove away. She pulled over on the outskirts of the town, shaking with fear and adrenaline. Sneaking up to doors in the dark was not something she enjoyed.

She thought through what she had just done. Suppose Barry was at home? His car wasn't there, but maybe it was in the garage. Even if he's not there, suppose Angie, terrified of him, gives him the package when he gets back? He'd know straightaway who was behind it. She felt a shiver of fear. But then, he'll know that anyway, when he comes for his money . . . For an instant, Lisa wondered if she should take the rest of the money and escape herself. But the thought did not last; she had a life now, and she had Nicola. Nothing was going to separate her from her daughter again. Even so, she was frightened of Barry.

'You've done it now. You can't undo it. And it was a very good thing to do,' Lisa heard Dawn's voice whispering in her ear, and she felt strength flooding back into her body.

'What if somebody saw me? There's CCTV on some of those houses.'

'So what? You weren't doing anything illegal. The only person to be concerned about is Barry, and we can deal with him,' Dawn whispered.

There was no sign of her light, but Lisa was not surprised

by this: she was parked at the side of a busy main road, with traffic and pedestrians going by.

Lisa laughed, more from relief than any other emotion.

'Well, I'm glad you think we can deal with him. I'm not sure how we're going to do that, mind.'

'One bridge at a time,' Dawn whispered. 'Now, get yourself home and try to relax. You have done well.'

'Will she escape?' Lisa asked.

'I can't predict the future,' Dawn said. 'She has free will, just as you do, but I know her angel will be telling her to get out and save herself and her children. We have to hope that she listens.'

Lunch with Nicola was a great success. Lisa was at Shenley's first, and she felt a surge of joy as Nicola walked in, with Lisa's pink scarf wrapped round her neck. They hugged and kissed, and Richard, peering out from the kitchen, also felt a rush of pleasure. It was wonderful to see Lisa looking so animated and obviously happy.

'Here's your scarf. I forgot to give it to you when you came to the house,' said Nicola, unwrapping it from round her neck as she sat down. 'You left it at the hospital when you disappeared without saying goodbye.' She was smiling when she said the words, and there was no hint of reproach.

'Yes,' said Lisa. 'I didn't want to interrupt your mum and dad.'

'They really like you,' Nicola said, and Lisa smiled. It was all going better than she could ever have hoped.

'I think you should keep the scarf. It suits you,' she said.

'Oh, can I? It feels . . . I know this sounds schlocky, and Giles would laugh at me, but it feels nice to wear something of yours.'

They chatted over lunch about clothes, shoes, make-up, their jobs. Nicola told Lisa that she wanted to get accepted on a course to become a veterinary nurse.

'I love working at the practice, but I'm only a receptionist, and I'd like to have a real job with the animals. My boss says I'm naturally good with them – and I love them. When I get my own place, I'm going to have a cat.'

'I thought you were moving to Leeds?'

Nicola shook her head and looked at Lisa shyly. 'Not now. Not now I've met you. Maybe one day – I do want to live in a city one day, just to see what it's like, but not just yet . . . Anyway, Tracey was going to share a flat with me and she's met this new guy and she's mad about him and she wouldn't move now, not even if I levered her out.'

They went through the ins and outs of Tracey's love life, and Nicola told Lisa about her own ex-boyfriend, and how it had all ended after two years.

'So I'm footloose and fancy-free – just like you,' she said.

Lisa laughed and glanced up. Richard was behind the counter, sorting out a bill with a customer. As Lisa caught his eye, he raised his coffee cup in a toast to her and she grinned back. Life was sweet.

After Nicola left to go back to work, Lisa lingered, waiting for Richard to bring the bill across to her. I owe him an explanation, she thought. She also wanted, badly, to talk about Nicola.

It was as if, having kept her secret for all these years, she now wanted to sing from the rooftops about her.

So when Richard came across, she said, 'Can Michelle cope if I buy you a coffee?'

'Sure,' Richard said, gesturing around the half-empty café. 'As you can see, we're not exactly run off our feet.' He sat down. 'It's good to see you looking so happy,' he said tentatively. He was still not sure how much he could say without provoking her defensive reaction, but just lately she seemed so much more open.

'Yes, I don't think I've ever been happier. At least, not for many years,' she said.

Richard stayed silent, prompting her to continue.

'That girl, the one I meet here . . . she's my daughter.' As she said the words, she looked up at Richard anxiously. It was still such an enormous statement to make.

'Well, I'm not surprised. You look like two peas out of the same pod. But she doesn't live with you?'

'No. I . . .' Lisa was relieved when Michelle brought two cups of coffee over to the table. It gave her chance to gather her thoughts, and pluck up her courage. She took a deep breath. 'I gave her up for adoption when she was a baby, and I've only just met her again,' she said, gabbling the words as quickly as she could. She didn't raise her head, but stirred her cappuccino as if her life depended on it.

Richard, moved at how difficult this was for her, stretched his hand out and covered hers. 'Don't worry,' he said. 'It's all right. I can tell, just by looking at you both when you are together, that you are going to be OK. You're going to get on. And whatever happened, well, you did it for the right reasons.

God, you must have been very young, to have a daughter of that age. I'm sure it was the right thing for both of you.'

'It was the right thing for her, and that's what counts,' said Lisa, turning her face up to meet his eyes. 'As for me – well, it probably screwed up my life, but that doesn't matter now. Because she's here, and she likes me.'

Richard nodded and squeezed her fingers. He didn't care that Michelle had told the chef, who had joined her behind the counter to watch their boss holding hands with one of the customers. He felt touched and honoured that Lisa was confiding in him. He was proud to be seen holding her hand.

But Lisa gave a sudden start, pulled herself free and looked at her watch. 'God, I'm twenty-five minutes late. How can I ever tell the others off about their long lunch breaks?' She was smiling as she said it, and Richard smiled back.

As she stood up, he said, 'I don't think you have screwed your life up, but I'd like to hear more about it. Will you tell me more on Sunday?' Then he added, in case she felt he was prying, 'And I can tell you how I screwed mine up.'

'Yes . . . yes, I will. I'm . . . I'm just grateful to you for listening today. I needed to tell someone.'

He waved away her attempts to pay the bill and she hurried out.

Someone, he repeated to himself. She needed someone. Would anyone have done? Was I just the nearest person, or did she choose me?

He wanted to think he mattered to her, but he was still not sure.

21

Escape for Angie

Lisa had a day off on Friday, and she had plans. She was going to go to the hairdresser to get her highlights done, and maybe she would treat herself to a French manicure. Then she was going to browse around the shops looking for something to wear for her date with Richard on Sunday. She smiled self-consciously at the idea that it was a date; it was just another driving lesson, she told herself. But she was secretly hoping that it would turn into something more and she wanted to look her best.

She intended to have a lie-in, but she was woken early by Dawn gently shaking her. The room was bathed in Dawn's light.

'Come on, sleepy head. We've got things to do.'

Lisa looked bemused. 'But I've got plans.'

'So have I,' said Dawn, 'and mine are more important. Get some breakfast and get dressed – we haven't got a lot of time.'

'Where are we going?'

'Leeds.'

'In the car? Only, I haven't had my practice drive with Richard yet . . .'

Dawn smiled. 'No. We'll go on the bus. I know how nervous you are about the traffic. Besides, going on the bus is part of my plan.'

When Lisa was dressed, she walked, with the invisible Dawn beside her, to the market square, where the Leeds bus, a white double-decker, was waiting, engine turning over. There were a handful of passengers already on board, mostly women with shopping bags.

'Where to, ducks?' asked the driver, a cheerful young man with his company cap pushed to the back of his head.

'Leeds, please,' said Lisa.

'I like a girl who goes all the way,' said the driver, with a broad wink. Lisa smiled back, wondering how many times he had made the same joke.

She walked to the rear and settled in a seat. There was nobody else this far back. She felt the gentle pressure of Dawn next to her and gave a giggle, covering it up by bending down as if she was picking something off the floor.

'I'm so used to you being with me, I nearly bought you a ticket,' she whispered to Dawn.

'One of the many advantages of being an angel – I get to travel free,' Dawn replied. She sounded slightly anxious. 'Come on,' she whispered, 'where are you? You're going to miss the bus.'

'Who are you talking to?' said Lisa, as the driver straightened his cap and touched the button to close, with a loud hiss, the double doors.

'Oh . . . oh dear,' Dawn whispered, but at that moment there was a hammering on the side of the bus and, before it could move off, a breathless Angie was at the door, clutching her young daughter in one arm and trailing a folded-up pushchair from the other. Her friend Shaz panted up, holding the hand of Angie's son and carrying a large bag. The driver, with a grin, opened the doors.

'You're cutting it fine, love,' he said genially. 'Another couple of seconds and we'd have been off.'

Shaz followed Angie on board and helped her stow the pushchair and the bag. 'Don't go yet, mate,' she said. 'I'm not going with you.'

'That's a shame,' said the driver, giving her the same wink he'd given to Lisa. 'I'd let you ride for nothing.'

Shaz and Angie clutched each other as best they could, with the little girl sitting on Angie's hip.

'You take care. Keep in touch, but only if you can. Look after yourself,' said Shaz. Then she delved into her pocket and produced a bag, which she gave to the little boy. 'Here's some sweets, Adam. Don't eat them all at once or you'll be sick. Be a good boy for your mummy.'

'Hurry up, can you?' said the driver amiably. 'They'll be grumbling in the villages if I'm late.'

After one more quick hug, Shaz left the bus and Angie made her way to a seat in front of Lisa, the little boy holding on to her coat with one hand and his bag of sweets with the other.

Angie plopped down gratefully and pulled him on to the

seat next to her. Both the children were quiet, their large eyes open wide.

'There,' said Angie, settling the little girl on her lap and pulling off her gloves and hat. 'It's warm in here – you don't need these. You'll be glad of them when we get off.'

'Where are we going, Mummy?' asked the boy. 'Are we on holiday?'

'Yes, we're on holiday,' Angie said.

'Will Dad come?' Lisa saw his face turn, apprehensively, towards his mother.

'No, Dad won't come this time. Not again. Dad won't be with us any more.'

'Not ever?' said the boy, his eyes even wider.

'No. From now on it's you, me and Ellie. That's all. Just us three. Isn't that nice?'

The boy nodded, obviously pleased.

'All you have to do is be a good boy today, because we've got a long journey, and you'll be tired. We'll all be tired.'

'Are we going on a train?'

'Yes, we're going on a long train ride. Here – here's your train.' She delved into her handbag and pulled out a small blue Thomas the Tank Engine.

'I wish we could have brought all the other trains, Henry and Gordon . . .' He trailed off.

'I told you, Mummy has to carry everything and she's only got two arms. We'll buy more trains when we get to our new home.'

The boy brightened. 'New trains.'

'Yes, all Thomas's friends.'

'I wanted to go upstairs on the bus,' said the boy.

'I know, but we were late, and whose fault was that? I kept telling you to hurry up with your breakfast. You weren't finished when Auntie Sharon came to collect us. And with the bags and the pushchair . . . we were very lucky the driver waited for us.'

The bus jolted and bumped across the cobbled streets and out of Allerby on to the Leeds road. Before long it diverted to another village, and then another. Lisa enjoyed the trip; when she had gone to Leeds by bus before, she had always caught the express, which went straight down the main road. Meandering around the countryside took longer but was much prettier. More people squeezed on board at every stop, so that eventually Lisa had an elderly lady with a large shopping bag sitting next to her, and with the noise of the bus and the chatter of other passengers, it became increasingly hard for her to listen to Angie's conversation with her children.

At one stage, she glanced at the young woman in front and caught her staring out of the window, biting her lip. Don't have second thoughts, Lisa silently begged her. Keep going. You've done the hardest bit, just by making the decision.

The bus eventually pulled into the shiny modern bus station at the rear of Kirkgate Market in Leeds. Lisa followed Angie as she struggled to get the children, the bag and the pushchair off.

'Here, let me help,' Lisa said, taking hold of the large bag and the pushchair. 'You get the children off and I'll bring these.'

A young man, hearing the exchange, turned and came back to help Lisa, and between them they got Angie and all her possessions off. Lisa watched her as she made her way to the special bus service that connected the coach station with the railway station.

Unsure what to do, Lisa pretended to study a bus timetable until she heard Dawn whisper in her ear, 'Follow her. Go to the station. Make sure she gets the train.'

Lisa felt like saying, 'What can I do if she doesn't?' but knew that people would look at her if she started talking aloud.

She heard Dawn chuckle. 'Don't forget, I know what you're thinking as well as what you say out loud. You won't be able to force her to get on the train, but I think you will feel happier if you see this through, and you know she has done it,' came the whisper in Lisa's ear.

She dashed across and jumped on the interchange bus, linking the bus and train stations, just in time. Angie gave her a quick smile, recognising her as the woman who had helped with the bags. When they arrived at the station a few minutes later, Lisa missed the chance to help again because the bus driver was going off duty and he swung Angie's heavy bag and pushchair on to the pavement for her. Angie opened the pushchair and put her sleeping daughter into it, slinging the heavy bag on to her shoulder and telling her little boy to hold the side of the pushchair. Lisa felt very moved by her plight: she could see how difficult it was, travelling alone with two children, without the trauma of heading off into an unknown future. At least you will all be safe, she thought.

She dawdled again, so that she was behind Angie as she went into the station and headed for the ticket office. Lisa positioned herself two places behind Angie in the queue and was able to hear her ask for one adult and two child singles to Truro. She argued briefly about whether her little girl needed a ticket, but the man at the window insisted she did. Angie shrugged and handed over a bundle of notes. As she walked away, Lisa was being called to an empty window, but she shook her head and left the queue.

She watched Angie pop into Marks & Spencer and come out with a bag of sandwiches and drinks, then head off for the platform. To Lisa's surprise, there was a direct train from Leeds to Truro and it was already in. She watched as Angie struggled down the platform, now with the carrier bag of food to manage as well as everything else. When the family finally hauled themselves on to the train, the little boy dancing excitedly around Angie, Lisa turned her back and walked slowly out of the station.

'There you are. A job well done. A new life in front of them,' Dawn whispered.

Lisa found a café for a baguette and a coffee, realising she had not had breakfast and now it was lunchtime. She smiled as she noted that the bread was not as fresh nor the coffee as strong as Richard's. What now? she silently asked Dawn.

'Now you can have some fun – shopping,' Dawn said.

The trendy Granary Wharf area was adjacent to the station, and Lisa knew it and loved it from her years in Leeds. Happily, she wandered around and bought herself some silver earrings and a bangle, before making her way to the Corn Exchange to buy new trousers and a top for her meeting with Richard on Sunday.

From time to time she thought about Barry. Was he home yet? Had he noticed they had gone? Had Angie left him a note?

Hopefully, she had covered her tracks well and left no clues as to where she and the children were going. Cornwall was about as far away as she could get, and Lisa fervently hoped that Angie would make a new life and that Barry would never find them.

Content, and with arms full of shopping bags, she made her way back to the bus station, pausing in the market to pick up some fresh fruit. The meandering journey back was even more enjoyable than the first bus ride, because now she had, like Dawn said, a strong sense of a job well done.

Now, Lisa told herself the next morning, there was only one more thing to do to make her life complete. She had to get rid of Barry. With a shiver of revulsion, she pressed his number in her phone. As soon as this is over, I'll delete him for good, she told herself.

'Yeah, what do you want?' Barry's voice sounded angry. Lisa realised her name had come up on his phone screen, so he knew it was her.

'I want you to remove your property from my shop,' she said as coolly as she could.

'*Your* shop? That's a laugh. If your boss in Leeds knew what you'd got in the oven . . . well, it certainly wouldn't be *your* shop then.'

'And it wouldn't be your money, either. As soon as the cops hear about it—'

Barry cut her off. 'I've told you before, it's not hot money.' He spoke forcefully, pausing between words.

'Yeah, you did tell me, but if the police aren't interested, I guess Chet Ainsworth would be.'

There was a slight pause. Lisa could hear Barry's intake of breath.

'You threatening me, you little cow? 'Cos if you are—'

'No, I'm not threatening you. I'm just telling you to get your goods off my premises. And then I don't ever want to see you again.' Lisa's voice sounded cool, and she felt in control, but her heart was racing.

There was another pause. 'We'll see about that. I'll come round after you finish work, then, shall I? Does that time suit you? I wouldn't like to do anything that didn't suit you.' His voice was loaded with sarcasm and Lisa felt a tremor of fear. 'You know how much you like a little bit of Barry's special treatment after a day's work.'

Lisa shuddered, appalled once more at the memory of finding this man attractive. 'That will be fine. I'll expect you,' she said, again surprising herself by how controlled her voice was. The phone clicked off.

Barry had said nothing about his family disappearing, but then Lisa had not expected it. He was no longer close to her, no longer confiding in her. Not that he had ever really allowed her to know much about his private life. She gave a short snort of laughter when she realised that, just a few months ago, she would have welcomed the disappearance of his wife and children for completely different reasons, hoping that she could get even closer to him.

How deranged was I? she asked herself.

'Not deranged, just very lonely,' Dawn whispered.

'And a lousy picker of men,' Lisa said aloud.

'Well, yes, that too.' Dawn's laughter tinkled around Lisa like a thousand tiny bells ringing.

Lisa was pleased that she had made the phone call; she knew she had to get this final piece of her life sorted out. Nevertheless the prospect of Barry turning up after work that day was worrying, especially as he would be in a foul mood. Angie's desertion, then her, Lisa, challenging him to remove the money . . . he's not going to be in a good place, Lisa thought. And that's putting it mildly. She shivered.

All that morning at work, she found herself rehearsing the scene. Barry was not going to simply arrive and take the money and go. He would be violent, she was sure of that. He had nothing to lose now; he wasn't going to sweet-talk her. He might – and this was an even worse thought – force her to have sex. And he knew, as bullying men always know, that she'd be reluctant to call the police. She should not have been hiding the money in the first place, and secondly, she would be too ashamed to admit her involvement with him.

Wild ideas came to her. Perhaps she could lock up early and leave the parcel of money on the doorstep? No, what if someone else picked it up? What if someone called the police and they thought it was a terrorist bomb? What if, when Barry arrived in his car, she threw the money out of the door and then barricaded herself in the building? But he'd break the door down, she knew. Barry wasn't going to be satisfied with just taking the money and getting out of her life.

When it was time for her lunch break, she could not face going to Shenley's. She wanted to see Richard – she was looking forward to telling him about the stale baguette and stewed coffee she had had in Leeds – but she didn't want him to see her in this state. She couldn't hold a proper conversation; all morning she was so agitated that when Anne went next door to buy coffees, she made sure Lisa's was decaff.

'You've not given up the hard stuff, have you?' Richard asked, when she ordered it.

'No, it's not for me. It's for Lisa. She seems very worried today. I don't think she needs anything to make her more wound up.'

'What's bugging her?' Richard asked, carefully avoiding Anne's eyes so that she would not realise how concerned he felt.

'Dunno. She's a lot friendlier than she used to be, but she doesn't confide in me,' said Anne. 'She's a bit of a closed book, that one, but she's definitely got something on her mind.'

When she took her break, Lisa walked into the town and bought a sandwich. She did not feel at all hungry, and the very thought of eating made her stomach fall away, but she knew that she must try: she needed all her strength for this evening.

The market was on in the town square and she wandered around the stalls, trying to take her mind off her problem. At the toy stall, she saw a set of Thomas the Tank Engine trains and she brightened; she hoped the little boy she had seen on the bus was now happy in his new, peaceful, violence-free home. She felt a surge of compassion for Angie. She knew what it was like to have to make a new life surrounded by strangers. It will come right, give it time, she silently told Angie.

'Oi, you, Lisa, or whatever your name is.'

The shout came from the other side of the market, and looking along the gap between the stalls, Lisa spotted Barry's old friend, the owner of the Italian restaurant, hurrying towards her. Her heart sank. Connections with Barry were what she was trying to sever.

'Oi, wait there,' the small, plump Italian yelled as Lisa turned to walk away.

She hesitated. The easiest thing was to speak to him, not make a scene. She waited until he panted up to her.

'*Buongiorno*, Enrico,' she said.

'Where ees 'e?' the Italian said, not bothering with any of the niceties. 'Where ees that fucking boyfriend of yours?'

A couple of people, browsing at the nearest stall, turned and looked.

'If you mean Barry, I've no idea. I don't have anything to do with him any more,' Lisa replied, keeping her voice low and level.

'When did you last see 'im?'

'Ages ago,' Lisa replied truthfully.

'Liar.' The Italian spat the word out and roughly took hold of Lisa's arm. He pulled her away from the market stalls, Lisa walking as quickly as she could to keep up with him, struggling to make it look as if they were walking together naturally. Enrico thrust her against the stone wall of an impressive bank building, jarring her back. He put his face very close to hers. 'You tell 'im this from me. 'E don't answer ees phone for me. So you tell 'im. I want what ees mine. 'E knows what I mean. You tell 'im I'm coming looking for 'im.'

'I don't see him any more. I don't have anything to do with him,' Lisa protested.

Enrico looked at her and his expression showed that he did not believe her. He pulled her face closer to his. 'You tell 'im. You tell 'im soon. I'm not the only one looking for 'im. 'E's in deep shit. You tell 'im.' He dropped her arm abruptly, turned and stomped away.

Lisa, shaken, stood still for a moment, composing herself. Glancing around, she could see that nobody had taken any notice of their little confrontation. She walked slowly through a cobbled alleyway to the park and sat on one of the benches. In the summer, these benches were full of office girls in bright dresses eating their lunches under the dappled shade of the trees, but today, when there was a biting-cold north wind, Lisa was the only one sitting there, and the trees were bare skeletons. She ripped the cellophane wrapper and took a bite of her sandwich, but struggled to swallow.

'What am I going to do?' she said out loud. 'He's going to be in a foul mood and he's going to want to take it out on someone.'

'You need help. You shouldn't do this on your own.' It was Dawn's voice and Lisa felt a warmth down her right side, telling her that Dawn was there, on the bench next to her.

'What do you mean? The police? I don't think they'll turn up until afterwards, if something terrible happens,' Lisa said.

'No. You need a friend. Someone who loves you and cares about you. Someone who is on your side.'

'You?' Lisa asked.

Dawn gave her familiar rippling laugh and the sound alone relieved some of Lisa's tension.

'No, not me. I can never help you in a physical way.

Remember when Nicola was being assaulted? All I could do was guide you there – I couldn't join in the fight.'

'Who else is there? I'm quite a loner, in case you hadn't noticed . . .'

'There is someone who is in your corner, someone who would like to be invited into your life, if only you could let yourself trust him.'

'Do you mean . . . Richard?' Lisa could hardly say his name.

'Yes, Richard. He cares about you more than you realise.'

Lisa shook her head vigorously. 'No, no, definitely not. I don't want Richard to know all the sordid details of my relationship with Barry. I'm too ashamed. I couldn't bear it . . .' Her head slumped forward and tears rolled down her cheeks. To her, involving Richard would mean throwing away all her hopes and dreams of a new, different life. He would be horrified and would run a mile from a woman like her. She knew he had seen Barry at the shop, but he had no idea that she would do something so low as to store money that was the proceeds of Barry's criminal life.

Dawn said nothing, leaving her to sob for a moment or two. Then Lisa, pulling herself together, glanced at her watch. 'I have to be getting back soon.'

'And you will go to see Richard this afternoon. He will help you tonight. He wants to help you. He knows more about you than you realise.'

'What do you mean?' said Lisa sharply. She felt a flush of embarrassment creeping over her; the thought of Richard knowing the worst about her was deeply humiliating.

'Remember that night you went for drink with him and

he asked you who the small girl was he had seen walking with you?'

'Yes.'

'And you stormed out, too upset to think about it. You have put it right out of your head. But answer his question now: who is the little girl he has seen with you?'

Lisa turned to stare at Dawn, who could not be seen, but whose presence could still be felt against her side. 'It must be you,' she said tentatively. 'That's what I thought when I ran out on him in the pub. But how could it be?'

'Well, it's like I said, sometimes people do see your angel. What I didn't tell you at the time, because you weren't ready to hear it, is that you can only see somebody's guardian angel if you love them enough. Some people just see a glow around the person they love. Others, much more rarely, catch a real glimpse of an angel.'

'And so Richard really did see you?'

'Well, what other little girl have you walked around with?'

'He could have meant Nicola.'

'No, he's seen Nicola, of course he has, and he's worked out just who she is. But this was different. Remember, he spoke of seeing a "little" girl. Richard definitely got a glimpse into the realm of angels and he saw me walking by your side. Lisa, he is a very special person. He is a good man, and he truly loves you. Nobody sees another person's angel unless there is real, pure love there.'

Lisa sat in silence for a few moments. A deep feeling of joy slowly crept over her, and for the first time, she allowed herself to open up to her feelings for Richard.

'Oh, Dawn, I think I love him, too. In fact, I know I love him. I just never thought he would care deeply for me. I didn't let myself hope.'

'He cares more deeply than you can imagine,' said Dawn. 'Your past experiences have made you build a wall around your true feelings, to stop yourself getting hurt. The wall has helped and protected you at bad times, but unless you open a gate in it, you will never experience true happiness and true love. Let Richard through the wall. Believe me, I know what is right for you.'

The wave of happiness she was feeling showed on Lisa's face. Despite the bitter weather, her cheeks glowed.

'Oh, Dawn . . .' She could not find any words to express her feelings.

'Now, you must also believe me that Richard is the person to help you. You must tell him your problems. He will be there for you.'

22

Confrontation

Richard was worried. First, Anne had told him that Lisa seemed very anxious, and then she had not come into the café for lunch as usual. Even on the days when she dashed to the bank or the supermarket in her lunch break, when she did not have time to sit down for a meal, Lisa would usually pop in to buy a sandwich. Richard was aware how much he lived for these meetings with her, however brief.

He knew her routines. He was always at the café early, to take delivery of the day's food orders, to open up for the early workers who wanted coffee and croissants, and get the chef started on prepping the meals, and he knew exactly when to pour himself a mug of coffee and stand at the window, surveying the street and watching for her arrival next door. Sometimes when he saw her, he gave her a wave. Other days he dodged back before she spotted him, for fear that she would think he was spying on her.

Halfway through the morning, one of the staff next door

would come in for takeaway coffees and he always felt a pang of disappointment when Jodie or Anne pushed the door open. At least he could usually turn the conversation round to Lisa when he chatted to her staff. Just hearing her name made him feel involved with her.

Then, at lunchtime, came the high point of the day. If she came in late for a meal and the café was not too busy, he would sit with her. Otherwise, he would simply enjoy the feeling of her being in the same room. From time to time, as he glanced at her, their eyes would meet and he was sure he recognised a spark of interest in her. Just lately, with the purchase of the car, he had been getting even closer to her. Sitting next to her for her first drive in Maisie had been exquisite torture for him. He had struggled to confine himself to one prim kiss, when every nerve in his body had longed to take her into his arms, run his hands through her tousled hair and kiss her with more passion that he had ever felt before.

Now he had the prospect of a whole day with her, on Sunday. It was supposed to be another driving lesson, but he had been making careful plans. When they got into Leeds, he knew exactly where he was going to take her for a superb lunch. One of the best restaurants in the city was run by a friend of his, and he would make sure that Richard and his date got the best of everything.

Afterwards, Richard had hazy plans of a slow drive back, touring some of the prettier bits of the Yorkshire Dales, stopping for tea at one of the inns he knew where there would be a roaring log fire. And then . . . and then . . . and then . . . He did not dare frame thoughts of what would come next, but he really hoped that by the end of the day he would be able to claim a different relationship with Lisa. He knew how difficult and prickly she could be, so he was determined to take it slowly, but he had been feeling buoyed up by the way everything had been going lately.

And yet now, today, everything seemed to have gone wrong again. Anne said she was in a bit of a state, and she had not come in at lunchtime. Richard feared it was something to do with Barry Shields. He hadn't seen him around for a while, but was he still on the scene? Was she the sort of woman who preferred the adrenaline-charge of a violent bad boy to someone tame and respectable, like himself? If so, he should give up his hopes. Sunday was perhaps, after all, nothing more than a driving lesson to her.

He began to feel wretched. If she wanted nothing to do with him, and she carried on working next door, life would be hell. At the moment, he lived on hope; if that was dashed, what would he do? Would he be able to be so close to her, to see her and talk to her on a daily basis? For the first time since his father was ill, Richard began to think about moving away, getting a job elsewhere.

He was polishing the coffee machine, his pride and joy, vigorously when Lisa came in at half past three in the afternoon, and at first did not realise it was her. Michelle, his waitress, hesitated before stepping in to serve her. Even though she was seventeen, and totally preoccupied with the dramas of her own hectic love life, Michelle knew that Richard had a soft spot for the manageress of the shop next door and always liked to serve her himself.

'Shall I do this one?' she said.

Without looking up, Richard replied, 'Yep, it's what you're paid for, isn't it?'

He'd been tetchy all day, but Michelle was not used to being spoken to like that and flounced sulkily over to take Lisa's order for a coffee and a toasted teacake.

'She says can she have a word with you,' Michelle said to Richard, with a note of triumph in her voice. See, she was saying in her head, you should have served her yourself in the first place.

It was only then that Richard turned, half expecting to see a saleswoman trying to interest him in a new line of biscuits. He froze momentarily when he saw Lisa, who was studiously avoiding looking at him. He did not expect to see her sitting down in the café in the middle of the afternoon: the most he could ever hope for at this time of day was that she popped in to treat her staff to cakes.

Recovering quickly, he walked across, smiling. 'Having a well-earned break?' he said. 'I missed you at lunchtime – were you too busy in there to take time off?' He knew that the shop had not been busy, and he had also seen Lisa walking up the street towards the market square, but he needed an icebreaker. And, perhaps, he was also testing her, to see how honest she was with him.

'No, I took a break, but I had to go into the town. I ended up buying a sandwich from the sandwich shop – nowhere near as good as yours.' She smiled at him. 'And on that subject, I had a baguette and a coffee in Leeds yesterday and it wasn't a patch on yours.'

Richard gave a wide grin. 'And I bet it cost more, too. Seriously, though, whenever you are under pressure like that, just put your head round the door, shout out what you want and Michelle will bring it to the back entrance for you. Or I will. Anyway, what were you doing in Leeds? Not practising driving in traffic without me, I hope.'

Lisa laughed. 'No, I wouldn't dare. I went on the bus.'

Before Lisa could say any more, Michelle arrived with her coffee and toasted teacake.

Richard turned to her and said, 'Can I have my usual, Michelle?'

The girl was relieved that he seemed to be back to his cheerful self again and said, 'Coming up, boss.'

Lisa's face had grown serious, and she was looking down at her coffee, stirring a spoonful of sugar into it very slowly.

'I've got a favour to ask. A big favour,' she said.

Richard's heart leaped. He would do anything to be involved with this woman. 'Fire away,' he said.

'I made a bad mistake. I was new in Allerby. I didn't know anybody. I guess I was lonely. Anyway, I . . . I started to go out with . . .' She was struggling to find the words, her eyes staying fixed on the frothy coffee.

Richard leaned across and put his hand on hers, squeezing very gently. 'I know. I know him. Barry Shields. He was at school at the same time as me, in the same class as my sister. It's a small town, remember.' He gave a short laugh. 'He was a bastard then, too.'

Lisa glanced up and met his gaze.

'Don't blame yourself. He always had a way with girls. Shirley had a thing for him for a while. Seems that bad boys know all the right cards to play.' He said it ruefully, and it was Lisa's turn to squeeze his hand. There was nobody else in the café except Michelle, who was standing behind the counter transfixed. She couldn't hear a word of what they were saying, but they were holding hands, and that was enough. She had Richard's coffee ready, but wisely decided to drink it herself and not interrupt them.

'No, he doesn't have the right cards . . . I mean, yes, he did get me to go out with him, and it took me quite a while to see through him, but no, he's not got the right cards. He's not got . . . What do you call it in cards when someone wins?'

Her confusion made Richard laugh. 'A full house. Royal flush. A winning hand. Top trumps. Take your pick. I'd have guessed you weren't a poker player, somehow.'

Lisa smiled, too. She was still feeling very nervous, but Richard was making this easy. She knew, though, that she had not yet reached the really difficult bit.

'I've broken up with him now,' she said.

Richard felt relieved. He had been worried that her disappearance at lunchtime was for an assignation with Barry. 'That's great,' he said. 'I'm really—'

Lisa interrupted him and again looked down, pulling her hand away from his comforting grip. 'I've got a big problem.' She took a deep breath and gabbled the words out as quickly as she could, as if by getting it over faster she would not give herself a chance to change her mind and run away. 'I let him store something in the shop. I know I shouldn't have done it, but it's hard to refuse him. He's violent. He made me do it. I should have called the police, I know. I was frightened of losing my job, losing friends . . . losing you.'

Richard's heart leaped at the last two words and he grabbed her hand again, this time cradling it between both of his. 'And now he wants it back?'

'Yes. He's coming tonight, after the shop closes.'

'And you would like me to be there, to back you up?'

Lisa nodded mutely. 'I'm scared of him.'

'I'm not. He's just a bully.'

Lisa nodded. 'But it's more complicated.'

She told him about the money, and how she had taken £6,000 from it to give to Barry's wife.

'And that's why I went to Leeds yesterday. I followed her, on the bus, and I watched her and the children get on to a train.' She lowered her voice to a whisper, even though there was nobody to hear. 'They've gone to Cornwall.'

'About as far away as they can get. Let's hope it works out for them,' Richard said. 'But that was very brave of you, and a really good thing to do.'

'Yes, but I don't feel very brave about the consequences, now they're only a few hours away. He'll go ballistic when he finds I took the money. It's vital he doesn't find out what I did with it. He's got to think I just took it. And he's not going to be a happy bunny, I can tell you.'

She had not raised her head, but Richard could tell from her voice that she was fighting back tears. He freed one of his hands and leaned across the table, tilting her chin to make her look at him. 'You have nothing to worry about. I can sort out

Barry Shields. Don't forget, I'm a trained fighting machine – that's why I'm in the third team at football.'

The joke broke the tension and they both laughed.

Lisa reached across and they now held both hands. 'Thank you,' she said.

Richard was desperate to kiss her, but at that moment the bell on the door pinged and an elderly couple, carrying several bags of supermarket shopping, came in. Lisa and Richard sprang apart.

'Ey up, Richard, lad,' said the old man, not noticing their confusion. 'We'll be having our usual.'

Richard stood. 'Got the taxi on order?' he asked.

'Yes, he's picking us up in half an hour,' said the old lady. 'Good time for tea and scones.'

'Coming up,' said Richard. He looked at Michelle, who was still in shock. 'Jump to it, young lady. You know how Fred and Eva like their tea – so strong the spoon stands up in it.'

'Good lad,' said the old man.

Lisa stood up and walked across to the counter.

'You haven't eaten your teacake, young lady,' said Eva, shaking her head. 'No wonder you're such a slip of a thing.'

'I'm taking it back to work with me,' said Lisa. She smiled at Richard, who handed her a paper bag to put it in. He waved away her attempt to pay.

'Six o'clock,' he whispered, as Michelle went out into the kitchen. 'I'll come the back way.'

Lisa went back to work feeling very happy. It wasn't the thought of Richard being able to handle Barry – she was pretty sure he could, but that wasn't what was making her feel so up. Her real joy came from having, at long last, confided in someone about the money. And, even more, from the fact that Richard had heard her confession and had not run a mile. He seemed to know more about her than she had realised – he even knew Barry. She smiled when she remembered how he had held her hands.

It was a lot to take in, but luckily the afternoon trade was very light. Jodie and Anne whiled away the time gossiping about Jodie's wedding preparations. The big day was finally in sight, and Jodie's excitement was catching. Every day, Anne and Lisa were treated to more bulletins about guest lists and flowers and the teenage bridesmaid whose growth spurt had meant endless alterations to her dress.

Lisa tuned out from it all, thinking only of her tender moments with Richard. Was it possible that he really loved her, despite what she had told him? Dawn said he did, and Dawn always knew these things.

'Thank you, Dawn,' she whispered, as she rearranged the window, with her back to the others. She thought she heard, very faintly, the tinkle of Dawn's laughter.

She let the other two go at a quarter to six. Although the shop stayed open until six, it was a dark, wet afternoon and it was unlikely they would get any last-minute customers, so she busied herself working out the day's takings. She had everything done by six, when she turned the sign to 'Closed' and locked the front door.

She walked through to the back and within two minutes heard a clattering noise, followed by a loud curse, from the yard at the back. She opened the door to see Richard picking up the dustbin, which he had landed on in the dark when he'd jumped down from the wall that separated the back of the restaurant and the shoe shop.

He laughed as the light from the door lit up the scene. 'Thank goodness you're a shoe shop – all you've got in this bin is boxes and paper. My bins are full of food waste,' he said. 'Much messier to land in.'

Lisa helped him pick up the litter, and then they went inside. As soon as the back door was closed, Richard took her arm, pulled her towards him and kissed the tip of her nose. He then let go; he wasn't going to push his luck. All he wanted to do was reassure her that he was here.

'Not exactly a superhero, am I?' he said, brushing down his clothes. 'I don't think Batman or Spiderman ever landed on a dustbin.'

Lisa smiled. It felt good just to be with Richard. She was still nervous about Barry, but her fear was mixed with happiness.

Before either of them had time to say any more, there was a loud and insistent banging on the front door.

'I'll stay out here at first,' Richard said. 'You go and let him in.'

Lisa felt her stomach lurch. She walked across the shop. She could see Barry standing in the doorway, his back turned to her, a thin plume of smoke rising from his cigarette. The Jaguar was again parked on the double yellow lines outside. As she unbolted the door, he turned, ground the cigarette under his foot and thrust the door open even as she was still bending to release the bolt at the bottom. The door hit her and sent her reeling.

'Get up, you stupid cow,' said Barry, without any other greeting. He grabbed her arm and hauled her to her feet, pulling her face close to his and glaring at her. Then he flung her away and she fell backwards and hit her spine on the counter. She let out a yell of pain.

'Hurt, did it? Good. That's just for starters,' Barry said. 'Let's see what we've got next.'

He moved towards her, fists clenched. At the same time, the door at the back of the shop opened with a familiar creak. Barry paused and turned.

'Hello, Barry,' said Richard. 'Long time no see.'

Barry's face registered surprise for a moment, which instantly turned to a sneer. 'Well, here's a turn-up for the books. Richard Shenley. A man who likes poncing about serving old ladies with pretty cakes. What are you doing here? Sniffing around our little Lisa?'

Richard was walking slowly across towards Barry, saying nothing. Lisa scrabbled her way to the far side of the counter.

'Well, I wouldn't waste your time,' Barry continued. 'She's not worth it. I've had better shags from—'

Richard launched one of his fists at Barry, catching him off guard. Barry jerked backwards, but the blow was not hard enough to knock him over. He quickly recovered and, letting out a roar, launched himself at Richard.

Richard sidestepped and Barry crashed unsteadily towards the opposite wall. A display stand collapsed, littering the shop floor with children's shoes of all styles and colours. Barry turned, and as he did so, he pulled a knife from the pocket inside his jacket. It was a short knife, with a six-inch blade.

'Ah, I might have known. Never one for a fair fight, were you, Barry?' Richard said.

The words angered Barry, who crossed the floor towards Richard, the knife held ready in his right hand. Richard did not flinch. As Barry got close, he lunged towards Richard, who parried the blow and moved aside again. Then he delivered another punch, which made contact with Barry's jaw and jerked his head backwards. Barry was caught off balance and stumbled, tripping over a small red shoe and ending up sprawled on the floor. Richard quickly bent over and grabbed the knife.

'OK, on your feet,' he said to Barry, who got up, his fingers carefully exploring his jaw. 'What do you want?'

'I want what's mine. She knows,' he said, turning towards Lisa with a vicious scowl on his face. 'I'll get it.' He made a move as if he was going to the kitchen.

'Stay where you are,' Richard said.

He was glaring at Barry, the knife in one hand and the other clenched into a tight fist.

'I'll get it,' said Lisa, sidling past the two men and going into the kitchen. She removed the carrier bag from the oven, and when she re-entered the shop, neither of them had moved.

'I've taken a donation for charity,' she said.

'You what?' Barry's face flared with anger and he stepped towards her.

'Stay exactly where you are,' said Richard, his voice hard and menacing.

Barry halted, glancing at the knife.

'Not a huge amount. Six thousand pounds. You've still got most of your money.' Lisa threw the parcel on to the floor.

'You little cow—' Barry began.

'That's enough,' Richard snapped. 'And get this clear – you make any trouble about this, you show your face round here or at Lisa's flat again, and you'll pay a much bigger price than six thousand.'

'Oh, yeah?' Barry's anger had boosted his confidence. 'What you going to do, lover boy? I'm on my own tonight, but when I come back, I won't be . . . And you'd better have my six grand waiting for me,' he said to Lisa. He bent down to pick up the package.

'I don't think so,' said Richard. 'You're forgetting quite a lot. You're forgetting the police, but more importantly, you're forgetting Mr Chet Ainsworth. Always brings his daughter and his grandkids in for tea and cakes in my café when he's visiting his family back here in England, or didn't you know that? Always leaves a big tip. Very nice man. Likes a chat about the football. Often asks about my dad – they played a bit of footie together, a long time ago.'

Barry blanched. He clutched the package to him and began to move backwards, towards the front door, never taking his eyes off Richard.

'It's all right. You can turn round. I'm not one of your lot – I won't stick a knife in your back. Besides, you might trip over the shoes,' Richard said, and laughed as Barry stumbled again.

Barry turned and went out, and within seconds they heard the door of the car slam and the engine roar into life. Richard and Lisa stood stock-still for a few moments, both of them breathing deeply.

Finally Richard burst out laughing, and Lisa giggled, too, with relief.

'Good job I watch a lot of gangster movies,' said Richard.

'Is that true, the bit about Chet Ainsworth?'

'Well . . . I may just have made that bit up. He did come in the café once, but I didn't talk to him. The chef told me who he was. I don't think he's ever met my dad in his life, but, you know, they're about the same age, so it's possible.'

Lisa laughed. 'You did very well. Thank you so much. I'd never have survived without you.'

Richard took a small bow. 'At your service, madam. Binman, the superhero who is always on hand to rescue damsels in distress.'

Lisa laughed again and flopped down on one of the red benches that lined the shop. She felt completely drained. Richard sat down opposite her, still holding the knife.

'What are you going to do with that?' Lisa asked, nodding at it.

Richard looked at the knife as though he had only just seen it. 'Oh well . . .' He turned it over. 'It's actually a kitchen knife, so I think it will join the others in the knife block next door. There you are, I've gained a new knife. It's been worth it.' He laughed again.

Lisa began to pick up the shoes from the floor. She righted the display stand and put everything back in its place. Richard watched her. As she put the last shoe on the stand, Lisa closed her eyes. She suddenly wanted to cry, so she bit her lip hard. Richard walked across, put his arms around her from behind and then turned her to face him.

She began to sob. He pulled her head against his chest and whispered, 'It's OK. It's over. He won't come back. It's all behind you.'

As Lisa's sobs abated, he gave her a gentle squeeze and then said, 'Come on. Go out the back and put your face on. I'm taking you out to dinner. We've got a lot to celebrate.'

23

Lisa's Mum and Dad

Later that night, when Lisa arrived home, she found the flat bathed in a familiar, welcoming light. Despite a relaxing and happy meal with Richard, and a few glasses of wine, she was still shaky with nerves. The encounter with Barry had fired her adrenaline and now she was crashing, slowly coming to terms with the momentous events of the day.

Richard had been very understanding: he had done no more than give her a gentle kiss when he drove her home. She'd invited him in, but he could see how tired she was and said no.

'We have all the time in the world in front of us,' he said.

She was relieved. She knew she was falling deeply in love with him, but she was determined to break her bad habit and stop rushing into things. He was right: time was on their side.

She sat down on the settee and immediately the light in the room concentrated itself into the shape of Dawn, who cuddled up next to her. She turned her cherubic face to Lisa, and Lisa looked once again into those beautiful eyes, which were filled with life, love and light.

'Nearly there,' Dawn said, in that lilting, gentle voice that now filled Lisa's dreams.

'What do you mean?' Lisa asked.

'The jigsaw puzzle is nearly complete. Just one last piece to put in place.'

Lisa frowned. 'I'm too tired to work out what you mean,' she said.

Dawn laughed, the high, sweet notes of her laughter filling the room. 'Yes,' she said gently, 'you are very tired, and tonight you will sleep in my arms again. You have worked very hard, and so have I. My work is almost over.'

Lisa gave a start. 'What do you mean? You're not leaving me, are you?'

'No, I will always be with you, whatever happens to you, but I have had a very big task in the last few months and it is not quite over.'

'You mean you've helped me find Nicola, saved her from danger, helped me get a good relationship with her, got me out of a terrible relationship and brought me together with Richard. I really know and appreciate everything you have done, but what else is there?'

Dawn did not reply, but just looked into Lisa's eyes. Slowly, she realised what Dawn meant.

'Oh, my mum and dad.'

'*Our* mum and dad,' Dawn corrected her. 'They have suffered a great deal in their lives. You have it in your power to make the end of their lives much happier.'

'But . . . after all this time . . . I'm too ashamed . . . I couldn't face them . . . They wouldn't want to see me.'

'Of course they want to see you. It's all they have wanted, dreamed about and longed for since you left home. As for you being ashamed, don't you think their love and happiness is more important than your embarrassment?'

Lisa said nothing. Dawn folded her wings around her sister and carried her through to the bedroom, lying her gently down on the bed. Instantly, without even taking her clothes off, Lisa was swallowed into the tranquil oblivion of a deep sleep. In her dreams, she saw her mother's face, and when she woke, refreshed, her mother's features were still before her eyes.

The next morning, as she got ready for work, Lisa fretted about the phone call she had to make. She felt very alone and scared, even though Dawn was with her.

'You need support,' Dawn said. 'Remember that Richard wants to be involved in your life, in *all* of your life. Why don't you talk to him first?'

After the drama of the night before, Lisa was not sure how to greet Richard when she walked into Shenley's to buy coffees the next day. Should she speak about it? How would he feel about her now, having had time to think about it all? The café was busy, with a queue at the counter. Should she just pretend nothing had happened?

She needn't have worried: Richard simply gave her a wide grin that reassured her and made her want to fling her arms around him and hug him. How could she, Lisa Heywood, who always chose bad men, have found such a great guy?

'Because you deserve him,' Dawn whispered in her ear.

When it was Lisa's turn to be served, she noticed, with a start, the bruises on his knuckles.

He winked and said, 'Busy night last night, rearranging furniture.' Then he leaned across the counter and whispered, 'And faces.'

Lisa smiled. She didn't care who was listening – Michelle was also serving, and there was a line of customers.

'How about supper at mine tonight? Just to prove that you're not the only one around here who can cook.'

'Sounds great. I'll just consult my social secretary to see if I have a window . . . Yes, you're on. What time?'

'Seven thirty? Give me time to rustle up some food.'

'I won't eat all day, to make sure I've got an appetite.'

It was a lovely evening, but there was a knot of nerves in the pit of Lisa's stomach the whole time. Before this relationship went any further, Richard had to know the whole truth about her.

'I feel I've unloaded so much on you already – Barry, Nicola – but I've got even more baggage . . .' Lisa finally said, over the baked Alaska pudding that had caused Richard to clap his hands with approval and offer her a job in his kitchen.

Richard looked at her steadily, his blue eyes locked on her grey ones. The table was between them, and he did not stretch out his hand to her or move towards her.

'Lisa Heywood, I want you to know that I am in love with you. I love you. I want to shout it from the rooftops, but I think a man of my age might look a bit ridiculous – and besides,

I might get up, but I'd probably never get down again. You'd end up calling the fire brigade.'

Despite her nerves, Lisa smiled. The words were everything she wanted to hear, but she could not relax into her love for Richard until he knew everything about her. He was so close to his father and his sister; how would he feel about someone who deliberately turned their back on loving parents?

'You must have realised you can tell me everything. I want to know you, everything about you,' Richard was saying, still looking straight at her. Lisa's head was bowed, but he leaned across the table and tilted her chin towards him. 'I know you are not going to let me kiss you until you have said whatever is on your mind, but it won't change how I feel about you.' His tone was serious. Then he added, 'So get on with it, girl, or I'll die from lack of a snog!'

Lisa smiled, took a deep breath and launched into the story of her life. When she told him about Dawn's death, Richard gave a start. Could that be the mystery child he had seen with her? Lisa guessed what he was thinking.

'Yes, she's still with me. She's my guardian angel. I feel she's always by my side,' she said lightly. One day, she would tell him the full story of Dawn's visits to her, but there was enough other stuff to deal with tonight.

Richard nodded. 'You say you've messed up family relationships, but it seems to me that's one that you've held together all these years. And I think the other one, the relationship with your mum and dad, is only a phone call away.'

'Yes, I'm going to call them . . . I'll do it tomorrow. It's too late now.'

Richard glanced at his watch. 'It's only half past nine. Do it now. No time like the present.'

Lisa nodded. She knew she was only putting it off because she was scared and nervous. Would they want to hear from her? Perhaps they were better off without her.

'Do it now,' Richard insisted, bringing the phone across to her and pulling his chair round the table, next to hers. 'Do you know the number?'

'Oh, yes . . . I've never forgotten it . . . Unless they've changed it. What if they've moved?' Somehow, down all the years, the thought of her mum and dad being anywhere other than their familiar little home had never occurred to Lisa.

'You won't know if you don't make the call,' said Richard, gently squeezing her shoulder. Secretly, he, too, was worried: what if one or both of them had died, or was very ill? Perhaps the stress of losing both their daughters had caused them to split up?

He kept his worries to himself. 'Come on. Press the numbers in. I'm right next to you, remember?'

Margaret Heywood got up from her easy chair and started re-arranging the cups and saucers on the tray set out on the coffee table.

Her husband, Bill, grey-haired now but still strong-looking, said, 'Leave it, Mags. It's fine. Stop fussing.'

'But they're late.'

Bill glanced at his watch, the one he had been given when he retired last year. 'Only a minute or two. They'll be here. Our Lisa was always late.'

He thought back to the last time he had seen his daughter, the day before she had vanished from their lives. For months, even years, they had both felt sure she would return. They hadn't talked about it much. Just as when Dawn died, Bill and Margaret dealt with their grief separately and in different ways. But they had not drifted apart, as so many couples do when overwhelmed by tragedy.

After several years, when they both knew that Lisa was grown-up and probably settled with a family of her own, they retreated from even thinking about it. The birthday, the one Lisa shared with Dawn, had always been a time of mixed emotions. Now they ignored it completely, although Bill always made sure that Margaret had plenty to keep herself occupied on that day.

There were many painful times: when their nieces and nephews got married, when Bill's brother proudly showed them his first grandchild, when new acquaintances innocently asked if they had children . . . Bill was not a deep thinker, but it did seem to him that life had been very unfair. All the worry about having babies in the first place, then the tragedy of Dawn's death and then losing Lisa . . . It didn't seem right for one couple to have so much sadness. He felt, in some way he could not explain, that he had failed Margaret, whose only ambition in life had been to be a good wife and mother.

Margaret was just as puzzled by their misfortunes, and in turn she felt she was to blame. She spent hours picking over her relationship with Lisa, wondering if they had been too harsh or too soft. She worried that, after Dawn's death, they had been overprotective of Lisa, causing her to rebel so much later on. Or maybe Lisa had just never got over the death of her twin.

The phone call last night had taken them both by surprise. After Lisa vanished, Margaret had insisted on having a phone extension in their bedroom, in case their missing daughter rang when they were in bed. For weeks she had left the back door open at night, so that Lisa would always be able to get in. It was only after a spate of burglaries in the area that Bill gently persuaded her to allow him to lock it.

'If she comes home in the night, we'll hear her ring the bell,' he'd told his wife.

In the early days, they had tried to find her. The police noted her down as a missing person and circulated her details, but because she had clearly left of her own free will, probably with a boyfriend, and she was over sixteen, they didn't spend too long looking into Lisa's disappearance.

Bill and Margaret contacted the various charities and agencies that helped trace missing people, but drew a blank. A kind woman at the Salvation Army explained to them that, even if they did trace Lisa, they would not be able to put Bill and Margaret in touch with her unless she agreed.

In those days, every time the phone rang they both leaped up, then suffered a thousand disappointments when it was not their daughter's voice on the other end.

As the years wore on, hope faded. Secretly, without ever mentioning it to Margaret, Bill was relieved that the police had not come knocking on their door with news of a body to be identified. Somewhere, he was sure, Lisa was alive, and all he could hope was that she was happy.

Margaret, too, never spoke to Bill about her hopes and fears, but she occasionally daydreamed about the grandchildren she might have. She'd given up hope of ever seeing them, but she wondered about them.

So the phone call, when it came, was a complete shock. It was late by their standards; nobody ever rang them at half past nine at night.

'Is that you, Dad? It's Lisa here,' said the voice on the other end.

There was a silence.

'Are you there? I know this must be a shock, but . . .' Lisa said.

'Yes . . . yes . . . I'm here.' Bill sat down with the phone cradled to his ear, and Margaret, walking into the room and seeing his pale face, instantly feared that something terrible had happened. Perhaps his brother had died, or one of the nieces and nephews had had an accident. Lisa was no longer the first thing that sprang to her mind.

'Is it really you, Lisa?' Bill asked.

Hearing the name, Margaret gave a little cry and dropped the mug of tea she was carrying, its contents spilling over the pale carpet. She slumped down on to the sofa and watched Bill's face.

'Yes, Dad, it's really me. I . . . I . . . I'm sorry it's been so long.'

Bill's voice was gruff with the effort of holding back tears. 'Don't worry about that. How are you? Where are you? Are you all right?'

'Yes, I'm fine,' Lisa said. 'How's Mum?'

Bill, now engulfed in tears, did not reply but thrust the phone at Margaret.

'Lisa? Is that you, Lisa?' Her mind was racing. Could it be some terrible joke? A hoax? Could anybody be that cruel?

'Yes, Mum, it's me. Are you OK? Is Dad OK?'

'Yes, we're both fine.'

Suddenly, with so much to say, they ran out of words. The gulf was too vast; how do you fill in nearly twenty years in a polite telephone chat?

'I'd like to come and see you,' Lisa said, after a long pause. She, too, was holding a tissue to her face to mop up the tears that were cascading down. Richard, at her side, squeezed her shoulder.

It did not take long to arrange to visit the next day; having made contact, neither Lisa nor her parents could bear a longer delay.

Richard's car pulled up outside the terraced house in Wolverhampton where Lisa grew up. As she had thought, her parents had never moved, and the street felt both the same and alien to Lisa. Nothing much had changed, yet everything was slightly different from her memories.

The hour-and-a-half journey had been agony for Lisa. She had not slept much, and she had been too anxious to eat.

Richard was very reassuring: 'It's fine. Of course they want to see you. You know they do. Just relax . . . It will be OK. It will be lovely.'

In Lisa's bag she had the photo of Nicola that had dropped out of the letter Nicola had sent her, just a short time ago. She wanted to show them their granddaughter.

Parked by the kerb, she hesitated before opening the door.

'Are you sure you want me to come in? I can wait out here in the car,' Richard said, leaning across to kiss Lisa's cheek. He knew how difficult this was for her, and he could see the tension in her jaw.

Her face was pale as she turned to him. 'No, if you don't mind, I'd like you to be there. I think it will make things easier . . . and, besides, I'm so proud to be with you, I want them to meet you.'

Richard's face lit up as she said these words. 'I'm more proud of you than you will ever know, my little darling,' he said. 'Come on, then – they'll have heard the car arrive and it's unfair to keep them waiting. Just remember, they're probably more nervous than you are.'

'I'm not sure that's possible,' said Lisa, with a faint smile.

Richard climbed out of the driver's side of the car. For a brief moment Lisa hesitated, before stepping out.

'Thank you, Dawn,' she murmured under her breath.

'Off you go,' Dawn whispered back. 'They're waiting, and they've done too much waiting already. Go to them. And hug them for me, too, will you?'

As Lisa walked up the short crazy-paving path to the front door – she could remember her dad laying the slabs – the familiar green door opened and Bill and Margaret, side by side, were suddenly in front of her. They looked older and greyer; Bill was slightly stooped and Margaret a little bit heavier. Their faces were the same, though: the mum and dad who had held her hand when she was little, read bedtime stories to her and Dawn, tickled her feet, stayed by her hospital bedside when she was ill.

For them, she, too, was their little Lisa: a small girl now grown into a woman, but the same in so many ways.

No words were spoken. Tears poured down the cheeks of all three. Richard, standing at the gate, watched them with a lump in his throat.

Finally, Bill stepped forward and took Lisa in his arms. It was a long, hard hug, from a man who was not given to demonstrative gestures. Next, as she disentangled herself, Lisa embraced her mother and the two women sobbed on each other's shoulders.

It was Bill who spoke first, across the shoulders of the two women.

'Come on in, lad,' he said to Richard. 'The kettle's on for a brew.' Then turning to Lisa, who was still clutched in her mother's arms, he said softly, 'Welcome home.'

ALSO AVAILABLE IN ARROW

Angels

With a foreword by Gloria Hunniford

In Greek *Angelos*, in Latin *Angelus*, and in Hebrew *Malak*. Three names, one meaning: *Messenger*. But we know them simply as Angels. Artists have painted them, choirs have sung about them, poets and authors have written about them. For many they bring messages of love and reassurance. And a promise that we're not alone.

Angels contains inspirational and compelling stories of modern-day Angelic encounters, and includes a unique interview with bestselling author and angel expert Glennyce Eckersley, who tells of some of her own experiences. From the truly astonishing story of the man whose angel brought hope as he lay trapped and burned after a horrific accident, to that of the soldier whose angel saved him from a bullet. Every encounter is different, but in each, the radiant truth shines through: there are angels everywhere ready to help us, supporting us with gentle love and care when we are at our most vulnerable.

Based on the TV series *Angels* produced by Liberty Bell Productions Limited

arrow books

ALSO AVAILABLE IN ARROW

Angels in my Hair

Lorna Byrne

Angels in my Hair is the autobiography of a modern-day mystic, an Irish woman with powers of the saints of old.

When she was a child, people thought Lorna was 'retarded' because she did not seem to be focusing on the world around her, instead Lorna was seeing angels and spirits.

As Lorna tells the story of her life, the reader meets, as she did, the creatures from the spirit worlds who also inhabit our own – mostly angels of an astonishing beauty and variety – including the prophet Elijah and an Archangel – but also the spirits of people who have died.

This remarkable book is the testimony of a woman who sees things beyond the range of our everyday experience.

'Those who see angels are close to being angels. In this book, Lorna beautifully and graphically describes angels and how they work.' William Roache, MBE, author of *Soul on the Street*

'Nobody is going to argue with her underlying message of love and compassion and forgiveness and her hopes for "peace among nations and peace in families".' *Irish Times*

'The world has discovered a modest mystic that it might do well to listen to.' *Daily Mail*

arrow books

ALSO AVAILABLE IN RIDER

An Angel to Guide Me

Glennyce Eckersley

Glennyce Eckersley is one of our most loved angel experts. In *An Angel to Guide Me*, she explains how angels communicate with us through the five senses of sight, hearing, smell, taste and touch, as well as the mysterious sixth sense of intuition.

Amazing true stories collected from around the world show how many of us have had incredible angelic experiences that appear to have been tailor-made for us, speaking to us individually through the senses in the ways we recognise and understand the best. These stories are illustrated by inspirational exercises, affirmations and quotations, which will help readers to connect with the angels themselves.

From 'Visions of Angels' to the 'Touch of Angels' and 'Angels of the Soul', it becomes clear that the angels are indeed all around us, ready to communicate with us through the gateways of our senses whenever we are willing to welcome them into our lives.

ALSO AVAILABLE IN ARROW

How Could She?

Dana Fowley

A frightened girl sits on the stairs. It's Christmas Day. Fear gnaws at her stomach. But there's nowhere to run and hide. She can hear them downstairs. Laughing like they have nothing to be ashamed of. She knows it will be over quickly. Still, the horror of it never goes away. At least today she can look forward to opening her presents. Afterwards, her mother will indulge her because it's Christmas. And for just one day the girl won't wonder, 'How could she?'

At just five years old, Dana Fowley learned that there was no one she could trust and nowhere she could escape to. She and her younger sister endured years of terrible abuse, subjected day after day to unimaginable attacks, and most horrifying of all, their own mother did nothing to protect them.

Only now is Dana's nightmare coming to an end. In June 2007 the shocking truth was finally exposed and Dana's lifelong suffering was revealed. She bravely testified against her own mother and the world was at last forced to open its eyes. This is Dana's story of survival.

arrow books